Though None Go with Me

a novel

BOOKS BY JERRY B. JENKINS

The Left Behind series, with Tim LaHaye
'Twas the Night Before
Rookie
The Operative
The Margo Mysteries

JERRY B. JENKINS

NEW YORK TIMES BEST-SELLING WRITER OF THE LEFT BEHIND SERIES

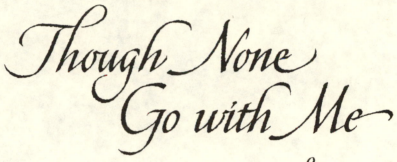

Though None Go with Me

a novel

ZondervanPublishingHouse

Grand Rapids, Michigan

A Division of HarperCollinsPublishers

Though None Go with Me
Copyright © 2000 by Jerry B. Jenkins

Requests for information should be addressed to:

📖 ZondervanPublishingHouse
Grand Rapids, Michigan 49530

ISBN 0-310-21948-5

This edition printed on acid-free paper.

Published in association with the literary agency of Alive Communications, Inc., 1465 Kelly Johnson Blvd. #320, Colorado Springs, CO 80920.

Interior design by Amy E. Langeler

Printed in the United States of America

99 00 01 02 03 04 /❖ DC/ 10 9 8 7 6 5 4 3 2 1

To Doug Barber, my friend,
an example of the believer in word and deed

Prologue

*T*he call that made Elisabeth cringe ever after at any ringing phone came just before midnight in the winter of her forty-fifth year.

Only the wealthy had extension phones in Three Rivers, Michigan, in 1945, and Elisabeth Grace LeRoy Bishop had not numbered herself among them for decades. Unsure how long the phone had been ringing, she ignored her slippers and tugged her robe on as she hurried stiff-legged toward the stairs. The hardwood creaked as her feet lost feeling on the icy floor. The thermometer outside the kitchen window had read nine below just hours before.

There was no one else to waken anymore in the big house on Kelsey Street. "Keep ringing, phone," she whispered, "unless you bring bad news."

At the bottom of the stairs Elisabeth breathed a prayer and picked up.

"Mother Bishop, it's Joyce. We've had an accident."

Elisabeth clutched her robe tight at her throat. Her daughter-in-law sounded calm enough, but . . .

"Tell me you didn't lose the baby."

"I'm fine, so I assume the baby is too."

Elisabeth hardly wanted to ask. "And Bruce?"

She heard her own heart as Joyce hesitated. "Bruce seems okay, but he's trapped in the car."

"Oh, no! Did you—"

"The police are on their way."

"Thank God. Where are you?"

"Not far. M–60. We were coming back from visiting—"

"At this hour? Joyce! You're due in what? A month?"

"The road looked clear, but at the big curve over by—"

"I know where it is."

"There was ice. We slid into the ditch. Bruce steered away from the water. He somehow swung back up onto the road, but we flipped over."

"Oh, Joyce!"

"He seems fine, but the wheel and the dashboard have him pinned."

"I'll come."

"Please don't. I'll call you as soon as we get home. He didn't even want me to tell you."

"Just like him. How did you get out?"

"I crawled out the window. We weren't far from a farmhouse. The people are so nice. I hated to wake them."

"Call as soon as you know anything. And have someone check you over, honey."

Elisabeth stood in the darkness of the living room, staring out at the streetlight on the corner. What a marvel, throwing off ten times the light of the gas lamps lit by hand, one by one at twilight, when she was a child. Back then a year could pass before she saw more than three automobiles. Now everyone had one. Some two. Imagine! Well, a flipped horse cart wouldn't have trapped Bruce.

The weight of a lifetime of strife overcame Elisabeth, and she lowered herself to the floor, her face in her palms, the backs of her hands pressed against the gritty carpet. "Oh, God," she began, "you have protected Bruce from so much. You must have great things in mind for him. He is completely yours. Let the police be your agents, and may they get there even now to rescue one who wants above all to serve you."

Elisabeth would not sleep. She alternately paced and sat on the couch in the stillness.

Since childhood, prayer had been as natural to Elisabeth as breathing. And during that time, God had required much of her, allowing her to be tested until she was forced to rely solely upon him. Her underpinnings had been ripped away with such regularity that she had often been tempted to settle into a life that didn't shake its fist in the Enemy's face.

Elisabeth didn't want to change her past. But as she shivered in the wee hours of a bitter morning, she struggled with God yet again, as she had so often before, over the safety of her son. She had accepted so much, suffered so much, given so much, that surely God would grant her deepest, most heartfelt wish now, would he not? Hadn't everything in her life and Bruce's pointed to her son being a *living* sacrifice?

She had long wondered whether there was any benefit, this side of heaven, for a lifetime commitment to obedience. Now, after years of service, of countless hours in the Word and in prayer, Elisabeth found herself at yet another crossroad. She had thought she understood grace, had told herself she understood sovereignty. But unless God spared her son, seemingly unhurt yet trapped in a twisted car on M–60 in the middle of a winter's night, she feared there was something about God she still didn't understand—and didn't like.

Part One

Chapter One

"Apart from a healthy birth," Elisabeth's father had told her, "no good news comes after dark." He should have known. Tall and portly, Dr. James LeRoy was Three Rivers's most popular general practitioner.

Her own birth, on the first day of the new century, had come after dark. Her father had told her the story so many times it was as if she remembered being there. "Your mother went into labor so quickly that I had to deliver you myself. I hadn't planned to. I didn't trust my instincts over my emotions. Your mother was—"

"Vera!" Elisabeth blurted.

"Yes. She was young and frail and worked hard to produce you, a healthy child. But her own vital signs—"

"She was sick."

"Yes."

"And what did you do, Daddy?"

"Hmm. I'm not sure I recall."

"Yes, you do! The bundling part."

"Oh, yes. I bundled you in a blanket and allowed you to exercise your lungs in the parlor while I tried to save your mother."

"Your wife."

He nodded. "I begged her not to leave me, not to leave us. All she wanted was to talk about your middle name and her own epitaph. I pleaded with her to save her strength."

"And what did she want you to call me, Daddy?"

"We had settled on Elisabeth, after her own mother," he said. "It had seemed too soon to worry about a middle name."

"But she thought of one."

"Yes, sweetheart. 'Call her Elisabeth Grace,' she said, 'after the grace that is greater than all our sin.' And on her tombstone—"

"I know, Daddy. It says, 'My hope is in the cross.'"

"If I hear that story one more time, I'm going to vomit!" first-grade classmate Frances Crawford hissed, shaking her ringlets. "All you talk about is your dead mother."

Breath rushed from Elisabeth, and her eyes stung. "Little girls oughtn't say 'vomit,'" she managed. "Daddy says the proper word is 'regurgitate,' but at least say 'throw up.'"

"'Daddy says *regurgicate*,'" Frances mocked.

"Regurgi*tate*," Elisabeth corrected, but Frances skipped away. Elisabeth pursued her. "You're lucky you've *got* a mother!"

Frances stopped to face her. "Just quit bragging about your father and quit bein' so—so—churchy!"

This time when Frances ran off, Elisabeth let her go. Churchy? They were in the same Sunday school class! But *Elisabeth* was churchy?

Three blocks from Dr. LeRoy's rambling mansion on Hoffman Street—not far from Bonnie Castle—the slender steeple of Three Rivers Christ Church rose above the first ward. That pristine monolith, old as the church itself, came to serve as a reminder of God's presence in Elisabeth's life.

Her father had often recounted how she talked every day about going to Christ Church. She toddled along to play in the nursery when he attended Wednesday night prayer meetings, Sunday school, and morning and evening services. "You skipped on the way to church and tried to pull me along faster," he said. "And once there, your eyes shone at the little sanctuary, the pictures on the wall, and every nook and cranny that seemed to offer something of God."

Her father and his older, widowed sister, Agatha Erastus, raised Elisabeth. Aunt Agatha did not share their love of the church. "I cannot worship a god who would take my own daughter at birth and my husband in the prime of his life," she often told her brother in Elisabeth's hearing.

"You're depriving yourself of God," Dr. LeRoy said.

"Housework, cooking, and looking after your little one is more than fair trade for food and shelter," she said. "Getting scolded is not part of the bargain."

"I worry about you, Agatha," he said. "That's all."

"Worry about yourself and your motherless child."

"I thank God you're here to help, but don't be filling Elisabeth's head with—"

"You'd do well to not associate God with my coming here, and when you start worrying about who's filling your daughter's head, start with the man in the mirror. I saw the reply from the last missionaries she tried to lecture."

Elisabeth saw her father blanch. "I'll thank you to keep out of my mail," he said. "Now I'd like to be alone a while."

"What's she talking about, Daddy?" Elisabeth said. "We heard back from the missionaries?"

Her father hesitated. "Show her!" Agatha crowed. "You're always telling her honesty is the best policy. Show her the effect she had on the missionaries."

Dr. LeRoy waved his sister off, but Elisabeth followed her father into his study and insisted on seeing the letter. He sighed and handed it to her, but she could not read cursive writing. He read it to her.

"Dear Dr. LeRoy, my husband's letter of thanks precedes this, so I trust you know we're grateful for every kindness from you and from the church. I feel compelled, however, to exercise Matthew 18 and inform you that the letter from your daughter, well intentioned though it may have been, was offensive. For a six-year-old, and a girl at that, to take it upon herself to counsel us and admonish us to remain strong and true in our faith evidences naivete and impudence of the highest order . . ."

Her father had to explain what the words meant. "But I was just trying to 'courage them," she said, tears welling.

"I know," Dr. LeRoy said, gathering her into his arms. "People just don't expect it from one as young as you."

Elisabeth would be forever grateful for her father's tutelage—prayer upon waking, prayer before every meal, prayer at bedtime, memorizing verses (thirty before she was five), and the recitation of the books of the Bible. Her dour and sour aunt was Elisabeth's first evangelistic target. She prayed aloud at mealtime for Aunt Agatha's soul, sang to her, even preached to her, setting up a tiny sanctuary of chairs, dragging in the milk box as a pulpit.

Fewer than a hundred people attended Christ Church in those days. Elisabeth knew them all, knew who belonged to whom and what they thought about her needing a mother. Many believed it unhealthy for a "pagan aunt" to raise her, while others knew just the right prospect for her father. But no one, Dr. LeRoy said, could ever replace Vera, and Elisabeth believed him with her whole heart. Though she wanted a mother as badly as she had ever wanted anything, no one could match her image of the mother she'd never known.

If Frances Crawford was sick of Elisabeth's recitation of her birth story, she acted doubly ill when Elisabeth began reciting every Bible story by heart. Elisabeth identified with the children. Baby Moses. Young David. Samuel. The boy who gave his lunch to Jesus. The children Jesus called to himself. How she longed to be protected from harm, hidden in the bulrushes, to be brave, to be called of God, to give something to Jesus, to sit on his lap. When she asked her father about girl stories, he reminded her of Jairus's daughter, whom Jesus raised from the dead.

"I want to be raised from the dead," she said. "But I'd have to die first, wouldn't I?"

Her father smiled sadly. "And I could not abide another loss."

"But Jesus would give me back to you. He could give Mommy back to you."

That made her father look sad.

Elisabeth loved everything about church, which made her frustrated by her own sin. After sitting through the stories and lessons in Sunday school, she strove to be perfect.

"Mine is better than yours," Frances announced one morning, holding up her Sunday school drawing. Elisabeth found herself so angry she could not speak.

I hate you, she thought. *You're stupid and you're wrong.* Worse, Frances was *not* wrong, and Elisabeth felt the deep sting of jealousy. She ignored Frances the rest of the morning.

Back home she felt glum. She couldn't imagine ever liking Frances again. "Daddy," she said, "Frances doesn't live in the first ward, does she?"

Elisabeth's heart sank at her father's squint. "What does that have to do with anything?" he asked.

"We're richer, that's all," she said. "Right? Rich people live here and poor people live in the other wards."

Her father set down his book. "Come here," he said, welcoming her to his lap. Elisabeth felt guilty even sitting there. "We're very fortunate to live in a fine home in a nice neighborhood," he said. "But where someone lives and what that might say about their means has no place among friends. Where a person lives says nothing about their character or their heart, does it?"

Elisabeth shook her head, embarrassed. She felt awful.

"Three Rivers was separated into four wards years ago so fire departments could be established in each one," her father explained. "That way they didn't have to worry about crossing the rivers or the railroad track. That these wards have become characterized by the level of income of their residents was hardly intended by the city fathers." Elisabeth had little idea what her father was talking about, and it seemed he wanted to say more. When she looked the other way, he let her wriggle free.

She felt terrible for hours. To Elisabeth, even those things merely selfish or wasteful were wrong. But to hate her friend, to be jealous of her? Elisabeth worried that God would stop loving her, cast her out, send her to hell.

That night when her father tucked her in, her remorse burst from her in tears. "I want to be perfect! Why can't I be?"

Elisabeth didn't understand everything her father told her then about Jesus being perfect so she didn't have to be. But she did believe that God would forgive her, and she couldn't wait to apologize to Frances.

"You're sorry for *what?*" her friend said the next day.

"For being jealous and thinking bad thoughts about you."

"I didn't even know."

"But I did. And God did."

"All right."

"Um—Frances, did you feel bad about saying your drawing was better than mine?"

Frances made a face and shrugged. "It *was.*"

Elisabeth found school almost as exciting as church. She loved reading and learning and was drawn to her teachers. She craved their attention and approval. Nothing short of perfect marks satisfied her. Frances was not as good a reader and didn't seem as smart, but still she sometimes got better grades. Elisabeth soon strove to compete rather than simply to learn.

Her life became frustrating. It wasn't that she didn't have a mother—she was used to that. She had a wonderful father, and she wanted to grow up to be a woman of God. But she didn't get it. Why was it so hard? Why couldn't she live only for God and not for herself? Why couldn't she be what she knew God wanted her to be?

"Daddy," ten-year-old Elisabeth said tearfully one night, "I don't think I'm a Christian."

Still in his three-piece suit, as usual, he settled his huge frame on the edge of her bed. "You're the best Christian I know," he said.

"Then you don't know me."

"Have you done something dastardly, Elisabeth?"

"I don't know what dastardly means, but I sin all the time."

Her father hesitated. "So do I," he said finally.

"You do?"

He nodded. "Sometimes I perform my tasks for the applause of men."

"The applause of men?"

"I do it for attention, to be admired and respected."

"What's wrong with that?"

"I should be doing it as unto the Lord. The Bible says we are to humble ourselves in his sight and *he* will lift us up."

"But you're not selfish, are you, Daddy?"

"I usually hide it, but I'm often frustrated by patients who come to me with minor ailments at the end of the day and make me late getting to you."

"That doesn't sound like sinning," she said.

"Tell me what *you* mean by sinning," he said.

"I can be awful," Elisabeth said. "I lose my temper, talk bad about people, want my own way. I'm jealous of anyone who does better than I do in school. Sometimes I actually hate Aunt Agatha. Why do I keep doing that?"

He shifted his weight and the bed creaked. "We keep sinning because we're sinners, honey."

"But Jesus died for my sins. Why am I still a sinner?"

Her father gently stroked her hair. "You remind me so much of your mother," he said. "She was light-haired with skin as fair as porcelain."

"Aren't our dishes made of that?"

He nodded. "Imagine your mother's face as delicate and beautiful as the teacup your aunt uses."

Elisabeth sighed. "I want to be a Christian like Mommy."

Her father embraced her. Her cheek lay against the wool of his vest and his watch chain tickled her neck. "Just like you, your mother worried and worried about her faith until it all came to her one night in our little church."

"What came to her?"

"She heard the truth, that's all," her father said. "She'd heard it all her life, but she didn't catch it until then."

"I want to hear the truth," Elisabeth said.

"Such wisdom from a wee one," he said, pulling back to look at her. "Tell me what it means to be a Christian."

"To believe in Jesus," she said. "And to live for him," she added quickly.

"Is that so?" he asked. "The Bible says we are known by the fruit we bear. You try to live for Jesus, Elisabeth. I know you do."

Elisabeth scowled. "Doesn't God want me to?"

"Sure, but why?"

"Daddy, I'm asking *you*."

Dr. LeRoy stood and stretched, and Elisabeth did the same. His yawn was contagious too, but she fought sleep. If her own mother had the same problem she did, and *she* had found the answer, Elisabeth would not rest until she found it too.

Her father sat again. "Listen carefully, Elisabeth. Your mother finally realized what grace was all about. It means we don't have to please God, because we can't."

Elisabeth was confused. "You mean we're not supposed to try to—"

He cupped her face in his hands. "We try to live godly lives to show our thanks to him for grace. Nothing we can do on our own can please God. You know the verses."

"'For by grace are ye saved through faith,'" she said, "'and that not of yourselves: it is the gift of God: not of works, lest any man should boast.'"

"We're saved by the grace of God, Elisabeth. Living godly is noble. But don't do it for any reason other than to thank God for the gift of grace. Otherwise, you're still trying to earn his favor."

Chapter Two

*L*osing her mother in childbirth had been a blow, but Elisabeth lacked little else. Despite her father's counsel, even as a child Elisabeth learned that the first ward was the place to live. "The riffraff in the other wards gossip about first warders," her aunt said. "But you know they strive to move up here themselves."

Elisabeth felt priceless when her father's countenance brightened at the sight of her at the end of the day. "Homework report," he would announce, and she brought him up to date. "Um-hm," he repeated, studying her work.

"Are you tired, Daddy? You're breathing hard."

He inhaled deeply. "Be sure to get more exercise than I do," he said. "And be careful of your diet." He patted his ample belly. "This is a self-inflicted handicap, but such things are also genetic. You'll have to be careful."

Her father's height camouflaged his true weight, which Elisabeth guessed at nearly three hundred pounds. He changed the subject. "Isn't learning an adventure?" he said, a smile burning through his haggard face. "Education gives us a passion for life!"

She nodded, aware of his stare. Normally he lingered over her schoolwork, making sure she understood the material, but now he just gazed at her. "You look more like your mother every day."

"Those smelly ladies at church pretend *they're* my mother," she said, shuddering at their smothering embraces.

"They're just affectionate."

Elisabeth shrugged, not letting on that she always shut her eyes and imagined her own mother. She had not even told Frances about that.

Aunt Agatha did not hug her, and for that Elisabeth was grateful. She had heard her aunt sobbing in her bed, railing against God for taking her loved ones. That made Elisabeth cry too, and at times *she* raged against injustice—against the unfairness, for instance, that Frances Crawford enjoyed both a loving mother *and* a father.

But Elisabeth would not complain. She remembered what her father had told her: "Always look on the bright side. Half the people I treat would be helped merely by a more positive outlook."

"I know," she said. "See?" She flipped to the back of her school writing tablet, where she had listed, "My blessings: God. Christ. Holy Spirit. Bible. Church. Father. House. Warmth. Brain. Curiosity. Books. Lamp. Food. Bed. Clothes. Training Hour. Friends. Aunt Agatha (sometimes)."

When Elisabeth's body began to change, her father seemed to change too. He grew more careful around her, speaking more circumspectly.

"Who's going to tell me about the things of life?" she said.

He looked away. "Such as?"

"You know. Men, women, husband and wife things."

"There's time for that," he said, busying himself in one of her books. Elisabeth wondered if she had broached a subject not proper to discuss.

One day her father sent her to a nurse friend of his at the hospital for a physical exam. Elisabeth blushed when the woman gave her a cursory once-over and said quietly, "Your father has asked that I explain what you might expect for your monthly cycle." The nurse also gave her a booklet on sexuality.

Elisabeth was so embarrassed she could not look at her father or speak to him for days. And it seemed that was fine with him.

They became cordial again, then more familiar, and were soon back to a friendly routine. He had to be as aware as she that there was a subject neither would acknowledge. Elisabeth wanted to ask if it was customary for one's mother to discuss such matters, but she dared not broach even that. She told Frances, "I will speak frankly to my children, at least my daughters, about these things."

With Elisabeth's increasing knowledge of the mysteries of life, her view of God and faith began to mature as well. "I finally understand the virgin birth," she whispered to Frances. "Don't laugh, but I always thought a virgin was just a young woman."

Frances shook her head. "Mary kept Jesus from being born with Adam's seed."

"I finally understand how Jesus qualifies to be the spotless sacrificial lamb of the Old Testament," Elisabeth said. She found that miracle every bit as dramatic and impressive as the Resurrection, and suddenly the picture of redemption and salvation began to crystallize. How often had she heard Pastor Hill say that one death could cleanse the sins of all, "because the lamb that was slain was the infinite God of the universe"?

The truth of it hit Elisabeth hard one humid summer Sunday night when the pastor preached on the subject of the cross. He asked the congregation to "close your eyes and imagine Jesus hanging there just for you." In the dark silence Elisabeth trembled, believing that if she had been the only person in the world, Jesus would have died just for her. When Pastor Hill whispered, "He loved us, every one, as if there was but one of us to love," she burst into sobs.

Barely thirteen, Elisabeth developed a hunger to understand everything about God. She made an appointment with Pastor Hill and was shocked to find him nearly as embarrassed to talk to her about the deeper things of God as her father had been to talk to her about the secrets of life. Jack Hill had been pastor of Christ Church since long before Elisabeth was born. It was he who had brought life to the doctrine of grace, giving such peace to Elisabeth's mother.

Pastor Hill was tall and knuckly, a hardware store clerk Monday through Saturday mornings. His office, such as it was, occupied a tiny alcove off the dining room in a modest parsonage in the third ward, where he and his wife had raised six children. Elisabeth and the pastor sat with his pine desk between them. He wore his Sunday suit, stiff collar pressing his Adam's apple. She wondered if he spent his afternoons dressed like that, studying and preparing his sermons. She would be impressed if he had dressed just for their meeting, but she thought it imprudent to ask.

"I just want to know if I have it all," Elisabeth exulted, accepting his offer of a chair and fanning herself as she spoke. "I always loved the faith, but I thought so much of it was a mystery, like the Trinity."

Pastor Hill stared at the wall behind her. "Much of the faith is indeed a mystery," he said. "Salvation itself is a mystery, as Paul writes."

"But it's less mysterious now, Pastor. You make everything so clear."

The pastor sat back, clearly embarrassed. "Well, Elisabeth, you've had wonderful training at home, and I know from your teachers and my own observance that you know your Bible."

"I only thought I knew it. There's so much there! I, uh, just wondered if there are more secrets or mysteries."

Pastor Hill studied her. He hollered to the kitchen. "Margaret, could you join us?" His wife was red-faced and stocky with raw fingers, her hair piled atop her head. She was sweating through her blouse as she dried her hands.

"Margaret," he said, his voice thick. "You know Elisabeth, of course."

"I've known her all her life, Jack," she said, smiling. "The spirit and image of her beautiful mother."

"But did you know she is an answer to prayer? Have I not been praying for years for a young person in love with Christ?"

Margaret nodded. "You have."

Elisabeth hadn't come to be singled out. "Is there more of God?" she managed finally.

Mrs. Hill smiled but appeared on the edge of tears. "There is all of God that you want," she said.

"The Trinity and salvation," she said, nodding. "I'll accept the one by faith, but the other is much clearer now."

The pastor seemed amused. "I have studied Scripture since Bible school and find salvation God's greatest mystery. I'm grateful Paul writes that we 'may know.' I rest in that."

Elisabeth immediately said, "First John 5:13, 'These things have I written unto you that believe on the name of the Son of God, that ye may know that ye have eternal life, and that ye may believe on the name of the Son of God.'"

Pastor Hill nodded, moisture from his forehead collecting in the creases beside his mouth. "Unfathomable love and grace is beyond me and most everyone but young girls."

Elisabeth scowled, wondering if he was criticizing her naivete.

His sad smile was like his wife's. It was as if he could read her mind. "I pray you will always stay close to Christ, despite any cost. True devotion requires sacrifice."

"It hasn't so far," she said, and that made him smile again.

He gazed at her, and she wondered if the meeting was over. She had more questions now than when the conversation had started. He reached for his Bible. "I need to tell you," he said, "that when you feel drawn closer to God, you must remain open to his call. The nudging in your spirit may be evidence that God wants more from you. And Jesus said that to whom much is given—"

"'Of him shall be much required,'" Elisabeth said. "'And to whom men have committed much, of him they will ask the more.' Luke 12:48."

"You are remarkable," the pastor said, leafing through his Bible. "Elisabeth, Paul counts all things but loss compared to knowing Christ and knowing the power of Christ's resurrection. The power that raised Jesus from the dead can work in our lives. Think of it! But see what follows. As Shakespeare would say, here's the rub. Read it."

"'. . . and the fellowship of his sufferings.'"

The pastor appeared to look upon her with pity.

"What does it mean?" she said.

"The more of God you want, the more of Christ you'll get. Most are content to stay out of the deep water."

"I can't tell if you're warning me or encouraging me."

"Both, Elisabeth. God does not call us to a closer walk to make our lives easier. Pray about your desire for a closer walk," he said. "I know few with the stomach for the cost. If you are called, you must go. But the rewards are few."

He seemed to rouse from a reverie and smiled at her. "There have been costs," he said. "But I am without regret."

Elisabeth wanted to ask what his walk with God had cost him, but she dared not. "I've taken too much of your time," she said.

"Not at all," he said. "Let me pray for you before you go. Margaret, would you be so kind." Mrs. Hill laid her hand gently on Elisabeth's shoulder as the pastor knelt. A lump rose in Elisabeth's throat.

"Fairest Lord Jesus," he began, "to you who promise to be both mother and father to the orphan, I plead for a touch on Elisabeth's life. She seeks a closer walk. May she be willing despite a cost you never reveal in advance, lest we faint at the weight of it. May she follow completely the one in whom there is no change, neither shadow of turning."

The pastor remained kneeling as if too spent to rise. Mrs. Hill's cheeks shone with tears, and Elisabeth could not even express her thanks.

Chapter Three

Elisabeth walked home at twilight. She was about to cross to the other side of West Michigan Street when she saw Will Bishop ahead on his bicycle, gas lamp lighter held aloft. In knickers and cap, he pretended not to notice her, as usual. They had known each other all their lives. One of her earliest memories was of tussling with him in the church nursery.

Elisabeth thought of avoiding him for his sake, not for hers. Poor Will was painfully shy. She couldn't decide what would be best, to spare his having to acknowledge her or to educate him in the social graces. She decided on the latter.

"Good evening, Will," she said, stopping before him as he prepared to light a lamp.

"Oh," he said, as if surprised. He left one hand on the handlebars and touched his cap with the other, seeming to forget he was holding the long wick. "Hullo, Elspeth."

"Careful there," she said. "Don't set yourself afire."

"No'm," he said.

"I'll let you shorten my name," she said. "But you must not call me ma'am until I'm older."

"Sorry." He looked away miserably.

"I'm teasing, Will. Call me anything you wish, as long as you call me your friend."

"Okay," he said. "Better keep going."

"Nice to see you, Will," she said.

"Yes'm," he said, "I mean, friend."

Elisabeth wished she could tell him about her visit to the pastor, but did boys ever even think about such things? She could barely get him to look at her, much less converse. She had once made the mistake of asking Will about his father, frequently the object of unspoken prayer requests. Will had merely shaken his head.

In youth group one night, a girl suggested a young people's activity might include an outing to see Mr. Bishop at the State Hospital in Kalamazoo. The youth group fell silent when Frances Crawford (who had lately earned the nickname Big Mouth) offered, "Isn't that where they send the loonies?"

Dr. LeRoy later assured Elisabeth that Mr. Bishop was "no loony, which is certainly not a term anyone should use for a mental patient anyway. He suffers from an undiagnosed memory malady, and it would serve you and your friends better to pray for him than to call him names."

"Should we visit him?"

"I'm afraid he wouldn't know us."

Elisabeth's friends said Will was handsome, but caring about that seemed frivolous. Frances accused her of being too serious and "way too spiritual. No boy's ever going to be interested!"

Elisabeth was impressed that Will seemed willing to work. He had a paper route, which he threw after midnight while outing the gas lamps he had lit just before sundown. He had his own little scavenger company, selling wagons full of stuff to the junkyard. And he volunteered to carry groceries, never charging but accepting tips. Elisabeth wondered if he said two words to his customers. She glanced back at Will as she headed home.

Still full of emotion from her visit with the pastor, Elisabeth was disappointed to find her father not home. It was just her and Aunt Agatha. The dreary woman seemed to need a target for her moods. "Where've you been, young lady? Your dinner's long cold."

"I didn't mean to make you worry."

"About you? That's a laugh. Did your father know you would be late?"

"I didn't expect to be."

"So, where were you?"

"Father knew where I was. Is it necessary for you to know?"

"I'd have been whipped, talking to an elder with such insolence. I'm entitled to an answer because I'm one of your guardians."

"I was at Pastor Hill's home," Elisabeth said, dropping onto the couch. "I'd love to tell you about it. He believes it's possible for a Christian to be called to a—"

"I don't need every detail!" Aunt Agatha said. "Your plate is on the stove, and don't expect company. I've already eaten."

"I'll manage," Elisabeth said.

"And don't think I won't be telling your father what time you waltzed in here. The street lamps are already lit, forevermore!"

Elisabeth wouldn't deny that her aunt could cook—in fact, she took pleasure in saying so. The old woman clearly didn't know how to take compliments, but they certainly defused her. "Delicious as always, Aunt Agatha," Elisabeth called from the kitchen.

"It would have tasted even better fresh!"

"That's why I'm so sorry I was late!"

"Let that be a lesson . . ."

"Where is Daddy, anyway?"

"You're old enough to quit calling him Daddy. You sound like a baby."

"It's a term of endearment," Elisabeth said. "Like when I call you Auntie."

"You can lay that to rest anytime, too," Agatha said. "Doctor Daddy is at the hospital in Schoolcraft, no surprise. Said you shouldn't wait up."

"What's he doing there? Does he have a patient there?"

"I don't manage his day, Elisabeth! It doesn't strike me odd that a doctor is at a hospital!"

Elisabeth was still wondering about her father later while reading her Bible. Being hungry for it, despite having read it daily as a duty for years, was new to her. She dressed for bed and sat reading and praying.

She had come a long way in a few hours, from believing she had the Christian life figured out to fearfully considering some divine call. But to do what?

No wonder her friends criticized her for acting older. She *felt* older. Elisabeth remembered fondly when Frances and her other friends were also interested in Bible stories and memorizing verses, Sunday school picnics, prayer meetings, camp, even protracted meetings.

"Protracted meetings!" Aunt Agatha repeated at dinner when she'd heard the phrase one too many times that summer. "James, I swear, it sounds like a dental society meeting."

Her brother chuckled. "Agatha," he said, "that would be an *extracted* meeting. *Protracted* merely means they are extended for as long as the guest speaker is drawing a good crowd and God seems to be working—"

"I know what it means, James! I was raised in the same home as you."

"I wish you'd come," he said, filling his plate again. "This year's speaker knew Mr. Moody personally."

"You don't say," she said. "Get Dwight Moody here and I *will* join you."

"Moody's been dead since '99."

"As if I didn't know that! Prop up his corpulent corpse, and I'll be on the front row."

Dr. LeRoy stared at her. "That's disrespectful, even for you."

"Even for *me?*" Aunt Agatha said. "What does that mean?"

"Who speaks ill of the dead, let alone of the greatest evangelist who ever lived?"

"You're putting Moody ahead of the apostle Paul?" she said, ignoring her food.

"How can you know so much of the Bible and turn your back on God?"

"We've been down this road," she said. "You know well that I didn't turn my back on God. He turned his back on me."

"I'm about to do the same," Dr. LeRoy said.

"He did to you what he did to me!" she wailed. "How could you forgive him for taking your Vera? She was just a child!"

"The Lord giveth and—"

She slapped her fork on the table. "Stop with the platitudes! More power to you if you let God tear your life apart and come back for more. When he took both Kathleen and my Godfrey, he took all he's going to get."

"I wish that were true."

"You two go to your protracted meetings and leave me in peace."

"You know what I'm going to do there, Aunt Agatha?" Elisabeth said brightly.

"Besides roast in the August heat, pray tell."

"Pray for you."

"Just to agitate me?"

"No. Because I care about you, that's all."

"That's all. That's all. You got that empty expression from your father, and you'd do well to expunge it from your vocabulary."

"You're changing the subject," Elisabeth said, "that's all."

Even her father had to laugh, but he wound up apologizing to his sister. "I'll never really turn my back on you, Agatha," he said. "I love you even when you're ornery."

"That puts you one up on God."

Dr. LeRoy shook his head. "No one will ever love you like he does."

"He has a strange way of showing it."

"His ways are not our ways. God works in mysterious—"

"I swear," she said, standing and beginning to clear the table, "you have a platitude for every occasion."

The banner, hung between two trees in the yard of Christ Church, announced the annual protracted meetings in August of 1913. Handbills and the newspaper revealed the meetings would feature well-traveled speaker Dr. Kendall Hasper. He was reputed to have taught at Mr. Moody's school in Chicago, at the famed Ravensway College in Great Britain, and at gatherings of missionaries on every inhabited continent.

The *Three Rivers Tribune* carried a feature on him. His exposure to foreign lands should alone draw huge crowds, the paper said, but "the world traveler also brings a message of hope and revival that should be uplifting to the entire community."

Elisabeth always looked forward to the protracted meetings. A tent was erected but used only in the rain. A potluck picnic preceded each meeting, which began with the sun still high and hot and ended under a black sky. Rarely did sundown bring a chill in August.

Over the years, Elisabeth had been held spellbound under thundering evangelists and had tried to stay awake while missionary executives told secondhand stories from the field. She enjoyed speakers with flair, as long as they didn't strut. She had inherited that aversion from her father, who said, "The primary trait of a man of God ought to be humility."

Elisabeth's friends had never before complained about having to wear their Sunday-go-to-meetin' clothes to protracted meetings. But now that they were young men and women, dress became an issue, especially with her girlfriends. They wore what they were told, but they groused, especially Frances.

Tradition allowed those Elisabeth's age to sit with each other for the first time, rather than with their parents, provided they behaved. Elisabeth wasn't sure she wanted to sit with Frances and her other friends. They were conspiring to pass notes. She didn't want to feel like a schoolmarm, as they labeled her. But Elisabeth was disappointed that church had apparently come to mean something different to her friends than it did to her.

Regardless, Elisabeth felt strangely warmed when Frances and Lucy, a younger girl, shyly approached a few minutes before the meeting. "May Elisabeth sit with us, Dr. LeRoy?" Frances asked in her most obsequious tone.

"It's all right with me, ladies. The choice is hers."

Elisabeth gathered her Bible and her notepad and followed the girls to the other side of the makeshift aisle. It touched her to feel wanted. She knew she was different, that her vaunted maturity had alienated many friends. Elisabeth wasn't trying to act superior. She was serious, that was all.

The young people knew the curmudgeons among the congregation, those who seemed to think being a Christian meant being miserable. Her fun-loving father had disabused Elisabeth of that notion; she dreaded becoming one who wagged a finger at anybody having fun.

As soon as she settled in on the aisle next to Frances, Art Childs—one of the older boys—spotted Elisabeth's notebook. "Paper!" he whispered, grinning as he dug in his pocket for a handful of stubby pencils. Elisabeth pressed her lips together and shook her head, hugging her notebook to her chest. "Oh, pardon me, Miss Pastor!" Art said.

Elisabeth glanced down the row, and even the girls were ridiculing her. At the far end Will Bishop sat taking it all in. He looked somber, staring at Elisabeth as if he understood, his father's huge Bible in his lap.

The piano had been rolled to the side of the platform inside the church so Elisabeth's piano teacher, Mrs. Stonerock, could play with a clear view from the window to the song leader. They never risked carrying the piano into the weather.

With the first strains of the music, a crowd twice the size of the Sunday congregation looked expectantly to the platform. After a brief welcome by Pastor Hill and congregational singing, he introduced the special music. A long-nosed woman from a church in White Pigeon held her music before her in both hands, and with heaving chest produced a contralto soprano that needed no amplification.

Mortified, it was all Elisabeth could do to keep a straight face. She knew she should admire the woman's willingness to serve God, but all was drowned out by the swelling vibrato. Elisabeth's friends covered their mouths and turned colors.

A chuckle tickled her throat, and Elisabeth prayed she would not humiliate herself or her father across the aisle. Appearing to corral a smile, he raised an eyebrow when the singer modulated. Elisabeth felt a guffaw coming, and when her father turned and winked at her, she lost control.

Clenching her teeth left the rush of air nowhere to escape but through her nose. With her notebook and her Bible against her chest, she heard her own honking snort when everyone else did, and all she could do was drop her stuff, bury her face in her hands, and pretend to weep. Which made her friends laugh all the more.

Miss Soprano was so enraptured that her eyes were closed, her face beatifically pointed heavenward. The young people collected themselves as the solo ended, and Elisabeth busied herself helping Frances and Lucy pick up her things. She feared her father's scowl, but he pursed his lips and pantomimed a delicate applause that made her bury her face again.

Finally, mercifully, it was time for the honored guest. Elisabeth was tormented by giggles that threatened to expose her every time her mind drifted to the soloist. She hoped with all her might that Dr. Hasper could somehow captivate her.

Small and bespectacled, he was not what she had expected. He spoke directly, and she found him as articulate as a man of his experience should be. He was not a strutter. Dynamic and magnetic, he spoke with an urgency and authority that deflected attention from him to his message. He bounced on the balls of his feet and preached from a Bible limp from use.

After his introductory remarks, he read from the Old Testament. "Listen," he said, "to this proclamation from Joshua 24: 'And if it seem evil unto you to serve the LORD, choose you this day whom ye will serve. . . . but as for me and my house, we will serve the LORD.'"

Hasper paused and looked from face to face. When his eyes met Elisabeth's, she held her breath. "Beloved," he said, "we are into the second decade of the last century of this millennium. The great swelling of commitment to Christ that characterized the Moody era, spawning evangelistic campaigns across this land and in Great Britain, should not have died when Mr. Moody died. Wherever I go I encounter Christians with one foot in the kingdom and the other in the world. Where are the Joshuas who will choose to unashamedly serve the Lord God and have the courage to so say?"

Elisabeth felt the heat of his sermon as Hasper perspired through his suit jacket. He offered illustrations of men and women who had made their choices, some to live for Christ, others not. "As God told the church at Laodicea, 'because thou art lukewarm, and neither cold nor hot, I will spew thee out of my mouth. . . . As many as I love, I rebuke and chasten: be zealous therefore, and repent.'

"I challenge you, make some decision. What will become of the kingdom if we do not continue bravely carrying the torch? My dread is for those who say they believe and know the truth and yet live as close to the world as they can. Are you in or out, enlisted or AWOL, on fire for God or only lukewarm?"

Hasper rolled on, barely raising his voice but making every syllable heard. Elisabeth had taken not one note, yet she would not forget a thing. "Make a commitment tonight," he said, and Elisabeth felt a tingle in her spine. She had already committed her heart. She was ready to commit her life. Would anyone take seriously a young woman making such a commitment? Elisabeth believed with everything in her that God knew her heart and would take her seriously.

Kendall Hasper stepped from behind the lectern. "Man, woman, boy, girl," he said, "do you remember Henry Varley's pronouncement to D. L. Moody? 'The world has yet to see what God can do through a man wholly consecrated to him.'" For the first time, Hasper raised his voice, and his words came with the resounding timbre of conviction. "Even more profound than Varley's challenge was Moody's reply. 'By the grace of God, I'll be that man!' He took the challenge! The ripples from his leap into God's ocean ebb and flow around the world to this day!

"Will you stand for Christ by God's grace even if you have to stand alone? Can you say with the hymnwriter, 'I have decided to follow Jesus'? 'Though none go with me, still I will follow'? Can you say with Joshua, 'As for me and my house, we will serve the LORD'?"

Elisabeth trembled. Her heart and soul screamed yes, and it was all she could do to keep it from her lips. She wanted to leap, to shout, to run down the aisle. When Hasper concluded, "Would you make the rest of your life an experiment in obedience?" she stood. It was as if God himself had spoken to her.

He wanted her. And she wanted the deeper walk, the higher plane. She would go anywhere, do anything. Elisabeth wanted to stand for Christ, to follow Jesus, to serve the Lord, and above all, she wanted to make her life an experiment in obedience.

She hurried up the aisle before Hasper had invited anyone. She fell prostrate, sobbing, pouring out her heart to God. She didn't care what anyone else thought or said or did. She would obey God in every situation for the rest of her life. She would pray to know his will, and she would follow it, no matter what.

Facedown in the grass, Elisabeth was only vaguely aware that others had joined her, that Hasper was still speaking, that the piano was playing and people were singing. She felt the presence of God, and that only.

A woman knelt and put an arm around her. But from above Dr. Hasper said, "Allow me to speak to that young one."

Hasper helped her into a folding chair and got another for himself. He asked her name and her spiritual history. "I could tell God was dealing with you before you ever moved into the aisle," he said. "I find that those who cannot wait for the invitation have made lifetime commitments."

"I want my life to be an experiment in obedience," she said.

"Praise God," Dr. Hasper said. "You will need his power every step. You have not chosen the path of least resistance, but if you could be dissuaded by that, you would not have come forward."

Dr. Hasper prayed for her, concluding, "If Elisabeth is never known outside this little hamlet, I pray you would do a work in her and through her that would shake the world for your name and bring glory to you."

Hasper stood and shook her hand. "God go with you."

She could not speak. She looked past him to where Will Bishop had just finished praying with an elder. Will smiled and strode away with what appeared to Elisabeth as unbounded joy.

Chapter Four

*E*lisabeth felt warm all over as she and her father silently walked home. The sky was inky, the moon a sliver, yet the thermometer on their back porch read eighty degrees. Elisabeth was so full, felt so clean and renewed and invigorated and resolute, that she wanted to tell the world—starting with her father and even Aunt Agatha. But her aunt was already snoring, and her father seemed distracted.

They sat on the front steps and sipped water chilled with ice shavings. "You did some business with God tonight," he said. "That's good. Those are the kinds of decisions and commitments I can't make for you, but which mean as much to me as any you could make."

Elisabeth pressed the glass against her cheek and glanced at her father. He seemed sad somehow, despite what he was saying.

"Are you all right, Dad?"

He shrugged. "A little tired."

"You're working too hard. But can you be happy for me tonight?"

He put his arm around her, something he hadn't done for a long time. "I am," he said. "I told you I was. At least I meant to."

Elisabeth was troubled. She wanted to talk about the meeting and her decision, but his mood threw her. Leaning into his great, warm mass made her feel safe and loved, like when she was a little girl.

"Ah, I'm going to miss you," he said.

She cocked her head and pulled back so she could look him full in the face. He avoided her eyes. "Where am I going?" she asked with a laugh. "Did you think I signed up for missionary work tonight?"

He shook his head. "We won't always be together, that's all. I miss you already."

Elisabeth sensed he was hedging. "I have five more years before college," she said.

"I know. I just hate to think of our ever being apart. But we have to be realistic. Someday you'll be as eager to get away from me as I was to get away from my parents."

"Never," she said, settling back into his embrace and gazing at the sky. "But if I become a brat, you'll force me out, banishing me from your kingdom."

She felt his squeeze. "You're already a brat," he said. "I'm trying to be serious here."

"I'm listening," she said. "You really want to talk about five years from now?"

He shrugged and fell silent. Finally he said, "I'm already in my forties, and I regret not having taken better care of myself."

"You've been too busy taking care of everyone else."

"I've used that excuse myself, but now I have no choice."

"No choice about what?" she said.

"Taking care of myself."

Despite the still air, a chill made her shudder. "What are you saying?"

"These extra nights at the hospital have not been for work," he said.

She pulled away and set her glass down. The ice shavings had melted. "Don't make me ask," she said, suddenly feeling old.

"I've been undergoing tests."

Elisabeth could not speak. Her spiritual high disappeared in a wave of nausea. "Tests?" she managed, her voice weak. It was as if she were watching and listening rather than actually engaging in this conversation.

"Cancer," her father said, the dreaded word hanging in the moist air.

She held her breath and stared at him, as if willing him to say more. He glanced at her and looked away.

"What?" she said. "What do we do about it? People survive that, don't they?"

"Sometimes."

"Then you'll—we'll—do whatever we have to do to—"

"I waited too long, sweetheart," he said, and he tried to embrace her again. Elisabeth stiffened.

"What does that mean?" she said.

"Don't pull away from me now," he said, reaching for her. "You've heard that a doctor who treats himself has a fool for a patient. By the time I knew I needed to consult someone, my illness was advanced."

Elisabeth was reeling. "Surely, you have time."

"My doctor gives me about eighteen months."

"Daddy!"

"You are strong, Elisabeth. God will be with you."

The condensation on her glass had disappeared in rivulets on the wood slats of the porch. She felt as if she too sat in a pool of her own emotions. She hung her head. "Could your doctor be wrong?"

Her father shook his head. "I've seen the test results. Without a miracle, some breakthrough—"

"That's what I'll pray for."

"This will not be easy on either of us," he said. "But it will comfort me to know you will be all right," he said. "Thankfully, my affairs are in order."

"I'm not interested in any of that," she said. She buried her face into his chest and wept. "I just promised God I would make the rest of my life an experiment in obedience. Look what it got me."

"Surely you didn't expect me to live forever."

She knew he couldn't mean to sound so cavalier. "In a year and a half I will be only fifteen."

He nodded. "I want to see your mother, and I long to see Jesus, but in truth I'd rather stay with you for now."

A spiritual fountain had washed over Elisabeth just an hour before. Now it had given way to a gnawing emptiness in the pit of her stomach. They sat in silence for several minutes until, without a word, they rose in unison to go inside.

Elisabeth's spiritual decision had been real, and it produced in her a hunger and thirst for God and his Word she had never before experienced. Her pastor and the evangelist had warned her not to expect spiritual highs, but rather to expect opposition from the Evil One. While she felt a deep sense of joy that she had made the right decision, her foreboding grew only worse as her father deteriorated.

First he lost weight. For a month or so he looked healthier, definition coming to his features, his large frame evidencing lean musculature where puffiness had been.

But he grew tired and weak; his face paled. By the spring of 1914 he was homebound and had quit seeing patients. Elisabeth hurried home after school every day to tend to him and to spell Aunt Agatha, who used the situation to fuel her tirade against God. "Your father was not just a believer," she told Elisabeth. "He was also devout. Look where it's got him. Don't you worry. I expect he'll provide for me, and you may rest assured that I will provide for you."

By late 1914, Dr. LeRoy had to be hospitalized. The church had prayed, visited, helped out, and now seemed merely to await the awful news. They still cared, Elisabeth knew, but the novelty had worn off. She felt she alone was watching him die.

Maddeningly, Aunt Agatha began redecorating the house. It was nothing major at first, but eventually it became clear she was slowly stockpiling her brother's belongings. His shoes and clothes were boxed and stored in the dank cellar. His room was rearranged as a guest room, and to Elisabeth it appeared Agatha herself was planning to move in there as soon as her brother passed.

One night after Christmas Elisabeth trudged home from the hospital in the dark. She slipped onto the back porch, removed her boots, and stepped into the warm kitchen without a sound. After visiting her father and knowing his time was short, she was not in the mood to talk. Aunt Agatha was.

"I have not seen your father's will, remember," her aunt said. "But you are not of age, and until you are I foresee no one else who might administrate his estate. Regardless how he compensates me for my years of service, I do not intend to take advantage."

Elisabeth had been relying on her commitment to Christ in the big issues of life, giving over to God her fear and anger about her father. Lately, she had been working on infusing the same thought process to every encounter. Clearly she was not to be catty. But when Aunt Agatha mentioned that she would "like to buy this house from your father's estate," Elisabeth didn't have time to pray or reflect. Her face flushed and she knew she looked stricken.

"I'm sorry," she said. "But I had not heard that my father was selling the house."

"I said I would buy it from the estate," Aunt Agatha said. "In, ah, due time, of course."

"So it isn't that Daddy died since I saw him a few minutes ago and you forgot to inform me?"

"Forgive me for being presumptuous, Elisabeth," Aunt Agatha said. "I just want to plan ahead."

"How convenient that there is something to plan for."

"That's what I thought."

Elisabeth was hardly in a festive mood on New Year's Eve. She knew 1915 would bring her father's death, and all she wanted for her birthday the next day was time with him. She was surprised to see at the desk the same nurse who had shared with her the facts of life two years before. The woman quickly put away what she was working on and followed Elisabeth to her father's room.

"Your daughter is here," she said, though Elisabeth had never been announced before.

Her father opened one eye. "And were you able to—"

"Yes, Doctor," the nurse said, and Elisabeth nearly wept at her tone. Her father was on his deathbed, yet his nurse still treated him with deference.

"Daddy," Elisabeth said, accepting his fragile hand.

"Your present will be here in a minute," he said.

"You're my birthday present."

"Naw, I'm not," he said. "I just take your time."

"Don't say that."

"Anyway, would you believe I went out and shopped for it last night?"

"Of course," she said. "And I assume you had a date too."

He forced a smile and fell asleep briefly. When he opened his eyes he said, "I dreamt I saw your mother again."

Elisabeth had resigned herself to the fact that this was for the best. She did not want him to suffer longer. He looked past her to the nurse, who handed him a paper sack. Inside was a thin, wrapped package, tied with a ribbon. "Open the card first," he said.

Elisabeth was crying already. The card had been handwritten, she assumed by the nurse, but her father had dictated it.

Elisabeth, you are the joy of my life. May you live to a ripe, old age and have to be told when your time comes. Your mother and I will await you at the eastern gate of the city that was built foursquare. Love, Father. Isaiah 25:8–9.

Elisabeth looked up the passage in her father's Bible. "He will swallow up death in victory; and the Lord GOD will wipe away tears from all faces; and the rebuke of his people shall he take away from all the earth; for the LORD hath spoken it. And it shall be said in that day, Lo, this is our God; we have waited for him, and he will save us: this is the LORD; we have waited for him, we will be glad and rejoice in his salvation."

In the package Elisabeth found a simple blank journal with cardboard covers. "Record your journey," he said. "Someday someone might find it encouraging."

"What do you want for *your* birthday, Daddy?" she said.

"I want to wake up in heaven."

She had quit telling him not to talk about the inevitable. "I'll miss you," she managed.

Ten days later she arrived home from school as her aunt was leaving the house, bundled against an icy wind. "He's gone," she said. "The hospital needs us."

Elisabeth stood shivering in the snow as her aunt moved past. Agatha stopped and looked impatient. Elisabeth had thought she was prepared for this day, yet the pain bit a hole in her that would never be filled. "I'm sorry for your loss, Aunt Agatha," she said quietly.

Agatha Erastus squinted and cocked her head. "Yes," she said. "Thank you. And the same to you for yours."

At the hospital, her father's nurse friend, red-eyed, handed Elisabeth a business card with the name and address of a lawyer on the front and a note scribbled in pencil on the back. "Please give to Elisabeth at the appropriate time."

As Aunt Agatha signed papers, Elisabeth sat alone with her memories. Pastor Hill soon joined her. He simply sat and wept with her. His was the most poignant response of the hundreds who attended the funeral. The only other who knew enough to say nothing was Will Bishop, whose own father was near death.

Two weeks later Elisabeth came home from school to find her Aunt Agatha stewing in the living room with a well-dressed man in his late forties. "Won't speak to me, Elisabeth," Agatha said. "Only to you."

Marlin Beck, Esq., whose card Elisabeth had been given at the hospital, rose briefly to greet her. "I have been assigned executor of your father's estate," he said, settling back down. "Much to the consternation of your aunt, I'm afraid."

"And we'll see what *my* lawyer says about that," Agatha chirped.

"He'll find the documents in order, ma'am," Beck said.

"My brother was in no condition to draw up a will. I couldn't get him to so much as look into—"

"Pardon me, Mrs. Erastus, but there was no need. He had prepared his will very early on in his illness and was of sound mind. You would be ill-advised to contest it."

"Are you *my* lawyer now as well?"

"I beg your pardon. But you might wish to hear the will before deciding to contest it."

Elisabeth eyed her. "Do you *have* a lawyer, Aunt Agatha?"

The old woman turned away. "I can easily retain one."

"You would contest your own brother's will?"

"If necessary!"

"I'd let you have everything before I'd fight you over one shoestring," Elisabeth said, desperate to keep from raising her voice.

"Miss LeRoy," Mr. Beck said, "I urge you not to speak from emotion. Your father precluded eventualities such as this by having his affairs put in order. I should think everyone involved would desire to accede to his wishes.

"Those wishes, as outlined in his will, were that his entire estate be put into a trust for Elisabeth and that she be given full access to it at age eighteen. In the meantime, his sister is to be allowed to stay in the house in exchange for her guardianship. The property is not to be sold before Elisabeth is of age, and its disposition will be solely at her discretion."

Mr. Beck read, "'It is my expectation and hope that my daughter, Elisabeth Grace LeRoy, shall treat my sister, Agatha LeRoy Erastus, with the Christian charity she deserves for the rest of her natural life.'"

"How do you interpret that, Mr. Beck?" Agatha demanded.

He seemed to fight a smile. "How much Christian charity do you deserve?"

"That's not amusing."

"Dr. LeRoy was a plain-speaking man, Mrs. Erastus. I expect he wishes Elisabeth to provide reasonably for you in gratitude for your years of service."

Agatha pursed her lips and shook her head. "I came here years ago in the midst of my own grief and had to be reminded every day of the precious baby daughter I lost. I was paid not a dime for virtually raising this ungrateful child myself."

"Ungrateful?" Elisabeth said. "If anything I've ever said or done has made you think that either I or my father were un—"

Aunt Agatha waved her off. "I ought to have the right to buy this house," she said.

Horrified at the depth of her aunt's disdain, Elisabeth snapped, "Fine!"

"Excuse me, Miss LeRoy," Mr. Beck said. "Legally the house is not yours to sell until you are of age. In the meantime, it is under my purview, and I am charged with retaining it for you."

"I'll sell it to you as soon as I'm able," Elisabeth told her aunt, determined to keep peace.

"At fair market value, of course," Mr. Beck said.

"At whatever price Aunt Agatha feels is fair," Elisabeth said.

"Oh, my," Mr. Beck said, putting away his papers, "I beg of you to carefully—"

"We both heard her loud and clear, Mr. Beck," Agatha said.

"Yes, but—"

"My niece will honor her word. She always does."

Mr. Beck shook his head and took a breath to speak, but Mrs. Erastus cut him off. "Unless you have other business specifically related to the will or your purview, as you put it, I'll thank you to leave my house."

"If it's your house already," Mr. Beck said, rising. "I prefer to leave. But I promise you, I'll fight for my late client's wishes, and you may—"

"Good-by, Mr. Beck," Agatha said.

Elisabeth believed God would have her honor her aunt, even if Agatha didn't deserve respect. Being cordial to her, let alone loving her, was a chore Agatha made more difficult. Elisabeth sympathized with young people who grew frustrated at home and couldn't wait to get out. Agatha reminded Elisabeth almost daily of her promise to sell the house.

"At fair market value," Elisabeth said.

"Those were the lawyer's words, not yours," Agatha said. "You said at whatever price I thought was fair."

Not sure what she was going to do about her foolish promise, Elisabeth found herself more aware than ever of every detail of the only home she had ever known. She knew every squeak on the stairs, every depression in the floor. She loved the highly polished lacquer on the great banister, the feel of the flocked wallpaper in the parlor and front room. If Elisabeth indeed had to sacrifice this place to a promise made in anger, she would memorize every detail of it. But as she walked slowly from room to room, running her finger over every surface, from the bricks around the great fireplace to the plaster walls of the kitchen and the tile in the bathrooms, Elisabeth felt the bitterness of Aunt Agatha's stare.

Elisabeth found it a relief that summer to be gone nearly every night for training hour activities at church. Will Bishop often sat near her but hardly said two words to her. She spent most of her time deflecting the attentions of Art Childs, who seemed to always want to sit with her, walk with her, talk with her. "Can we walk in the woods tonight after the meeting?" he suggested one day.

"No, Art. No, thank you. All right?"

She feared she had humiliated him. He looked at the ground and busied the toe of his shoe rearranging the dirt. "Well, no, it's not all right, but I get the message."

"There's no message, Art," she said, feeling awful as he forced a smile, then turned from her. "It's just, I—"

"It's all right, Elisabeth," he said. "I know you can do better."

"It's not that at all," she called after him, but he didn't look back.

There was, Elisabeth had to admit, a young man she wouldn't have minded strolling with. Five years older, he would be a junior that fall at a small Bible college in Grand Rapids. He had been invited to both sing and speak every night for a week, and his dark eyes and light hair captivated her nearly as much as his obvious devotion to God did. How strange to see a young person so bold and unashamed of his faith.

But Benjamin Phillips seemed to have eyes for no one, even the classmates who came with him to help out. More than one mooned over him, but not even the girls Elisabeth's age could detect favoritism. Art Childs tried vainly to best him on the baseball diamond, and Frances Crawford said she was convinced Benjamin had his eye on her. Elisabeth was certain his affections were set on things above.

"I guarantee he'll write to me," Frances said more than once. "I may have to write him first, but you watch. I got his address."

Later it came out that she had copied the address of the school from a pamphlet. She wrote him twice before receiving a cordial reply. "He's conceited after all," she told Elisabeth.

"Why do you say that? Let me see his letter."

Frances handed it over with a knowing look. Ben had written, "Forgive me if I can't immediately put a face to the name, Francine. I met so many wonderful kids at your church. I agree it was a refreshing time in the Lord, and thanks for your kind comments about my role in the program. God's best to you. Warmly in Christ, Benjamin P."

"He doesn't sound conceited at all," Elisabeth said. "He seems perfectly wonderful."

"He didn't even remember me!"

"Should he have, Frances?"

"We shook hands after the service one night, and I told him I might come to his school."

"I'm surprised he didn't propose on the spot."

"That's not funny, Elisabeth. He should have remembered. I told him my name."

"We all did."

Chapter Five

The pain of the loss of her father was never far from Elisabeth. She busied herself in church work, playing the piano, singing in the choir, teaching a Sunday school class—one year young girls, the next young boys. She joined the junior missionary society and took her turn writing to missionaries, though she soon found herself the only young person who stuck with that.

Her lingering grief drove her closer to God. Her friends sympathized, but even Frances never seemed to know what to say. Elisabeth tried to be cordial and appreciated any attempt to comfort her, but mostly she found solace in prayer.

Few wanted to hear that, she realized. Pastor Hill explained that "praying without ceasing" was actually attainable. He said Paul's expression meant "keeping the line open all the time. But our connection to God is not a party line. Corporate prayer is one thing, but to pray without ceasing means to keep your private line open to God every waking moment. Keep him at the forefront of your mind. Know he is with you, watching, listening, available for counsel in the secret places of the heart."

Those secret places were where Elisabeth felt so needy, so fragile. She told Frances one day, "I sometimes feel apart from God for no reason." Frances's face showed sympathy as if she had heard Elisabeth, but she said nothing. "How about you, Fran?" Elisabeth pressed.

Frances shrugged. "We *are* apart from God, aren't we?" she said. "I mean, someday we'll be with him in heaven, but that's a long way from here. I don't think God wants us walking around with our heads in the clouds all the time."

Elisabeth was astounded that Frances seemed content to, in essence, leave God out of her life outside of Sundays and Wednesday nights. Elisabeth found comfort in the Psalms and other passages, but still she felt alone. Aunt Agatha badgered her to get out more, to mingle, to start setting her sights on a life's mate. That last surprised Elisabeth, and she had been unable to hide her reaction.

"Why, thank you," Elisabeth said.

"What?" her aunt said. "You assume I think you too young? The sooner you're married, the sooner you're on your way."

Elisabeth fought to keep from reacting angrily, though that cut deeply. How had she allowed herself to walk into it? She was hardly at a point where she was interested in finding someone with whom to share her life. In truth she feared becoming a hermit because of that lack of interest.

"Why don't you get lawyer Beck to dip into your trust and install a telephone in this house?"

Elisabeth shook her head. "Too extravagant," she said. "Snyder's Pharmacy has a phone if we have an emergency, and we haven't had one since Daddy died."

Drifting farther and farther from her friends at church and school, Elisabeth looked forward to Bible camp each summer forty miles to the north. Something about the place and the atmosphere and the people her age from other churches invigorated her, brought her out of herself.

From the moment the little Christ Church caravan turned onto the long, dusty, unpaved road that led to the camp, Elisabeth felt rejuvenated. She stood in line in a musty, wood-paneled hall, signing in. Then she walked the grounds alone, finding her cabin, her bunk, meeting her counselor. Briefly greeting friends from previous summers, she remained alone as long as she could, immersing her senses in the unique atmosphere.

The sandy soil near the lake, the slap of dozens of screen doors from cabins to mess hall to meeting house, the sound of the wind in the trees—all these recalled memories that allowed her to leave her grief in Three Rivers. The oppressive nagging of Aunt Agatha stayed there too. Her friends might have stayed behind as well, because she tended not to spend a lot of time with them during camp week. Elisabeth's spiritual antennae were tuned to others as devoted to God as she. First conversations with new acquaintances told the story. Did they talk about clothes and the opposite sex, or did they talk about Jesus? Some exuded spiritual superiority, which did not jibe with her view of devotion. But many were humble, serious about their faith, strange and wonderful young people who longed to pray and talk of God. With these new friends, she could steal away late at night, not for mischief but actually to discuss the message they had just heard. Elisabeth felt as if she were getting a glimpse of heaven. Here were serious-minded students, interacting mostly with strangers, yet unafraid to speak of their loyalty to Christ.

She couldn't deny that a major draw that summer was the renowned Ben Phillips. Elisabeth loved to hear him preach and sing, but mostly she was still simply impressed that a college student was so overt about his faith.

Fewer and fewer of the young men in her church went to camp each year, but one who never missed was Will Bishop. His father had died in the spring of 1916, apparently leaving no estate. Elisabeth marveled that Will was able to get a week off from his various jobs to get to camp at all. He spent his afternoons that week working maintenance, which must have been, Elisabeth deduced, how he paid the fee. He was the only other camper from her church who joined Ben Phillips and the others for what they called "prayer and sharing" late each night. Poor Will looked exhausted and never said a word. When they prayed around, he was skipped because he was either dozing or simply silent.

One night Will was late and someone asked about him. "He's from my church," Elisabeth said, and quickly told the story of his father and of Will's industriousness.

"Does he ever say anything?" someone asked.

Elisabeth smiled. "He's just shy."

Ben Phillips, who was not only guest college speaker and musician but also helped supervise the camp for the summer, spoke up. "I can't get him to say more than a word or two. But the other night, when we were feeling sorry for ourselves because we are oh-so-spiritual that we can't have fun like everyone else—remember?" Several nodded, smiling. "And instead of going straight back to our cabins we played Capture the Flag? Did you notice that Will didn't play? He just wandered off to his cabin. I figured he was tired from working all afternoon."

"I was afraid he thought we were being unspiritual," someone said.

"Here's what happened," Ben said. "I broke away from my team and circled far around the west row of cabins, then noticed a light in one of the windows. As I tiptoed by, there was Will on his knees by his bunk. He had fallen asleep." Ben paused and shook his head. "I'll tell you something: I'd love just once to fall asleep praying."

Elisabeth was proud of Will, glad she knew him, happy to call him a friend, though they often went months hardly speaking.

She loved those late-night sessions. Besides spiritual matters, they discussed issues of the day. One late night in the summer of 1917, a dozen or so like-minded campers sat before the fireplace in the fellowship hall discussing the war in Europe. "How long before it affects us?" a girl said.

Elisabeth had read in the newspaper that President Wilson had established a neutral policy toward what had become known as the Great War. Wilson said Americans should be "impartial in thought as well as in action," but that was becoming more and more difficult. In 1915 Britain's blockade of Germany and Germany's retaliatory submarine attacks had actually cost some American civilian lives.

"I think most of America is on the side of the Allies," Elisabeth said. "Realistically, how long can the United States remain neutral?"

Congress had approved a war resolution against Germany, but President Wilson, whose reelection motto was "He kept us out of war," would not let America officially join the Allies. Yet just a few months before, in May of 1917, a military draft had been initiated.

"All we can do is pray," a girl said.

Several others nodded, but Ben raised a hand. "At the risk of sounding overly dramatic," he said, "some of us may be called upon to do more than that. General Pershing wants a million men in Europe by this time next year. I just graduated and want to go on to seminary. But if I get drafted—"

"Surely they won't take a seminary student," someone said.

"Maybe you can be a chaplain."

"Or you could—"

Ben interrupted. "I'm not looking for a way out. I'm just saying some of us will be asked to do more than pray."

"Get married!" someone said. "They're not taking men with families."

Ben smiled. "No prospects. Anyway, that would be a pretty bad reason for getting married."

It was close to midnight when the meeting broke up. As the group drifted out into the night, Elisabeth battled her emotions. She wanted to talk to Ben, to let him know that she would be thinking of him, praying for him. But she didn't want to appear forward. She had been as intrigued with Ben as anyone—even Frances Crawford, who had by now gone through a series of summer romances—but Elisabeth's concern for him carried no ulterior motive.

She was in the doorway with only Ben behind her when she hesitated. Ben had turned, apparently to turn out the light, and bumped into her.

"Oh!" he said, his hand gentle on her shoulder. "I'm sorry, Elisabeth. I didn't see you."

She couldn't get over that he knew her name. He seemed as embarrassed as she. She assured him it was her fault as they stepped into the night and he locked the door.

"I, uh, just wanted to tell you, Mr. Phillips, that I—"

"Mr. Phillips!" he said. "I'm not that much older than you. Please call me Ben."

"Okay," Elisabeth said, glad a dim light on a nearby pole did not make plain her red face. She wanted to ask how he knew her name, but she finished her thought. "I will be praying about your war. I mean, your future, whether it means war or not. For you, that is."

Elisabeth wanted to start over, to fix it. But she said nothing.

"Well, thank you," Ben said.

They stood there awkwardly, and as her eyes grew accustomed to the dark, she found herself studying his two-toned shoes. He was dramatically handsome and trim, with a flair for class without flash.

"I'm sorry," he said. "May I walk you?"

"I'm over the rise there," she said, grateful hers was the farthest cabin from the hall.

They strolled slowly, and he was uncharacteristically quiet. It couldn't be that he was as nervous as she. It was all she could do to keep from asking how it was that he was twenty-two and still single, let alone apparently not dating. Surely he had a girl at home.

"I didn't know you knew my name," she said. He stopped and looked at her, as if in shock. "Well, I didn't," she said.

"Everyone knows who you are, Elisabeth."

"Go on," she said.

"Don't be coy," he said. "You stand out."

Elisabeth was dying to ask in what way, but she would not. She looked down. "Really, how did you know my name?"

"Truthfully? I asked your friend the first summer I was here."

"My friend?"

"Francine something?"

"Frances? Frances Crawford?"

"She wrote me once."

"You asked Frances my name? She never told me that."

"I asked her not to. You were what, fourteen?"

"Fifteen."

"I was twenty."

She wanted to say, "So?" but the whole conversation made her woozy. "So you knew my name but never spoke to me?"

"Your father had died, wasn't that it?" She nodded. "And to be frank, high school girls often become enamored with college men. I dared not risk that."

"Of course not. You wouldn't want someone like me to become enamored with someone like you. A college man."

"It wasn't that," he said in the darkness. "You were so young, and, of course, grieving. I could have been misunderstood."

"By whom?"

"You, of course. And there are rules about speakers fraternizing with campers."

"And those have been rescinded?"

"Ah, no. But this was unplanned. I mean, you approached me. Well, you didn't approach me, but—"

"*You* ran into *me*," she said.

"Guilty," he said. "But you said you wanted to speak to me."

"And now I have. And so I should go. My cabin is just over there."

He looked at his watch. "We have ten minutes till lights out."

"But you wouldn't want to be seen fraternizing with a camper," she said. "A high school girl."

"I'm sorry," he said. "I didn't mean to offend you."

"I'm teasing, Ben. I'm not very good at this."

"At what?"

"Social graces."

"People love you here," he said. "It's obvious."

"I'm barely sociable at home."

"Maybe you're in your element here."

She cocked her head. "I do love it."

"But you've got a fella back home."

She shook her head.

"But Francine, Frances, told me—"

"Told you what?" Elisabeth said.

"A young man from your church . . ."

"Who?"

"A couple of years older. He was with you the last two summers."

"Art?"

"That's it."

"Art Childs?" She laughed aloud. "Actually, Art and Frances have begun seeing each other."

They stood by a big tree in front of Elisabeth's cabin. Ben looked at his watch again and seemed to study the ground. "I wish I'd known that," he said.

She held her breath. "Why?"

"I might have broken the rule."

"Ben!"

"I mean this year, not then."

"And what made you think I would be interested?" she said, amazed at her own nonchalance.

He smiled. "I would have taken my chances."

"We really should call it an evening," she said.

"May I finish my thought?"

"I think not."

"Tomorrow night?" he said.

"That would be willfully breaking the rule."

"I'll clear it first," he said.

"With whom?"

"My boss."

"Reverend Shaw?" she said. "I'd be mortified."

"But I'll be within the rules, which is only right." He was walking away.

"Ben, please don't."

He stopped and turned. "Elisabeth, the choice is yours. It's your right to decline."

Decline? Elisabeth could not imagine.

She quietly slipped into the cabin, but as soon as the door was closed, the giggling began. "We must know everything," her cabin mates demanded. "How did you do that?"

"Do what?"

"Catch Ben's eye."

"We were the last ones out and he walked me back, that's all."

They weren't buying, but neither was she talking.

Elisabeth was good for nothing the next day. She forced herself to keep from watching for Ben. That night in the fellowship hall she wanted to acknowledge him but not appear eager. He never glanced her way, though he gave the devotional and seemed to make eye contact with everyone else. Elisabeth feared she had scared him off. She had amazed herself at the things she'd said. Other than Will Bishop, she had never talked to a boy alone.

Elisabeth was so disheartened that she believed everyone could see it on her face. She waited again, careful not to be the only one left when Ben closed the door. When the others moved on, it seemed he noticed her for the first time.

"Oh, Elisabeth," he said, "I'm sorry, but I asked Reverend Shaw, and he denied me permission to interact with you."

Elisabeth fought for composure, the embarrassing ramifications sweeping over her.

"I assumed that would make you happy," he said.

"Happy?"

"You didn't even want me to broach it with him, so—"

This was her fault. She had ruined it by feigning lack of interest. "Yes, but—"

"I'm just kidding," he whispered. "Actually, Reverend Shaw said he wondered how long it would take me to notice someone as beautiful and spiritual as you."

Elisabeth blinked. She didn't know whether to be thrilled or insulted. Apparently that showed.

"I'm sorry, Elisabeth," Ben said. "I had to clear it anyway, just in case. How else could I justify walking with you tonight?"

He touched her elbow and guided her to the door, slowing to let everyone else out first. Some stared and smiled, others whispered. Elisabeth wanted to tell them to mind their own business, but there was no such thing at camp.

She felt awkward as a newborn calf, stumbling into the night, unable to form words. She was thrilled Ben had taken the initiative, but could she ever be the person he thought she was? If not, how would she keep his interest? Elisabeth would be herself, as her father had encouraged her. "You are irresistible when you are you," he would say. If only she might one day hear that from Ben Phillips.

Ben stopped outside the door and stood before her, palms up, brows raised. "I've cleared it, so now it's up to you. May I walk you?"

Elisabeth exhaled, but before she could respond, a voice startled her.

"Excuse me."

"Will!" Ben said, shaking his hand.

"Good devotional tonight, Ben," Will said, and he nodded to Elisabeth.

"Will," she said.

"I was just wondering if you needed someone to walk you to your cabin."

"Oh, I—"

"I mean, the others are already gone, and I—"

"Oh, yes. I appreciate that. But no. I, ah, Ben here has just offered, so I'm all set."

Will looked down. "Okay, then."

"But thank you, Will. Thank you very much. I appreciate it."

"Thanks, Will," Ben added.

"Sure thing," Will said, his face crimson as he backed away.

Chapter Six

Elisabeth had no idea what to expect from Ben Phillips. Could his mind and heart be filled with her every second, as hers were with him? It couldn't be. Otherwise, how could he think or say or do anything not revolving around her? Yet he did. He still taught and sang and led the late-night gathering of the devout.

Had he wanted to sit with her at meals in the noisy mess hall or walk around camp with her during the day as other couples did, she would have been thrilled. But one of the Reverend Shaw's caveats was that they not become "an item."

"We're both too busy anyway," Ben said. "Or we should be."

Elisabeth agreed, appreciating his sensibility and practicality. And any time she wondered whether their lack of time together—save for half an hour or so just before midnight each night—revealed a level of ardor on his part less than her own, she need only recall his gaze.

But their relationship, such as it was, was embryonic. By the end of the week they had not held hands. He would touch her briefly as they walked, but only to courteously direct her. At times she felt like embracing him; occasionally she imagined his kiss. She prayed much about this, worried that her affections had been displaced from God to Ben. Yet she felt no guilt. Only concern. Perhaps this was right. She would need a husband one day, and who better than a godly man like this? Surely, if she maintained her priorities—and Ben seemed as eager as she that they both do that—God would look kindly on the possibilities.

Elisabeth was careful not to express her heart. She planned for their parting a comment that merely said what a wonderful week she had had and that she considered his attention a highlight. She longed for some expression from him, not of love at that too-early place, but of some interest in writing, perhaps of his traveling to Three Rivers, something, anything.

The end of the week approached, and nothing of the sort was suggested. He was the perfect gentleman. She caught herself smiling, amazed that part of her actually wished that just once he wasn't perfect or wholly a gentleman. If he allowed himself the recklessness to say one thing he wouldn't otherwise say if not for their soon parting, she would treasure it.

By their last evening together Elisabeth hoped for something to take with her as comfort to her heart that this had not been merely a week's diversion for him. It certainly had been more than that to her. But rather than express any emotion, Ben simply left her with, "Reverend Shaw asked me to have you visit him in the morning."

"What time? We leave at noon."

"I'd say the earlier the better."

"What's it about?"

"I'll leave that to him."

"But you know?"

"Of course."

"And you can't prepare me?"

"He asked that I not."

"This is maddening, Ben."

"It's not worth worrying about. You'll see."

After breakfast Elisabeth made her way to the administrative offices, housed in a creaky little building that also served as the repository of athletic equipment. Reverend Shaw, who directed the camp for the whole summer with Ben Phillips as his assistant, was an itinerant preacher the rest of the year.

"Come in, my dear," he said, rising when she appeared in the door-way. "You're aware I knew your father, are you not?"

"You told me at the funeral."

"Of course. Well, let me get right to it. Is there a chance you could stay on with us for the last six weeks of the summer?"

"Stay on? No, I—"

"There's an opening on the policing staff, and I asked Mr. Phillips to be on the lookout for a woman of good character who might enjoy serving the Lord this way."

"He recommended me?"

"Highly. If I'd had a brain I'd have suggested you myself, but I get so busy, I was barely aware this was the week you were here."

"But you approved Ben's, um, fraternizing—"

"Miss LeRoy, you would have even less time together if you accepted this position, but of course you would be in closer proximity to Ben here than at home. Naturally, I would not want you to accept the offer based on that . . ."

"Naturally."

"So?"

"I'm at a loss. I would have to ask my aunt. And I was going to work at the pharmacy during the school year, beginning the week before school."

Elisabeth was at a loss for more reasons than that. She wanted more than anything to stay at camp six more weeks, to live with other staff, to see campers of all ages coming and going. Who was she kidding? Proximity to Ben had become her priority. "I'll send a note home with Will Bishop, asking my aunt to inform the pharmacist. But I must tell you, I was not even aware you had a police staff here. I know nothing about police work."

Reverend Shaw laughed. "You'll not be a gendarme. We use the term in the classic sense of policing an area. It is more genteel than calling you a washwoman. There is no glamour in it. You will help wash dishes three times a day, clean the dining hall and kitchen, and scrub the outhouses."

Elisabeth nodded, already imagining the tradeoff. She was not afraid of work, and she had scrubbed more than one outhouse growing up. If this was the price to be on the same campground as Ben, she would do it.

"It's not a volunteer position, by the way. But I don't imagine you could finance a college education on a dollar a day."

"Oh, my."

"That's only six days a week, mind you."

"For six weeks," she said. "Thirty-six dollars goes farther than it used to."

Reverend Shaw stood. "I like a young woman with a sense of humor. If your aunt doesn't send the real police back for you, consider the matter sealed."

Elisabeth told everyone she saw. Several suggested it was because of Ben. "Wrap him around your little finger," Frances said, too loudly.

Elisabeth feigned ignorance. "I'll be too busy to see him much anyway."

She wrote Aunt Agatha: "If for some reason you cannot accommodate this, I apologize for asking and will return as quickly as possible."

Elisabeth sealed the letter and sought out Will Bishop. "Could you see this gets to my aunt?"

"You're not riding with us?"

Elisabeth explained.

"You'll need a ride home at the end of the summer. I'll come get you."

"Oh, Will, thanks. But—"

"I insist," he said. "I have my own truck now. Used but a good one."

"You'd have to take off work . . ."

"Elspeth," he said, "let me do this, will you?"

"Thanks, Will."

Elisabeth did her laundry and settled into her new quarters by the time her friends left at noon. Her supervisor gave her a list of duties that appeared to include about ten hours' work per day, Monday through Saturday. She and her compatriots had the choice of doing the supper kitchen work during or after the evening meeting, so they could attend if they chose. She had to decide whether to be available for the meeting or for a little time with Ben after that. She decided to talk it over with him.

Elisabeth found Ben out front of the administrative offices, readying his staff to greet the new campers, more than a hundred boys from age eight to ten. "My favorite week," he said.

She smiled. "I came to ask about my schedule."

"I'm glad you did. This week's pianist is ill and not coming. Could you fill in?"

Elisabeth was to play three times each day, including for the evening service. She would still be expected to do everything else assigned to her.

The only sliver in her schedule came after the evening service and her kitchen work. Assuming the meeting was over by eight and her work by ten, that might give her more than an hour with Ben. But she also had to rise long before breakfast.

Elisabeth wished she was bold enough to ask Ben straight out, "So when will I see you?" Rather, she said, "That doesn't seem to leave much time for anything else."

"It sure doesn't," he said, looking past her to a cloud of dust boiling up from the gravel half a mile away. "Here come the first of them. We'll have to play the schedule by ear."

Elisabeth had lost his attention, but she understood. He was a man of priorities and commitment and conviction. But as she set about her chores, she allowed herself to wonder if he had charmed her last week merely to enlist her help for the rest of the summer.

By the evening meeting, Elisabeth could not imagine working from six in the morning until ten at night for six weeks. Only love could motivate her, and if it had to be her love for God rather than for Ben, so be it.

There would be no practicing the piano. She would have just enough time to splash her face with water and change her clothes before playing songs by sight from the hymnal. Exhausted, she sat at the bench grateful that Mrs. Stonerock had taught her well. Elisabeth dozed during the prayer. She wished she could slip into the kitchen to get her work done once the singing was over, but she was expected to play for the final song too. She couldn't leave and come back sweaty.

The boys filled every chair in the auditorium, so she had to sit on the piano bench with no back support, wishing all the while she was back in her cabin, stretched out on her bed.

Elisabeth was quickly transported, however, when Ben went from master of ceremonies to soloist and then speaker. Elisabeth was stunned at his ability to communicate with young boys as easily and powerfully as he had the high schoolers from the week before. He was funny and engaging, yet challenging. He had the boys' attention and they seemed to love him.

Until the closing prayer she forgot her fatigue and the work that still lay ahead. She felt privileged to be there, impressed anew with the spiritual side of Ben, and eager to see him later, if only for a few minutes. She marshaled enthusiasm for the last song, then hurried back to her cabin to change and then down to the dining hall and into the kitchen. The giant pots and pans, the massive stoves and ovens looked even more enormous in the otherwise empty kitchen.

Peeved that the crew had left her more than her assigned duties, Elisabeth felt obligated to leave the place ready for breakfast preparation. As she did her work and that of at least two others, she rehearsed how she would state her case the next morning. "I'm warning you," she said silently, "I will do only my work from now on. If the place is not shipshape for breakfast, don't blame me."

Her back ached as she mopped the floor, and it seemed as if Christ himself spoke to her heart. *For whom are you working?*

"Not for everyone else," she said. "Never again."

The question came again.

"For you, Lord," she whispered.

She kept working, hoping for some sense of peace, of assurance, of favor. God's only response was to stop asking the question. *Of course,* she thought. *I already answered. If I'm working for him, I will obey him. If there's work to do, I'll do it. And if there's been an injustice, vengeance will be his.*

Such, Elisabeth decided, was a life that was an experiment in obedience. But certainly there would be some small reward. There had to be some sort of payoff this side of heaven for a life of true devotion. Surely Ben was waiting at the end of this grueling day.

She finished after eleven and caught a glimpse of herself in the mirror on her way out. Her faced was streaked with grime and sweat. Her work dress was nearly soaked through. Elisabeth was desperate for a few minutes with Ben. Simply unburdening herself, telling him what she had endured, would put things back into perspective. She would be able to sleep without dreading the early wakeup.

But there was no way she could see him looking the way she did.

Elisabeth hurried back to the cabin, where her coworkers were already sleeping. She was tempted to rouse them, to tell them what she had done and demand to know why it had all been left to her. But she merely grabbed fresh clothes and hurried to the creek, where she disrobed and dove in. The water was so cool and refreshing it made her weep, but time was fleeting. She felt vulnerable in the bright moonlight and feared being seen. She quickly dried and dressed and tied her hair atop her head, then wrapped her clothes in her towel and set out to find Ben.

But the camp was dark. She didn't know where his cabin was and didn't want to—she could never explain being found there, bothering his mates to rouse him. The administration building was dark too, as was the tiny cabin behind it where Reverend Shaw and his family stayed.

Elisabeth felt faint as she made her way back up the path toward her cabin. She prayed that Ben would be somewhere waiting for her. He was not. It was midnight and she had to be up by six. In fact, if she wanted to get in her time of Bible reading and prayer, she would have to be up before that. There would be no other time, day or night, to make up for lost time in the morning.

Elisabeth dropped her bundle on the floor, sat on her bunk, lay back without changing into her nightgown, and fell asleep unhappy. Her eyes popped open at five-thirty, and her mood had not changed. Her cabin mates still slept, and she was grateful for the time. After freshening up, she sat on a wooden bench just off the path and read and prayed. She asked God to lift the gloom from her, to remind her again that she was working for him, and to help her examine her motives for having stayed at camp.

When she arrived at the kitchen she was furious to find that only her supervisor was there. "Your teammates have overslept again," she was told. "Would you go get them for me?"

Elisabeth stared at the woman. Everything in her wanted to scream, "No, I will not!" She did her job and still managed to get up early. If they couldn't get up on time even though they went to bed early and did less work, she should not be expected to roust them out of bed. But she remained silent.

The woman stared back. "Do you follow directives or do you not? I'm shorthanded, but I'll fire you before I'll allow you to be impudent. Need I remind you that we're working for the Lord here, and that—"

"No, ma'am. I'm sorry. Right away." Elisabeth wished she could demand to know who the other girls were working for, still asleep, lazy, no account . . .

"Good girl."

Elisabeth ran up the path, sobs climbing from her chest. Impudence? *For the Lord,* she told herself over and over. *For the Lord.*

When she got to the cabin the other girls were hurriedly dressing. "First one up is supposed to wake the others!" one said. "You trying to make us look bad?"

Elisabeth said nothing. Did they really want to be awakened when she got up? Maybe she'd find out the next morning. She headed back down.

"We don't have time to wait for them," her supervisor said. "Let's get cracking." Again Elisabeth did her work and theirs.

After breakfast dishes and dining hall cleanup, Elisabeth policed the outhouses until lunch. She barely had the energy to eat, but lunch revived her and she was able to manage her afternoon chores. She was determined to talk with Ben before the evening service, regardless how forward she appeared. She hurried through her work, changed quickly, and found him at the front of the auditorium chatting with someone about the program.

She tried to smile when he looked up at her, but he motioned he would be a minute. Finally he broke free.

"I really wanted to see you last night," she said.

"Me too," he said. "You got my note?"

"Note?"

"I left it in the screen door of the kitchen last night. I had a home-sick camper and by the time I got over there it was eleven-fifteen and you were gone."

"Thanks, but I never got it."

She wanted him to suggest trying again that night, but he just looked at her. Her reserves were gone. Feeling bold, she said, "Tonight?"

"Oh," he said, "that was in the note too. The reverend and I have an errand in Paw Paw and won't get back until after midnight."

Elisabeth wondered if she would see him at all that summer. "Well," she said. "Safe trip."

"Thanks."

And that was it. No apology. No wishing he could see her. No set-ting a time for the next night. He handed her a slip of paper listing the hymns for the evening, and she trudged back to the piano.

The boys were filing in, so Elisabeth opened to the first selection. It was "My Savior's Love," written just a dozen years before by Charles H. Gabriel. Elisabeth sight-read the music, silently running her fingers across the keyboard. She was about to turn to the second selection when she caught sight of the lyrics. She had sung the song many times at Christ Church, but suddenly the truth of it pierced her.

She had been so self-possessed, so worried about the offenses and slights of the last day and a half that her mind had been derailed from God. What had she endured compared to what Jesus had gone through for her? The song seemed to slay her. She stared at the verses through pools of tears and found herself playing the song softly but with deep expression.

The music soothed the rambunctious boys. Elisabeth was unaware that her playing had also caught the attention of the platform until Ben stood at the pulpit and raised his arms, asking that the boys bow their heads and listen. He began to sing just above a whisper in a voice so filled with emotion that Elisabeth felt the presence of God.

She was amazed anyone could hear either the singing or the play-ing, but there was no other sound. From the corner of her eye she saw her coworkers emerge from the kitchen and stand silently in the back as Ben sang:

I stand amazed in the presence of Jesus the Nazarene,
And wonder how He could love me, a sinner, condemned, unclean.
For me it was in the garden He prayed: "Not My will, but Thine";
He had no tears for His own griefs, but sweat-drops of blood for mine.
In pity angels beheld Him, and came from the world of light
To comfort Him in the sorrows He bore for my soul that night.
He took my sins and my sorrows, He made them His very own;
He bore the burden to Calvary, and suffered and died alone.
When with the ransomed in glory His face I at last shall see,
'Twill be my joy through the ages to sing of His love for me.
How marvelous! How wonderful! And my song shall ever be:
How marvelous! How wonderful is my Savior's love for me.

When Ben finished, even the young boys remained silent. Others on the platform had knelt by their chairs. Ben said, "I feel led to cancel what we had planned for tonight. Just let me tell you what those words mean and invite you too to stand amazed in the presence of Jesus."

He walked them through each verse as Elisabeth continued to play. He explained what it meant to be condemned and unclean and then ransomed by a Savior. He invited boys who wanted to receive Christ as their Savior to come forward and pray with counselors. Dozens did.

Nearly spent, Elisabeth went back to the kitchen where the team was cleaning up. "That was something," one of them said.

"I forgot to give you this," Elisabeth's supervisor said. "It was on the door this morning, but I was so distracted by the others being late …"

Elisabeth thanked her and peeked at the note. Under his signature he had added the reference, Philippians 1:3–6.

Thankful her father had early started her on a path of memorization, she let the verses resound in her mind as she finished her tasks:

"I thank my God upon every remembrance of you, always in every prayer of mine for you all making request with joy, for your fellowship in the gospel from the first day until now; being confident of this very thing, that he who hath begun a good work in you will perform it until the day of Jesus Christ."

What a perfect way to end the day! The spiritual truth of the verses fit with the song she had just played and the experience they had all shared. The idea that Ben was thanking God upon every remembrance of her was thrilling too. Physically drained, Elisabeth cheerfully finished her work and headed for a longer night's sleep. She was in her nightgown and nearly asleep when her last bunkmate arrived.

"Ben Phillips is looking for you."

She sat up. "Where?"

"Auditorium. He said if you were in bed to not bother you."

"It's no bother," Elisabeth said, changing quickly.

"It's not that important."

"It is to me."

She was breathless by the time she reached Ben. "I didn't mean to bother you," he said. "You must be exhausted."

"I'm fine."

"Reverend Shaw and I are not expected in Paw Paw until later, so I had an hour. I should have assumed you'd want to rest."

"I'd rather spend time with you," she said. "If you don't mind."

"Do I look like I mind?"

They sat on the same wooden bench where Elisabeth had read that morning. It seemed ages ago. "The meeting tonight was worth this whole summer," she said.

"But you're only two days into it."

"Still . . ."

"You did it."

"I just played the music, Ben. The words got to me. What happened was God's doing."

"Wasn't it a privilege to be used that way?"

She nodded.

"Lord, we're grateful," he said, and she quickly bowed her head and closed her eyes. But he said no more. She believed it the most poignant and heartfelt prayer she had ever heard.

Ben looked at his watch several minutes later and said, "I'd better hook up with the reverend." Their hands brushed as they rose from the bench. "I'll see you off," she said.

"I'll see *you* off," he said. "You need your rest."

He walked her back up to her cabin and said goodnight. She giggled.

"What?" he said.

"I'm awful."

"Tell me."

"I was just wondering what I might do tomorrow evening to cut short the meeting."

"You *are* awful," he said. "But I hope you come up with something."

Chapter Seven

*A*unt Agatha's letter arrived near the end of the week. After a volley assuring Elisabeth she was enjoying her solitude, she urged Elisabeth to keep her eyes open for a suitable match, "perchance someone able to abide your fancy of pie in the sky by and by."

Elisabeth had to smile. Was Aunt Agatha unknowingly angling for her to marry into the faith?

Elisabeth quickly adjusted to the routine and felt she had gained the kind of discipline her father had tried to instill in her. The work was torturous, the hours unbearable, and her coworkers lazy and selfish. She told Ben she was trying to guard against spiritual superiority. "I know the testing of my faith brings patience and that I should count it all joy. But when I return kindness for evil, even if I don't get kindness back, I feel some sort of victory."

"It *is* a victory," Ben said. "But you're right to guard against smugness."

"I know," she said. "And I'm proud that I know."

"Rascal," he said.

Elisabeth soon felt at least two weeks behind in her sleep. But she was maturing. She worked harder than ever, and she benefited from hearing Ben speak nearly every night. He would make a fine pastor. It was beyond her how he could speak on so many different topics to different age groups and always find something challenging and interesting to say.

When she received permission to practice in the auditorium during a rare free moment, Ben joined her on the piano bench. "How am I supposed to concentrate?" she asked.

"I was hoping you wouldn't," he said.

"Is that what you call being a good influence on a young person?" she said.

"I hope so."

When he rested his hand in the middle of her back, she fought to keep from increasing the tempo. Though she feared perspiring under the warmth of his palm, she hoped he would never take his hand away. But as she finished the song, he withdrew his hand.

The next time he sat with her, however, he seemed nervous. He said he had only a few minutes. Halfway through the second song, he stood and leaned toward her ear. "Keep playing," he whispered, "I have to go."

She nodded, her eyes on the music, and he brushed her cheek with his lips. She froze, laboring to concentrate as he left. Though the kiss thrilled her, it had been his, not theirs.

After the evening meeting he seemed awkward, avoiding her gaze as they strolled the dirt pathways that rimmed the camp. When they were alone he said, "I apologize. I had no claim to kiss you. I mean, I didn't even give you the opportunity to refuse me."

"Or slap you," she said.

"I was afraid you might say that. Forgive me?"

"I have too many options," she said, brushing a mosquito from his forehead. "I could have refused you or slapped you, and now I can forgive you. What's your preference?"

"The latter."

"Denied."

"It's too late to refuse me. Slap me as hard as you want."

"I can't forgive what I don't consider an offense. I will be offended next time, however, if you feel you have to steal it."

"I didn't mean to."

"Of course you did. You didn't give me the chance to refuse or to give it freely."

"And would you have?"

"I was not given the opportunity to find out."

"Shall I try again?"

She glanced down the pathway toward the lights near the center of the campground. No one was coming. "I wish you would."

The sensation of his lips on hers left her breathless.

The end of the summer came so quickly that Elisabeth hardly had time to prepare for parting with Ben. Stealing away behind the administration building, beyond curious eyes and the cacophony of dozens of farewells, they embraced fiercely.

"I'll write," he whispered.

"Me too," she said. "Every day. And you'll come see me?"

"First chance I get."

"I can't wait," she said.

Ben fell silent, holding her so tight that she knew he hated separating as much as she did. "So this is what Shakespeare meant by 'such sweet sorrow,'" she said. Though neither had spoken of love, she had fallen for Ben. His embrace told her he felt the same about her.

Only moments after Ben and his friends pulled away from the camp, Will rumbled up in his truck. Elisabeth was glad to see him. She only wished he were more forthcoming; he could be a quality friend. He loaded her stuff and opened her door, helping her in. It was as if she had grabbed a tree branch. She was amazed at the strength and size of his hands. He had to have died a thousand deaths, she thought, to let her touch him. As he climbed behind the wheel he avoided her gaze and did not return her smile.

"I really appreciate this, Will," she said.

"You're welcome," he said, wrestling with the gearshift. "Good summer?"

She told him how challenging and yet beneficial it had been, but she said nothing about Ben. "And what about you?" she said. "How's your work going? Your mother? The rest of the family?"

"Good. She's okay. We're all living together now, you know, Ma and me and my married sisters and their families. Taking in boarders too. Everybody's busy."

It was the most he had said in one burst since she'd known him. She tried to engage him further, but he would only answer questions, not offer more. Tired of the effort and full of fresh memories of Ben, Elisabeth looked out the window as if studying the sunset, deciding not to turn back unless Will said something.

After about fifteen miles of silence, she jumped and turned when he spoke. "Just basically been working," he said.

He was staring at the road. "Have you?" she said. They had been through this. Everybody was fine and he was working more than ever. She had told him she had always admired that about him. Maybe he wanted to hear that again.

"Yep," he said. "Seems like it's all I do. Work. 'Course we've still got senior year."

It was the first conversation he had initiated with her in more than ten years. She had to reward it. "Yes," she said. "I'll be glad when that's over. Won't you?"

"I sure will. I was hoping maybe we could get married then."

Her eyes grew wide. "You're getting married?"

Will looked left, then back to the front, still avoiding her eyes. "I was hoping."

"Who's the lucky girl? Someone I know?"

He pursed his lips and shook his head.

"I know," she said. "That Burke girl, the redhead?"

"I wish you wouldn't do that, Elspeth," he said, clearly angry.

She hadn't seen this side of him but was delighted he was asserting himself. "I'm sorry, Will, but this is exciting. I don't mean to make a game of it. Just tell me."

"Is that your answer?" he said, his voice flat and hard.

"My answer?"

"Is that how you turn me down?"

A chill washed over her. "Oh, Will, I'm so sorry. I wasn't sporting with you. I didn't realize what you were saying. Please forgive me."

"Okay, but then will you?"

"Oh, Will."

Elisabeth wished he would pull over so they could talk face to face. But he was on paved road now and they seemed to be flying. She couldn't imagine what he must have gone through to broach the subject.

"I've been praying about it," he said, sounding encouraged. "I believe it's what God wants for us."

Elisabeth sighed. Why did this have to happen? The day she committed the rest of her life to God, she learned her father was dying. Now the day she knew she was in love with Ben Phillips, Will Bishop announced his intentions.

"Will, I'm flattered. And you must know I'm very surprised. Thank you for such a compliment. I'll never forget that you asked me."

"Sounds like you're saying no."

"I'm sorry."

He stared straight ahead, his body stone rigid except to steer. "Can I ask why?"

Should she tell him something she hadn't told even Ben? She had no choice. "I'm in love, Will."

"But not with me."

"I like you a lot. I always have, and I always will. I admire you. You're going to make someone a great husband."

"But not you."

"No." It pained her to be so direct, but anything less would have been cruel.

"Ben Phillips?"

"Yes."

"Engaged?"

"No. We've only just—"

"I hope not, after just part of a summer."

"Of course. But I love him, Will."

"Does he love you?" It wasn't a challenge. Will simply sounded devastated.

"I believe he does."

Will shook his head. "That makes two of us then," he announced. "And until he asks you and you say yes, I don't guess I'll be giving up."

Elisabeth rubbed her forehead with both hands. "Will, I want us always to be friends. If you hound me, it'll ruin that."

He was suddenly animated, glancing back and forth between her and the road. "But it's right, Elspeth. I know it. And someday you will too."

They were on the outskirts of Three Rivers. "So God has told you but not me," she said. "Is that it?"

"Seems like it."

"Don't you agree that until he tells me, I should not say yes?"

"Of course. Has he told you to say no?"

"I didn't even know to pray about it," she said.

"Now you know."

"Well, sure, yes. But God would also have to give me feelings for you that I haven't even considered. I have to be frank, Will. I don't see it."

Will downshifted and turned a little too quickly into Elisabeth's neighborhood. "Has God told you to marry Ben?"

"It seems he's part of us. We have so much—"

"But has God told you?"

"Not yet."

"Then I still have a chance."

Poor Will. There was no arguing with him. She shook her head. "Tell me you won't pressure me."

"I shouldn't have to," he said. "God will tell you."

"And if he doesn't?"

"He'll tell me to forget about it. But he already told me, Elspeth."

"What if he tells me to marry Ben?"

"He won't."

"But what if he does?"

Will pulled in front of Elisabeth's house and parked. "If God told me something, and I was sure of it, I'd do it."

"There you go."

Both hands on the wheel, the truck idling, Will stared straight ahead. "I already told you what God told me."

Conversing with the taciturn Will Bishop was surreal enough. That they were discussing love and marriage left Elisabeth reeling. "This is making me uncomfortable, Will."

He opened his door. "God will give you peace about it. Until he does, I promise I won't bother you."

"Thank you," she said, and she meant it. She leapt from the truck before having to take Will's hand again.

She and Will saw each other at school every day and even had two classes together, though they sat nowhere near each other. Will gravitated toward accounting and bookkeeping classes, telling her he was hoping to get a desk job someday where he could work long and hard and make good wages without working his body to death.

Meanwhile, Elisabeth and Ben were deeply in love and saying so in their daily letters. Then came a letter that Elisabeth wished had been a phone call, or even a visit. She hopped onto the couch and tucked her feet beneath her as she unfolded it. "I've been drafted," Ben wrote simply, and her hands began to shake so she could hardly read. The tears didn't help either.

"I can only imagine you're as upset as I am," he wrote. "Maybe more. But this is where our faith is tested. God knows. Trust him."

That was Ben. He said he was upset, but he sure seemed to get over it quickly. He *was* more spiritual than she, and as she sat there trying to calm her racing heart, she imagined the worst. *What kind of a spiritual baby am I?* she scolded herself. Ben would be ashamed of her.

"I've already been assigned chaplain's assistant at Grand Rapids Memorial Hospital, awaiting deployment."

Deployment? That sounded so, so military!

"I'm prepared to go wherever I'm sent," he wrote, "but I'm praying for something stateside."

"So am I," Elisabeth wrote back. And she prayed as she had never prayed before.

Ben promised to visit Three Rivers over Christmas, and Elisabeth couldn't wait. Communication between her and Aunt Agatha had been strained to the breaking point. She needed above all to simply converse with someone who loved her.

Marlin Beck reminded Elisabeth that the housing decision was still hers.

"I mean to do as I said," she told him. "I can tolerate my aunt until I sell and move out."

"But clearly her intention now is to move you out on your eighteenth birthday. You'll have six months of high school left."

"Surely she'll let me stay until I graduate."

"Make it a condition of the sale."

"No conditions." She told Beck she was a Christian and had pledged the rest of her life as an experiment in obedience. "At the very least that means I must be true to my word, even if I spoke too hastily."

"I consider myself a Christian too," he told her. "And there is a huge difference between being charitable and being a doormat. Jesus was walked upon only when he allowed it. May I remind you that the one time he erupted in righteous indignation concerned inappropriate use of funds?"

Elisabeth did not want to be taken advantage of. But neither would she quarrel over temporal things, especially things that belonged to the father who had taught her to hold loosely to material goods. Mr. Beck tried to Dutch uncle her into exercising her faith by honoring her father's wishes and doing the just and right thing. Elisabeth felt powerless and would not discuss it, except in her letters to Ben.

Ben first broached the subject of marriage circumspectly in a letter. "We should not even talk about a future together until I know how risky my assignment might be," he wrote. Elisabeth appreciated it. So much was unclear. Long range, Ben wanted to attend seminary and become a pastor. Short term, he had to remain flexible due to America's increased involvement in the war.

He was so practical, Elisabeth thought. She wanted above everything to marry him, but he had not asked yet. As right as the prospect of their marriage felt, she appreciated his unwillingness to risk her being widowed just months after their wedding. She tried to keep from her mind that he might die, but it was futile. She prayed the war would end before he was assigned and that their murky future would become clear.

Elisabeth also prayed that Will Bishop would find a wife and that God would make it plain that Will had simply misread the first signal. If by some bizarre twist Will was right, if God had really impressed on his heart that Elisabeth was in his future, God would tell her too. Wouldn't he?

One Sunday in December, Frances Crawford and Art Childs stopped Elisabeth on her way out of church. Frances waved a diamond ring in her face. So eager herself to marry, Elisabeth had to fake a smile. "When's the big day?" she said.

"After graduation," Frances said, beaming. "Art's already a welder with the railroad." Elisabeth was impressed that Art seemed to have become a serious young man and was now back in church regularly after a season of spotty attendance.

"I want you as my maid of honor," Frances added, and Elisabeth was stunned. They had drifted apart, but maybe there was hope for their friendship yet. Frances had to know that Art pursued Elisabeth first, but she also knew of Elisabeth's interest in Ben. "Or will it be matron of honor?" Frances said.

"Not that soon," Elisabeth said. "But I'll be honored either way."

Will Bishop blossomed with his new interest in accounting. He worked part-time at a local manufacturing plant while maintaining his many side businesses. Elisabeth noticed that he had begun speaking up in Sunday school and training hour, evidencing things he had learned from his own Bible study. He was cordial to her, but his eyes betrayed his pain. She could only hope they would one day be friends again.

Ben arrived a few days before Christmas at the Lake Shore and Michigan Southern depot. Elisabeth met him with great fanfare and they walked arm in arm to a nearby boarding house. She waited in the lobby while he settled in, then they walked home to meet Aunt Agatha.

Elisabeth was eager to see whether Ben could work his considerable charm on this tough case. "Aunt Agatha Erastus," she said, "Benjamin Phillips. Benjamin, this is my father's sister, who has devoted her life to raising me."

"Not my whole life, thankfully," Agatha said, nodding but not offering her hand. "But what's a body to do in such a situation? Out of tragedy rises responsibility."

"Which, carried out, is godly virtue," Ben said.

"Yes, well, I don't know about that."

Before dessert Agatha maneuvered the conversation to the future. "Are you clear about the disposition of Elisabeth's estate?"

Ben looked at her, open-faced. "Begging your pardon, Mrs. Erastus, I frankly don't see how that's any of my business."

"Then let me be frank with you, Mr. Phillips. If you wait long to make it your business, the house portion of it will have been disposed of."

"I told him all about that," Elisabeth said.

"Just so he has no designs on it or the proceeds from it."

Elisabeth raised her brows. "There'll be precious few proceeds if you pay only what you believe is fair."

Aunt Agatha glared. "I was talking about when I sell it."

Elisabeth was stricken. "You'd sell this place?"

Agatha laughed. "What do I need with a house the size of a barn? It's an investment, child."

"Surely, you'll take into consideration the feelings of your niece," Ben said. "Does it make sense for her to sell it to you for whatever price you set and then you turn a fast profit on it?"

"You said yourself it was none of your business," Aunt Agatha said.

"Maybe I'll buy it back myself!" Elisabeth blurted.

"Then don't sell it," Ben whispered.

"I've given my word," she said.

Ben tried to help Elisabeth cope with her aunt. He went so far as to visit Marlin Beck, and he returned agreeing with the lawyer that Elisabeth had confused meekness for weakness. "Your aunt is walking all over you and the memory of your father."

"It's my own fault," she said.

"Only if you let it happen."

"It's already happened. I can't go back on my word."

Elisabeth worried that Ben would consider her too immature to become his bride. That fear was eradicated Christmas Eve when they walked in the snow to the corner of Adams and North Main, where Bonnie Castle had been transformed from a private residence to the new Three Rivers Hospital. Ben brushed snow off a wrought iron bench and they sat huddled and shivering.

"Elisabeth, I love you," he said. "I want you to be my wife."

"Are you asking me to marry you?"

He laughed. "Was that not clear?"

"I thought we had decided to wait—"

"Until my disposition, yes. That's why I don't have a ring for you tonight. I won't leave the continent with a fiancée waiting. But I wanted you to know my intentions, and I want to know if they have basis."

"Basis?"

"I need to know you'll marry me when I return."

"I will."

They fell into a long kiss. "It will have to be our secret until we make it official," he said at last.

She nodded. "No one would understand if we announced now and I had no token . . ."

"Nor a visible fiancé."

"Some are becoming engaged despite the dangers. Some even marry, worried they may never again have the chance."

"My faith is stronger than that," he said. "Anyway, their reasons are shallow if they guarantee themselves only a few weeks together."

Elisabeth felt that same urgency, but she would not admit it. "I'll wait for you," she said. "As long as necessary."

Ben left the day after Christmas, and Elisabeth busied herself at the pharmacy and the library and the church. She was tempted to take Mr. Beck up on his offer to legally preclude Aunt Agatha's attempt to wrest the home from the estate. But as much as she wanted to honor her father's wishes, when she prayed about it she felt led to follow through with her commitment. She didn't dare ask if her aunt was intent on moving her out as soon as she turned eighteen. Elisabeth's birthday was a holiday anyway. Nothing legal could happen that day.

Among Elisabeth's Christmas cards was one from Will Bishop. On the back he wrote, "Elisabeth, regardless of what the future holds, I wish you all the best that God has for you, now and forever. If you ever need anything at all, with no strings attached, please do me the honor of asking. Your friend, Will."

Elisabeth was taken with the simple beauty of the sentiment and thankful that Will had acceded to her request not to pressure her. A tear surprised her and raced down her cheek. She blinked away the sting and prayed for Will. His old question echoed in her mind—not whether God had told her she was to marry him, but rather, whether God had told her she was to marry Ben.

Elisabeth did not believe God spoke audibly anymore. But she knew when God impressed something on her heart. Had she prayed about marrying Ben? Only that God would spur him to ask, and that had been answered. Had she sought God's will? She couldn't say she had, but did she need a loud signal for every decision?

On the other hand, this was not just another decision. Ben had asked. She had answered. And while it seemed she prayed without ceasing about anything and everything, she felt discomfort in her soul. For the briefest moment she was glad Will was not right there demanding an answer. As forward as he had been and as uncomfortable as he had made her that summer, his question—the one about seeking God—was legitimate.

Everything about Ben, except his immediate future, fit neatly on a list of everything Elisabeth looked for in a life's mate. He was spiritual, mature, bright, articulate, caring, moral, ethical, motivated. She had examined her heart. She loved him. It was a first love, yes, initially perhaps infatuation or a love of being in love. But she had gotten to know him, and she loved him all the more. What more did she need or want from God on the matter? Could there be anyone more perfect for her?

Surely God had thrust Ben into her path. She smiled. Actually, she had been in Ben's path. What kept her from praying specifically about marrying him? How did that jibe with her commitment to obey Christ in everything? Had something deep down kept her from leaving it with God?

Worse, was she again setting a course where she felt bound to her word, even if she had acted impulsively, apart from God's wisdom?

Elisabeth shook her head and stood, placing Will's sweet card into a basket with the others. There was no reason to doubt her yes to Ben Phillips. She was sure that if she asked God to give her complete peace about it, he would. Someday, she might do just that.

On Monday, December 31, 1917, a document was delivered to Elisabeth at home. "This is to inform you that a check has been written to the First National Bank of Three Rivers by Mrs. Agatha LeRoy Erastus in exchange for the title deed to the house that legally becomes yours tomorrow. Please plan to appear at the closing of the transaction at 1 P.M., Wednesday, January 2, 1918."

Included in the envelope was a birthday card from her aunt. Under Agatha Erastus's signature, she had written:

"Please evacuate the premises of all your belongings by the end of the day, Thursday, January 3."

Elisabeth had been put onto the street by the only remnant of her family. Hands trembling, she replaced the documents in the envelope and wished she could talk to Ben. What she really wanted was to be held by him, to announce to the world that they were marrying right away. Instead she merely wept and tried to pray, her spiteful aunt not twenty feet away, working in the kitchen.

Elisabeth had already accepted this. It may not be right; it certainly wasn't what her father had in mind. And she couldn't imagine it was God's plan. But she would rise above it and go quietly.

Where, she did not know.

Chapter Eight

*E*lisabeth heard the slam of a car door and watched Marlin Beck march to the porch. Apparently he had been served the same papers.

"My authority ends the day you turn eighteen," he whispered fiercely to her at the door, "but I beg you not to let this happen. I will have failed your father."

"You didn't fail him," Elisabeth said. "I did."

"Well, by heaven, I'll have my say anyway. Do you know the market value of this house?"

"I don't care."

"You don't care that it's four times the amount of your aunt's check? It's a travesty. Let me in."

Elisabeth stepped aside and stood gazing out as Mr. Beck stomped through the house behind her. "Mrs. Erastus! This is criminal! If your niece would say the word, I'd have *you* on the street tomorrow!"

Elisabeth turned at the unhurried footsteps of her aunt. "Are you joking? That would violate her sacred code. She'd no longer be a martyr, the last attribute she would sacrifice."

Beck wheezed, bereft of a comeback. Red-faced, mouth pinched, he swept past Elisabeth. She opened the door, but he stopped. He looked at her with disgust, then at Aunt Agatha. "*That* I have to give you, Mrs. Erastus. Yes, *that* would be difficult to argue. But could you please tell me why? What has this child done so despicable that in the middle of winter you would put her out of the house she was born in?"

The woman eyed Beck as if wondering whether she owed anyone an answer. "My own daughter would be about her age," she said. "Kathleen is gone. This one will survive. Mine had to die, but this girl's been dealt every blow God could bestow, yet she blithely prances through life, feeling no pain."

"No pain?" Elisabeth said, hating the whine in her voice. "I—"

"Mrs. Erastus," Beck said, "yours is an act of greed as plain as I've seen in a career. You care no more for your own niece than you care what I think of you."

"I certainly care nothing about you, sir."

"Hallelujah! A badge of honor I can wear home." He turned to Elisabeth. "Dear, you need not appear at the closing. I'll handle it." She nodded, unable to speak. Beck added, "The proceeds won't go far. I hope Snyder is paying a livable wage. Where will you go?"

Elisabeth cleared her throat. "Maybe Aunt Agatha will rent me a room."

"For Pete's sake!" Beck roared. "My wife and I would take you in before I could abide that!"

"This place will be sold within the week," Aunt Agatha said. "Why do you think I need her out by Thursday?"

Elisabeth stormed to her room, stuffing everything she could find into two trunks and a suitcase. She was stunned when Mr. Beck followed and began helping. "If you stay in this house one more night, I'll sue you myself—for stupidity."

In spite of everything, Elisabeth had to laugh. Beck shook his head. "Is she right? Are you hopelessly cheerful, regardless?"

Elisabeth shrugged.

"Seriously, where are you going? Where may I transport your things?"

"To the front porch for now. I may need a ride to Central House or—"

"Please, Miss LeRoy! A single young woman? That place has a saloon."

"Three Rivers House, then."

"Better. I know the proprietors. But won't you stay with my wife and me until you make other arrangements?"

"I'll manage, but thank you." Elisabeth couldn't imagine staying in a stranger's home.

Beck looked at his watch. "I'm sorry," he said, "I'm running late." He lugged the trunks to the porch and was gone.

Elisabeth strode to the cellar, found a box, and took it to her room. She sat on the edge of the bed, her eyes filling at the thought of the years she had spent there. It had been her only bedroom her whole life. How many times had her father sat where she was sitting? Talked with her. Prayed with her. Held her. Let her cry. Taught her. Loved her. She breathed a prayer of thanks, pleading with God to not allow her to be bitter toward her aunt. Elisabeth was already losing that battle.

She pulled on her heavy winter coat and sat again. "Lord," she said, "I still want to obey in everything. Tell me what to do. Pastor could find someone to take me in, but I hate to ask. Don't let me be proud."

And with that came the answer. Elisabeth was nearly rocked by the force of it. By simply asking to be shielded from pride, she was deeply impressed with what to do. "No, Lord, please. This is not of you, is it? Tell me it's my penchant for martyrdom."

But she received no such peace. She filled the last box and muscled it out the front door, then stepped back inside. From the basket on the piano she sifted through the Christmas cards, selecting those addressed to her alone. She tucked the stack in her pocket, took a deep breath, and called out for her aunt.

"What do you want? I'm in the kitchen."

Elisabeth wiped her face and caught sight of her reflection in the oval, concave photograph of her mother near the front door. Standing there in her snug coat, collar high on her neck, hair up and pinned back, Elisabeth thought herself a full-grown woman, tall, straight, and—incongruously—confident looking. She shifted her focus so her mother's face replaced her own. Vera LeRoy had a softer, more complacent countenance. She had been not much older than Elisabeth when the photograph was made.

Elisabeth wanted to ask Aunt Agatha why she was hiding in the kitchen. There was nothing on the stove, not even anything before her on the table. Elisabeth wished she could force her aunt to acknowledge her own wickedness. Rather, she said, "Aunt Agatha, I want to thank you for all you've done for me."

"Oh, please," Mrs. Erastus groaned. "You were a job, and you know it. I needed room and board. You were the price."

"You helped raise me, and I appreciate it."

"You're a fool."

"Clearly. But I didn't want to leave with you unaware that I appreciated—"

"All right!" Agatha said, turning away. "Now go."

Elisabeth hoped her aunt averted her face to hide tears, but she knew better.

Will Bishop lay in the snow in his fourth ward driveway under the very truck he had used to drive her home from camp months before. "Must be wet and cold under there," Elisabeth said, standing at his feet.

"Elspeth?"

"How'd you know?"

He slid out from underneath, his hands red and raw. "Universal," he said.

"Universal?"

"U-joint. Slipping and sliding in the snow is awful for 'em."

"You don't say. Will, may I speak with you?"

He struggled to his feet, attacking his greasy hands with an oily rag as he led her inside the huge, ramshackle house. He and his mother, his two married sisters, their husbands, and a passel of kids under ten shared it with boarders. Rent was cheap and you got what you paid for. Mrs. Bishop was not known as a fastidious housekeeper or a great cook.

"I'm selling my house in two days," Elisabeth said.

Will narrowed his eyes. "You can imagine I have all kinds of questions. Your aunt. Your timing. Your boyfriend. Everything."

Elisabeth was shocked at how easily he conversed, compared to just that summer. Maybe branching into bookkeeping and accounting, or taking more responsibility in his family, had produced this.

"Will, I have a card in my pocket with a precious promise on it."

"Anything, Elspeth. You know that. I can have the truck running in an hour. Where ya going?"

"I'd like room and board here, no discounts, and no questions."

He concentrated on his hands with the rag. "One condition. I need your forgiveness for this summer."

"Oh, Will, that's all right."

"No, you need to know I was sincere. Probably just misguided."

"Well, I appreciate it. I still want us to be—"

"I'm not saying I was wrong, but Pastor helped me see—"

"Pastor Hill knows?"

"I'm sorry, Elspeth. He won't say anything. Anyway, it was wrong how I went about it, and I don't blame you for being upset."

"Thank you. I forgive you."

"You sure you want to stay in the same house? School's not exactly walking distance. If I drive you, people will talk."

"I don't care. People know I have a, an, um, boyfriend."

Elisabeth hated taking Will from his many jobs, even for the few minutes it took to move her into a room at the end of the hall on the second floor. Shabby as the house appeared outside, the inside was in the midst of Will's remodeling. Everything worked. Plumbing. Electricity. Heat.

That night Elisabeth penned a note of thanks and information to Mr. Beck, then wrote a long letter to Ben. She concluded, "It would mean so much to me if I could tell Will of our betrothal. I trust him, and as his classmate and lifelong chum, I think it's important for him to know our intentions."

Ben's reply arrived a week later: "My precious Elisabeth, I must urge you to keep our secret. If you trust Will, I know I would too, but I hardly know him. There's nothing I'd rather do than tell the world of my love for you and yours for me. But you know most so-called secrets are merely things everyone is told one at a time.

"There's a reason for my reticence. My orders have arrived. My assignment is so clandestine that military censors will read this letter. I am allowed to tell you only that I will not be stateside. I shall write you at every opportunity and you may write me at the military post office below, though there is no guarantee how quickly or regularly I will see your mail.

"I will count the days until God allows us to be together as man and wife. All my love, Ben."

Elisabeth shuddered. She prayed for him, carefully avoiding seeking word from God whether she had made the right decision to accept his proposal. She loved him more than ever, and while she was aware of the many Scriptures that called worry sin, it became a sin she committed around the clock.

A few days later Elisabeth read in the *Three Rivers Tribune* the text of President Wilson's address to Congress of January 8, wherein he reminded them and the nation that the United States was not technically one of the Allies. He also reiterated that General Pershing had been told to keep a separate and distinct identity for his force. Yet Wilson also put forth fourteen points for peace, ideals that seemed designed to strengthen the cause of the Allies.

So the U.S. was knee-deep in the war after all, Elisabeth told herself. This was the war to end all wars, but it seemed ludicrous to send young men in the prime of their lives to fight thousands of miles from home. The cause seemed just, and, she asked herself, who else should go? Surely not younger men. Will was exempted not only because he was still in high school, but also because he was the only male child of a widow. Both his brothers-in-law, despite being husbands and fathers, fearfully awaited assignment. Art Childs and several others from church were already overseas.

Taking her cue from the relentless Will Bishop, Elisabeth filled her days. Mr. Beck banked the modest check from the painful sale of her childhood home for her, and she noted curiously a new family moving in just a few weeks later. She prayed they would cherish it as she had. Where Aunt Agatha relocated, Elisabeth had no idea.

Elisabeth bided her time, waiting to get through high school and marry Ben. She wrote him nearly every day, sending her letters to a central military post office as directed. As weeks passed and she heard nothing from him, she worried more. If absence was the true test of love, she passed. She loved him and longed for him more every day.

Elisabeth rose early each day, knowing that if she did not read her Bible and pray then, she would be too exhausted later. She volunteered to help Mrs. Bishop in the kitchen, which meant setting the table for between seven and ten people every morning and helping cook breakfast. Mrs. Bishop proved wary and fearful, shyer than Will had ever been. She rarely smiled and looked as if she believed everyone was out to take advantage of her. She did not understand why Elisabeth wanted to help and often reminded her that "this doesn't mean you don't have to pay your rent."

Then it was off to school in Will's truck. As he predicted, people began to ask if they were an item. Both assured everyone they weren't and the speculation soon stopped. Word spread that Elisabeth had exercised her freedom upon her eighteenth birthday and sold her house. That she sold it to her own aunt, lost her shirt, and saw it sold again right out from under her somehow never got out. The news and the gossip moved away with Aunt Agatha. Ironically, Elisabeth earned a reputation for shrewdness for what she and her lawyer agreed was the most foolish thing she had ever done.

In a vain attempt to take her mind off Ben, she busied herself in school and church like never before. Her work at Snyder's often extended to closing time and locking up. Will seemed to have a sixth sense about her schedule. Often—never with her arranging it—he was waiting in the truck when she was finished work or was leaving church.

She still did a lot of walking, because he was busier than ever too. But he seemed an agent of God when she needed one most. If she felt energetic, she walked home. But when the stress of her loneliness or schoolwork or work in general caught up with her, her ride was often waiting.

She always expressed her heartfelt thanks, and Will, to his credit, never made her feel obligated. Knowing he would never accept a tip, Elisabeth tried to recompense him by rounding up her rent payment. But her bill was always lessened by the same amount the next time. Finally she confronted him.

"Will, you're being too kind. You must allow me to compensate you for all the extra trouble."

"It's no trouble, Elspeth," he would say. "I'm happy to do it."

"But I feel bad. I—"

"Listen to me," he said. "When I say I'm happy to do it, I mean I would be unhappy if you didn't let me. If it helps you out, that makes me feel good."

Impulsively, Elisabeth embraced him. What a dear, dear friend! He had become a man before his time. Will did not return the fleeting hug, but she wondered what Ben would think. She wouldn't want him embracing a friend of the opposite sex, even without romantic feelings.

After a month without word from Ben, Elisabeth wrote his mother. Mrs. Phillips responded, "We have heard nothing either, dear, and the local military office tells us this is normal. They say no news is good news. We sure want to meet you, however, having heard so many wonderful things about you from Benjamin. Is there any chance you might come up this way, or might we meet you somewhere?"

Elisabeth saw not one open day on her calendar for months and so kept her reply encouraging but nebulous.

By March, despite her determination, Elisabeth became nearly beside herself with worry. She wanted to know where Ben was and that he was all right. Surely someone could tell her. She fired off letters to every official she could think of, receiving kind and timely replies that either evaded the question or assured her she would get word in due time. "No news is good news," she read over and over. Well, it wasn't good news to her.

Like many other men in town, Will's brothers-in-law worked at the Sheffield Car Company plant, assembling railroad cars. They largely ignored Elisabeth, and their wives barely spoke to her. It was as if they were jealous that their children were smitten by her. Will's sisters were several years older than Elisabeth, and after marrying "outside the faith," as their mother said, they left the church as well. It was clear the couples resented having to raise their broods in their mother-in-law's boarding house, and all they talked about was getting their own places someday.

Elisabeth played with Will's nieces and nephews every chance she got, teaching them songs and telling them Bible stories. One of the brothers complained, but Elisabeth responded by offering to take the children to Sunday school every week. For whatever danger the parents saw in her filling the kids' heads with religion, the idea of Sunday mornings to themselves sold them on the idea.

The kids loved piling into the back of Will's truck, and Elisabeth saw yet another surprising side of him. He was wonderful with the children—patient, loving, kind. He took them to Snyder's to pick her up after work one Saturday and bought them all phosphates. One ordered one too many. When he leaned in the window at a stop sign to tell Will he felt sick, he proved it all over Will and the cab of the truck. Not only did Will not respond with revulsion or anger, but he also quickly cleaned up the boy and the truck, all the while comforting him and telling him it was all right.

By May, Elisabeth was exhausted from her schedule and from worry over Ben. She wrote the War Department in Washington, demanding "information on his well-being if not on his location. If you do not want a determined fiancée making a personal excursion to Europe to find her man, you'll respond posthaste. Most sincerely yours, a loyal and praying citizen, Elisabeth Grace LeRoy."

Ten days later she received a telegram from the War Department: "MISS LE ROY: BE INFORMED PVT. PHILLIPS ASSIGNED EUROPE. SPECIFIC LOCATION CLASSIFIED. NO REPORTED ACTION OR CASUALTIES. HAS RECEIVED YOUR MAIL. TRIP ILL ADVISED."

Elisabeth had coerced a response from the lumbering government. To both her bemusement and consternation, the telegram had arrived COD.

She wondered why he was receiving her mail and she was getting none of his. Had he written? Might he have lost interest? Come to his senses? Had a word from God? Dare she pray about the same? Not until she checked back with his parents.

She wrote them again, telling of her experience with the War Department. "That's a relief," his mother responded. "You're very resourceful. We didn't know where to turn except to the Lord. We have received no mail from Ben either."

It was Elisabeth's turn for relief. If he had changed his mind, he certainly would have told his parents, wouldn't he? But parents of the servicemen at church were getting letters, some even from overseas. What must Ben be involved in? She scoured the newspaper every day for clues.

Unable to sleep one Saturday night in late May, Elisabeth poured out her heart to God. "I had no idea what my commitment to you would bring," she said. "I'm determined to obey you in every instance, but except for Ben, my life has been nothing but trouble from the moment I turned it over to you. I know life abundant doesn't mean happiness all the time and that you're trying to teach me something. But can't I know your will? Can't I have some peace? Please tell me I did the right thing when I pledged myself to Ben. I feel obligated to honor that. I love him and want to be his wife."

She rolled onto her stomach and propped herself up by her elbows to look out the window. Elisabeth had communicated with God frequently enough and for enough years to have an inkling where she stood. She lay her cheek on the pillow, believing God had forgiven her getting ahead of him. Yet she felt no confirmation about marriage. That didn't mean she had been wrong. But she hated God's silence on the most important issue in her life.

She felt suddenly compelled to pray about Will. Was this God's answer to her request for confirmation about Ben? She thanked God for Will's friendship, for his character, for his work ethic, for his servant spirit. It was as if God were saying, "You think *you've* had it rough? He committed his life the same night you did, and look what *he's* been through. You lost your father. So did he. You lost your home; he shares his with family and strangers."

Elisabeth was at a loss. She was not about to pray, "Should I marry Will?" She didn't have those kinds of feelings for him. She would go mad if God weren't clearer. "Should I marry Ben?" she blurted.

She didn't sense a clear yes or no. She simply felt she had gotten ahead of God by promising herself to Ben. But she had known that and already asked forgiveness for it. Now she just wanted God's blessing on her commitment. Apparently, it didn't work that way.

She had been wrong for having promised before praying about it, but was marrying Ben wrong? She could not conceive of that. If she was to marry Will rather than Ben, God would have to give her a love for him that transcended what she felt for Ben. Was that possible?

This would be easier if Ben was a cad or Will ignorant. Choosing between good and bad was easy. How did one choose between better and best? And how had it come to this? Since when was she deciding between Ben and Will? She had already made that decision.

Enough military men were getting Dear John letters because their women grew tired of waiting. That was not her problem. She had not even known of Will's interest in her until she had fallen in love with Ben. Yet months before Ben asked her to marry him, she had known of Will's intentions and even his conviction that it was of God.

Elisabeth put her feet on the floor and sat with her head in her hands. Was this the adventure of faith she had signed on for? Was this what it meant to make her life an experiment in obedience? What if God made it clear she had made the wrong choice and that she *was* to withdraw her acceptance of Ben's proposal? There was not a doubt in her mind that Will was eager to step back into the picture. Neither God nor Ben had given her the freedom to tell Will that she had accepted a marriage proposal. There had to be some reason for that.

If God led her away from Ben, how would she ever tell him? Would he understand if she said it was God's idea? And what would she do with her love for him, her passion, her longing to be his wife?

Elisabeth tried to sleep, hoping and praying that she was simply as young and confused as she felt and that somehow God would make it clear that she should marry Ben. Wherever he was.

Chapter Nine

Elisabeth woke Sunday with the dread fear that something had happened to Ben. She could not talk to nor even look at Will. Was this why God had given her no peace about Ben? Not because he was an unsuitable partner, but rather because he was not going to come back? She could think of nothing else.

The children were excited about Sunday school. Their parents slept in, which put pressure on Mrs. Bishop, Will, and Elisabeth to corral the children, feed them, and get them ready. Halfway through breakfast, Mrs. Bishop had had enough. "I don't feel like going now myself," she said. "I'd just as soon go back to bed."

"Aw, Ma," Will said. "You know you want to. Go get ready. I'll handle the kitchen." She stared as if she didn't really want the obstacles removed. "Go on, now," he said. "Wear that dress I got you."

Will cleared the table and poured a pan of hot water in the sink. "Let me do that," Elisabeth said, but he suggested if she could just keep track of the kids for ten minutes, he'd be right out.

"And you kids," he said, making them all stop and look at him with expectant smiles. "Whoever's the quietest and sitting the straightest when I get out there gets a phosphate tomorrow after school."

They squealed and lit out for the truck. Elisabeth followed, but she too was stopped by a word from Will. "You all right?"

Standing at the sink in a shirt and tie, a dishtowel tucked in his belt, he looked at her with such concern that she nearly wept. "I'm worried about Ben," she said, as if it were an admission.

"Any news?"

"No."

"Then assume the best. Anything I can do?"

She couldn't speak. She didn't want to turn away, but neither did she want to burst into tears in front of him. As if to spare her the embarrassment, he turned back to the dishes. Elisabeth needed to follow the children, but she felt riveted. Staring at Will, busy at the sink, it was as if she had seen this before. Or would see it again. She could not pull away.

Then it hit her. With an alarming chill she pictured herself growing old with him, working with him in the kitchen. In the yard. In the car. The view was stark and clear. This wasn't a vision; it was more an impression, some foreknowledge, an absolute assurance. She knew that if she merely said the word, told him she was available and would marry him, the deed would be done. They would have a family of their own.

When he turned toward her, she shook herself from her reverie and forced herself down the stairs. What had that been all about? Did she love Will? Could she? Should she learn to? It made no sense. Will Bishop?

The kids ran around the yard, but Elisabeth knew they would snap to as soon as Will came. She had to get her mind on something else before he came down. She sat in the cab of the truck, her Bible and Sunday school lesson on her lap. She tried to concentrate, to remember the points she wanted to make to her young girls that morning. It was no use. Here came the kids. They had seen or heard Will bounding down the stairs, and they leapt into the back of the truck, stiff and straight and still.

Will made a huge show of examining each of them like a drill sergeant, and they all fought with all their might to keep from grinning. Mrs. Bishop came down looking surprisingly sporty in the dress Will had bought.

"Everybody wins!" Will said, and the kids cheered. His mother slid into the cab, putting Elisabeth in the center next to Will. He excused himself each time he had to move the gearshift lever on the floor between them. Elisabeth had never felt more self-conscious. On the way home she would sit by the window, with his mother between them, if she had to climb over the top of the truck to do it.

Will walked his mother to her class before heading to his own, and the kids raced to their respective spots. Elisabeth taught fourth-grade girls in a tiny room off the fellowship hall in the basement. One of Will's nieces, Sue, with short brown hair and huge, dark eyes, was new enough to church and Sunday school that she alone would have made it worth Elisabeth's while. Sue stared at her, listening to every word, eager to find verses in the Bible Pastor Hill had given her.

During class, Elisabeth briefly forgot Ben and Will and her turmoil. In church she found herself directly in front of Will. She knew it was her imagination, because a man like Will had loftier things on his mind, but she felt as if his eyes were boring a hole in the back of her head. She couldn't concentrate. When the congregation stood for the closing hymn, she used the occasion to look sideways. From the corner of her eye she couldn't tell what he was looking at. Next week she would sit behind him. Or beside him. Anywhere but in front of him.

The hymn was "In the Cross of Christ," which Elisabeth loved because it reminded her of the mother she never knew. Pastor Hill suggested they sing all four verses *a cappella*, and Elisabeth was struck to hear Will's clear voice behind her. In all their years growing up in that church, she could not recall having heard him sing.

His pure tenor voice captivated her, and his emotion moved her to where she could barely articulate the words herself:

In the cross of Christ I glory, towering o'er the wrecks of time;
All the light of sacred story gathers round its head sublime.
When the woes of life o'ertake me, hopes deceive and fears annoy,
Never shall the cross forsake me; Lo! It glows with peace and joy.
When the sun of bliss is beaming light and love upon my way,
From the cross the radiance streaming adds more luster to the day.
Bane and blessing, pain, and pleasure, by the cross are sanctified;
Peace is there that knows no measure, joys that through all time abide.

Lurching toward her graduation from Three Rivers High School, set for Saturday, June 8, 1918, Elisabeth found it difficult to focus on her many duties. She maintained her schedule and her disciplines, but everything seemed futile. The only bright spot in her life had come in the middle of May when Mrs. Phillips responded to her graduation announcement and invitation to the ceremony with the surprise news that she and her husband planned to come. "What an appropriate occasion to meet our future daughter-in-law," she wrote. "My husband and I shall handle all our own arrangements so you need not worry after us, and we look forward to it with great anticipation."

Friday, May 31, Will picked her up from Snyder's after work and said, "I have good news."

"That I could use," she said wearily. "Tell me it's a letter from Ben."

"It is."

"Don't tease me, Will."

"I wouldn't."

"You're serious? Did you bring it?"

"I thought you'd want to read it by yourself."

His blasted kindness and consideration! Of course he was right. It had been so long since she had heard from Ben, she believed she could jump out and run and beat Will home. Alone in her room minutes later, she tore open the envelope, crying before she could unfold the page. The letter was dated May 16, fifteen days before.

Dearest Elisabeth,

How could you have referred to me as your fiancé in a letter to no less than the War Department itself? Don't you know that puts me in a different category here—special treatment and all the rest—which I definitely do not want? The engagement was announced to my company, which has hazed me mercilessly. I thought we had agreed to say nothing to anyone. You sure chose the wrong target!

Part of me is thrilled that so many here know, but I suppose it's futile to expect the news won't sweep through our families and friends in the States. I feel such a fool, having given no token of my pledge and now having the world know I put you in the untenable position of promising yourself to a soldier overseas.

Make no mistake, I am more committed to you and our future than ever, and I want the ring bestowed and the ceremony accomplished within a week of my return, if you'll still have me. I wish I knew where your mind and heart were, because I have received no communication from you and can't know whether you have received mine. No one here has heard from home, so I take some comfort that I am not alone. I am anticipating a sack of mail when it finally comes. If nothing else, your gaffe with Washington tells me how you view me. Officially or not, you call me your fiancé.

Things are heating up here, and as you don't know where I'm writing from I can tell you that some resolution—at least as it relates to U.S. troops—should be forthcoming within a month.

Loving you and missing you,
your devoted Ben.

How she loved him! It hurt to be scolded, especially when she only had his best interest in mind. She folded the letter and kept it with her, peeking at it several times that evening. Will did not ask to see it, though he did ask if all was well.

"Better than well. Ben's fine!"

"I'm glad for you," he said. "Any idea where he is?"

"None."

"There was something in the paper today about the first American offensive of the war."

"He predicted that! Let me see it."

"There were casualties, Elspeth."

"How many?"

"It doesn't say."

He handed her the paper and she read of the May 28 action. General Pershing delivered reinforcements to the French on the Marne, while fifty miles to the northwest in Cantigny, American troops were successful against the veteran Eighteenth Army. The U.S. reported light casualties in both operations.

So it had begun. Elisabeth couldn't guess where Ben might be, but what were the odds he was in on the first two U.S. offensives in France? And if so, was he safe? The paper told of a massive buildup of both German troops and U.S.-supported Allied troops along the

Marne. Elisabeth wished she hadn't read it. The letter had assuaged her fear, but now she would worry all the more.

"Mother kept a plate warm for you on the stove, Elspeth."

"Thanks. What did you have?"

"I don't know. I'm eating late tonight."

"Really?"

"Just going out."

"Got a date?" Elisabeth asked, teasing.

She froze when he nodded. "Lucy from church."

"Lucy?" Elisabeth said unnecessarily. A pretty sophomore who wore glasses. "Why, uh, why so late?"

"I didn't want you to have to walk home is all. She didn't mind. She understands I'm kinda watching out for you. We're just going to have the special over at Three Rivers House. Better get going."

"Have a nice time."

Elisabeth walked stiff-legged to the kitchen and found her meal, which she only picked at. What was wrong with her? She was engaged, soon to be a high school graduate, then to marry as soon as her fiancé returned from the war. She didn't love Will Bishop, had no claim whatever on him, and didn't deserve one if she'd wanted it. She couldn't be jealous of Lucy. Yet she was. Flat jealous and wallowing in it.

She trudged upstairs to her room, tried to pray, tried to read her Bible, tried to write a letter. Finally, she gave up on it all and collapsed into bed. It was not late enough for sleep, but she slept anyway, for lack of anything else that made her feel anything but terrible.

I'm a rotten, awful person, she told herself. *I can't have what I want and I don't want what I have.*

On the Friday afternoon before graduation, Will asked if she minded if Lucy rode with them the next day.

"Oh, Will," she said, "that wouldn't be fair to Lucy. I'll find a way. If the Phillipses get into town early, I may go with them."

"But what if they don't? Anyway, you don't want to invite yourself along, especially with your future in-laws. It'll be okay. Lucy understands."

If Lucy were anything like Will, she probably would be bigger about the situation than Elisabeth would. It was too far to walk and too late to arrange for a ride with anyone else.

That night a light tap on her door awakened Elisabeth. "Don't open, Elspeth," Will said. "I'm just slipping a message under the door. The Phillipses phoned you at Snyder's, and the delivery boy brought a note."

Elisabeth flipped on the light and squinted against the brightness. *I hope they're still coming,* she thought.

The note read, "E. L., a Mrs. Phillips called and said she was sorry she missed you and to tell you they were still coming regardless. They'll see you after. A.W.S."

Regardless, she thought. *Regardless the weather? Regardless what?* She was glad she had not counted on them for a ride.

By noon the next day, as most of Three Rivers readied itself for the graduation ceremonies, word spread that the war had taken a dramatic turn in favor of the Allies, due in large part to U.S. efforts. A major German offensive had been thwarted and pushed back, and while it might take months to accomplish, the momentum had shifted and it seemed certain Germany would be defeated.

To Elisabeth the whole town seemed optimistic about the safe return of many young men, so graduation would be more festive than ever. The male graduates likely need not worry about their draft status, despite the Selective Service Act.

Elisabeth watched for signs of affection between Will and Lucy during the crowded ride. She saw nothing and scolded herself for caring. Worrying about Will Bishop's love life was far from where she ought to be by now in her spiritual life.

She won several class awards, including the plaque for the student most inspirational to classmates as an example of a dedicated scholar. She nearly burst with pride for Will, who looked terribly embarrassed to win both Most Improved Student and the Accounting Club award.

Elisabeth scanned the crowd for the Phillipses, wondering if she would recognize them by seeing Ben in their features. Many students had out-of-town guests and relatives, however, so she quickly gave up.

His parents would know who she was because she had been announced several times even before being presented with her diploma.

After the students tossed their caps, signed each other's annuals, tearfully embraced, and posed for photographs, Elisabeth told Will she had a way home and that she would see him later. As he walked off with Lucy, she carrying some of his stuff but neither showing more than appropriate familiarity, Elisabeth decided meeting her future in-laws would cap a fairly happy day.

A couple older than she expected stepped in behind Pastor and Mrs. Hill as they shook her hand and congratulated her. "That inspirational award has gone to someone from Christ Church for six years running," the pastor said. "Congratulations and thanks for keeping it in the family."

"Oh, Jack," his wife said. "Let's not boast. It was Elisabeth who won it."

As the Hills greeted other graduates, the couple approached. He was dressed in clerical garb, she in a long, black dress. Their faces were drawn, their eyes red. Elisabeth stepped gracefully through formal introductions but found it disconcerting that Mr. Phillips seemed so serious and his wife had an accusatory tone reminiscent of Aunt Agatha.

"This has been quite a day for you," the woman said. Perhaps she was one who believed too much attention only swelled a young person's head.

"Thank you. I'm humbled." Elisabeth couldn't keep from smiling. She wished they could share her joy.

"You seem to be holding up remarkably well."

"Well, it's not easy, Mrs. Phillips, as you know. But this has been a wonderful day. I'm sure you've heard the good news from the front."

"We heard," Mr. Phillips said, shoulders slumped. "A day late and a dollar short."

"I understand there's reason to be optimistic," Elisabeth said, determined not to let them spoil the moment. "Anyway, it makes my day to meet you both. Ben speaks so highly of you."

Mrs. Phillips stared at her. "You say that in the present tense."

"Well, he has and he will. I heard from him a week or so ago. The letter was a couple of weeks old, but—"

The Phillipses looked at each other, and Ben's mother interrupted. "You haven't heard from the War Department?"

"Oh, yes. Some time ago. Ben was none too pleased that I spilled the beans . . ."

Mrs. Phillips disintegrated into tears, quickly finding a chair where her husband knelt next to her, gathering her in and glaring at Elisabeth. "We didn't bring the letter," he said. "We assumed they had copied you. We knew all about the fiancé business, but they must have found out the engagement was not official if they didn't communicate with you directly."

"But they did. I got a telegram. That's what upset Ben so. He—"

"You've not heard that Ben was lost at sea."

"That he was what?"

"We thought you knew. We called you last night."

"What are you saying?"

"His transport ship sank. Only six survivors, all officers."

Elisabeth found herself on her hands and knees, her head spinning. People came running. She was helped to a chair, fanned, and given water. Nothing helped. The shock, the grief, the horror of it hit her like a sledge, and she could not catch her breath. She had so many questions. This couldn't be! She must have seemed so callous to the Phillipses.

"In a way, I'm glad," someone said. Elisabeth looked up with a start at such a ridiculous comment. It was Ben's mother. "I'm just saying, dear, that it was probably for the best that you didn't know before your big day."

My big day? Elisabeth thought. Her big days, from the day she was born and lost her mother, all carried horrible memories. She felt cursed.

Elisabeth fought to regulate her breathing. This was too much to take.

"Coming today has been more difficult than we imagined," Mr. Phillips said, "and was probably ill-advised. We'd like to get back directly. May we drop you somewhere?"

"I'll take her," Pastor Hill said. "As soon as she's ready."

He stepped back so she and Ben's parents could say their good-byes.

"I don't know what to say," she said.

"If you loved him like we do," Mr. Phillips said, "you know how we are suffering."

"It's such a loss to the church, to the world."

"We try not to think about that," Ben's mother said. "The loss is deep enough in our own hearts."

"I know."

"We're sorry," she added, "that we had to be the ones to tell you."

Elisabeth waved her off. "May I ask, ah, no—I'm sorry."

"No, please."

"Have they found him? Will they—"

"Ship him back?" Mr. Phillips said. "They make no promises. We will have a memorial service next week, to which you are invited."

"Oh, I don't know," Elisabeth said, feeling faint again.

"We would be honored," Mrs. Phillips said.

"Then I will be there."

Pastor Hill drove slowly and his wife sat in the back, cradling Elisabeth as she wept. "Poor child," she repeated. "Too much, too young."

"Will you be all right?" the pastor asked as he walked her to the door.

She meant to nod but wasn't sure she had. "Is this what you meant by the fellowship of his sufferings? Is this all there is to the committed Christian life? Just tragedy and disappointment?"

"Not all, but let's be careful to blame this neither on God nor on your commitment. That ascribes evil to him and too much power to you. Satan is the author of death. God is sovereign. That is a difficult truth right now, but rest in it during the dark night of the soul."

Elisabeth nodded, desperate to be free of the overwhelming sense of evil that surrounded tragedy.

"If we don't see you in church tomorrow, we'll understand. But if you find yourself up to it, you'll be surrounded by love and care."

"Would you do me a favor?" she said. "If you say anything—"

"I will announce it, of course."

"Would you make clear that the man I lost was my fiancé, the love of my life. It was our secret, but I want it known."

The pastor hesitated, looking down. "You don't think that might open him to criticism for—"

"Maybe," she said. "But I want no question that we were committed to each other forever."

As she made her way inside, Elisabeth felt the eyes of everyone in the household. No one said anything, but all—even the children—looked at her with pity. She stopped on her way upstairs, put her hand on the railing, and turned to face them. They looked away, everybody but Will, whose liquid eyes locked onto hers.

"I'm all right," she said quietly. "Thank you for caring."

Her Bible lay open on the bed stand. She ignored it, locked her door, and undressed. Despite the warmth of the evening, she put on a flannel nightgown. As she approached the bed, her legs gave out and she tumbled to the floor. She wept bitterly, careful not to be heard, worried that the sound of her fall would concern the family.

Elisabeth crawled into bed and curled into a fetal position. "God," she prayed silently, "I don't understand this. I don't like it. And I don't know where you are right now. If this is your answer about whether I am free to marry Ben, I'm sorry I asked."

She heard footsteps on the stairs and held her breath. Someone approached the door, the floor creaking. There was no knock. The steps retreated to the stairs, but there was no sound of descent. Elisabeth lay waiting. Nothing. She was exhausted, but would not sleep this night.

She crept to the door and put her ear near it. Still no sound. She carefully unlocked the door and turned the knob, opening it an inch. In the darkness of the hall, silhouetted against the streetlight outside, sat Will on the landing, his back to her.

"I'm all right," she whispered.

He didn't turn.

"Get some sleep, Will," she added.

He nodded but did not move. Elisabeth pulled her robe from a hook on the back of the door and moved to the stairs. She sat next to Will on the top step. His chin was buried in his hands and he stared out the window, tears on his cheeks.

She could barely speak. "Thanks for caring so much."

He drew in a labored breath, covered his eyes, and sobbed quietly. She reached to comfort him with a light touch on his heaving shoulders.

He wept for her, which made her weep for him. And there they sat, supporting each other in a moment of pain and grief so deep that Elisabeth could not imagine living through it. Without a true friend like Will, how could she?

She left her hand on his shoulder until his sobs subsided, then sat with him the better part of an hour. Twice she told him, "Go now. Get your rest." But he did not move.

Finally she said, "I'd better get to bed," and he nodded, still not moving, not looking at her. She returned to her room. Every hour or so she rose and peeked out to see Will still there. By the wee hours he was dozing with his head against the railing. At dawn he was on his back on the landing, his legs extending down the stairs. She tiptoed out and covered him with a comforter, lifting his head and slipping a pillow beneath.

She decided he was the most gallant man she would ever have the privilege to know.

Chapter Ten

$\mathcal{E}$lisabeth felt beyond repair. Her confusion over Ben was a fleeting memory, and snatches of it made her wonder if she had contributed to his death. She was now horrified by war stories and avoided the newspaper; despite that over the next several months the Allies and the U.S. pushed to victory.

She was haunted that so many of those who drowned on the transport had never been accounted for. By fall, more than twenty percent had still not been found. Ben's miraculous return became a recurring dream that ended as a nightmare, for either he was unreachable or she awoke just as they embraced. She sweated through her nightclothes and awoke in tears, wondering how she could go another day without him.

Elisabeth was determined to follow through on her commitment to Christ, though she alarmed herself with a nagging resentment toward what she felt God had allowed. Other than not having cleared her marriage decision through prayer, had she not been obedient? Even that had been an act of omission rather than commission.

She worked at communicating with God every waking moment, but she heard only silence back. She knew death was the devil's business and not God's, yet something told her she had been responsible for this. The Bible became a textbook, uninteresting, hard to get into, impossible to stay with. She prayed for a renewed hunger and thirst for it, but all she seemed to crave was more sleep.

Elisabeth worked full-time at Snyder's now, and while she had taken the rest of the summer off from her responsibilities at church, she was soon back to work there too. Many Sunday mornings she felt hypocritical, earnestly trying to impress upon her class the truth of Scripture while not feeling it in her heart.

The last five years of her life had been an experiment, and the experiment had failed. What had she hoped to gain by total obedience? Favor? Reward? That went against everything she knew. And she had to admit that her father, her pastor, and even the evangelist Hasper had warned her she had chosen a hard path. It had sounded glamorous. Now, in the thick of it, she did not feel fit for battle. She hung on for dear life, fearful of defeat.

"I haven't seen Lucy in a while, Will," Elisabeth said in the truck after work one night in September.

"We were just friends, Elspeth."

"And you and I, Will?"

He hesitated. "Do you have to ask?"

"Yes."

"Always friends, I hope."

An influenza epidemic ravaged Three Rivers that fall, affecting nearly every household. All over town, people of all ages died. Some fell ill in the morning and died before nightfall. Others suffered for days, only to survive. Area hospitals and clinics were full, the schools closed. Health department quarantines and police curfews were established in the hope of keeping infected people away from healthy ones. The pharmacy ran short of medicine, and eventually Elisabeth herself was stricken.

She felt so bad about bringing the disease into the Bishop household that she pleaded with Will to find somewhere for her out of town. But he cared for her himself, bringing food and tonics up to her, checking on her around the clock, even—to her abject embarrassment—policing her chamber pot.

She grew so ill at one point that Pastor Hill visited, wearing a surgical mask. Elisabeth was delirious, conscious only that she hated to face Will. During lucid moments she pleaded for news of others in the house. When a doctor finally got around to her, she established rapport as daughter of the late Dr. James LeRoy. She then coerced him into admitting that two Bishops, a niece and a nephew, had been hauled away by the mortician in the previous ten days. Elisabeth was inconsolable, though the doctor assured her their diseases had incubated much longer than hers had. "Naturally you will grieve, ma'am, but you would be wrong to feel in the least responsible. It's more likely they infected you than the other way 'round. I worry about Will, however. He has eluded this killer strain so far, but he is exhausted, and I fear for his immune system."

"You must insist he stop caring for me," Elisabeth pleaded. "He won't listen."

"Everyone else in the house is down, young lady. Don't you realize he's caring for you all?"

"I have some money," she said. "The lawyer Mr. Beck has access to it. It's not much, but it will pay for nursing care for a few months. Please tell me you'll see to it."

The doctor shook his head. "You couldn't find medical care in this state for all the money in the world. We're stretched beyond the limit. I'm working twenty-hour days myself, and half the hospital staff is home sick. If you're a praying woman, please do. It'll take a miracle to keep this monster from destroying the town."

The next day Elisabeth was so determined to spell Will that she tried to make it downstairs. Fever had so swollen her joints that she collapsed on the steps. She remained there, refusing to call for help despite her chill, hot flashes, and nausea. She prayed she would not be discovered there, having expired or eliminated—deciding the latter would be worse.

When Will finally came upon her, she could only cry, "Please! Get someone to help you!"

Elisabeth hid her face as he knelt and lifted her wasted frame like a baby. He struggled to keep his balance at the top of the stairs and she could tell he had lost strength. He placed her gently on the bed and covered her. She felt unworthy and wanted to say so, but Will had long since quit responding to anything she said.

When he left with her chamber pot yet again, she sought God with all her heart, pleading to either die or recover quickly enough to relieve Will before he himself died.

Her fever broke in the middle of the morning three days later.

The house was silent, the sun high. Elisabeth crept out of bed, weak and shaky. She pulled on her robe and slowly, carefully made her way downstairs. The house smelled of medicine and death. The brothers-in-law, greasy with sweat, were loading the truck. She resented that they were healthy enough for that but had never, as far as she knew, helped Will with the rest of the family.

Will's sisters shared bedrooms with sick children. Will lay on a couch in the living room, asleep. Elisabeth tiptoed past him to the front door and peered out. The men looked angry and none too healthy themselves. They had been so standoffish around her that she didn't even know which was which. She opened the door and the sweet, fresh air hit her like an elixir.

"You still contagious?" one asked.

"I don't think so," she said. "What's going on?"

"We bought Will's truck," one said. "Movin' south. We've both lost kids, and now with Miz Bishop gone, it's time to head out."

"Miz Bishop?"

"Died overnight."

"Oh, no."

"It's for the best."

"The children?"

"Lost two each."

Elisabeth nearly toppled. And what of the one in her Sunday school class? "Sue?" she asked.

One hung his head. The other looked at her, and she knew.

"Do you know whether Will has caught the flu?" she whispered.

"Doesn't look like it. A miracle for sure."

Elisabeth loved but also feared the cold wind. "You'll see that those kids get to church and Sunday school wherever you're going, won't you?"

"Yes, ma'am."

Within a week, the house was empty save for Will and Elisabeth. The first night they were alone he moved to the Central House. "I'll check on you," he said. "But I can't stay here and have people talk. I'll advertise for boarders, and when we get some, I'll move back in."

The town grieved its losses for months. Elisabeth slowly regained her strength, went back to work and church, and made a project of scrubbing the huge old house from top to bottom. Will called her occasionally and gave her rides in his new used car. But he was busy with his side jobs and his starting accounting position at Fairbanks-Morse, a railroad car assembly plant which had just consolidated with the Sheffield Car Company. He had not actually been inside the house since the day he moved out.

Late in November he stopped by Snyder's as Elisabeth was closing up. "It's good to see you," she said. "I have a surprise for you."

"I came by because I've got one for you," he said. "Two families answered my ad today. They'll be here next week. This weekend I have to get the house in shape."

"Need me to cook for them?" Elisabeth said, climbing into the car.

"I wouldn't ask you. I told them they had use of the kitchen, but their rent includes only bed, not board."

Elisabeth was relieved. She didn't need cooking chores on top of everything else. "It'll be good to have you back," she said. "I can never thank you enough—"

"Please, Elspeth. You'd have done the same if you'd been the healthy one."

She hoped that were true.

"It's been lonely in that old place," she said. "Thanks for protecting my reputation."

"I wouldn't have had it any other way."

"I should compensate you for what you had to pay to stay somewhere else."

"Don't start with that," he said. "It was my choice. I could have evicted you."

"Or married me and killed two birds with one rent check."

He did not appear amused. "Don't joke about that, Elspeth," he said, crossing the Michigan Avenue bridge over the Portage River into the fourth ward. "You're in mourning for a year."

"I have to wait till next summer for you, Will Bishop?"

"Don't tease me."

"I'm sorry," she said. For once she wished she'd kept Ben's and her secret. Once it was known that she had been engaged to him, she was expected to mourn his death for a year. Of course, she *would* mourn. In fact she wondered if she would ever be over it, or over Ben. But she was also coming up on nineteen years old, and there was not another man in the world she would look at twice besides Will Bishop.

Did she love him? With all her heart. How could she not? They had so much in common, not the least of which was that they were both orphans. He was so proper and traditional that she knew he would not even ask to see her socially until June of 1919.

He pulled into the driveway. "You never told me your surprise," he said.

"It's inside."

"We shouldn't be in there together at this time of night," he said. "I'll wait."

"Where do I look?"

"Anywhere."

Elisabeth was thrilled to see the lights come on as he rushed from room to room. Soon he bounded out, the first time she had seen him grinning in months. "Elspeth, you're the berries! What's that smell in there? Where'd you get disinfectant and whatever else it is I can't make out?"

"I used ammonia for the first scrub down, then covered it with witch hazel and vanilla extract. You'd be surprised what you learn at a pharmacy."

"I have to pay for the materials and all that labor."

"Nonsense, Will. Don't you dare insult me by mentioning that ever again. I could paint this place with three coats and still owe you my very life. I could *never* repay your kindnesses."

He held up a hand. "All right," he said. "I'll abide by your wish if you'll abide by mine. We're even. We don't owe each other a thing."

"I owe you a lot more than you owe me," she said.

"You've already violated our agreement," he said, smiling.

"Okay," she said. "Truce. You want to call it even, we're even."

He thrust out his hand to shake on it. She took it in both of hers.

"I'm looking forward to getting back home," he said.

"This is starting to feel like home to me too, Will." She wanted to add, "And next summer you'd better come courting," but she had been forward enough for one evening.

Elisabeth counted the days until the boarders arrived. With her renewed health and anticipating getting to know Will in a new way, it seemed she had unlocked the gates of heaven. Her prayer life became sweet, and she looked forward to reading her Bible again.

Still she worried. Elisabeth hated being alone in the huge house overnight, and she started at every noise. Four nights before the boarders were to move in, she was sound asleep in her bed with every window and door locked. During the wee hours she was startled wide awake. What had she heard? Breaking glass? From where? She bolted upright and sat still, squinting at her alarm clock. It was five before two in the morning.

More noise. The back door downstairs. She held her breath. A rattle of the door, maybe the lock being jimmied. This was not the wind or the house settling or her imagination, excuses with which she had calmed herself before.

Elisabeth crept from her bed—her whole body trembling—and painstakingly opened her door to listen. She prayed whoever was down there was unaware she was in the house. Who kept anything of value in unheated upstairs rooms anyway? "Lord," she prayed silently, "if it's a burglar, let him look around down there and be on his way."

Heart cracking against her ribs, Elisabeth could not slow her breathing. When the door downstairs banged open she could tell at least two men were in the house. One said, "Somebody's living here. Look at this kitchen."

One shushed the other and Elisabeth had to cover her mouth to keep from whimpering aloud. Why couldn't they realize they had chosen a poor home and just leave? They had to be strangers. Who breaks into a fourth ward home when first ward mansions are just across the river?

What if they came upstairs? *God, help me.*

Elisabeth tiptoed to her closet and found the bucket, a mop, and a half-full bottle of ammonia, which she dumped into the bucket. Her eyes and nose smarted from the noxious fumes. She set the bucket and mop quietly near the door, which she closed within an inch of the jamb.

Elisabeth heard one of the men say something about "upstairs" and feared she would collapse from fright. Heavy clomping at the base of the stairs told her the man was large, old, or drunk. "I will not go easily," she told God. "Give me strength."

Standing in the darkness she could see through the slightly opened door to the landing midway up where the stairs turned. Elisabeth nearly squealed when the man reached that landing. He was big and slow and ponderous, wearing a navy blue shirt and pants and huge, dark boots. He wore a navy cap as well.

As he reached the top landing a few feet from her door, Elisabeth immersed the mop head in the ammonia and stood back. She held the mop like a baseball bat, the ammonia sickening her and dripping softly onto the floor. She was amazed how heavy the sodden mop was, holding it that way.

When the shadow of the big man's head appeared in the crack of the door, she swung with all her might. The business end of the mop seemed to move slowly, but it picked up speed with the momentum her adrenaline provided. As the man's nose poked through the opening, she smashed his face with a mop head full of undiluted ammonia. He screamed as the door swung open and he staggered back into the railing, which met him at the hip and cracked under his weight.

Elisabeth now held the mop like a poker, her left hand down the handle a couple of feet. The tortured intruder blindly lurched toward her, and Elisabeth charged. It was kill or be killed.

She drove the dripping mop into his face again, snapping his head back and making him reel. He stumbled backward again, so she parried and thrust again, this time catching him in the sternum as his weight carried him back. He broke through the banister and went screaming off the ledge from at least eight feet. His big body resounded as he slammed onto the stairs and tumbled the rest of the way down.

Elisabeth stepped out to see if she had killed him. Seeing him lying there motionless, she assumed she had. Dogs barked and through the window she saw other lights come on in the neighborhood. The injured man's compatriot hollered, "What's going on up there?"

Ammonia Face groaned and his friend recoiled.

"Come on up here," Elisabeth shouted, surprising herself, "and you'll wind up right beside him!"

She didn't know what she'd do if he hurdled his friend and came after her. Being on higher ground seemed an advantage, but how long could she fend off two men with a smelly mop?

"That's enough for one night, Edgar," the latecomer said, and he yanked his friend off the floor, steering him toward the back door. "Whew! Have you wet yourself?"

"That's ammonia, George! Don't you know anything?"

"You want to see my shotgun?" Elisabeth called after them, wondering where in the world she came up with that. When she saw the men run through the alley toward the west, her knees buckled and she slumped to the floor.

"Hello?" came the voices of an older couple next door. "Have you had trouble here?"

"Yes!" Elisabeth called out. "Call the police! And Mr. Bishop at Central House!"

The clumsy housebreakers were arrested twenty-five minutes later at the hospital at Bonnie Castle, seeking treatment for Edgar's eyes and assorted contusions. Like the fools they were, they used their real names and were quickly identified. The pair had been fired late that afternoon from the Hazen Lumber Company and admitted they'd heard of an abandoned boarding house assumed ripe for picking.

Will took Elisabeth to Pastor Hill's home, where he and his wife happily took her in and insisted she stay until the boarders arrived at Will's. "I lied to those men, Pastor," she said. "I implied I had a shotgun."

"Do you want to ask their forgiveness?" he said, smiling.

"But what about driving that poor man over the railing?"

"I wish I'd seen it," the pastor said.

"But seriously."

"Seriously? You had no idea they were bumblers who likely would have done you no harm. You asked God to help you. You operated biblically."

"Biblically?"

"Jesus said it is more blessed to give than to receive."

"Jack!" Mrs. Hill scolded. "She's scared and she's serious."

"She needs a good night's sleep in a safe home," he said. "And she's found it."

Elisabeth did not drift off until the sun streamed through the window in the Hills' guestroom.

By the following summer, Elisabeth had settled into a routine she found wholly satisfying. Two poor families, a traveling book salesman, and two female students of the Sage Business College kept the Bishop Boarding House hopping. Will did well enough at Fairbanks-Morse that he could afford help, and so a cleaning lady and a cook also moved in.

Elisabeth still suffered bleak moments when the tragedies of her life occupied her, but overall she believed she was maturing. She was happy at church, fulfilled if not challenged in her work at Snyder's, and enjoying the bustling activity at home. She'd had to discourage the advances of the book peddler, first informing him she was still in mourning over her fiancé and finally admitting that her heart was already set on another.

"May I ask whom?" he said.

"Forgive me for not answering," she said, "and I'll forgive you for asking."

Elisabeth saw Will at breakfast and frequently rode home with him after work. She soon quit hiding her loving glances and knowing looks. These were not returned, however, and she had to resist the temptation to remind him that her official period of mourning was about to end. Telling him would spoil everything.

"Are you melancholy today?" he asked her one Sunday morning, early in June.

"Actually I'm quite well today, Will, thank you. Do I appear out of sorts?"

"No. But it was a year ago today we heard the news."

She loved that he included himself. "God has been good," she said.

"From anyone else that would sound hollow," he said.

"I never say that lightly."

When Will still had not made any advances toward her a week later, Elisabeth grew frustrated. Had she not been forward enough, clear enough in the fall when she first broached the subject? She had spoken inappropriately then and would not do so again, but surely his memory could not be that bad.

The Fourth of July, with its attendant social activities, came and went, and Elisabeth began to despair. Her admiration for Will had blossomed first into true love and now longing. They belonged together, and she wanted the world to know. She wanted to be seen in public with him, to date him enough to make holding hands expected. She wanted him to court her, to hold her, to kiss her.

Obedience had been a bitter pill, and while Will's reticence didn't compare with the loss of her father and her fiancé, what was she to do with herself? She was interested in no one else, and had no interest in a future as a spinster. Did she not deserve some modicum of happiness? Would God deprive her now of the man he had placed in her path since childhood?

It was August before Will Bishop made his move. Elisabeth was so used to being disappointed that she almost missed it. He began at dinner with other boarders present. "Have you heard about the homecoming parade September 1?" he asked. He was looking at Elisabeth, but he had not addressed her.

Book Man answered. "Sorry I'll have to miss it. Should be quite a spectacle."

"What is it?" Elisabeth said idly.

"A celebration honoring the returning soldiers and sailors from the Great War."

Elisabeth was stricken; memories of Ben's loss washed over her. She put her fork down but did not want to draw attention to herself by leaving the table.

"The whole town will turn out," Will said.

Elisabeth wanted to say, "Don't be so sure."

"I'd love to take you," he said. Elisabeth was not paying attention.

Someone said, "Did I just hear Will ask to escort Miss LeRoy?"

Elisabeth looked up with a start. Will was smiling at her. "Yes, you did," he said.

Elisabeth burst into tears.

Chapter Eleven

*E*lisabeth skipped breakfast to avoid seeing Will. She walked all the way to the drugstore, then felt faint by midmorning. She ate half a box of mints, which normally settled her stomach. These only intensified her hunger until every notion in the store looked edible.

If I can scare off burglars, she told herself, *I can endure hunger until lunchtime.* During her half-hour break at noon, Elisabeth planned to slip next door for a sandwich at the counter of the five and dime. Meanwhile, she would wait on customers, run the cash register, sweep floors, and do whatever else she was told.

And she would feel sorry for herself.

By eleven-thirty, with store traffic virtually nil, Elisabeth was woozy. Granted permission to move up her lunchtime half an hour, she gratefully hurried next door. The elderly Gertrude flashed a smile as Elisabeth sat at the counter. "Early today, aren't we?"

"Famished!"

"The usual?"

"Please."

Dr. James LeRoy had been fond of saying, "Hunger is the best seasoning." Elisabeth had never found that truer than today. But her father had also been skeptical of any remedial claims for Coca-Cola, though many swore by it. Going by his further pronouncement that "it certainly shouldn't be harmful, enjoyed in moderation," Elisabeth ordered one as a sort of dessert.

"Shall I make it two?" Gertrude said.

"Oh, my, no."

"You're about to have company."

Elisabeth looked out the window. Will's car sat in front of the drugstore. Sure enough, a minute later he had been directed to the five and dime. She stiffened but was impressed with his sense of purpose. He entered with such determination that she was transported to a childhood memory of his buying penny candy in this same store, too shy to speak, pointing to his selections and handing over his coins.

Now he removed his cap, ran a hand through his hair, and nodded to the women. "I'm sorry I didn't get here in time to take you to lunch, Elspeth," he said.

"To ask me, you mean," she said, feeling testy.

"Of course. Would you join me at a table?"

Elisabeth hesitated, as if thinking about it. How perfect that he had left his office to seek her out. Gertrude busied herself, appearing to try to conceal a grin.

"I'm nearly finished, Will," Elisabeth said.

"Which means you will or you won't?"

Elisabeth sighed and rose. Will carried her drink and her napkin to a table, pulled out her chair, then excused himself while he got a Coca-Cola for himself. "You should eat," she said.

"*I* had breakfast."

She raised a brow. "To what do I owe the honor?"

He sipped and dabbed his mouth. "You leave the dinner table in tears and ignore me this morning, but this is an honor?"

She leveled her eyes at him. "It's always an honor to see you, Will. Especially when you're man enough to apologize."

He leaned forward. "I'm new at this, Elspeth. I didn't even realize what I had done until a couple hours after dinner. I wasn't thinking."

"You know then why it would be impossible for me to go to—"

He straightened. "Are you going to make me grovel?"

"No," she said. "I'm sorry. I just—"

"No, Elspeth, I'm the one apologizing. I don't mean to make this your fault. But yes, of course I understand how inappropriate my request was."

"Especially in front of people."

He gazed at her, unsmiling. "You *are* going to make me grovel."

"No!" she said. "Will, I'm forgiving you. I just want you to know the extent of the pardon."

Finally he smiled. "I have to get back," he said.

"Aren't you going to get some lunch?"

"I'm all right. Thanks for asking. I'll walk you back."

"I can't tell you how much this means to me, Will," she said on their way out.

"Yes, you can. You can allow me to find a suitable occasion we can enjoy together."

"I would enjoy that."

He stood awkwardly in front of Snyder's. She had been seen alighting from and entering his vehicles for months, but everyone considered theirs a familial relationship, a friendship of convenience and proximity. She was the bereaved fiancée, he the old chum who had taken her in.

But now they stood in the noon sun, she feeling as if the world was watching and he apparently even more self-conscious. With a grin he thrust out his hand, she shook it, and they parted.

He would, she decided, make a fine husband.

Their courtship was just long enough to be appropriate, but they were soon seen together so often, hand in hand, sometimes arm in arm, that Elisabeth assumed all of Three Rivers merely awaited the wedding announcement. She knew Will enough to know that he had dated only one other person, the fleeting Lucy, and that they had never progressed to so much as holding hands. Elisabeth had kissed only one other man, and while Will confessed he didn't like to dwell on that, he understood. "You were in love, you were engaged. Naturally you were affectionate."

They took long evening walks until they had talked themselves out. Their first kisses were tentative. He had no experience, she little more. Without words, she taught him to be gentle, to give as well as take a kiss.

There were few revelations in their extended talks. Elisabeth and Will had known each other so long that the only catching up they had to do was revealing what each had thought about the other at various ages. "I always thought you were the prettiest girl in the church," he said one evening as they sat on a wooden bench near the Rocky River.

"Didn't everyone?" she teased.

"And the humblest."

Families strolled by, the adults fanning themselves as kids skipped rocks on the river and taunted each other. A little girl jumped in fright, to her brother's glee, when a fish leaped from the water and splashed back in.

"I considered you just another boy, after wrestling with you in the nursery and enduring your roughhousing."

"By the time I was ten," Will said, "I knew I would marry you."

"You did not!"

He nodded. "Positively."

"How did you know?"

He shrugged. "I just did."

"God didn't tell you *that* early, did he?"

Will laughed. "Not until summer camp. I should have kept that revelation to myself, shouldn't I?"

"You scared me."

"Don't I know it." He shook his head. "I was such a fool."

"No, you weren't." She settled into his embrace, smiling at kids who giggled and pointed. Though the sky was still light, a pale moon appeared.

"I had been in love with you for years by then," he said.

"Since you were ten?"

"No. I knew I was going to marry you at ten, but I didn't know anything about love. I fell in love with you the night you went forward at the protracted meetings."

"You went forward too!"

"We were kindred spirits, but I wouldn't have known what to call it."

He stood and tugged her toward a walkway shrouded by a leafy canopy. It was cooler there and quiet. They walked with fingers entwined, serenaded by cicadas. "I fell in love with you gradually, Will."

"Once you had no other options."

"Careful."

"I didn't mean that the way it sounded. I feel blessed now, because you have many other options. But you were not free, once you began seeing Ben."

"By choice." She stopped and leaned back against a tree. The bark felt cooler than the air. "I didn't want to be free."

"Of course."

"I really believed I loved him."

"And I'm sure you did." Will thrust his hands deep into his pockets and appeared ill at ease with where the conversation had led.

"Come here, sweetheart," she said, reaching for him. He stepped closer but kept his hands in his pockets. She cupped his face in her hands. "I can tell you honestly, and not just because he's gone, that I never loved him the way I love you."

"Elspeth . . ."

"It's true. It was not the same. And why should it have been? It was not meant to be."

"You thought it was."

"Sure I did."

"Even after I told you you were to marry me."

"Did you even know I had fallen for Ben when you told me that?"

"I was afraid you had, but I didn't know. All I knew was that he had walked you back to your cabin the night I offered to."

Elisabeth pulled his face to hers and kissed him. "I fell in love with you watching you with your family, especially your mother and your nieces and nephews."

He sat back and studied her. "Not long after you moved in."

"Not very long."

"You fell in love with me then." It was more statement than question.

"I did."

"Are you sure?"

"I'm sure."

"In love?"

"As a matter of fact, I was terribly jealous of Lucy."

Will stood and moved away, staring into the distance. Elisabeth went to him. "What is it?"

"I was so heartsick over you at the time."

"I sensed that, but you didn't pressure me at all."

He put both hands on his head, as if in agony. "There was a reason for that! You were taken, remember?"

"You didn't know I was engaged. I had told no one."

"But you had pledged yourself."

She nodded.

"Ben didn't die until June last year," Will said.

"I should have said I began to see the real you, to understand the depth of your character, to appreciate you."

"You said you fell in love with me while you were engaged to Ben."

"I did, didn't I?" Will appeared in turmoil. "You were partly to blame," she said. "You told me God intended us to be together."

"I should never have said anything."

"But you made me think. You were right, I had not prayed about it. The truth is, Will, I never had peace about marrying Ben. I don't know what I would have done if he had come back, ready to push ahead."

"You would have had to marry him or break your promise."

"I'm afraid so."

Will put his arm around her waist and walked her back to the river's edge. The sky was growing dark. "There we were," he said, "living in my house, me loving you beyond all reason and looking for reasons to show it, and everything pointed toward your marrying Ben."

"It must have been awful for you, Will."

"Apparently it was worse than that for you."

She nodded, remembering that her troubling feelings for Will and her lack of peace about Ben had been swept away by the news of his death. "You were so sweet when I was grieving."

"I was grieving too. It was an awful loss, and I wondered if my prayers had caused it. I was so convinced you and I belonged together that I prayed every day that God would make it clear to you. Well, he sure did, didn't he?"

"Ben, you can't think that way."

He winced. "Do you realize what you just called me?"

"Oh, Will, I'm sorry. We need to put this behind us. I was not meant to marry Ben. If he had come back, God would have found another way to put you and me together."

"You might have broken the engagement?"

"I would have had to. I could not have married him with conflicted feelings."

It seemed everyone else had drifted from the riverbank. "Your grief was so deep."

"I loved Ben. I still grieve over him. But I did not love him the way I love you. You deserve to know that."

Elisabeth wanted to reestablish good memories associated with her birthday, and so she set the wedding day for January 1, 1920, at Christ Church. As a courtesy she invited her Aunt Agatha, who, Marlin Beck informed her, had moved to Sturgis. Elisabeth received no response.

It was the coldest day of the year, but the skies were clear and the sanctuary full. Beck and his wife attended, as did Dr. LeRoy's nurse, who hurried in late and quickly approached the bride, who was moments away from her grand entrance from the foyer. She whispered in Elisabeth's ear, causing her to burst into gales of laughter.

"What?" Frances Childs demanded.

Elisabeth shook her head, desperate to settle down and refusing to repeat what she had just been asked, especially in front of Pastor Hill. He would also enter from the back in a departure from protocol, as Elisabeth had selected him not only to officiate, but also to give her away.

"As your matron of honor, I command you to tell me what she said!"

Only after the ceremony, when the two had a moment of privacy, did Elisabeth tell Frances. "You remember who she is?"

"Of course! The one your dad got to tell you about you-know-what. Now what did she say?"

"She asked if I needed a refresher course before my honeymoon!"

Frances squealed and doubled over.

"If you tell a soul, Frances, I swear—"

"If? If? I can't think of a soul I *won't* tell!"

She went away laughing. Elisabeth felt as if her blush would never dissipate. Every time Will asked what was so funny, she burst into laughter anew.

They honeymooned in a cabin at a little lodge outside Plainwell. She was nervous and felt conspicuous when they checked in, assuming the proprietor and everyone he knew were aware of their business. But she found Will so considerate and gentle that she knew she would cherish living with him forever.

Upon their return, Elisabeth was puzzled when Will drove not to his big old home in the fourth ward, but to a beautiful estate in the first, not far from where she grew up.

"What's this?" she asked.

"Your wedding present."

He had to be joking. They parked in front of sprawling, palatial estates that backed up to the Rocky River and were owned by bankers, doctors, and industrial moguls. In fact, immediately to the south was the well-known Porter home, which featured "Lover's Bridge," a rustic footbridge that led to an island in the river.

"Which one would you like?" Will said.

Elisabeth's eyes were glued to the one before her. "This would suit me just fine," she said.

"That's a relief. It's yours."

She laughed. "And have you arranged a tour? I'd love to see it if we have time. We must get home soon though, mustn't we?"

But Will was out of the car and coming around to her side. As she stepped out she noticed keys in his hand. "Will. What is this?"

He took her arm and led her up the icy front steps and onto an expansive Victorian porch. The roofline was all angles and gingerbread. Elisabeth was falling in love with the place, still unsure what to make of it and not wanting to get her hopes up. It was impossible they could afford something so extravagant and more than they would need until they had half a dozen children.

Will unlocked the door. The house was bare, but the fireplace in the living room blazed. Someone had been put up to that. She could only hope it was a realty agent who knew better than Will that this was beyond his reach.

The interior was even more impressive than the exterior, everything freshly painted, scrubbed, and waxed. Elisabeth enjoyed the beauty, imagining what she would put where. Will was maddeningly silent, grinning, and—she feared—wasting their time. He had proved to be a bright man, a fast riser within Fairbanks-Morse, the youngest manager in their history, and much more handsomely paid than she ever dreamed he would be. But perhaps he was still naïve. Maybe because he had never lived in this ward he was under the impression that a person could take out a mortgage on a place like this and help make the payments by taking in boarders.

By the time they reached the kitchen Elisabeth had had her fill of the excursion and was through dreaming. "We really should go, Will."

"We really should stay," he said.

"No, really."

"Just one more room," he said.

She sighed and followed him to a glassed-in sunroom in the back. She looked past the tarpaulin-covered piles that filled half the room, apparently belongings that had yet to be moved. Elisabeth was struck by the wide lawn that led to the river and the tree-lined horizon beyond. The sun would set over those trees and create an enchanting vista. "It's gorgeous," she said. "All right? Can we go home?"

"We're home, Elspeth. Look here."

He pulled the tarpaulin off the piles and she saw it was his things and hers from the other house. "We need to talk," she said. "This is ridiculous."

Will found two chairs that looked shabby in their new surroundings, and set them next to the window, facing each other. Elisabeth reluctantly sat across from him, and he took her hands in his. "Will, I don't need this. I don't want this. We're sensible, middle-class people."

"You were raised in this neighborhood," he said.

"Not on this street I wasn't. This is above me. I wouldn't feel comfortable here, knowing the hole you had to put yourself in to get it. We'll look silly, rattling around in here—"

"Until we start filling it."

"You can't take in boarders in this neighborhood."

"I meant our own family."

"Will, we'd live under the mortgage for years and we'd never be able to live up to the expectations of the—"

He let go one of her hands and put a finger to her lips. "If I can't persuade you," he said, "I'll put it back on the market tomorrow. But hear me out. I have been saving every spare penny since I was a child. For years that meant just a few cents a week, but then it became dollars. When my father died we had some tough years, but the boarding house was cheap and quickly paid for, and you know I did most of the work myself. I sold the house and the business. If we went back there, we'd have to pay rent.

"I've had my eye on a place like this since I was twelve years old. I didn't say anything because I didn't want to disappoint you if I never achieved it. My life's dream was to go into our marriage with only a small mortgage. I make a good salary, and our only debt is a mortgage that will pay off the balance in ten years, about the same amount we would have paid for rent or for a smaller home in another ward."

"Which would have suited me perfectly."

"That's one of the things I love so much about you, Elspeth. But even without you working, we can easily make the payments, cover other expenses, and even save. I've worked toward this my whole life, but I'm not married to it. I'm married to you, and all I want is to make you happy. Tell me what would make you happy, and I'll do it without looking back."

"You'd sell this place and we could set up housekeeping in a normal house?"

"If that made you happy."

"But I want *you* to be happy."

He smiled and shook his head. "I'm happy if you're happy."

"That gets us nowhere, Will. Tell me what you want."

"You know what I want. I want to give you this."

"That would make you happy."

"That would thrill me."

She studied him, loving him all the more. "Then I accept."

"Really?"

"Absolutely."

"And all your objections?"

"I'll get over them. I might feel self-conscious for a while, but who wouldn't love this place and be grateful to God for a husband so kind?"

Will slumped in his chair. "I was afraid you were going to refuse."

"When have I ever refused you, darling?"

He smiled. "There was that night on the way back from camp."

She laughed. "Obnoxious as you were, who knew you were right? I'll never refuse you again."

Elisabeth settled in more quickly than she could have imagined as the only matriarch on the street without professional help. She decorated rooms, arranged furniture, and set about preparing the home to entertain. She reminded Will often that she could only feel comfortable in such opulence if she shared it as a gift from God. Her Sunday school classes, the choir, the missionary society, their friends, Will's coworkers, just about anybody and everybody was welcome to parties, dinners, or even to stay overnight. Visiting speakers at church and other dignitaries learned to call the place their home away from home. To the consternation of some of the snootier neighbors, the Bishop home became a catalyst to bring a new class of people into the neighborhood.

Elisabeth's days were full and rich, and for the first time since she had made her lifetime commitment to Christ, she felt God was smiling upon her. She knew she didn't deserve it, that she hadn't earned it. But she believed God would honor obedience and dedication. All right, perhaps the sacrifice part was in the past, but hadn't she had—as Pastor Hill's wife once lamented—too much at too young an age anyway? Maybe she had already had her allotment of turmoil for one lifetime. She occasionally felt the guilt of living in such comfort, but neither was she possessive or worshipful of it. The more she was able to give, the happier she was.

Elisabeth rose early enough every day to send Will off with a hearty breakfast. Every other day he walked all the way to the factory, so he was in the best shape of his life. She, on the other hand, busy as she was, was eating well too and found herself picking up the occasional pound. No one else, not even Will, noticed. But she did.

When Will was gone she spent an hour in the sunroom reading her Bible and praying. Then she sat at the piano, brushing up to accompany the singing at church—and improving her memory of every verse of every song in the hymnbook. It was an unusual ability and one that never ceased to amaze Will. During congregational singing, she never looked at the hymnal and never missed a word. Soon she even played from memory. Hymn lyrics had become nearly as dear to her as her Bible, and she loved meditating on them.

Elisabeth was busy at church and in the community, and near the end of their first year in the new house, few would have believed that she was yet to turn twenty-one. Elisabeth was an established woman about town, married to a most successful and prosperous young husband only a few months older than she.

On her twenty-first birthday Will took her out for dinner and gave her a beautiful necklace. "I have something for you too," she said.

"A present for me on *your* birthday?" he said.

She nodded. "Just a bit of news I hope you will like. Sometime around the end of July I should be able to refer to you as Daddy."

She loved his dumbstruck look. "You mean it?" he said, a little too loudly.

Elisabeth put a finger to his lips. "That's not the kind of a thing I'd tease about."

She suffered a difficult pregnancy and a nearly unbearable summer of heat. On July 25 she gave birth to a son they named—not merely with Will's permission, but with his insistence—Benjamin Phillip Bishop. He was a sickly, colicky baby who kept them up all hours, causing their first angry words and heated argument, yet they loved him with all that was in them.

Benjy, as Elisabeth called him, nearly wore her out, and by the time he was two she confessed to her physician that she wasn't sure she was ready for another child. Her beautiful home had been reorganized to accommodate an energetic, curious, extremely strong-willed and messy toddler. She spent most of her day keeping track of him and trying to discipline him.

Will proved a good and attentive father. Elisabeth, though, because of her lack of time to take care of herself, felt unattractive. Pregnant with their second child by late 1923, Elisabeth suddenly felt older than her years and worried about maintaining the idyllic marriage she and Will had begun. But he was wonderful about getting home at the same time every night and spelling her so she could have a break and get some rest.

May 15, 1924, Elisabeth Vera was born, and the Bishops called her Betty from the beginning. Just about the time Benjy had shaken all the physical ailments from his infancy and had become a stubborn and tireless three-and-a-half year old, Betty was diagnosed with chronic asthma that the doctor predicted would plague her all her life.

Elisabeth was distraught but determined to provide for all of her children's needs, whatever they might be. As exhausting as these first two were, Will still looked forward to a house full. In her more rational moments, after a good night's sleep or when the babies were napping, she realized that Will was right. He acknowledged that she had the tougher job, but this too would pass, and they envisioned a big happy family of children who would come to Christ and serve God. That, she and Will agreed, was their highest calling.

Late that fall Elisabeth asked Frances Childs to come and watch the kids while she went to the doctor yet again. While she held her suspicions until she knew for sure, she hoped Will would be more excited than she was about yet another pregnancy. She could not tell him of her growing despair. She knew she would get over it and love the child.

Part Two

Chapter Twelve

On the way home from the doctor's office, Elisabeth prayed for the grace to accept yet another child and the emotional freedom to share Will's likely excitement.

She could not deny God's obvious blessing in her choice of a marriage partner: Will seemed always to rise to the occasion, being patient and kind with her even when she was testy. It was difficult even to fault him over the division of duties. She handled the household and he worked full-time, and after several years of marriage and two children, he was still quick to help and even to anticipate when she needed it.

Elisabeth had in her mind a vision of the perfect mother, and she feared she had never matched it. In fact, she was more sympathetic every day to the temperament of Aunt Agatha. Elisabeth wondered if she had been as challenging a baby or toddler as her two were. If she had been, it was no wonder Aunt Agatha turned her out the first chance she got.

With that realization came a wave of gratitude. Why had she never thought of it before? As she walked up the front walk—eager to know how Frances had made out with the children and also conjuring a way to break the new baby news to Will—she stopped briefly and surveyed her beautiful home in a new light. She had always been thankful for it, but she had seen it as something Will had done for her. Yes, he was the wonderful husband God had provided, but now for the first time she understood that this place, this house, was God's recompense for the loss of her childhood home.

The fiasco with Aunt Agatha had been Elisabeth's fault. She had spoken recklessly and then felt obligated to stand by her word. She had been walked on and allowed the wishes of her dear father to be over-ruled. And yet because in the end she had acted honorably and not in her own interest, God had blessed her. Elisabeth didn't know what a theologian would say about that logic, but she believed it nonetheless.

Frances seemed relieved that Elisabeth was home, though she was ahead of schedule. "The children sleeping?" Elisabeth said.

"They are now," Frances said flatly. "But they've been down only ten minutes."

Elisabeth was alarmed at her friend's tone. "Everything all right, Fran?"

Frances was busily collecting her things. "Frankly, no. I'm afraid I'm going to have to ask that you find someone else next time."

"What is it? Trouble?"

"Just the usual. I'm scared to death I'm not going to get the steamer right for the little one, her breathing is so labored. And I cannot concentrate on her when Benjy is up and around. He doesn't listen, doesn't obey. He has such a mind of his own, and, Elisabeth, I know it's only a stage, but I cannot handle him. I don't know how you do it."

"He's a handful for me too."

"Sometimes I think it's a godsend that Art and I have so far been unable to—oh, Elisabeth, forgive me. I'm not implying it would have been better if you hadn't been able—well, bless you. In an emergency, call me. But otherwise . . ."

Elisabeth walked Frances to the door. "I understand."

"And you won't hold it against me?"

"Of course not."

"You had a phone call, by the way."

"Oh?"

"Mrs. Phillips. It had to have been Ben's mother, don't you think?"

Elisabeth racked her brain. "That's the only Phillips I know."

"She's quite eager to talk with you. She asked me to tell you to expect her."

Elisabeth was at a loss. "In person?"

"I told her I couldn't say whether you were prepared to entertain a guest, but she was not dissuaded."

"I wonder how she got my number."

"She said she called the drugstore and they gave her your married name. I hope they weren't out of line."

"Not at all."

Elisabeth expected Will at six. Betty was up wheezing by four and Benjy shortly made his noisy appearance. How could she possibly see Mrs. Phillips, and what was so important? Elisabeth had never followed through on her promise at Ben's memorial service to keep in touch, but neither had the Phillipses.

With dinner on the stove, Betty in her arms, and Benjy testing the back door lock, Elisabeth saw a late-model motor car pull up out front. Mr. Phillips came around to open his wife's door but then returned and waited behind the wheel.

"My goodness, you've married well, haven't you?" Mrs. Phillips said as Elisabeth welcomed her in.

"Not so well as it might appear," Elisabeth said, "but we're happy, and we do love our house."

"I'm sorry to barge in, dear. In fact, when we learned you had married, my husband urged me to leave you alone. But you deserve to know. I would not have wanted you to find out and wonder why the news had not come from us."

"News?"

Mrs. Phillips pulled from her purse a letter from the War Department. "Let me hold the baby while you read it. She's not contagious, is she?"

Elisabeth smoothed the sheet before her and read, "Dear Mr. and Mrs. Phillips: A critically ill unidentified man, long assumed a derelict, has languished for years in a British clinic. Thought to be in his thirties, he was pulled half-eaten and barely alive from the English Channel during the war. Because he was rescued so far from action, bore no clothing, and carried no identification, the prospect of his being a serviceman was ruled out. Due to severe amnesia, he has only recently been able to communicate, and British authorities now believe he may be American military. We're asking next of kin to some victims of the Great War to provide any clues that might help us determine if he is one of ours. If he is, you may rest assured that we will do all within our power to bring him home and get him the best care possible."

Elisabeth could not speak. She traded the letter for the baby.

"We're on our way overseas," Mrs. Phillips said.

"It's him?" Elisabeth said, her eyes stinging and her head light.

She nodded. "We informed them of the unusual formation of three small moles on his forearm that look like a tiny footprint. They told us that was one of his few unaffected areas above the waist. They will confirm with dental records, but we have no doubt."

"I—I—I don't know what to say." Elisabeth felt as if she were dreaming.

"That you're glad to hear he's alive would be a start," Mrs. Phillips said, brusquely handing back the baby.

"Of course! I'm just, just—"

"Shocked, I'm sure. And you're married. And a mother."

Elisabeth wanted to defend herself, to ask Mrs. Phillips if she had expected her to wait for Ben's return. Was this possible? How could it be? Who could have known? What would she have done if she'd known earlier, knowing God was steering her toward Will anyway? How would Mrs. Phillips have endured *that* crisis?

Dumbfounded and knowing she sounded so, Elisabeth said, "Well, thank you for telling me."

"Shall I keep you posted, or would you rather I had not informed you at all?"

"No, of course, Will and I will be eager to hear if he's all right."

Mrs. Phillips smoothed her skirt and leaned to look out the window at the car. "We already know he's not all right."

"I know, I mean, yes, tell us when he gets home and when he might receive people."

"You want to see him then?"

"I, uh—certainly. Yes, of course."

To Elisabeth's horror, Will pulled in the drive, slowing nearly to a stop when passing the Phillipses' car. With his suit jacket draped over his arm he shook Mr. Phillips's hand as the man stepped out. She could only imagine the conversation.

"We'll let you know, then, if you're sure," Mrs. Phillips said as she left. Elisabeth could think of no proper response.

Benjy called for his mother. Betty cried in frustration just trying to breathe. Something was boiling over in the kitchen. Will came in studying the lay of the land. He gave Benjy a cracker and soothed the baby as he followed Elisabeth to the stove.

"Elspeth, I'm—I'm speechless."

"Will," she said, "I can't even eat now." And suddenly she was crying, worried what Will would think of her reaction, yet having no control over it.

"Go up and lie down," he said. "I'll feed the kids and we can talk."

Elisabeth lay rocking in her bed, hearing Will inexplicably patient with the kids while he did her work and his, got the kids to bed, and even did the dishes. Her joined her in bed two hours later.

"I didn't know what to say to his mother," Elisabeth said. "And I don't know what to say to you."

"I'm as stunned as you are, Elspeth. I'm glad he's alive. I hope he recovers and becomes the man he was meant to be. I don't know any other way to respond. Did his mother expect that you would be waiting for him?"

Elisabeth shrugged.

"Does she want you to leave me and give him a reason to get better?"

"Don't, Will."

"How old is he by now?"

"Five years older than we are."

"Twenty-nine or so then. A lot of life ahead. He can still go to seminary, become a pastor, whatever he wants."

Elisabeth turned her back to Will and curled up. "He might have been better off dead. Who knows what he looks like, how much of his body he can use? How much of his mind is left? Can he think? Study? Speak?"

Will turned out the light and draped his arm over her. "Did you introduce his mother to Ben's namesake?"

"It never crossed my mind. Did you mention Benjy to them?"

"I didn't think of it either. I was just too—"

Betty wailed. Elisabeth sighed and began to get up. "Let me," Will said.

Elisabeth was too tired even to thank him. She covered her ears and breathed a prayer of thanks for her husband. As he moved past the door and headed downstairs with the baby, Elisabeth suddenly sat up. "Will?" she called out. "Something else I forgot. I'm due again."

He returned and sat beside her on the bed, Betty whimpering in his arms. "When?"

"Late May," she mumbled. "Maybe early June."

"I won't ask if you're as excited as I am."

"Thank you," she said, drifting off.

Over the next several months, Will and Elisabeth received letters and newspaper clippings about the return to Grand Rapids of Ben Phillips. "His motor skills and speech have improved remarkably," his mother wrote. "He has asked about you but does not want you to see him until he is out of the hospital. I have not told him of your situation for fear of a setback. He is expected to be able to come home in the fall."

Elisabeth wrote back with her best wishes and the news that it would be unlikely she could get away until sometime early in 1926, given that she would soon be the mother of three. Soon the letters from Grand Rapids stopped. "Whenever you want," Will told her, "you should plan to go see him."

"I'll have to tell him."

"The truth never hurt anyone."

"I couldn't tell him the whole truth."

"That you would not likely have married him anyway? He doesn't need to know that. But he can't blame you for getting on with your life."

Bruce James Bishop was born Monday, June 1, 1925, named after Robert Bruce—a favorite historical character of Elisabeth's—and, of course, after her father. Exhausted and guilty about not sharing Will's enthusiasm over another baby, still she was taken with Bruce from his first squall. A healthy, beautiful boy, he had olive skin, large dark eyes, and a full head of hair. The first time she cradled him to her breast he seemed to look deep into her eyes. She experienced a feeling similar to that strange day when she felt she had been granted a glimpse of her future with Will.

It was as if she could see Bruce as a compliant, obedient, bright child. She discounted it as wishful thinking, but the image would not leave her. Every time she held the newborn, she ascribed to him wonderful character traits like patience, honesty, and kindness. She had a feeling he would be curious and fun-loving. She prayed he would be a man after God's own heart.

Elisabeth was deeply grateful he was physically perfect. She felt sorry for Betty and the malady that would dog her her whole life. She also enjoyed that the new baby seemed more of a cuddler than the other two, never pulling away but rather seeming calmed by nuzzling Elisabeth, the closer the better.

Her premonitions proved accurate. Bruce made parenting a pleasure. As the older two became more difficult, Elisabeth looked forward to interacting with her youngest. He loved to be held; he cooed and tried to talk to her from the first, smiled earlier, crawled earlier, even seemed to understand the word no.

Will told Elisabeth he noticed that she had more energy and was quickly back to her old self. "We should think about another child," he said.

"I don't know," she said. "We shouldn't press our luck."

In the fall of 1926 a letter arrived from Ben Phillips addressed to Mrs. Will Bishop. So he knew.

"Dear Elisabeth," it read, "I trust you and Will are doing well and prospering in the Lord. I hear wonderful things about you and him and your family.

"Put to rest any fear you may have about my reaction to your marriage. Clearly God was in this, and while I don't understand my loss of so many years, I continue to rest in him. I will finally be going to seminary this fall with only a slight limp and scars visible only in the neck area. I may never know how I survived, but I am grateful for a second chance and feel much like Lazarus must have felt. My goal is still to preach, and I feel gratitude beyond measure that God has restored my memory and my mental faculties (such as they are!).

"My warmest greetings to Will. (You're a lucky man, friend.) I would love to see you both when it's convenient and you feel it appropriate. It might be awkward for us all, but my wish is that we might be friends and fellowship together as brothers and sister in Christ."

The letter made Elisabeth cry. Will shook his head. "That's about as big a man as I ever hope to meet."

Will's work and his involvement both on the school board and the city traffic commission, not to mention church activities, kept him busy nearly every night of the week. He often told Elisabeth he hated to go out after dinner and leave her and the children again. But she was proud of him. He was a leader in the community and had recently been promoted to comptroller of the company, the youngest senior manager by fifteen years. Some saw him as the eventual president of Fairbanks-Morse.

Elisabeth felt as if each day was a long week, highlighted only by the time she spent with Bruce, and she collapsed into bed every night, waiting for Will to get home. To his credit, he still was first to rise when one of the children needed something in the night.

They wrote Ben and arranged to see him as soon as his school year was over in the summer of 1927. Elisabeth included pictures of the children, and Ben wrote back exulting over the one named for him.

Despite her fatigue, Elisabeth was delighted with her family as the time drew near for the big visit. She loved Will more every day, the depth of his character showing in so many ways that she wondered if she would ever be able to fathom it.

She worried about Benjy, now almost seven. His first grade teacher threatened to make him repeat the grade, then insisted on passing him so she would not have to deal with him anymore. He was not below average in intelligence but seemed incapable of sitting still, following rules, or being quiet.

Poor Betty was another matter. Barely three, she was miserable, unable to understand why merely breathing had to be so difficult. She had been to specialists and was on so much medication that Elisabeth wondered if she wouldn't be better off in a sanitarium or a different climate. She could not be cheered, nor be made to smile. She lacked interest in much of anything and sat sucking her fingers, her nose and eyes running.

Bruce was wonderful. He greeted his mother with a smile every time he saw her, reached to be hugged or carried, kissed her without being coerced. He seemed to see each day, indeed each room, person, or new situation as an adventure. His very countenance seemed to ask, "What's next, what's fun for us now?"

He talked in sentences by his second birthday and loved being the center of attention. He was the favorite of the young people at church, and teenagers competed to hold him and interact with him. Few babysat him a second time, however, because Benjy and Betty came with the package. Elisabeth grew desperate about them, praying she would not fail them. Bruce was easy.

Pastor Hill's wife, now in her sixties, agreed to move into the Bishop home and watch the children the weekend Elisabeth and Will went to Grand Rapids. Will had volunteered to let Elisabeth go alone. "I trust you," he said, smiling.

"*I* don't trust *you*," she said. "Imagine this place when I got back." He feigned offense. "There is no way I could see Ben without you, Will. I don't know what I might do or say. I haven't seen him in more than nine years."

They followed Ben's directions to a small apartment complex near the seminary on the east side of Grand Rapids. Elisabeth could barely breathe, imagining Ben watching from the window. "You look wonderful," Will said as he walked her to the door. "He'll be thrilled to see you."

"That's the last thing on my mind."

When Ben opened the door, the years evaporated for Elisabeth. He smiled and shook their hands warmly. His hair was thin and gray, way too early for a thirty-two-year-old. He was only slightly smaller than she had remembered him, and his limp was more pronounced than she expected. His voice did not have the timbre it had when he was younger, but he said it was improving.

"It's been so long!" he said. "How remarkable to see you both!"

Will seemed bemused. Elisabeth didn't know what to say. "It's as if you're back from the grave," she tried. "Well, I guess you are."

"I knew this would be awkward," Ben said. "I don't know what else it could be. But tell me about yourselves."

Elisabeth was glad for the diversion. She bragged on Will, fearing she sounded as if she were trying to justify her choice. But she was proud of him and often spoke of him this way.

"God has blessed you," Ben said. "He has blessed me too. I'm doing well in school, getting opportunities to speak. Many churches are looking for pastors, so I should have little trouble finding a place to serve."

"You'll do well," Will said. "I still remember your messages at camp."

"How kind of you. Maybe someday *I'll* remember them!"

Ben and Will laughed, but the enormity of what Ben had endured washed over Elisabeth. The tension of seeing him again pushed her past the brink. She didn't want to sob in front of him, and she pulled a handkerchief from her handbag just in time to bury her face in it.

"I'm sorry," Ben said. "I didn't mean to treat this lightly."

Elisabeth collected herself. "Forgive me," she said. "This is all just so bizarre. I cannot imagine what it must have been like for you."

"In some respects I'm thankful for the amnesia so I can't imagine it either."

"You never resented it, wished you had died?"

"I was confused and frustrated for so many years, I didn't know what to think. When my memory began returning, it was as if I was living my life over again. I couldn't wait to contact my loved ones, to climb all the way back. It still seems to have happened quickly."

The scar that ran from the nape of Ben's neck to his Adam's apple was high-ridged and deep red. He said doctors concluded it had resulted from the bite of a large sea creature. "I won't show you the other scars," Ben said. "I can hardly stand to look at them myself."

At the end of the evening, Ben walked them to the door. "Your pastor there in Three Rivers—Hill, is it?"

"Yes."

"I understand he may be moving on."

Elisabeth flinched. Pastor Hill had been there since before she was born. She couldn't imagine the place without him. "He's not mentioned that."

"I may be mistaken," Ben said. "But at the seminary we were looking at a list of the pastors in this region who may soon start moving south or phasing out. We do that just to consider opportunities."

Elisabeth shot a glance at Will, who appeared nonplussed.

"Oh, don't give it another thought," Ben said. "I would never see myself as a candidate for that pulpit anyway."

"Why not?" Elisabeth said, relieved but curious.

"I can't imagine serving the church where my former fiancée and her family attend. Too distracting. For me and the congregation."

"Probably so."

"Anyway, a church that size would probably be too selective to consider me."

"I think you'd have your choice," Will said. "Once a church has heard you."

"That's kind, but older, more established congregations almost always insist on a family man, at least a married man."

"Well, you're still young. There's plenty of time for that."

Ben smiled and shook his head as he ushered them out. "Oh, no, that's not in my future. No, sir. Anyone other than who I had would never compare."

Elisabeth sat silent for several miles. "How was that supposed to make me feel?" she said finally.

"Since you brought it up," Will said, "all things considered, he spoiled a perfectly cordial reunion."

"So my marrying ruined his life."

"He just might feel that way."

"But it was the war! How long was I supposed to wait? Would he like to know that I would not likely have married him anyway?"

"You're overreacting," Will said, checking the rearview mirror.

"But what an awful thing for him to say."

"How do you think it made *me* feel?"

"I can only imagine, darling. You stole his fiancée and since no one else will ever do, he'll be a lonely cripple the rest of his life."

"We're being a little hard on him," Will said. "I wouldn't have wanted to marry anyone but you either."

When they neared home Elisabeth reconsidered her reaction to Ben's comment. "I should be flattered, I suppose. It wasn't as if he planned to say it. Any number of women would find him a worthy husband."

"You almost did."

"Almost."

At home Elisabeth detected relief in Mrs. Hill's eyes. "How were they?" she asked.

"A challenge. But that little one! He dropped off God's own tree, didn't he? I'll take him home with me any day of the week."

"No you won't," Elisabeth said. "He's all mine."

"Say, Mrs. Hill," Will said, hanging their jackets, "I trust Pastor knows how much he's appreciated. Does he?"

"Oh, I think so. People are mostly kind. There will always be critics. It comes with the territory, as they say."

"I just hope he's planning to stay with us a long, long time."

Mrs. Hill's eyes darted. "There are days when we tire of the flooding, the snow, the cold. And this is a long time to have stayed in one church. But I think Jack has a few more years in him."

A week to the day after their visit, a letter arrived from Ben. Elisabeth opened it nervously. It read, "Dear Elisabeth and Will, I laid awake for hours after your visit, thrilled how God has blessed you. The insensitivity of my last remark crushes my conscience, and I beg your forgiveness for implying that losing you had irreparably damaged me. While it's true I cannot imagine sharing my life with another, blurting that was crass and the wrong way to end a wonderful evening. If you can find it in your hearts to forgive, I would like to put it behind us. In Christ, Ben."

They agreed that Will should respond with a simple note of thanks for the evening and an assurance that Ben should not give his parting comment another thought. They would watch his career with interest, trusting God to put him into a pastorate that complemented his many gifts.

Elisabeth thought often of Ben and the odyssey of their relationship, but she never again mentioned his name to Will. She tucked the memories in a deep corner of her mind and heart, assuming she would never see him again and deciding that that was best.

Chapter Thirteen

*T*he Depression hit Three Rivers in 1929 like a Michigan tornado. The neighbors on both sides of Elisabeth moved away in the night within weeks of each other, rumors saying both men had lost fortunes in the stock market. Elisabeth's only hint had come when the wife to her west said, "I suppose your husband's company will save you from losing *your* house."

Elisabeth was so unversed in the issue that she didn't even respond. Within days, the woman and her husband had disappeared, and a holding company had come in to secure what was left of the home.

Fairbanks-Morse took a tremendous hit, sales dropping every month. Will came home more haggard every night. Barely twenty-nine, he looked ten years older.

"We laid off more men," he said one night. "Nearly a hundred."

"For how long this time?" Elisabeth said.

He hung his head and pressed his lips together, appearing to fight tears. "There's no plan to bring them back. I don't know what they're going to do."

"Should *you* start looking, hon?"

He shook his head. "We're safe at my level, but there'll be no raises for a while. We're asking mid-level managers to take a cut, and we can't cut them if we're not willing to take a hit too. And here we had only about a year to go on our mortgage."

"I know, Will. You've done great." She followed him upstairs, grateful the kids seemed preoccupied.

"Could have done better. We haven't watched the budget the way we'll have to now. We could have paid off the mortgage by now and been ahead of the game."

"You couldn't know this was coming."

"I'm the comptroller," he said, "yet I underestimated it." He stood and shook his head. "All F-M needs is one quarter where the demand for product matches one of the quarters from last year, and our fortunes turn."

But things grew darker. Elisabeth hated the look on Will's face when he announced the first pay cut. "It's severe," he said. "The car will sit until I get back to my previous salary. I'm willing to walk. Are you?"

"Whatever you say, Will. I believe God will see us through."

Elisabeth believed that had to be the worst of it, but banks closed and businesses failed every day. More neighbors went bankrupt. One day Will came home and, without a word, changed clothes and began digging a huge garden in the backyard. She rushed out. "What is it?"

"Can't you guess?"

"Another cut?"

He nodded and kept working.

"You love corn, beans, onions, and carrots, don't you, sweetheart?" she said. He nodded again. "Take a break and have a lemonade while you keep an eye on the kids. I'll be right back."

She walked to the grocer and returned with seeds and bulbs. "Will," she said. "We'll beat this."

His mood had brightened some. He showed her his lemonade, a couple of shaved lemon peelings in a glass of water. "I didn't even waste ice," he said.

His pay was cut again the next quarter and one more time the next. Inside a year his salary was reduced four times, parts of the plant had been shut down, and the workforce decimated.

"I'm still willing to work," Elisabeth said.

"We've been through that," he said. He took seriously the scriptural mandate for a man to provide for his family and for a mother to nurture her children. "Besides, your working wouldn't net us enough to be worth it, with babysitting and all. I appreciate it, but the discussion is over."

The final blow came at his next quarterly review. Despite being one of the senior officers, he told her, "If I choose to stay, my rate of pay remains the same."

"That's like a raise in these times," Elisabeth said.

He hesitated. Then, "The *rate* of pay is the same, but all they can offer is half a week's work."

"How do they expect us to live?"

"It's generous, Elspeth. You should see what this means to the men on the line. They're down to almost no pay and glad to have work."

Elisabeth found no shame in looking for bargains, pinching pennies, wearing clothes until they needed mending, and then wearing them some more. Businesses that extended credit gradually reduced the payments so people could pay at least something. Some credit loans were suspended indefinitely in the hopes that when the economy turned, people would remain loyal and do the right thing.

Elisabeth cut off the telephone service, even the newspaper. She no longer bought beefsteak. She expanded the garden to cover the entire backyard, and what could not be consumed or canned she sold for pennies, which she hoarded.

She made egg sandwiches for Benjy's lunch. He told her one day, "I traded mine for a meat sandwich."

"Meat?" she said. "Who can afford meat in their sandwiches?"

He told her the boy's name. "Will," she whispered. "They live in the fourth ward, and his father's out of work."

Will told Benjy, "Save a quarter of that meat sandwich tomorrow and I'll trade you a jawbreaker for it."

"Is that what I think it is?" Will said, sniffing the evidence the next day and showing it to Elisabeth.

She nodded. "Dog food. Canned horsemeat. Benjy! Come in here, please!"

In the midst of adversity Elisabeth felt closer to God than ever. She continued her open communication with him, rose early to read, and stayed as active in the church as her schedule would allow. Benjy caused her no end of grief, responding to neither discipline nor punishment and only a select few forms of positive reinforcement. She agreed with Will that rewarding him for merely acceptable behavior set a dangerous precedent.

Betty, about to start school, had improved not at all. The combination of medicines and humidifying contraptions had become so confusing and ineffective that Elisabeth began praying for a miracle. The poor child didn't deserve this, and Elisabeth worried that Betty would never know a normal life and never have a reason to smile.

Meanwhile, little Bruce was as engaging as ever, providing Will and her with diversion and entertainment. He was a generous, giving child, and she worried that he got less of her attention merely because he had fewer needs than the older two.

Will tried to maintain his civic activities, even adding a few volunteer positions. Elisabeth privately resented his increased time away during the evenings, but she knew service was part of his makeup. He had to do and to give and feel needed. She needed him too, but she couldn't complain. When he was home and had a spare hour before bed, he studied correspondence management courses from LaSalle Extension University.

"In times of adversity," he explained, "most people struggle to get by. I believe God would have me ready to advance as soon as the climate changes."

When their money was nearly gone, Will talked to the bank about refinancing the mortgage. He told Elisabeth it would help their case if the whole family showed up to illustrate the need. It was all she could do to keep Benjy reigned in while Will was pleading his case.

"I'm sympathetic," the loan officer told him. "But we simply don't have the capital. If I were going to extend credit to one customer, it would be you. You're the moneyman at the biggest plant in town. When this economy turns, you'll be back up to hundreds and hundreds of workers, and we want to keep doing business with you. My cards are all on the table, sir. I find myself in the unenviable position of having to turn you down flat and beg you to understand and not make me suffer for it later. If I had dime one, I'd lend it to you right now. In fact, if you need a personal loan, just between us, and anything short of a hundred dollars would help you, you name it."

That, Will told Elisabeth later, sounded too much like charity. "If I can't borrow against a piece of real estate like ours, I don't want a loan. We'll make it."

"You won't hold it against the banker, will you?"

Will shook his head. "If it wasn't for Fairbanks, Elisabeth, that bank would have closed a year ago. I *know* if they had it, they'd lend it to me."

Elisabeth wasn't listening. He had thrown her off. "What did you just call me?"

"Pardon?"

"You just called me Elisabeth."

"So?"

"Elisabeth! Will! You've never, ever called me Elisabeth."

He looked lost. "Isn't that your name?"

"Not to you it isn't! You've been working too hard, Will Bishop. You've called me Elspeth for longer than I can remember, and you're the only one I let do it. Now what's this Elisabeth?"

He smiled but looked embarrassed and seemed to try to cover. "You told me I sounded hick saying Elspeth."

"When did I ever say something like that?"

"In fourth or fifth grade."

She swatted his arm. "That doesn't count. You *were* hick then. Elspeth has always been your name for me."

"Yes, ma'am," he said.

She hugged him. "That was a new one, Will, I must say."

He went upstairs muttering, "Didn't seem that big a deal . . ."

Elisabeth found that while praying for her family, she mostly thanked God for Will and requested more rest for him. With Benjy she prayed for patience and a dramatic change in his behavior and, more importantly, his character. He was as difficult in church and Sunday school as in grade school, and she was embarrassed. Elisabeth herself had clucked about parents who didn't control their children. She knew people already considered her a failure.

For sickly Betty her prayers were simply for relief, for the child as well as everyone else in the family who suffered with her and because of her. Elisabeth loved her, but she found pity wearying. She could barely stand to watch and listen as the little thing wheezed and dripped and groaned and cried all day. It was hardly Betty's fault, yet Elisabeth battled resenting her for the incessant irritation.

Bruce was easy to pray for. She simply asked that God use all the incredible gifts he had clearly planted in the boy. By age four he was reading, conversing with adults, even doing sums. One day a pastry vendor pushed his cart past the house, advertising donuts two for five cents. Bruce looked at Elisabeth, beaming, and pulled a nickel from his pocket. He had been carrying it around for weeks. "You want a donut, Mom? Do ya, huh? Do ya?"

"You want to buy a donut for each of us?"

"I want to buy one for Daddy and Mommy and Benjy and Betty and me!"

"You can buy only two."

"Nuh-uh."

"Yes. Read the sign and figure it out."

Other kids and a neighbor lady had stopped the cart. Bruce looked at it, looked at Elisabeth, looked at his nickel, and set off. He stood at the edge of the little mob surrounding the cart until the vendor noticed him. "And what might I do for you, little one?" he said.

Bruce had the nickel hidden tight in his fist. "Can I just have one donut for a penny?"

Elisabeth was surprised. He knew full well the difference between a nickel and penny. She had laid it out for him on the table, showing him how many pennies equaled a nickel.

"Hm," the vendor said. "Two for a nickel comes to two and a half cents each." Bruce stood staring at him with a beseeching look. "But sure, I can give you one for a penny."

As the vendor grabbed one with a sheet of waxed paper, Bruce said, "Good!" and opened his hand to reveal the nickel. "I'll take five!"

The vendor roared and the crowd cheered as Elisabeth came running. "No! No!" she said. "Two will be fine."

"Are you kidding, ma'am?" the pastry man said. "The pitch alone was worth the loss of margin!"

"Please, don't feel obligated."

"Give the boy the five," a woman said, wiping her eyes. "I'd pay for 'em myself just for having seen a little businessman in the bud!"

Elisabeth finally let Bruce take the five donuts. He carefully set aside the three for the rest of the family and later took great pride in presenting them. Whenever he saw the pastry vendor he ran toward him yelling, "One for a penny?"

The vendor pretended to be irate and said, "No more of that from you, you little rapscallion! Now off with you!" and Bruce ran away, squealing with delight.

Money got so tight that Elisabeth began taking in laundry. Will was not happy about it, but he allowed it because, "at least you're here. And we *can* use the money." He helped out in a grocery store and sold soda pop from a stand on the beach after work and on Saturdays during the summer. He spent his two and a half days off each week working for the city's public works department, once tearing up and relaying pavement bricks for the installation of streetlights. He told Elisabeth he had not worked so hard since high school, but the extra fifteen dollars carried them another week.

Just when Elisabeth thought she could never love Will more than she did, she discovered another facet to his personality or heard another amazing story. He ran a small savings and loan department out of the office at Fairbanks for the benefit of hourly employees. It was small potatoes, and mostly men on the line invested for a small return or borrowed for emergencies.

Will mentioned that one day a worker requested a larger than average loan for an operation, the last hope for his ailing daughter. "We didn't have enough cash on hand, so I asked a couple of the guys who seemed to save regularly to put in a little extra if they could, so we could extend the loan. Not only would they be helping this man and his daughter, but also everybody who invested would share the risk. They did, and we made the loan. Today the man's daughter is improving."

"That's wonderful, Will. Do you realize you did that?"

"Yeah," he said. "I'm somethin', ain't I?"

"Seriously, how does that make you feel?"

"I wish someone would do the same for our company."

It seemed to Elisabeth that when one part of their lives improved, another deteriorated. The book of Job told her that "man is born unto trouble, as the sparks fly upward." She didn't expect clear sailing, only the knowledge that God was their rear guard. She didn't hesitate to remind him—as if he needed it—that she had made a pledge of obedience and that with his help, she intended to keep it.

When the Depression finally started to lift and Will went back to work full-time for about three-quarters of his old salary, Elisabeth felt as if they could breathe again. They would never be on easy street, but the Depression had taught her and—she knew—everybody else who had lived through it a valuable life's lesson, one they should have known all along: "Lay not up for yourselves treasures upon earth, where moth and rust doth corrupt, and where thieves break through and steal: but lay up for yourselves treasures in heaven, where neither moth nor rust doth corrupt, and where thieves do not break through nor steal. For where your treasure is, there will your heart be also."

"Lord," she prayed, "I want you always and only to be my treasure."

For months Elisabeth dreamt about running completely out of money. She and Will discussed often how that terrible season had affected something fundamental in their thinking. Never again would they take money for granted. Never again would they feel comfortable with their means.

Despite some financial relief, Elisabeth faced more trouble with the children. Benjy was forced to repeat third grade and responded with anger and mischief that alarmed the neighborhood, the school, and the church. Twice he was associated with suspicious fires, both times denying involvement; then he was caught red-handed setting fire to a wastebasket in the bathroom at church.

Betty had to be hospitalized three weeks in the spring of 1931, and other parents complained they didn't want the distraction of her asthma—which they wrongly assumed was contagious—in the classroom.

Bruce was a precocious first grader, smartest in the class and happy to play the role. He had to sit out of arithmetic and spelling drills so as not to dominate. He read the Bible and other adult books, especially encyclopedias, including the Book of Knowledge, which he methodically worked through, volume by volume.

In his spare time he ran a variety of businesses, from a lemonade stand to selling vegetables door to door. It seemed every moment of his day was filled with wonder and excitement. And he was eager to go to bed on time, because that meant he could read until he fell asleep.

One day that summer, as Bruce explored the rocks near the footbridge, Elisabeth toiled in the garden. What had begun as an economic necessity now seemed a frugal venture she might never give up. As she worked she hummed hymns and prayed and thanked God for bringing them through the Depression. It seemed the whole town was coming carefully into the light from the darkness of money woes. All of Three Rivers, indeed the whole of Michigan and most of the country, was breathing a collective sigh of relief. No one who had lived through the Depression would ever be the same.

Elisabeth kept an ear open for Bruce's whistling or singing or chatter. Even when alone, he kept himself entertained with running dialogues and commentary, making up stories and situations. Her thighs aching from squatting too long, she sat back and pulled off a glove to wipe her forehead. And she saw Bruce.

He hung precariously from the bridge by one hand, peering at something beneath it. Elisabeth started to yell but thought better of it. If she startled him . . .

She loved his curiosity, but this was reckless. She stood gingerly, hoping she could approach casually and tell him to carefully come back. He twisted for a better view, and before she had taken a step toward the river, his hand slipped, he swung and banged his head on the superstructure, and he dropped into the river. With a shriek Elisabeth ran toward the bank. Bruce was clearly unconscious, carried downstream by the swift current.

She sprinted toward the bridge, but Bruce was way past it already. Elisabeth could outrun the river, but she realized that once she plunged in she would never be able to swim fast enough to keep up. Where might he wind up? What might he hit? She could see his face, but not his mouth. If he came to and sucked in water in a panic, he would go under. She would lose him.

Elisabeth cried out, "God, help me! Help me save him! God! Please!" She had to get ahead of him before she entered the water to have a chance. She let her shoes fly off behind her and, gasping for breath, raced thirty yards ahead of him.

Her old yardwork dress, long-sleeved and ankle length, flapped behind her. As she neared the place of no return the edge of the river went from grass and sand to rocks, and she had to slow to keep from stumbling or cutting her feet. With nowhere else to go, she took a sharp right and dove into the water.

Her dress instantly doubled in weight and the skirt billowed like a submerged sail in the current. She fought to keep from being dragged downstream. She had to allow Bruce to catch her. Desperate, flailing, she maneuvered into his path, saw the strawberry scrape on his forehead, and even saw his eyes pop open. *Don't panic!* she pleaded silently. "Swim to me!" she screamed.

Bruce's eyes grew wide and he thrust out an arm to keep from sweeping past her. She grabbed him in a fierce grip he couldn't have broken if he'd wanted to. She wanted to scream but let him do that as she kicked hard and shifted her body weight till the river deposited her onto a collection of rocks.

They lay there, gasping, Bruce asking over and over what had happened and how he had gotten into the water. By the time neighbors got to them with blankets and towels and walked them back toward the house, everything was coming back to him.

"God must have something special in mind for you, young man," an elderly man intoned.

"Why?" Bruce said. "What do you mean? What does he mean, Mama?"

"You should have drowned, little one," the man said. "God saves people for a reason. He put your mama there because it wasn't your time."

"That's right," Elisabeth told him. "God saved you."

"You saved me, Mama!"

She eyed the river's rapid current with respect. "He let me help, that's all," she said. "I could not have saved you by myself."

The experience galvanized the family. Even Benjy settled down when the story was rehashed. Betty said over and over, "*I* could *never* stay above the water. I'm not playin' on that rickety bridge ever again."

"None of you are," Elisabeth said.

"I am," Benjy said.

"No, you're not," she said.

"Am too."

It was days before Elisabeth could sleep without the incident haunting her. Will prayed with her, and she pleaded with God for relief from the trauma. She also believed what her neighbor had said. Bruce was something special. God had huge things in store for him.

Will, like the rest of the men in town, still reeled from the lessons of poverty. But he seemed energized by being back to work full-time. He even added to his overloaded schedule a passel of additional civic responsibilities. "Why?" Elisabeth asked. "You already do more than enough."

"It's about being a good citizen," he said. "I can't stand people who enjoy the benefits of society without sharing in the responsibilities."

Will became director of the Three Rivers Tax Payers League, was elected to the school board, presided over the Rotary Club, and even spent a year as director of the Family Service Organization. Elisabeth hoped he wouldn't regret filling his days so full that he seldom got a chance to relax.

She watched him for signs of overdoing it, but his pace had been top-speed for so long, she hardly knew what to look for. One morning in the fall of 1933 he came to breakfast, read a portion of Scripture aloud as usual, encouraged the children, complimented Elisabeth on the meal, and headed for the door.

As was their custom, Elisabeth angled her way from her place at the table, and they embraced and gave each other a good-by kiss. Sometimes the children hooted. When they were younger they had often tried to squeeze between their parents. But by now Benjy was an angry, twelve-year-old fifth grader. Betty, nine, had been held back too and was struggling through third grade at a special school. Bruce, eight, was breezing through third grade.

As the kids watched them embrace at the door, Elisabeth slipped a hand around Will's waist and teased him. "Forget something today, Mr. Executive?"

He felt his waistband and blushed. "No belt," he said, clearly troubled. Will was the most buttoned-down person Elisabeth had ever known. He hurried upstairs and came down with his belt. As he rushed out the door, he said, "Good-by, Elisabeth."

She sang after him, "What did you call me?"

"I said good-by!" he said, still clearly embarrassed and, it seemed, disgusted with himself.

Chapter Fourteen

*E*lisabeth felt conspicuous: she and Will had the smallest family in their age group at Christ Church, other than Art and Frances Childs, who were preparing to adopt. The Childses were pitied, and of course rumors abounded about whose "fault" it was. But Elisabeth would rather have traded places with Frances than hear comments about her own situation. One woman, not realizing Elisabeth was behind her, went so far as to say, "When one's home in the first ward becomes more important than one's obligation to replenish the earth, well . . ."

Elisabeth wasn't about to have more children just to fulfill some unwritten rule. She and Will had always assumed they would have a large family, and she had not yet ruled out more children. But she was glad God had not given them more just yet. On the other hand, she thanked him every day that she had not stopped at two.

Bruce carried to church the same wonder Elisabeth had had at his age. At eight he became the junior pastor in his department, which included children up to twelve. In the adult services he sang lustily and told his mother that when he grew up he wanted to be a pastor, a missionary, or a choir director. She assured him she would be proud of him regardless.

Will was wonderful with the kids, as he had been with his nieces and nephews years before. Although he had no more success with Benjy than Elisabeth had, his attention was the only thing that seemed to cheer Betty. Bruce was easy, of course. He was curious about adult things. One night Elisabeth heard him quizzing Will about Fairbanks-Morse. Will came to bed two hours later marveling that "Bruce seems to understand more about the organization than some of our managers."

Elisabeth became convinced that Will was near exhaustion in December of 1933. Twice he had to return to the office after pulling into the driveway at the end of the day, having forgotten his briefcase. One morning he prepared to leave the house without his overcoat. It was seven degrees below zero.

At first Elisabeth teased him about it, calling him an absentminded professor. When she tried to speak seriously to him about it, he dismissed it, then seemed touchy. She suggested he think about trimming his schedule. He did not respond, but she was troubled by his look. She told herself it only made sense that a high-achieving man would be sensitive about any deterioration of his skills. And organization was certainly one of his.

Drawing attention to his memory lapses seemed only to make them worse. Elisabeth became more alarmed as the holidays approached. One morning Will arrived at the breakfast table barefoot, though otherwise dressed for work. The kids giggled and pointed, but he was oblivious.

After getting everything on the table, Elisabeth went upstairs and brought down his socks and shoes, setting them next to him without a word. After breakfast he stumbled over them and complained about things being in the way. Then he sat quickly and put on his socks and shoes. He left the house without kissing Elisabeth or saying a word. He had forgotten their good-by, the one she had enjoyed every weekday for more than a decade.

Midmorning he called her. "Elisabeth," he said—she chose not to correct him, "I feel as if I forgot something this morning. Did you say something as I was on my way out? Was I to pick up something for you?"

She bit her lip. "I just told you that I loved you with all my heart and couldn't wait to see you at the end of the day."

"Oh," he said. "Nothing I need to do then. No errand."

"No."

"Okay. I love you too, sweetheart."

That last sounded so normal that it thrilled her, but she feared she was fooling herself to hope this new phase would pass. The next morning Will arrived at breakfast wearing no tie and with his hair still wet. She pressed a finger to her lips when the kids looked at him and then at her.

"I'd like to read the Scripture this morning," she said, hurrying so he would have time to finish dressing. As soon as he finished eating she rose and went to him. "All right," she said, "you've got just enough time to dry and comb your hair and you'll be set to go." He grabbed his head, his face flushed, and he hurried upstairs.

Late that afternoon he phoned from the office. "Say hello to the new executive vice president," he said.

"Darling!" she said. "Really?"

"But it's a secret until tomorrow. Jake is going to announce it at the employee Christmas party."

"I'd love to be there."

"That would give it away, dear. And other wives are not invited. Better not."

"I'll want every detail."

That evening a phone call reminded Will of an important Tax Payers League meeting, already almost over. In the morning he wore mismatched shoes and Elisabeth had to remind him to shave. "And why don't you find another right shoe," she said. "I need to have that one repaired."

"What's wrong with it?"

"It's wearing unevenly. Wear the black one."

If he noticed she had steered him toward matching shoes, he didn't mention it. "Wish me luck," he said. "Big day."

"Luck?" she said. "It's all over but the announcement, isn't it?" He looked at her blankly. "Your promotion," she added.

"Right! Beloit."

"Beloit?" she said.

"That's where it is."

She stepped in front of him and put her hands on his shoulders as he picked up his briefcase. "I'm still sleepy this morning, hon," she said. "What is in Beloit?"

"Wisconsin," he said.

"I know. Beloit, Wisconsin. What about it?" He looked angry and tried to pull away. "Will," she said calmly. "You don't need to rush. You're ahead of schedule. Remind me what's in Beloit, Wisconsin."

"You know," he said abruptly. "Our other plant."

"Of course. What does it have to do with your promotion?"

"I'm not being transferred, am I, Elisabeth? I don't want to move to Beloit."

The room spun and Elisabeth held tight to Will. If he wasn't losing his mind, she was losing hers. "Sit down a minute, Will. Would you like me to call Jake and ask him what's going on?"

"Jake?" he said, as if he had never heard the name before.

"Your boss. Jack Jacobson."

"Jake!" he said. "He called?"

Elisabeth realized the kids were taking this all in. "Benjy! Make sure Betty is ready for the bus. Now!"

"*I'm* not doin' it," he said. "That's your job. Whatsa matter with Dad anyway?"

She glared at him so fiercely that he grabbed Betty's hand and ran upstairs. Bruce looked at her like a scared animal. "I'm getting ready, Mom," he said, and he took off too.

"Will," she said, trying to keep control, "you're frightening me. Now concentrate. You told me you had been promoted to executive vice president and that it would be announced today."

"At the Christmas party."

"Yes!" she said.

"Are you coming?"

"I asked you that, hon, and you said no."

"Why not?"

"Because no other wives are invited and it was supposed to be a secret."

He squinted at her and rubbed his forehead. "Now *you're* scaring *me*," he said. "Everybody knows."

"They do?"

"They're not supposed to bring their lunches, because Jake's treating everybody in the cafeteria."

"They know about the Christmas party, you mean."

"Isn't that what we're talking about?"

"And then Jake's going to announce your promotion."

"First he has to tell them about Donald going to Beloit."

Elisabeth feared she would hyperventilate if she didn't sit too. She pulled a chair alongside Will's. "So Don is going to Beloit. Is he being transferred?"

Will suddenly looked like his old self. He sighed, appearing frustrated that Elisabeth just wasn't getting it. "Don goes to Beloit, Franklin and Earl become vice presidents, I become executive VP, okay?"

She blinked. It made perfect sense.

"You got it now?" he asked.

"Yes, I do," she said. "Do you?"

He pursed his lips and shook his head as if he could hardly believe how difficult it was for her to grasp office politics. "Don't worry your little head about it, Elspeth."

So he was back to Elspeth. That so warmed her that she was almost ready to pass the whole episode off to his excitement over the announcement. Until he said, "Are the kids home yet?"

"You know what I think?" she said. "I think you need some rest. Would you like to lie down a while?"

He seemed to look through her. "How about let's get you up to bed, hm? I need to get the kids off to school and I need to make a phone call. So, come on. A nap sounds good, doesn't it?"

Will did not respond, but he let her lead him by the hand up to their bedroom. She sat him on the bed, knelt, and removed his shoes. He lay on his back, staring at the ceiling. She reached to loosen his tie but he pushed her hands away and did it himself. He covered his eyes with his elbow and his breathing immediately sounded deep and rhythmic. Tears rolled down Elisabeth's face as she draped a blanket over him. "Lord, let him sleep," she prayed silently.

As she went to round up the kids Elisabeth heard Betty's school bus. "Betty!" she called. "Are you ready?"

"No! Benjy locked me out of the bathroom!"

"Benjamin!" she hollered. "I told you to get her ready!"

"She takes too long!" he called out.

Elisabeth decided Betty looked ready enough and hustled her down the stairs and out the door, just as the bus was about to pull away. Elisabeth ran back upstairs and demanded that Benjy open the bathroom door. "Only if you promise not to kill me," he hollered.

"I promise I will if you don't open up," she said.

He burst out and rushed past her. "That'll be the day," he said.

"Where's your brother?"

"Digging in the back last time I saw him."

"If you're ready, get going to school. Bruce will be along."

She found Bruce in the backyard, having dug through the snow to the grass and soil. "Bruce!" she shouted.

"Mom," he said, "c'mere a minute."

"You don't have a minute. You've got to go."

"Mom, I've never been late in my life." It was true. "C'mere just for a minute." She hurried to him.

"Look at this," he said, lifting a shovel full of steaming earth.

"Yes, what?"

"Those tulips that come up here every spring? This is why. Those roots look frozen and dead, but they're not."

"From death comes life," she said.

"Uh-huh. I knew it was the same flowers, or from the same seeds. I just had to see what they were doing down there when they should have been freezing to death. After they bloom, they look dead, they shrivel up, the sun bakes 'em, they get snowed under, and they freeze. But in the spring they come back."

"May it ever be so," Elisabeth prayed silently as she wrapped Bruce in a tight embrace. "Now get going, young man. I'll put this back the way it was."

"Thanks, Mom!" he said, running off.

Elisabeth knew she should have a coat on, but shoveling the dirt back would take only a minute. She heard Bruce go in to get his stuff, then let the door slam when he ran out. "Bye, Dad!" he said. "Better get some shoes on!"

Elisabeth dropped the shovel and ran to the other side of the house. Bruce was running one direction to catch up with Benjy. Will was driving the other way in the dead of winter in his shirtsleeves and stocking feet, on his way, or so he thought, to being named the new executive vice president of the Fairbanks-Morse Company.

Elisabeth ran to the phone.

"I'm afraid Mr. Jacobson is not taking calls this morning," she was told.

"This is an emergency," Elisabeth said. "Interrupt whatever he's doing, please."

Jacobson was on the line a few seconds later. "Elisabeth, my dear . . ."

"Jake, I'm sorry, but it's Will." She quickly spilled the story.

"Don't you worry, Elisabeth, we'll watch for him. And if he doesn't arrive here, we'll have the police find him."

"This must come as a great shock to you, Jake."

"I'm afraid not, dear. I had been meaning to call you, but we didn't want to upset you. I was meeting with his colleagues when you called. We were discussing how to break the news to him about postponing today's announcement."

"He was right about that then?"

"Oh, yes. Not that long ago I would not have been able to think of a better candidate. Elisabeth, it's clear he needs immediate attention. As soon as we locate him, we'll get him to the new hospital. Can you get there?"

"I'll find a way."

"I'll send a car for you."

"Oh, Jake, that's not nec—"

"Nonsense. Be ready, dear."

Less than thirty minutes later a large, black F-M sedan pulled into the driveway. Jacobson himself alighted from the backseat to usher Elisabeth in. "Will pulled into the lot pretty as you please," he explained. "One of the security boys asked him to slide over and let him drive. Told him he had an important meeting with me off-site. He's in with the doctor already."

"What's wrong with him, Jake?"

"We'll know soon enough."

As they waited in the hospital, Jake said, "I was impressed that Will was willing to move, at least temporarily. You too."

"Move?"

"To Beloit."

"Beloit? Jake—"

A nurse interrupted. "Mrs. Bishop? Doctor Fitzgerald would like you to join them, please."

As Elisabeth entered, the doctor watched impassively as Will rushed to her and whispered. "What's the older boy's name?"

"What?"

"The older boy."

"What older boy, Will?"

"Our son! Our son! Betsy and Bruce and, come on, what's his name?"

She looked to the doctor who closed his eyes and nodded. "Benjamin," she said.

Will looked shocked. "*Benjamin?*"

"Benjy."

"Yes!" he shouted, whirling to face the doctor. "Benjy, then Bruce, no, then the girl, Bess, and *then* Bruce. See? I knew."

"Sit back down, Mr. Bishop, please." The doctor introduced himself to Elisabeth and pointed to a chair. She sat. The doctor continued. "Now, Mr. Bishop, if you will, please tell your daughter and I—"

"That's 'daughter and me,' Doctor," Will scolded. "You wouldn't say 'please tell I,' would you?"

"Very good. Please tell your daughter and me the name of—"

"She's not my daughter. My daughter is Betsy. Betty. Same name as my mom, I mean as my wife. This is my wife, Elisabeth."

Elisabeth bit her lip and looked at Dr. Fitzgerald. "He has always called me Elspeth. Always."

The doctor nodded. "Mr. Bishop, please tell your wife and me the name of the president of the United States."

"Lincoln."

"The president now, Mr. Bishop."

"Abraham Lincoln."

"And what year is this?"

"Nineteen hundred."

"Nineteen hundred and what?"

"Nineteen hundred and nothing."

"Abraham Lincoln was president seventy years ago, Mr. Bishop. Before any of us were born."

"I was born in eighteen ninety-nine."

"And how old are you, sir?"

"You're going too fast."

"This is the end of 1933. That makes you how old?"

"Don't tell me."

"Oh, Will," Elisabeth said, reaching for his hand. He ignored her.

"I'll get it," he said.

She turned to Dr. Fitzgerald. "Must you continue? I get the point. What can we do?"

"It's important we determine the extent of the dementia."

"Dementia, at thirty-four?"

"Thirty-four!" Will shouted. "I'm thirty-four!"

"Ask him who the president is."

"Will, you know who the president is, don't you? You didn't vote for him, but you're still hopeful, remember?"

"Woodrow Wilson."

"Not anymore. Who was elected two years ago and took office early last year? A Democrat."

"Roosevelt."

"Yes! Good!"

"Teddy Roosevelt."

"No."

"Yes! Teddy. San Juan Hill."

Elisabeth stood and embraced Will, fearing she had lost him forever.

In truth, Elisabeth realized, she *had* lost Will. He spent the next two weeks in the Three Rivers Hospital while she endured batteries of forms and interviews, trying to determine any injury, trauma, or stress-related incident that might have triggered a psychosis. While discussing with Jack Jacobson the symptoms that surfaced at the office, Elisabeth remembered that Will's own father had suffered the same malady, though not at so young an age.

Elisabeth's days became jumbles of housework, baby-sitters, trips to the hospital, meeting with Fairbanks-Morse over employee benefits, insurance, and the like. Christ Church people rallied round her, but at times she felt if she had to answer one more question she would explode. At the end of two weeks she had little hope of bringing Will back home. Dr. Fitzgerald asked that she come in at her convenience to discuss Will's transfer to the State Hospital in Kalamazoo.

"How long do you expect he'll be there?" she asked wearily, desperately short of sleep.

"Mrs. Bishop, may I get you something? A sandwich? Something to drink?"

She shook her head. "Do I need it? Am I not going to like what you're about to say?"

He sighed, rearranged a few things on his desk, and looked at her sympathetically. "The move to Kalamazoo will likely be permanent. We have a diagnosis, but of course, diagnoses are open to interpretation. We have studied the elder Mr. Bishop's records and compared them to your husband's symptoms and tests, so we feel fairly confident of our evaluation."

"I'm ready."

"We believe your husband has an acute degenerative disease of the brain."

"He'll get worse?"

"There is new research all the time, new medicine, new therapies. We never rule out hope. At this point, however, if he has what we fear he has, it is incurable."

"Does it have a name?"

"In lay terms it's senility, but in your husband's case it is premature and unusually aggressive. My colleagues and I are persuaded that Will's condition is exacerbated by what is becoming known among researchers as Alzheimer's disease, after the neuropathologist who first described it about twenty-five years ago. Only an autopsy can confirm this diagnosis. We should have a pretty good idea in a few months by

watching his symptoms, but if this *is* the disease Dr. Alzheimer has cat-
alogued, Will would be among the very youngest victims on record.
The two most common risk factors are advanced age and genetic disposition. He, of course, had only the latter. He might survive long
enough to benefit if someone finds an antidote, or, because of his rel-
atively good physical condition, he could live longer with the disease
than most. But I remind you, his rapid deterioration leads us to believe
that more than one disease is attacking his brain."

"I believe in prayer," she said, realizing her legs were crossed and
her foot had fallen asleep.

"As do I, but I feel obligated to tell you everything. Your husband's
core symptom is memory loss, which he is, of course, already experi-
encing acutely. The speed with which his deterioration is progressing
is as alarming to us as it is to you. The general course of this disease sees
the patient regress in language, reasoning, and even visual ability. In
short, adults regress to childhood with symptoms more acute every
year. Whereas your husband learned to crawl, then walk, then talk, then
control bodily functions, unless some cure or arrestor is found, he will
gradually, in essence, forget how to do those same things."

Elisabeth set both feet on the floor and fought to maintain composure. "You're telling me that without a miracle, Will will be in diapers."

"I'm sorry."

"And in ten years he'll be gone."

"That is harder to predict, because he is still so young." Elisabeth
stood. "Are you okay, ma'am?"

"I'm trying to find some ray of hope," she said, "some bright side
of my husband living longer as a helpless infant when death might be
the greatest blessing."

Elisabeth followed the ambulance that transported Will twenty-two
miles north to Kalamazoo. She had traveled the route before, of
course, but today it seemed particularly depressing. The blacktop road
was crumbling and the sparse farms bored her. Not even the Burma
Shave signs cheered her.

Once Will was settled in, she sat next to his bed. "I'm going to have
to go soon," she said. "I'd like to be home when the children get
home from school."

"Yes," he said, looking directly into her eyes as if he understood perfectly.

"I'll bring them to see you, maybe next weekend."

"I'd like that, Elspeth."

She felt a chill. "Will, you understand me right now, don't you?"

"Yes, I do."

"Do you understand what's happening?"

"No."

"Do you want me to explain it?"

"I'm hungry."

"You ate just before we came here. Dinner will be at six. You should be able to wait until then to eat. All right?"

He nodded. "I love you."

She stood and embraced him. "I love you too, Will," she said, sobs racing to her throat. "I love you with all my heart, and I'll be with you every step of the way."

"You'll go to Beloit with me?"

"I'll go anywhere on earth with you, Will. Just stay with me as long as you can."

"I can stay a little while longer."

She smiled through her tears and sat again, looking at her watch. "You can?" she said.

"What time is it?"

"About one-thirty."

"I can stay with you until two, Elspeth."

"Where are you going then, Will?"

"To a party. It's Christmas, isn't it?"

"Soon."

"It's the Christmas party at work."

"That will be nice."

"I'm getting promoted."

"Um-hm."

"Big boss."

"You'll be the big boss?"

"Yes. Jake is leaving."

"Is he? Where's he going?"

"Three Rivers."

She opened the drapes and brightness from the sunlit snow burst into the room. "Time for breakfast," he said.

"Dinner at six," she said.

"Dinner at six."

"I really should go."

"I'll miss you, Elspeth."

"I already miss you, Will. Where are you? Where have you gone?"

"Beloit."

"Do you know who I am, sweetheart?"

He was smiling, and except for the gibberish, she could pretend she was talking with her old Will. "I love you," he said.

"Yes," she said. "That's who I am. You love me."

Elisabeth wept during the whole drive home, her stomach aching from the effort. She prayed aloud through her tears, "God, heal him or take him quickly! I won't be able to stand to see him like this. I believe in you, trust you, want to obey you in everything. I'm committed for the rest of my life, but I'll need you if I'm going to survive this. It's more than I can bear alone."

She arrived ahead of the kids and a neighbor asked how things had gone. Crazily, incongruously, she said, "Oh, fine. As well as could be expected."

Why do I do that? she wondered. *How did things go? I just put my husband in an institution where he will slowly lose his faculties and die, that's how things went. I don't know what to tell my children, how I can prepare them for the man they'll see Saturday, how I'll raise them on my own, how I'll support us, how I'll maintain my own sanity.*

She put dinner in the oven and tried to freshen up. In the mirror she saw an old, humorless woman, eyes full of dread fear, hair pushed into place, bags under the eyes, skin drawn around the mouth. Elisabeth splashed water on her face and rubbed hard with a towel, bringing color to her cheeks. She would not be able to smile for the children. She was determined to answer every question honestly. She would not start down a path of half-truth or misdirection that would be impossible to navigate. She knew what it was to be raised by one parent, and she also knew what it was to lose her father. The children deserved the truth in exchange for all they would lose.

Betty arrived home first. Elisabeth tried in vain to cheer her. "When's Daddy coming home?" she whined.

"We'll go see him Saturday," Elisabeth said. "But he will not be coming home. He's very ill."

"When then?"

"Probably never."

"Is he going to die?"

"Not very soon, but eventually."

"Before you?"

"Probably."

"I want to see him now."

"Saturday."

Betty whined and busied herself upstairs. When the boys got home, Benjy terrorized Bruce, as usual. Bruce couldn't compete physically, but he was merciless orally.

"You only try to beat me up because I'm smarter than you!"

"Come here, you little rat. I'll kill you."

"Benjamin," Elisabeth said, "I don't ever want to hear those words out of you again!"

"He's a coward, making fun of me because I'm stupid, but he won't stand and fight!"

"Why should he? You're bigger."

"He better not forget it."

"Bruce, run along for a moment so I can speak with Benjy alone."

Bruce, probably assuming his mother was going to scold Benjy for bullying him again, stuck out his tongue and bounded upstairs. Benjy's threats echoed through the house.

Elisabeth had never had success sitting Benjy down and talking seriously with him, especially when he thought he was in trouble. But something about her carriage or countenance must have caught his attention. They sat across from each other at the big dining room table.

"I need to tell you about Dad," she said. "Things are going to have to change around here."

Chapter Fifteen

*B*enjy did not respond well to the news. Elisabeth saw fear in his eyes for the first time in years. Then came the defiance she was used to. He looked suddenly older, his physique developing, his voice changing, a shadow of hair on his lip.

"First of all," he said, "if you really want me to be man of the house, I want to be called Benjamin from now on."

"Fair enough," she said. "It might take some time to get used to that, so be patient with—"

"Just tell Ugly and Big Mouth, and I'll remind you anytime you forget."

"Benj—Benjamin, if I ever hear you refer to your sister and brother like that again, you'll lose every privilege you've got."

Benjy pushed his chair back from the dining room table and tilted on the back legs. "And I don't want to have to do all that Bible stuff all the time either."

"The memory work has helped you in school."

"Nothing helps. It won't be long before Big M—before what's-his-name passes me up, and he's four years younger."

"Well, you're not getting out of church or learning the Bible."

"Then I don't want to be man of the house, because I'm not going to do it, and then you're going to keep me in all the time."

Elisabeth was tempted to slap his face, which scared her. She had spanked the children, Benjy more than the others. But she had seldom done it in anger, and even then she had been able to keep from actually hurting them. She'd never hit one in the face, though Will had once backhanded Benjy in the mouth when he had sassed his mother for the umpteenth time.

She prayed silently but couldn't quit glaring at him.

"What?" he said.

"Don't you have any questions about your father?"

"Like what?"

"Anything. This is a rare disease, and he'll never be the same again. It won't be long before he doesn't recognize us."

"He hardly knows me anyway." Benjy let the chair drop forward, the front legs banging on the hardwood floor.

"How can you say that? He loves you! You've been hard to handle, but he's spent a lot of time with you. Your father has more character in one hand than all the other men you know, and if you just tried to pattern your life after his, you'd—"

"I'd wind up just like him. He does all this good stuff, loves God and all that, and look at him now. I don't want to see him that way."

"But you'll see him Saturday, Benjamin. He can still talk with us."

He scowled and turned away. "If you make me."

"He's failing so fast."

"I don't want to see him in any diaper."

"Don't be spreading that around, Benjamin. I told you it would come to that only so you would understand. Your father deserves dignity and respect, and no one should ever know the extent of his disease, unless it's someone who really cares."

"Yeah, like I would tell my friends my dad has to be fed like a baby."

Elisabeth shook her head. "It's certainly not his fault."

"'Course not. It's probably my fault, like everything else around here."

"Nobody's ever said that."

"So, what, does the man of the house have to take over all Dad's chores too?"

She was tempted to wish aloud that Bruce were the oldest. "I'm going to need a lot of help," she said. "I'm going to have to go to work."

"Great," he spat. "I get to shovel snow and rake leaves and all that."

"You've done that before."

"Not all of it!"

"We'll all pitch in."

"And what if I don't?"

"What does Proverbs say?"

"I don't know, but I'm sure you'll tell me."

"Chapter 21, verse 25 says, 'The desire of the slothful killeth him; for his—'"

"I know all the verses, Mom, all right? You calling me lazy now?"

"You're the one who said you might not help out. First Timothy 5:8 says that if anyone does not provide for his own, and especially for those of his household, he has denied the faith and is worse than an unbeliever. Second Thessalonians 3:10 says that if anyone will not work, 'neither shall he eat.'"

Benjy stood so quickly that his chair flew back and toppled. "Don't you ever get tired of all those verses?"

"Benjy—Benjamin—stop it! Honestly, I never dreamed of talking to my father that way, not ever."

"Then he wasn't like you."

"Pick up your chair and sit down here for one more minute."

He glared at her as he slammed the chair back into place and plopped into it. "I'll tell you when a minute's up," he said. She dreaded the day he would simply stop obeying. What would she do then?

"I want to know when you stopped caring what God thinks about how you act."

"I never cared."

"I don't believe that. You were in trouble a lot at church, but still you learned. You know all the stories, the songs, the verses. I thought you gave your heart to the Lord when you were little."

"I don't even remember that. If I did, I'm taking it back. I can't stand all that stuff, and anyway, look where it's got you and Dad."

"We wouldn't trade our walk with the Lord for anything."

"I sure would."

"It seems you already have."

"Time's up."

"I worry about you, Benjamin," she said as he stood.

"Yeah, yeah."

"I'll never stop praying for you."

"I knew that was coming."

"I need you to do two things for me before dinner. Send your brother down and then bring in more firewood."

He sighed loudly. "Bruce!" he shouted.

"I asked you to send him down. That means go get him." But Bruce was already on his way. "And don't mess with the fire. Just get more wood."

Elisabeth rested her forehead on the table, realizing she would never again be able to talk and pray with Will about Benjy. They had often wondered if he had the devil in him, but they believed if they loved him and remained firm, he would not turn from the way he had been trained.

Bruce dragged his finger across Elisabeth's back as he joined her. "How's Dad?" he said.

She smiled at him, her tiny ray of sunshine in a sky of storm clouds. But she couldn't stop the tears. That made him cry too, but he kept telling her, "It'll be all right, Mama. It'll be all right."

"Actually, it won't," she said when she was able to gather herself. "Bruce, I would never tell the normal child your age what I'm about to tell you. You're a special boy with a bright future for God, but with that comes great responsibilities. Do you understand?"

"I think so."

Elisabeth told him all about Will. She had rarely rendered him speechless and now feared she had done the wrong thing. He appeared to try to form a response but was unable to say anything. Finally he whispered hoarsely, "We can't see him until Saturday?"

She nodded. "I'll see him every day, but you kids must keep up with school and everything else."

His face contorted. She knew he wanted to comfort her. That was his way. He looked away, and his tears came again. "Isn't there anything I can do?" he managed.

"Just pray," she said. "And I'm going to need a lot of help."

He nodded, sobbing. She took him in her arms and they wept together.

Saturday was awful. Neighbors advised Elisabeth not to try to drive all the way to Kalamazoo with the temperature nearly twenty below zero. But she started the car early, giving it plenty of time to warm up, and it seemed to run fine. Blowing snow across the road left thick sheets of ice that sent cars and even trucks into the ditch. Elisabeth averaged barely fifteen miles an hour, and the trip took ninety minutes.

The weather was giving Betty the only degree of relief she'd had in ages, so at least Elisabeth didn't fear an asthma attack during the visit.

Elisabeth had made sure the staff knew Will's children were coming. He had been shaved and bathed and looked remarkably fit in the dayroom, where he sat near a clicking radiator.

"Look at you all," he said. "So cute."

"Thanks, Dad," Betty said.

Will smiled at Elisabeth and said, "Dad."

"You remember Benjy," she said.

"Benjamin," Benjy said, but she shushed him. "We need to help him remember," she whispered, "not make it harder."

"I'm Benjy, you're Dad," he said, scowling. Will smiled at him.

"Dad," Will said.

"And Betty. This is our daughter, Betty."

"Hi, Daddy," she said, still shy.

"Daddy," Will said.

Bruce looked as serious as Elisabeth had seen him in ages. It was clear he hated to see his father this way, disengaged, seemingly unaware and apathetic. She turned Bruce around and steered him toward Will. "And this is our baby—" Elisabeth began.

"Bruce!" Will exulted, throwing open his arms. Bruce hugged him fiercely.

"Figures," Benjy said, sitting several feet away. Elisabeth motioned for him to return, but he would not.

Will took Bruce into his lap, and while the boy was too big for that, he didn't protest but laid his head on his father's shoulder. After a while Will said, "I have to go soon. I'm going to a Christmas party."

"Here?" Bruce said.

"At work."

Bruce looked at Elisabeth, who put a finger to her lips and shook her head. "We need to get going too, Will. Say good-by to your children."

"Good-by, children," he said, still smiling, maddeningly looking no different than he had a month before. Elisabeth knew that would change.

Benjy drew a little closer, as if to see if his dad would acknowledge him. Will opened his arms for another hug from Bruce. Then he let Betty hug him. He opened his arms to Benjy, who came no closer but said, "See ya, Dad."

"Dad," Will said.

"I love you, darling," Elisabeth said, embracing him.

He did not return her hug but smiled and said, "I love you tomorrow. Every day."

"Yes, I love you. And I'll see you tomorrow and every day."

"Every day," he said.

"Can we pray with you, Will?"

"In Jesus' name, amen," he said.

"Gather around and let's hold hands, kids," she said. "Let's pray with Dad."

Benjy refused. Betty groaned. Bruce held Elisabeth's hand and reached for Will's, but Will said, "Dad," stood, and walked away.

An orderly asked Elisabeth, "Are we done here, then?"

"I guess," she said.

They watched as Will was led down the hall, telling the orderly about the Christmas party.

Thick smoke billowed from the chimney when Elisabeth pulled in the driveway.

"Benjy!" she snapped.

"Benjamin," he said.

"I left that fire low and told you to leave it alone."

"I did! There was a lot of wood already in there."

On the way into the house she argued with him. "Before dinner it was down to a couple of logs, which should be embers by now."

"I swear I didn't touch it, Ma."

She knew he was lying. She dragged him to the fireplace where a fire still blazed. "Benjamin, we were gone nearly four hours! I did not put that much wood in there."

"You just forgot, that's all. Or maybe somebody came over and did it for us."

"People don't do that. It's dangerous."

"Well, don't ask *me*."

"And where's the newspaper? You didn't kindle those big logs with newspaper again, did you?"

"I told you! I didn't do anything with the fire!"

"Just the same, you're off firewood duty." It had been years since Benjy had been accused of anything related to fire, but Elisabeth couldn't take any chances.

"Good!" he said. "One less job."

While the kids were getting ready for bed, Elisabeth stoked the fire and spread it out, letting it die a bit. She selected three large logs from the stack Benjy had brought in and set them aside. Before she retired, she would put them atop the accumulating bed of coals.

As she made the rounds of the children's bedrooms, as had been Will's and her custom, Benjy made it clear he wanted that to end too. "I don't need to be tucked in like a baby," he said.

"But I want to be sure you're praying and that you're all right and will sleep tight and won't let the bedbugs bite."

He groaned and rolled onto his side with his back to her. "Do whatever you want," he said. "But I don't need this."

She didn't have the energy to argue.

Elisabeth found Betty weepy. "Benjy said he didn't want to see Daddy ever again, and I said 'Me neither,' and now I feel bad."

"It's hard to see Daddy this way. And it won't get easier."

"I hate this. Why did God do this to us?"

"God didn't do it, honey."

"Then who did?"

Elisabeth didn't know how much Betty would understand of a fallen world. "Bad things happen to everybody. They test our faith. The important thing is how we react to them."

"My faith isn't too good."

"Sure it is."

"I'm sick all the time, Mama. Even when I can breathe, I'm still sore and tired of this."

"I know."

Betty fell asleep as Elisabeth prayed for her.

She tiptoed out and into Bruce's room. He put a bookmark in a volume of the Book of Knowledge and set it atop a pile of them next to his bed. "Dad's going to be worse every time we see him?" he said.

"I'm afraid so."

"I'm not going to like that. He's going to remember me as the one who hugs him, even if he doesn't recognize me."

"Probably."

"So I'd better keep going."

They prayed and Elisabeth slid his books closer to the head of the bed. "I don't want you tripping if you have to get up in the night. Now goodnight, sleep tight, and don't let the bedbugs bite. For if they do, I'll take my shoe, and beat them till they're black and blue."

How many times had he heard that and laughed with glee regardless?

As she headed toward the stairs, she saw Benjy dive into his bed. "I thought you were asleep!" she said.

"He was standing right behind you in the doorway when you were in here, Mom!" Bruce yelled.

"Shut up, Big Mouth!"

"Benjamin!"

"I mean, 'Shut up, Bruce!'"

Elisabeth ran a hand through her hair. How could three so different children have come from the same womb? Downstairs she swept debris from in front of the fireplace, set the logs, replaced the screen, and watched as the fire leapt. Back in her room she lay on her side of the bed. She would never again have to worry she was crowding Will or hogging the covers, but she avoided his side as if doing otherwise would besmirch his memory. She gathered his pillow to her breast, buried her face in it and smelled his essence, and cried herself to sleep.

She awoke gasping for breath, a child atop her, shaking her. It was Betty. She was wheezing so badly she could barely get out the words. "Mama! Mama!"

"The flue's probably shut!" Elisabeth said, pushing Betty toward the stairs. "Get outside where you can breathe! I'll get it open again!"

She followed Betty down the steps and tried to get near the fireplace. The smoke was so thick she couldn't see and didn't dare inhale, but one thing was frighteningly clear: the fire had escaped the fireplace, and that entire end of the room was on fire.

Betty stood frozen at the front door, coughing and gasping. Elisabeth recalled how dangerously cold it was as she backed toward the stairs. The oxygen from the open front door fueled the fire and it filled the room. "Betty! Get out! Go next door and call the fire department!"

Elisabeth eluded huge licks of flame that singed her hair as she charged up the stairs two at a time, screaming for Benjy and Bruce. "Get up!" she shrieked. "Get up! Fire! We've got to get out, boys!"

Benjy's room was the farthest, so she went to get him first, planning to grab Bruce on the way back. "Get up, Bruce!" she screamed as she passed his door. He lay motionless and she feared that the smoke had already gotten to him.

She burst into Benjy's room, yelling for him. Nothing. No movement. She felt all over his bed, then dropped to her hands and knees and checked underneath, then the rest of his floor and the closet, all the while frantically calling him. She hollered down the hall, "Benjy, are you up here? Get out! Get out now! Bruce, get up!"

She moved to Benjy's window and peered out. The neighbors' lights were on, Betty was huddled with a woman in the driveway, and it looked like Benjy was with a man. She raised the window and shouted, "Is that Benjy down there?"

"Yes!" the man shouted. "Firemen are on their way! Get out!"

Elisabeth whirled to see the hallway lit bright orange. The draft from the window had drawn the fire up the stairs. She tried to shut it but it was jammed. "Bruce!" she screamed. "Get up! Get out!"

She moved into the hall where the flames lapped at the walls around Bruce's doorframe. She leaped into his room and found him curled in a ball in his bed, the covers over his head. She yanked them off and used all her strength to lift him. He was limp as a doll and she was sure he was not breathing. She had forgotten how heavy a boy could be. How long had it been since she had carried him?

She slapped at his face and shook him, hoping to rouse him so he would be more than dead weight. But the fire burst in from the hall and enveloped her. She nearly dropped Bruce, flailing at a ribbon on her nightgown that had caught fire.

Elisabeth was out of options, standing there in the middle of the night with her youngest child in her arms, the two of them about to be incinerated. The fire, originated in the fireplace, fueled from the front door, and drawn by the open window in the back bedroom upstairs, was a raging monster hungry to devour everything in its path.

Elisabeth shifted to hold Bruce tighter, buried her seared face in his neck, and backed toward the window. The room was engulfed in flames now, and she had seconds to get out or burn. She felt for the window frame with her backside, then moved forward a step and drove herself back. The twenty-foot fall might kill them, but they had a better chance in the snow than in the inferno.

She was upright when she hit the window, the center of the wood frame catching her at the waist without any give. Her sleeves were afire, now her hair. She screamed, bent over as far as she could without dropping the boy, and backpedaled through the window, her seat smashing through the pane.

The back of her head caught the middle of the frame, and it seemed she was watching her own death in arrested time. Her dark-haired boy was sandwiched between her torso and her legs. She hung out the window, the arctic wind biting into the sweat on her neck. Her bare feet seemed but inches from her face, and again the draft drew the fire.

Elisabeth hung there for an instant, suspended between heaven and earth, the soles of her feet and the top of her head roasting while her seat and her back froze. If she couldn't dislodge the back of her head she knew it would serve as kindling to the holocaust. Mustering her last trace of strength and exhaling to make herself as thin as possible, even with a boy attached to her middle, she tucked her chin as deep into her chest as she could.

Gravity pulled her farther out the window, the window frame catching her hairline at the back and tearing it away from her skull. With the hem of her gown ablaze, Elisabeth rocked hard, felt her scalp tear free, and knew if she felt anything more, it would be a horrible collision with the cold, cold ground.

Elisabeth was amazed at the amalgam of images that passed through her mind in the next split second. She must look like a burning marshmallow, all white and puffy, flung off a stick at a midnight roast. Her instinct was to throw out her arms and try to turn so she would land any way other than on her back or her head. But she would never let go of the boy. She believed their only chance was together. Separate free-falling objects would likely both be smashed beyond mending. She and Bruce were in this together, for life or for death.

She was aware of smoke above, stars peeking through, the wind rushing up under her nightclothes, Bruce suddenly weightless as they seemed to float together. She hung on to him for all she was worth, and in the next instant the wind was driven from her lungs in a great gush and she heard the crack, crack, cracking of twigs and branches and then a big branch. The leafless tree on the east side of the house had broken her flight.

Bruce and her feet rotated above her as she continued to hold him tight. Even in the face of death, modesty made her grateful that any audience was on the other side of the house. She feared landing, unable to move, her nightgown over her head.

For a flash she thought she had stopped, lodged between branches, but they gave way and she rolled, another branch changing her direction yet again. Then she landed roughly on her side in the snow and felt Bruce's sternum smash into her ribs. That drove air from his lungs and he expelled smoky, blackened phlegm and mucus that allowed him to breathe.

A fire truck slid up to the curb, and half the crew sprinted for her, diving to douse the fingers of fire that flitted about her. She ached all over but was able to sit up, then help get herself on a stretcher as she watched the men attend to Bruce. He was shaken, puzzled, scared. But fine.

A nasty tear above Elisabeth's neck at the hairline in back would require stitches. Her feet and face and hands were blistered, her hair singed, her eyebrows and lashes gone. She had cracked a rib in back and one in front. And she had suffered damage to her upper spine that would never be accurately diagnosed or treated. It would bother her for the rest of her life, but she would also let it remind her of the night of the fire and another miraculous deliverance of her blessed son. God had allowed her to pluck him from the jaws of death yet again.

As she was carried to an ambulance, her attention was drawn to the west side of the house where a figure stood next to the neighbor man and jumped up and down, seemingly unable to stop. It was Benjy, shouting hysterically, laughing with each breath.

"What's that crazy boy saying?" a fireman said.

Suddenly the wind shifted and they heard him clearly. "Now there's a fire!" he screeched. "There's a fire all right!"

"I'd lock him up," another fireman said.

"I'd shoot him."

"If this turns out to be arson, he's the first one I'd talk to."

Which it was, and which they did.

The night had been so cold that the remaining shell of the house was ice encrusted for the next several days. Fire investigators found that there was still a pile of logs near the fireplace that had been only charred. The cause of the smoke and fire, they said, was a stack of huge books thrown on the fire that probably blocked the exhaust when the pages flew up to the wire mesh near the top of the chimney.

Bruce would never have done something like that, especially with his precious volumes. All the evidence pointed to Benjy, who denied the charge with everything he could muster. The closest investigators got to a confession, they said, was when he allowed, "If I had anything to do with it, it had to be in my sleep, because I don't remember anything about it."

Because of his age, nothing more could be done anyway. The most incriminating evidence: Betty said Benjy was already outside when she got there. He claimed he had heard someone yelling "Fire!" and he had run.

The family was shuttled from member to member of Christ Church during the months it took to rebuild the house. Elisabeth was never so glad to move back home, but she lived in fear for their safety as long as Benjy was around. She could hardly believe he was her own son. She loved him and prayed for him and scoured her memory for some key to his despicable behavior. And she was scared to death of him.

Elisabeth took the kids to see Will every Saturday for a few months until it became too difficult for all of them. He was soon unable to walk, to dress, to feed himself. His speech became childlike, then nonsense, then just sounds. He drooled. His hands and feet curled. He did not recognize his family, though sometimes he maintained eye contact with Elisabeth and with Bruce for several seconds at a time. Elisabeth detected wonder if not recognition, and she constantly talked to Will as if he could hear and understand.

She went back to work at Snyder's Pharmacy, accepting all the overtime she could get. Still she had to take in laundry again, and she even watched a few other children frequently. Anything for enough income to keep making the interest payments on the house, which she had restored after the fire to its original design. Elisabeth knew that would mean a lot to Will. Their clothes, the car, nearly everything else fell into disrepair and could not be replaced. But she vowed to keep the house. It represented Will to her if anything did.

With all she was doing, Elisabeth still somehow found time to keep coming to church. The new pastor, a young man named David Clarkson, fresh out of seminary with a wife and small children, urged her to cut back from all her service. And she did. Some. "But I'm going to be there Sundays anyway," she said. "I might as well keep teaching." Often she did her devotions and studied her lesson while sitting at the State Hospital with Will. Tomorrow and every day.

She no longer had the time or energy to go to choir practice or practice the piano, nor could she attend missionary society meetings. She tried to keep up her share of missionary letter assignments anyway, but often fell asleep in Will's room while writing.

Will had become helpless. She greeted him every day, opened the curtains, looked into his eyes, ran her hand through his hair, cupped his face in her hands, talked to him, prayed with him, and sometimes just stood and caressed him as he stared blankly. She knew her husband was somewhere in that wasted body, that shriveling frame that sometimes hummed but mostly grunted or groaned. Will hardly ever moved on his own and could not roll over.

Elisabeth held pictures of the kids before his face, never able to tell if he had an inkling what he was looking at. But she told him anyway. Countless people told her she needn't feel obligated to come every day or even at all. The pleasant chaplain, doctors, nurses, orderlies, other patients' visitors she had gotten to know, neighbors, her pastor, church friends, people from Fairbanks-Morse, coworkers, everyone had the same opinion: she should not come every day. The cost. The toll on her. "And dare we say it, Elisabeth—the waste of your time." They said they knew she meant well and that her loyalty was admirable, but . . .

What they didn't understand was that duty was only part of her motivation. Yes, she had promised herself to this man for better and for worse, for richer and for poorer, in sickness and in health. And she knew if she were the one ravaged by the disease, Will would be there for her every day. But beyond that, she *wanted* to be there. There was nowhere she would rather be.

She loved this man in the present tense. She didn't love only his memory. And while the grotesque body no longer looked like him and she could no longer communicate with him, couldn't everyone see it was still him? The man in the bed, the man in the diaper, the man whose very soul had seemed to leave him overnight was Will! Where else should she be? She had no interest in arguing the point. She knew that people meant to be helpful; fine, she would smile and listen. And while she did not counter, neither did she agree. Neither did she stop coming, driving from Three Rivers or taking the bus. Every day. Tomorrow and every day.

When she missed because she was ill, she could hardly wait to get there again. She repeated her routine every time and wondered if he was aware when she missed. It made no difference. If she was a fool, she was a fool. A fool for Christ, and a fool for Will.

Part Three

Chapter Sixteen

Benjamin became more than Elisabeth could handle. When he finally began the eighth grade—the first year of high school in Three Rivers—Elisabeth hoped being around older kids might help him mature.

Exhausted from a long day at the State Hospital with Will, Elisabeth made certain she was home when Benjy arrived from school that first day. She wanted to ask, "So how was it?" but his demeanor made the question moot.

"Ma, what's a *Rhinie* anyway?"

"A *Rhinie*? How are you spelling that?"

"How should I know? It's what the older kids call eighth graders, and I'm about to pop the next one of 'em who does."

Elisabeth told Benjamin that most schools have traditions for initiating newcomers, but he didn't want to hear it. She could tell he was embarrassed to be by far the oldest eight grader, and she feared he would make good on his threat.

The next day the school tracked her down through her emergency numbers, finally reaching her in Kalamazoo. "Mrs. Bishop," the discipline dean told her, "your son bloodied both a tenth grader and the physical education teacher assigned to break up the fight. Benjamin will be suspended for a week, and then one more incident will become a matter for the police."

The suspension punished her more than Benjy. What was she supposed to do with him for a week? She made him ride along to Kalamazoo, but he refused to go in and visit his father. Once she came out to the car during lunch, only to find that he had somehow hot-wired it and was joyriding around town.

By the end of the school year, Three Rivers High was glad to see Benjy go, but within a week he had been fired from a summer job and found enough mischief to get himself sent to the Audy Home for Juvenile Offenders in Kalamazoo. His sentence was to last until the next school year, when he was expected to make another attempt at passing eighth grade.

Seeing the bright side even of this, Elisabeth slept better without him in the house and visited him as often as was allowed on her way to or from seeing Will. He clearly didn't care whether she visited or not, and she could tell he was becoming more hardened than rehabilitated.

The next fall he returned to high school briefly, using home as a rest stop between parties and getting in trouble with his friends, many of whom had cars. When Benjy did make the occasional appearance at home, he smelled of alcohol and tobacco.

One morning at breakfast, the usually chipper Bruce looked as if he hadn't slept. "Reading all night again?" Elisabeth said.

Bruce shook his head. Betty, whom Elisabeth feared was becoming as petulant as Benjamin, gave her a look. "You didn't hear? You must sleep like a rock."

"Hear what?"

"Bruce was up all night again, tending to the prodigal."

"What are you talking about?"

Betty pushed away her cereal bowl and began a coughing jag that left her groaning and pounding the table. "I'm going to kill myself if you don't get me some relief from this!"

"Betty! Don't say that! I've tried and tried to—"

"Well, you've failed, Mom! You spend so much time bailing Ben out of the drunk tank and going ape over little Mr. Perfect here, you might as well let me die."

"Oh, Betty!"

"And since you slept through it, you might as well know that Bruce takes care of Benjy *every* time he comes home in the middle of the night to vomit his guts out."

Elisabeth didn't want to ask how frequently. She was losing Benjy and apparently Betty too, and worse, she was abdicating her most distasteful responsibilities to Bruce. Desperate to show Betty—who rose to leave—she was still in charge, Elisabeth said, "That's it! Benjy's out of this house."

Even sleepy Bruce looked up at her as Betty stopped. "You'd do that?" she said. "Ben bet me you'd never have the nerve."

Elisabeth was mad. "Well," she said, "you win."

"Can I tell him?" Betty said.

"I'll tell him," Elisabeth said. "Where is he?"

"I couldn't get him off the floor this morning," Bruce said. "He might still be in the bathroom."

Elisabeth found Benjy, a smelly mess, draped across his bed. "Get up and get out," she said. "You're no longer welcome in this house."

He did not stir, and she feared he was not breathing. She knelt to put an ear next to his face and smelled more than cigarette smoke. Benjamin reeked of gasoline and woodsmoke. What now? At least he was breathing. She wrote him a note, telling him she had come to the end of her patience and reminding him that she had prayed about this. She was on her way out the door—with him still dead to the world— when the Three Rivers Police called, asking if Benjamin Phillip Bishop was home.

"He's sleeping," she said. "What's he done?"

"You're certain he's asleep?" the desk sergeant pressed.

"Yes, now what?"

"We're coming to get him. If he is not there when we arrive, you will be responsible."

"For what?"

"Aiding and abetting a fugitive wanted for arson."

Benjamin had been identified by a neighbor of the same phys ed teacher he had assaulted the year before. The woman had seen him in the alley behind the man's house just before his garage burned to the ground.

Benjy's life as a free man was over. He would be in and out of jail for the next several years over a series of disorderly conducts, petty thefts, parole violations, and two grand theft autos; finally, an armed robbery would send him to the Michigan State Penitentiary in Jackson.

Elisabeth gave up trying to visit him there after the fourth consecutive time he refused to see her. Still she wrote him and sent him gifts and necessities at least twice a week. She proffered more prayer and shed more tears over that boy than the rest of her prayer list combined. She reminded him constantly that she and God still loved him unconditionally. His only reply, dictated to the prison chaplain, said he considered her "a raving religious lunatic."

Maybe she was, she decided. The chaplain wrote that he had discovered Benjamin had "never mastered reading, suffers from a puzzling inability to differentiate between similarly shaped letters and numbers, and seems still to possess the nervous energy of a schoolboy."

Elisabeth fired off this reply: "You may find any number of excuses for aberrant behavior, as this seems the fashion of the day. But as a man of the cloth you surely know that the root problem of base human nature is sin. No amount of remedial education or calming therapy will rehabilitate men who need to deal before God with their sin problem."

The chaplain let time pass before responding, but his reply humiliated Elisabeth. "You are apparently blind to your own narrow judgments. While I might agree there are no excuses for crime, being open to reasons outside the sinfulness of man might prove fruitful. You profess unconditional love, but have you ever looked beneath the surface? Is it possible the answer to how a hardened criminal could emerge from your family might be found in some less black-and-white area?"

Having finished her special school course by her sixteenth birthday, miserable, sickly Betty wanted out—out of Michigan, and out from under her mother's influence. "Where will you go?" Elisabeth asked her. "What has happened to you?"

"Thankfully, I met some students like me who are tired of being controlled by their families. We need to take charge of our own destinies so we aren't dependent victims all our lives."

Elisabeth bit her tongue. She wanted to say, "What about that oxygen bottle strapped to your side?" but she wasn't sure Betty's declaration of independence was all bad. Until Cliff.

Betty first exercised her self-announced freedom by insisting on her own hours, but Elisabeth was encouraged by her desire to do volunteer work in the church. She helped package foodstuffs for needy families and also coordinated a church food co-op, which helped finance social ministries. When Betty first mentioned Cliff, one of the co-op farm's truckers, his significance was lost on her.

But when Betty began referring to him more frequently, Elisabeth took note. "Who is this Cliff again?"

Betty sat filling her pill containers. "I told you, Mother. He's a truck driver. And he's just landed a long-haul job out of New Mexico."

"They let young drivers have those jobs?"

"I didn't say he was young. He's driven cross-country before."

"How old is he?"

Betty shrugged. "I'd sure love to live out west. Dry climate. They say lots of asthma sufferers go there for relief."

"Who's 'they'?"

"Everybody."

"Everybody like Cliff."

"Yeah."

"Do I need to meet this boy?"

"For one thing, Mother, he's no boy. He's a man."

"Are you dating him?"

Betty fell silent and went upstairs. Elisabeth called after her.

"Just leave me alone!" Betty shouted from the top of the stairs. "I'll bet Ben is happier in prison than he was here!"

Elisabeth couldn't imagine what she had done to so alienate her daughter. Betty rebuffed every attempt at reconciling, so Elisabeth finally confronted her. "You won't talk to Pastor with me and you refuse to tell me where you are at all hours of the night. Do I need to ban you from the house the way I did Benjy?"

"That worked well, didn't it?" Betty said. "He never came back either."

"What do you mean 'either'?"

"Just what I said." And she began packing.

Elisabeth did not want to plead, to break down, to show weakness. She had somehow lost Betty and didn't know why. And she couldn't risk pushing this girl farther away. *God*, she prayed silently, *I can't do this alone!*

That night Betty did not come home. Late in the afternoon the next day, when she found out Betty had not been at the church all day, Elisabeth was about ready to report her missing when Frances Childs called. "Betty asked if I would give you a letter from her."

"Where is she?"

"Shall I give it to Bruce when he brings Trudy home, or do you want to come get it, or what?"

"Bruce has the car."

"Art's working second shift, but he got a ride. I'll bring it over."

"I don't want to make you come all this way, Fran."

"Nonsense. I'm on my way."

Elisabeth could not mask her dread over the letter from Betty. She and Frances sat in the parlor as Elisabeth tore at the envelope.

"She's a very unhappy girl," Frances said.

"I know. Have you met Cliff?"

"Of course."

Elisabeth slid the letter from the envelope. It read: "Mother, by the time you read this, Cliff and I will be married. I know you dreamed of a big church wedding, but you would not have approved of him, no matter what I said. I'm going with him to New Mexico. Mrs. Childs can give you more details. I love you. I really do. Don't worry about me. Betty."

Elisabeth pressed her lips together as she replaced the letter. "'Don't worry about me'?" she echoed. "I haven't even met this man!"

Frances nodded.

Elisabeth glared at her. "You couldn't have told me? We've been friends since childhood, and you didn't think I should know?"

"I'm sorry. Betty asked me not to."

"She's a teenager! What does she know?"

"She knew you wouldn't understand."

"This man is going to take care of her? Does he have any idea—?"

Frances shifted in her chair. "There's no easy way to say it, Elisabeth. Cliff is older than you are, twice divorced, and a grandfather."

Elisabeth balled her fist, the letter crumpled between her fingers. "I could have it annulled."

"She's of age, Elisabeth. And Cliff claims to be a Christian."

"Lots of people do."

"Betty believes him. So do I."

"You would." Frances looked wounded. "Forgive me, Fran. I don't know why I said that. It's just, I'm so—I don't know what I am."

"It's all right, dear," Frances said. "Anyone would be upset."

Elisabeth spread her arms, raised her brows, and announced, "I'm a failure. That's all there is to it."

Frances rose and sat next to her, wrapping an arm around her. "I know this is a cliché, sweetie, but this too shall pass. No one can call you a failure when you have a son like Bruce. And let me tell you something, Betty has more of a head on her shoulders than you give her credit for."

Elisabeth folded her arms around her stomach and rocked. "That's not saying much."

Unable to afford train or bus fare and feeling unwelcome in New Mexico anyway, Elisabeth had seen only pictures of her son-in-law. Cliff was a large, swarthy man given to leather and red bandanas. It pained Elisabeth to see that Betty still had to carry a portable oxygen tank. She was mortified that Betty so enjoyed Cliff's grandchild that she had taken to calling herself a grandmother.

Against her own inclination, Elisabeth felt the urging of God to maintain contact with them. Believing this was part of her experiment in obedience, she forced herself to write regularly with news about the church, about Bruce, and even about Benjamin. She was intrigued, though skeptical, to learn that Cliff and Betty were members of a small Bible church in Albuquerque.

Thank God for Bruce, Elisabeth often thought. While it was clear her older two had always been jealous of him, she found it difficult to keep from praising him. Betty wrote that she hoped her mother was not "being as effusive about Bruce to Benjy as you have to Cliff and me." Weren't they proud that Bruce had finished in the top ten percent of his class, that he was a three-sport athlete (all-conference in baseball), and that she had become a sports fan just watching him?

Were they so small they couldn't be as thrilled as she that he belonged to the Bible Club, competed in speaking at Boys' State in Lansing, and taught his own junior boys Sunday school class? Why, he was only doing the things they should have done.

Elisabeth knew Bruce wasn't perfect. He'd had two speeding tickets, and even with his apparent ability to drive fast was often unable to get in by his curfew. He was never more than twenty minutes late. Art and Frances's beautiful adopted daughter was the love of his life. When Elisabeth instituted a rule that every minute he showed up past curfew would cost him an evening without Trudy, he was never late again.

But what she so treasured about Bruce was not just his many accomplishments. She loved noticing the open Bible on his bedstand. She cherished how he cared for her, talked with her, listened to her. He even went with her to see Will a couple of times a month. True, Bruce found it so painful to see his father, now curled into a pitiful mass of skin and bone weighing less than a hundred pounds, that he did not go near him and barely looked at him.

Elisabeth dug for her husband's curled-up fist every day, pried open the fingers, forced her hand into his, and lovingly rubbed and patted it as she spoke to him. Sometimes it was more than Bruce could take and he would leave the room. "Mom, he's gone," he would tell her on the way home. "I wish God would take him and spare you this torture."

"Do you think he suffers, Bruce?"

"I'd be surprised if there was brain wave activity."

"The doctor says there is or he wouldn't breathe on his own."

"But he's not conscious, Mom, and he hasn't been for years. He wouldn't know whether you were here or not. I know you come for yourself as much as for him, but—"

"Bruce, don't you, of all people, tell me to stop coming. He's still my husband and I still love him. I *need* him, need to be with him. I don't care whether anybody else understands, but I need you to support me."

"I'm sorry, Mom. I know."

One day she turned off the car in the driveway without getting out. "Do you remember him, Bruce?"

"A little, sure."

"Come on, you were old enough that you should still have some memories."

"It's hard to talk about, seeing him like that."

"He used to pray with you."

"Every night. I remember, Mom."

In December of 1941 the United States had responded to the attack on Pearl Harbor by declaring war on Japan. Elisabeth would never forget hearing, four days later, that the Axis powers of Germany and Italy had declared war on the U.S. The second great war to end all wars finally included the U.S., and the local paper predicted it would starkly affect commerce and manufacturing and the economy yet again.

Three Rivers, like the rest of the country, mobilized for the war effort. Elisabeth lost her long-time job at the pharmacy but quickly found a job making weapons at Fairbanks-Morse. Meanwhile, she had maintained interest payments on the home mortgage through the years but had never been able to further dent the principal. In January of '42, the bank finally called the loan.

Bruce, in the midst of his junior year of high school, urged her to sell and move into a smaller place. "It's just two of us now, Mom, and as soon as I'm eighteen, I'm enlisting."

"You're going to college. Anyway, the war will be over by then. Everyone says so."

"I'd go now if they'd let me. I want to be a marine."

Elisabeth tried to explain why the house was so important to her, telling Bruce the whole story of his father's gift to her the day they returned from their honeymoon. He was silent for several minutes, busying himself in his room. Then he asked for the name of the loan officer at the bank and permission to talk to him.

"Bruce, you needn't involve yourself. I'm making more money now, and maybe I can start paying on the principal."

But he insisted and she relented. He returned from the bank beaming. "You have to sign, because I'm underage, but look what he agreed to."

Elisabeth was dumbfounded. Bruce had renegotiated the remaining principal into an eighteen-month loan with much higher monthly payments. If they could meet the payments, the house would be hers free and clear by the time Bruce graduated from high school. "And join the marines," he said.

"And go to college," she said. "But how will I ever make these payments?"

"You won't," he said. "I will."

"You barely make enough for your dates now."

"I'm going to drop extra-curricular stuff and—"

"No! You love sports and all the rest!"

"Now let me do this, Ma. It's what I want to do."

"At least stick with baseball."

"I do hate to give that up with them counting on me."

"I'll let you do the rest if you stay with baseball."

He agreed and began spending nearly every spare minute shoveling snow, washing windows, mowing lawns, even clerking at F-M. By the time he graduated in June of 1943, the loan was paid. Bruce had been so busy he had nearly lost Trudy (though she thought his plan to become a marine was "dashing"). He was at the recruiting office the next day.

Elisabeth couldn't imagine another loved one off at war, but if the country had rallied around the cause the first time, morale now was ten times that. Adolph Hitler and his Nazi storm troopers signed peace agreements with neighboring countries, then made a mockery of them, smashing through Europe. Germany's agreement with Italy and Japan against the U.S. was the last straw. Prime Minister Churchill was standing against them in Britain, and America could do no less.

The tragedy was that too many young men were going and too few coming back. Though it had been a quarter century, the horror of what had happened to Ben Phillips seemed like only yesterday. She anticipated hours on her knees until Bruce was safely home.

The war machine seemed to gobble teenagers like appetizers, and already friends and neighbors had suffered losses. All over town, stars appeared in windows, signifying a son at war. Gold stars indicated he had paid the ultimate sacrifice. Three families at Christ Church had already lost boys in the war, and U.S. involvement was just heating up.

The marines loved a healthy young man with ambition and conviction like Bruce, and he came home from the recruiting office with orders to report to Parris Island for six weeks of basic training before shipping out.

"To where?" Elisabeth asked that evening as she served Bruce and Trudy dinner.

"I hope to the front," Bruce said. "Of course, there are lots of fronts."

"I'm hoping to an office somewhere right in the good old U.S. of A."

"Me too," Trudy said, her long, dark hair framing a thin, pretty face. "But Bru has the makings of a hero."

"He's already a hero," Elisabeth said. "And you remember your promise, young man."

"Straight to Moody's as soon as I get back. Then seminary. Then my first church."

"You forgot one step," Trudy said.

"Oh, yeah. Did you show Mom?"

"I was hoping she'd notice."

Elisabeth froze. "Let me see it," she said, and Trudy produced her left hand. "It's beautiful, kids. I knew this was coming, but I thought maybe you'd wait, you know, until—"

"Until he comes back. But there won't be any Dear John letter, Mrs. Bishop. We're in it for the long haul."

"There are no guarantees. You wouldn't want to be faced—"

"Here, look at the inscription." Trudy slipped off the ring.

"I can't believe I need bifocals already," Elisabeth said. "Let me see here."

Inside the band was etched, "Bru and Tru forever."

"How nice." She hated those ridiculous nicknames, but they had caught on with their friends and Elisabeth was powerless to stop them. "I prayed since before Bruce was born that his spouse would love God and want to serve him. I'll be proud to welcome you to the family."

Trudy was crying by the end of the night and promising to stay very close to Elisabeth while Bruce was away.

"I'll be fine," Elisabeth said. "A little lonely, but I'll keep busy."

Elisabeth's description of her life as lonely but busy soon began to seem inadequate on both counts. From the painful day she and Trudy saw Bruce off at the bus station—looking as young to her as on his first day of grade school—to the day she got word he was coming home, Elisabeth felt as if she were living in a tomb.

Oh, she loved her home. She had insisted after the fire that the rebuilt house duplicate the original design—except that the fireplace was now fake. When linoleum was the rage, she had it installed upstairs, hoping it would provide a little insulation between her feet and the wood floor. But how the place echoed when she was the only one there.

Trudy's promise to check in on her quickly faded. Elisabeth didn't blame her. They had given each other space and time at the bus station, and then Trudy joined her for a light lunch. Without Bruce it was awkward and uncomfortable. Trudy was a little too forward and more talkative than Elisabeth liked. She was also less inclined to bring up spiritual matters.

Trudy seemed overly interested in Bruce's "rising" within the Marine Corps. "Oh, I don't know," Elisabeth said. "Since he doesn't plan to make a career of it, I wouldn't mind seeing him blend into the crowd, keep his head down, come home in one piece."

"You don't know Bruce then," Trudy said, insulting Elisabeth more than she could know. "He'll never shrink from a challenge."

Elisabeth knew that well enough. In fact, she told herself, she knew Bruce better than Trudy would know him until they'd been married half a lifetime. *That boy was in my womb,* Elisabeth thought but dared not say. *I suckled him, taught him to walk and talk, led him to Christ, saved his life—twice!—and you have the audacity to say I don't know him?*

Chapter Seventeen

*F*inally alone again, Elisabeth fell into a routine she had not enjoyed for decades. She rose early for Bible reading and prayer, ate breakfast, and packed herself two lunches—one for noontime at the plant and the other to eat while sitting with Will at the State Hospital in Kalamazoo. She was as much a fixture there as the long-term employees, known by everyone. She knew they pitied her and likely thought her batty.

Elisabeth left the hospital most evenings in time to get back to Three Rivers for many church activities. Prayer meeting on Wednesday night was back on her schedule. She still taught Sunday school and also maintained frequent letters to missionaries, sharing their replies with Pastor David Clarkson for inclusion in the weekly bulletin. One evening she handed one to him in his office. He thanked her and asked if she minded a personal question.

In fact, she did mind. He was much younger than she, and Elisabeth believed a question that needed permission ought not be asked. "Go ahead," she said as she sat down.

"I was just wondering if you are aware that there are at least a couple of single men in our congregation—around your age—who have privately asked about you."

Elisabeth stiffened. Dare she ask who? "How would I know that," she said, "if it was private?"

"I'm sorry, I guess I should have asked if that would surprise you."

Surprise was not the word. Was it possible, after all these years of loneliness—? "What would surprise me, Pastor, is that you would allow it. You know I'm married, and if they don't, you should tell them. Can they not see my ring? Do they not know my history? My life is no secret."

He held up a hand. "Mrs. Bishop, I—"

"*Mrs.* Bishop is correct, sir, and I would appreciate it if you would not forget that." Elisabeth didn't want to forget it either, and the chill that went through her troubled her.

"I apologize, ma'am. I—"

"Accepted, but I'm shocked that you would even inform me of such inappropriate questions. What did they want, to know if I was dating in anticipation of my husband's passing?"

"No, I really—"

"Does everyone know he was originally given ten years to live? Is there now a death watch? Feel free to inform anyone insolent enough to ask that my doctor feels the disease has done everything it can to Will but kill him, so now it's a matter of how long he can last. He's only forty-four years old, so you can tell the hopefuls it could be twenty more years."

"Mrs. Bishop, I—"

"And while you're at it, you might tell anyone else who thinks it's their business that I have not looked to the right nor to the left since the day I married that man. I have never been interested in anyone else, and I can't imagine I ever will be."

It was true Elisabeth had never been interested in anyone else, but she wondered if she was being honest with herself about the future. Pastor Clarkson sat staring at her, apparently realizing it was futile to try interjecting a thing until she was really finished. Elisabeth was shaking. "I trust you know me well enough," she said, "to know that it is not my practice to fly off the handle like this."

He nodded. "Well, I—"

"I've embarrassed myself, and now—"

"Not at all."

"I would know that better than you, Pastor, if you don't mind my saying so. I shouldn't take it out on you. I get questions and comments about Will all the time, and I've long since quit stating my case."

"If you'll permit me . . ."

"I'm sorry. Go ahead."

"The fact is that I did tell both inquirers they were out of line, and for largely the same reasons you stated. But I mentioned it to you to encourage you."

"To encourage me?"

"This is difficult, Mrs. Bishop, but I talked it over with my wife, and she thought it would be appropriate to express to you. She even volunteered to be here when I said it, but since you happened to come by, well . . ."

"Whatever are you talking about?"

He blushed. "Let me get this out now. I'm sure you're aware that you're much beloved and admired around here." Elisabeth wasn't so sure. "But you may not get the encouragement the typical wife receives."

"God is good," she began.

"Now, excuse me, but I'm going to ask that you let me finish, because this is hard enough as it is." He smiled. "You probably don't have people telling you how attractive you are."

Sweat broke out on his forehead. Elisabeth's heart leapt and she laughed, a little too loud. How she had longed to hear that! But from this young pastor? "How attractive I am?" she said. "What does that have to do with anything?"

"People have always considered you beautiful," he said.

"Nonsense!" Could it be?

"Now, Mrs. Bishop, I've seen the photographs of you as a child and teenager, and you were very, very pretty."

Elisabeth had calmed down. "My father says I favored my mother."

"Well, then, she must have been beautiful, because you've gone past pretty now."

"I have, have I?" Elisabeth said, enjoying Pastor Clarkson's discomfort.

"Age has only enhanced—"

"I'm aging well, is that what you're telling me?"

"No, I—well, I wouldn't—"

"Yes, you would. You just did."

"I've not communicated well."

Elisabeth stood. "Actually, you have. I'd rather not dwell on it," she said, immediately convicted by that lie. "I know I look older than my years. To know there are those who believe otherwise is flattering, and I thank you for saying so."

"Thank *you*, Mrs. Bishop."

Elisabeth went home intrigued with how good it made her feel to know that some still found her attractive. "Surely, Lord," she prayed, "I'm on the edge of vanity."

After washing her face before bed, she stared at her too-early lined face. She still had what her father had called porcelain skin, and gravity had not given her jowls yet. She smoothed her hair back. *Agh!* she thought. *Too much thought of myself!*

Elisabeth went to bed, staying on her side of the mattress still after all those years, and wished Will would tell her she was still beautiful. That was all she cared about. Whatever she had to offer anyone belonged to Will alone. Lonely, starved for affection and touch, she missed him so much! How she wished he still shared her bed.

When next Elisabeth saw Will she was certain she detected a flicker in his eyes. She ran for the doctor who refused to even come and see. "Impossible," he said. "Mrs. Bishop, don't do this to yourself. The damage was done years ago and is irreversible. If we found a cure even now, it would have no effect on a man comatose for nearly a decade."

"Just look and tell me what I'm seeing then!"

"I'm sorry. I really don't have time. If he seems to be making eye contact, it's coincidence. He's not seeing anything. Nothing is registering. Please."

Elisabeth hurried back to Will's room. She took his face in her hands and stared into his eyes. He was staring back if there was a God in heaven! "Will," she said, "you see me, don't you? You know who I am! I love you and you love me, don't you?"

He struggled to nod! She screamed for a nurse, an orderly, anyone. "Will! You know me!"

He nodded without her help. There was a trace of a smile! A nurse's aide came running. "What's happening?"

"Look at him! He recognizes me! Nod, Will!" He nodded. "See?"

"Unbelievable."

"It's a miracle," Elisabeth said. "Thank you, Lord!" Did she have faith to believe he might actually improve? "Will!" she said. "Nod for me!"

He nodded and tried to speak. "Elspeth" came the raspy whisper.

She whirled. "Did you hear that?" But the aide was gone. She turned back to Will. "Say it again, Will! Say my name again!"

He was smiling, trying to sit up! He spoke again and she bent to listen. "You're dreaming," he said. "Elspeth, wake up. You're dreaming."

She awoke with a shudder that threw her writing materials off her lap and onto the floor. A big black man in an orderly's uniform stood in the doorframe. "You all right, Miz Bishop?"

Gooseflesh had risen on her arms. It had been so real! She nodded. "Yes, Charles. Thank you."

Charles helped pick up her stuff. "And how's the gentleman today?" he said.

She stood shakily and they gazed at Will. He lay in a fetal position, not moving, eyes open, staring out the door, unseeing.

"The same," she said. "The same as always."

Basic training was over, and the bad news arrived in a letter from Bruce. He was being shipped out. He couldn't say where, didn't know yet himself. But it would be overseas and it would be strategic. "Maybe they tell everybody that," he wrote, "but it sure feels like something big."

Elisabeth found herself melancholy. It seemed her prayers had been going only one direction for weeks. "I've given you my life," she said to God. "I'll try not to look at circumstances. But who would follow you wholeheartedly if they see my life as an example? Is heaven the only reward for a life wholly given to you? Have I not obeyed in everything?"

She should have known not to expect happiness. There was no payoff this side of heaven for a life of consecration. Others had tried to tell her. Would she have pursued obedience so resolutely if she had known how hard it would be?

How would a normal Christian life have been? Show up on Sunday and do your part. Maybe your husband is healthy and all your kids make you proud. When she was younger she would not have even entertained such doubts. Somehow now she found herself expecting more of God than he had given her.

With Bruce off to who knows where to engage in who knows what, and Betty more than a thousand miles away, Elisabeth received a letter from the chaplain at Jackson.

"Your son might be open to seeing you, finally," he wrote. "Unfortunately, what has sobered him was a knife fight in which he nearly killed a guard. Benjamin was to have begun annual parole board hearings next year in anticipation of his release in 1947, or before. This latest will likely result in a change of his sentence to life without parole. He is asking to be read your letters now, rather than throwing them away. He also now keeps the trinkets you send and eats the cookies. I may be wrong, but you might find him receptive to a visit."

Elisabeth wasted no time putting in her formal request to see Benjamin on the next visiting day, Wednesday, November 17, 1943, the day before Thanksgiving. But Benjamin vetoed the idea and did not suggest another date. Elisabeth sent him another package of goodies, including a Bible, and reminded him she still loved him and prayed for him.

She received several letters from Bruce in the Pacific theater, mostly when he was stationed in Hawaii. He warned her she might suddenly stop hearing from him, but not to worry. "That's easy for you to say," she wrote back.

He told her how much he missed her, how much he looked forward to getting home, and how he and Trudy anticipated bringing their children back to the big house someday. "She says you seem to be doing fine," he wrote.

How would she know? Elisabeth wondered, but she left it alone. The last thing she wanted was trouble between her and her future daughter-in-law. Trudy's mother invited Elisabeth for Thanksgiving dinner, but she begged off and drove to Kalamazoo. All the way there she regretted the decision. Art and Frances had become wonderful

Christians and good parents. From the State Hospital she called and asked if she could call on them the following Friday.

"We'd love it, Elspeth," Frances said, and the name pierced her.

"I go by Elisabeth these days, Frances, if you don't mind."

"Oh, I'm sorry. Anyway, we'll see you then."

Elisabeth sat gazing at Will. "Another holiday, love," she whispered. "Another year come and almost gone. Bet you're getting tired of this, hm? When you're ready to be with Jesus, you just go. Don't worry about me."

She brushed away a tear and realized she had turned a corner. She couldn't imagine having expressed that thought, given that permission, even a year before. Why had she so desperately hung on to the wasted body of a man once so vibrant and robust? The day would come when she would have to let him go whether she was ready or not, so she had to get used to the idea now. As well-intentioned but insensitive people had so often said, Will had been dead to her almost from the beginning. She prayed only that she be allowed the privilege of being there when he was ushered into the presence of Christ. That would be the greatest gift God could give her.

Elisabeth scoured the newspaper for stories about marine operations. Reports generally came several days after the fact. Often grieving families suffered anew when an account showed up on their doorstep with details of a battle that had already resulted in the dreaded gold star in the window.

At the Childs' home the next Friday, Elisabeth learned that Art read the paper the same way she did. "The other stuff doesn't interest me," he said. "But I like trying to figure out where Bruce might be. Did you see today's?" Elisabeth shook her head and he handed it to her, thumping a front-page story with his thumb. "Who knows?" he said.

The article told of the Central Pacific Offensive, a U.S. operation begun at the Gilbert Islands. Earlier that month, not long after Elisabeth had quit hearing from Bruce, U.S. task forces attacked Tarawa and Makin Islands. Makin was taken in just days, but the wire service reported that five thousand experienced Japanese jungle fighters were prepared to battle to the death at Tarawa. Elisabeth held her breath when she read that on November 20, the same number of U.S. marines arrived. She looked at Art and read, "'Fighting was ferocious and casualties high.'"

He nodded. "But you would have heard something by now. No news is good news, right?"

"I've heard that before," she said. "I wish it were always true."

Trudy arrived home about three hours later with two girlfriends, greeted Elisabeth, and disappeared. Elisabeth couldn't imagine how she could socialize and carry on as usual with her fiancé at war.

The following Saturday Elisabeth read that the problem at Tarawa was that air support had not been properly coordinated. However, the U.S. had finally taken the island on November 26.

Just before she was to leave for work on Monday morning, the sixth of December, Elisabeth's phone rang. The caller, who spoke with a thick southern accent, identified himself as Sergeant Howard of the United States Marine Corps.

"Oh, no," she said.

"Madam, this is not a bad news call."

"Oh, thank God." She had heard that death notices came in writing or in person, to prevent cruel hoaxes.

"It's not all good either, I'm afraid, but your son is coming home. If you can confirm that I am speaking with the mother of Bruce James Bishop, DOB six-one-twenty-five at Three Rivers, Michigan?"

"That's him. How bad?"

"He was not physically wounded, ma'am, to the best of my knowledge. He has been diagnosed with battle fatigue and has suffered, I'm reading here, 'possible sensory damage which will be better evaluated when oral function returns.'"

"He's lost his voice?"

"That's the way I interpret it, ma'am. That's usually not physical but psychological, and not uncommon with battle fatigue. Problem is, until he can talk, it's hard for them to know the extent of any hearing or vision loss."

"Is he in shock?"

"In a manner of speaking, ma'am. He was apparently involved in heavy combat and was traumatized. It's no minor condition. There are chances of complete recovery, but no guarantees."

"When can I see him?"

"He's been transported to Honolulu where he's being stabilized. From there, when he's up to it, he'll be flown to San Diego. He could be moved from there to Quantico, Virginia, Washington, D.C., or directly home, depending on whether we can find a suitable rehabilitation facility in your area. I need to warn you that transporting these boys from the Pacific is always tedious, and you may not know exactly when he's getting home till he gets there."

Elisabeth phoned the Childses; word spread through Christ Church, and a prayer vigil began to get Bruce home as quickly as possible. After ten of the most anxious days of her life, Elisabeth received a call from Sergeant Howard. "Miz Bishop," he said, "Bruce James is expected to arrive tomorrow at 1900 hours at the State Hospital in Kalamazoo. Do you know where that is?"

She smiled. "I'm sure I can find it."

Of course, Bruce was late. The last leg of his journey was routed from Chicago rather than Detroit as planned, and when he arrived, he was sedated and asleep. Elisabeth and Trudy embraced him and sat with him through the night.

"He'll speak as soon as he wakes up and sees me," Trudy said.

"I don't think we should overwhelm him," Elisabeth said. "You greet him first and I'll hang back."

Trudy paced the halls, then finally stretched out in a chair and fell asleep. Elisabeth kept watch in case he woke early. But Bruce didn't so much as twitch. She lifted his hand and held it in hers. It was the big, warm hand of a man. When had that happened? How she wished he would open his eyes and know she was there, know he was home and safe. He looked just like the pictures he'd sent from Hawaii, maybe a little more tanned and angular, hair starting to grow out.

Elisabeth prayed as she held his hand, thanking God for watching over Bruce.

"I thought *I* was supposed to wake him up," Trudy said, and Elisabeth jumped.

"He's not awake, dear. I'm just praying for him."

"Well, what if that wakes him up?"

"He's really out, Trudy. Yours will be the first face he sees, I promise."
Trudy didn't look so sure, but she soon slept again.

A doctor entered at six in the morning and checked Bruce's vital
signs. "He should wake up in an hour or so," he whispered. "His pulse
and respiration have increased, BP's up. He'll start moving, but don't
try to make him speak. He may try, but just let that come. You'll do
more harm than good if you rush him. They'll bring him some breakfast at eight, and I'll check back after that."

Elisabeth wouldn't have missed seeing Bruce's eyes pop open. As
the clock crowded seven, she stared at his face. His fingers moved. He
rolled his ankles. His head came off the pillow, then dropped back
down. Sunlight peeked through the venetian blinds and crossed his
face. He turned away, lids fluttering.

Finally he turned back toward the sun and let it bathe his face. He
opened his eyes and blinked slowly. Elisabeth woke Trudy. The girl sat
up, scratched her head with both hands, shook out her hair, and leaned
forward from the foot of the bed. "Hi, honey!" she said a little too loudly.

He looked right through her.

Trudy moved to the side of the bed. She tried to take his hand, and
though he did not pull away, it remained limp. Still he stared, and Elisabeth stayed where she was, a foot from his line of sight.

"It's me, Bru! It's Trudy! Welcome home, soldier boy!"

She pressed her lips together and sighed. Elisabeth started to protest
when Trudy cupped Bruce's face in her hands and tried to get him to
look at her. "Wake up, sleepyhead," she said. He lay back on the pillow and stared straight ahead. "Forget this," Trudy said. "Tell them
to call us when he's conscious."

"He's conscious, honey. He just won't be rushed."

Bruce followed Elisabeth's voice, and his eyes widened when he saw
her. She hesitated, not wanting to crowd Trudy or confuse Bruce. His
eyes locked on Elisabeth's. She smiled.

"That's your mom, Bru. Can you see her? Say hi to your mom."

Elisabeth shook her head, trying to remind Trudy that they weren't
to push him to talk.

"Fine," Trudy said.

Elisabeth slipped to his bedside and he turned to stay focused on her. How many thousands of times had she dreamed Will would follow her with his eyes? "I'm here, Bruce," she whispered.

Bruce's lips moved as if he was about to say something but couldn't form the words. His mouth curled with the effort and it appeared he might cry. That broke her heart. He took a breath, raised his chin, and appeared to try to open his mouth. He exhaled through his nose and shook his head.

"Shh," she said, taking his hand in both of hers. She rubbed the back of his hand. "There's plenty of time, Bruce."

Trudy backed away and watched from the doorway. "How long are you going to stay?" she asked.

"Probably until midmorning."

Trudy looked at her watch. "That long?"

"You need to be somewhere?"

"Kinda. By noon anyway, back in Three Rivers."

"I can get you there by then."

Elisabeth stayed by Bruce's side until his breakfast arrived. A volunteer, a redheaded candy striper whose nameplate read "Joyce," delivered it. She read from his chart. "He needs to be fed. Either of you want to do it?"

Elisabeth very much wanted to but thought she should defer to Trudy. She nodded toward her.

Trudy hesitated. "I thought he was all right."

"I'm just telling you what the chart says," Joyce said. "We don't feed him, he doesn't eat."

Trudy shook her head.

"I'll feed him," Elisabeth said, and Trudy walked away.

Feeding him like a baby came back to her as if the years had melted away. Elisabeth put one hand under his chin and spooned his food into his mouth with the other, tidying him up with each bite. Bruce would feed himself eventually, and the sooner the better. But to Elisabeth this was a privilege.

"Looks like you've had experience," Joyce said on her way out.

"Years," Elisabeth said. "I haven't seen you around here before. New?"

"In rehab, yeah," she said, smiling.

Late in the morning, while Bruce napped, Elisabeth and Trudy headed for the car. "I know that candy striper," Trudy said. "Fourth ward."

"Really? You didn't greet her."

"I told you, fourth ward. I think she might even live in a trailer park."

Elisabeth couldn't imagine the importance of that tidbit. "Would you mind driving, Trudy," she said, "since you got at least a little shut-eye?"

"You didn't sleep?"

"I was too excited."

"I've never driven one of these big, old ones. How about I just make sure you stay awake?"

Trudy was silent all the way home. When Elisabeth pulled in front of the Childs's house, Trudy started to get out, then hesitated. "You know what, Mrs. Bishop, I don't think I'm going to be able to handle this."

"Sure you will. He'll come around. I don't know where he was or what he saw, but God will see him through this and he'll get better, you'll see."

Trudy shook her head, tears in her eyes. "I feel awful, but I just, I just can't—"

"Trudy, honey, we need to be strong so we don't set him back farther." Trudy collapsed into sobs. Elisabeth patted the young woman on her back.

"I hate to admit this, Mrs. Bishop, but I can't help thinking Bruce was a coward."

"A coward?"

"He's not hurt!" Trudy said. "He's scared! Guys are getting wounded and dying over there, and he's back because he didn't like what he saw."

"For heaven's sake, child! He wasn't AWOL and he hasn't been accused of desertion. They tell me this is a common malady and very real."

Trudy looked up at her. "To come home early without being wounded?"

"If you know Bruce," Elisabeth said, "you'd know he's deeply wounded."

"I don't know if I know him or not," Trudy said. She reached for the door handle.

"You want to ride along tomorrow?"

Trudy hesitated. "I'll call you."

Elisabeth drove home wondering what she would tell her son if Trudy didn't call. Elisabeth had misgivings about Trudy, and they had been exacerbated by the previous twenty-four hours. But she couldn't imagine Trudy as one of those fiancées who disappear when things get tough.

The next several weeks were grueling for Elisabeth, but at least she had only one round-trip drive to the same place every evening. She spent most of her time with Bruce but always stopped in for several minutes with Will too. "If only you knew who was in the other wing," she told him. "If only I could make you understand."

To put her own mind at ease and, she hoped, to give her an advantage once Bruce started to talk, Elisabeth investigated what he had been through. She called Sergeant Howard and asked if Bruce had been at the battle on Tarawa.

"Did he tell you that?"

"He's not talking yet."

"How did you know then?"

"I read, sir. I want to know firsthand whether he has legitimate reasons to be home or whether he should still be there doing his duty."

Sergeant Howard's tone changed and his pace slowed. "I understand where you're going with this," he said. "Let me find out and call you back. You may rest assured that I will tell you the truth, either way."

Two days later he reported, "Not only was there no sign of cowardice or failure to perform, but Private Bishop recorded several enemy kills and was credited with heroism in the face of mortal danger."

"Kills?"

"How he avoided injury while exterminating at least six enemy soldiers at point-blank range is a mystery. But at least two compatriots credit him with cover fire that allowed them to escape with their lives, if not with all their limbs."

"It's no mystery to me, Sergeant. It was a miracle of God."

"I wouldn't argue that, ma'am. Your son was the only one unscathed in that sector. Eleven dead and sixteen critically wounded, all within his view."

"How close to him?"

"It's difficult to recreate these things, but it would not stretch the bounds of credulity to say that these men could all have fallen within an arm's length of each other."

"No wonder he was traumatized."

"Ma'am, you wouldn't want to dwell on what he might have seen and heard. There's nothing more pitiful than a teenager who knows he's dying, and no more helpless feeling than knowing you can do nothing for him. I imagine one of the things your son is going to have to deal with is the guilt of surviving."

"You sound as if you speak from experience, Sergeant."

"I'm speaking to you from a wheelchair, ma'am, my constant companion. Let's just say I'm half the man I used to be."

Unless Elisabeth was reading Scripture or singing hymns to him, Bruce struggled to speak. He face contorted into a mask of horror and grief and his lips trembled as if he were constantly on the verge of tears. "Which is what he is," his doctor told her. "If you've ever tried to speak while weeping and were unable to form the words, that's what he feels every second. He wants to say something, to explain, to make sense of it. He wants you to know what's wrong with him. We've learned from men who've come through this that the harder they try to speak and the longer they are unable to, the more frustrated and panicky they become. They come to believe they will never be able to speak again, and it scares them to death."

"What can I do?"

"Speaking to him is good. Talk soothingly, tell him there's lots of time to heal and recover and grow and that he mustn't push things. Remind him it will take time, and remember, when you're entertaining him—reading or singing or whatever—you're taking the pressure off his feeling obligated to talk."

From then on, any time Bruce labored to communicate with her, she sat patiently, touching him. When he grew agitated, she'd say, "Let's wait. There's time. We'll talk tomorrow. Let me read to you."

She read Psalms and sang hymns from memory. The day she thought to bring her Bible, his eyes lit up. She opened to the twenty-third Psalm and laid it before him. Later, when she reached to take it, he pressed his hand on it so she couldn't. That was also the day she told Joyce the candy striper to leave his dinner and see if he ate it on his own.

Joyce left it and Bruce waited and watched his mother, as if expecting her to feed him. "I'm going to sing to you," she said. "You have to feed yourself tonight."

As she sang he idly picked up his spoon and began with his dessert. "That's my Bruce," she said.

Joyce came in to see how they were doing and smiled when she saw him eating. She and Elisabeth had been getting him up and walking him to the bathroom each evening.

"Wait here a moment, Joyce," Elisabeth said. "I want to try something after this song."

She sang:

Open my eyes, that I may see glimpses of truth Thou hast for me;
Place in my hands the wonderful key that shall unclasp, and set me
    free.
Open my ears, that I may hear voices of truth Thou sendest clear;
And while the wave notes fall on my ear, everything else will disappear.
Open my mouth, and let me bear gladly the warm truth everywhere;
Open my heart, and let me prepare love with Thy children thus to share.
Silently now I wait for Thee, ready, my God, Thy will to see;
Open my eyes, illumine me, Spirit divine!

When Bruce finished eating, they helped him out of bed, each supporting an arm. "Let go, Joyce," Elisabeth said. "I've got him."

Joyce was reluctant but slowly pulled free. "Now, Bruce, I want you to stand on your own," Elisabeth said.

"He'll fall," Joyce said.

"Get your balance, son."

When Elisabeth pulled away, he reached for her and wobbled, fear in his eyes. "I'm right here," she said. "You can do it."

He shuddered and jerked to keep his balance, as if he might tumble any second. Elisabeth backed off, and there he stood. It would be a while before he could walk on his own, but for now he was standing unaided. And that was progress.

Chapter Eighteen

$\mathcal{E}$lisabeth dreaded the day Bruce would ask about Trudy. Apparently the girl had no stomach for adult life. Meanwhile, Elisabeth made it her business to get to know everyone who had anything to do with Bruce's care. She was especially interested in finding someone who would read Scripture to Bruce when she was not there.

Whispering at Bruce's bedside one evening, candy striper Joyce Adams told her, "I'm switching to mornings. I got a waitressing job in the evenings."

"But you'll still volunteer here?"

"I like helping people."

"You could help both Bruce and me if you would do me a favor."

"I will if I can."

"If I left you a list of verses, would you read them to Bruce when you have time?"

"Verses? Poems, you mean?"

"Bible verses."

Joyce hesitated. "I suppose."

"And Bruce likes to go and sit in the chapel when the chaplain speaks on Thursday mornings."

"I'll see that he gets there."

The next week, Joyce left a note for Elisabeth. "Bruce helped me find a verse today. I didn't know where Ephesians was, so I was looking in the front of his Bible. He reached over and turned to it for me. See if he'll do it again."

Bruce had stopped struggling to speak, and Elisabeth worried he had given up. "You can nod or shake your head, can't you, Bruce? Can you talk to me that way?"

He looked away.

"If you're not ready, just shake your head." She saw the hint of a smile. He had caught her.

"That didn't make any sense, did it?" she said. "Shake your head if you're not ready to shake your head! Mother is batty, isn't she?"

He shrugged and she saw the upturned lips again.

"That's progress, Bruce. When you're good and ready, I'll be here."

That gave her an idea. She had made him stand by backing away. She had made him eat by busying herself with something else and implying that if he was hungry he had to feed himself.

"I'm going to go see your father for a few minutes before I leave. I'll come back to say good-by, but only if you want me to."

He looked at her.

"Do you want me to?"

He held her gaze.

"I guess not. All right then, I'll see you tomorrow."

He lifted his chin and struggled. Had she made him regress? "All you have to do is nod. Otherwise, I'll see you tomorrow."

He struggled.

"You don't have to speak yet, Bruce. All I need is a nod."

He nodded. Though thrilled, she didn't make a big deal of it. "All right. I'll be back in a few minutes." He nodded again.

When she returned, she said, "I have some reading to do tonight. I could do it here until you fall asleep, or I could do it at home. I think I should leave, don't you?"

He shook his head. She knew it wouldn't be long before he spoke.

How long had it been since she had felt so needed? She read for a while. When it was past time that Bruce should be sleeping, she stepped to the side of his bed. "I'm praying for Joyce. You know who she is?"

He nodded.

The doctor was pleased with Bruce's progress over the next couple of weeks. He was still not speaking and strained mightily when he tried. But he got up and went back to bed on his own, fed himself, dressed and bathed himself, and even read.

"If you can read," Elisabeth said, as they sat in the dayroom, "you can write. Let's try something simple. Write your name. Or my name. Here. Try."

He sat staring at her, then wrote, "Where's Tru?"

"Do you really want to know?" she said.

He nodded.

"It's not good news."

He shrugged.

"Tell me one more time you really want to know."

He nodded again.

"She couldn't handle it."

He pointed to his ring finger.

"I've heard she's not still wearing it."

His face contorted as if he wanted to cry, and he leaned back on the couch.

"God knows," Elisabeth said.

Bruce turned away.

She wanted to tell him she knew from experience that God sometimes protects his children from wrong choices. But Elisabeth felt terrible. "I shouldn't have told you."

He sat up and wrote, "I asked."

"That's true. I couldn't lie, could I?"

He nodded and smiled ruefully.

"That's my Bruce."

He wrote, "I'll win her back."

Elisabeth hesitated. "That's the spirit," she said.

"Tell her I want to see her," he wrote.

She shook her head. "It's not my job to play switchboard for you two. You tell her. If you're not ready to talk, write it down."

Bruce wrote Trudy three notes over the next week, and Elisabeth mailed them. Trudy ignored them all.

In a note to his mother he wrote, "I want to talk to you."

"When you're ready," she said.

One afternoon a month later, pleading silently with God to loose Bruce's tongue, Elisabeth found him napping on a couch in the day-room. A long note to her lay in his lap. It read:

"Dear Mom, I want to speak so badly I could explode. I even want to talk about what I did, but it seems unspeakable. The doctor wants me to try something simple, but getting close to a normal word makes me want to cry. He suggested trying to whisper. Maybe when I'm alone I'll try.

"But there's nothing to talk about as important as what I went through. It's like I would be desecrating the memories of heroes if I spoke of anything else. I love hearing you speak. I love hearing Joyce Adams speak, even with that clipped accent and those choppy sentences (don't let her see this).

"You were crafty in telling her to look up that list of my favorite verses. They are my favorites all right, but wasn't it interesting that they were arranged just so? Romans 3:23, Romans 6:23, Ephesians 2:8, 9, etc., etc. You set her up, didn't you? All have sinned, sin leads to death, we can't save ourselves. Pretty neat. She's asking me all kinds of questions, and I'm scribbling answers and pointing her to new verses. The other day when she walked me down to the chapel, no one else showed up but the chaplain. He was almost not going to give his devotional, but I gave him a note, telling him I really needed it. She listened and took notes. She's close, Mom.

"She told me she wanted to test God and see if he would give me back my speech. I wrote her that it's not right to test God, but she said she was going to pray that if he were real, he would prove it to her. I don't see how he can ignore a prayer like that.

"The chaplain's retiring. I hope they get somebody else soon. I want to get out of here, but until I do, I want to keep going to that chapel.

"I'm spending more and more time wandering, lying around, sitting. I'm bored, but I'm so tired sometimes I can hardly move. They say it's part of my 'problem.' I feel so helpless. I want to get better fast, but I'm not supposed to rush it. I still want to go to Moody and serve God, but there's no sense studying to preach before I can say two words.

"I'm writing this with the sun at my back. That means you'll be here soon. I wish you'd sing me that song you said was new when you were a teenager. Remember it? That same guy who wrote 'When I Survey the Wondrous Cross' wrote it, and it always used to make me cry. I want to cry almost as bad as I want to speak, but I'm afraid once I start, I will never stop and wind up dead of dehydration.

"Mom, I need you to know that I did not lose my faith over there. But what we were doing could never have been what God had in mind for anybody.

"Right now I'm fighting to keep my eyes open, because I'm tired of napping during the day and not being able to sleep at night. I want to come home, and I know the doctor wants me to to, but I'm afraid. People will visit and they'll be uncomfortable and they'll try to get me to talk. I'll try on my own, and then maybe sometime when you're here, we—"

He had apparently fallen asleep at that point.

Elisabeth settled in across from him and began to hum the tune to "I Gave My Life For Thee." Then she sang softly:

I gave My life for thee, My precious blood I shed,
That thou might'st ransomed be, and quickened from the dead;
I gave, I gave My life for thee, what has thou given for Me?
My father's house of light, My glory-circled throne
I left for earthly night, for wand'rings sad and lone;
I left, I left it all for thee, has thou left aught for Me?
I suffered much for thee, more than thy tongue can tell,
Of bitt'rest agony. To rescue thee from hell;
I've borne, I've borne it all for thee, what has thou borne for Me?

Bruce opened his eyes and sat up, taking his mother's hands as she sang. He moved his lips, as if singing along. It was all she could do to continue when tears formed in his eyes, the first since his return. She sang the last verse as he began to weep aloud.

And I have brought to thee, down from my home above
Salvation full and free, My pardon and My love;
I bring, I bring rich gifts to thee, what has thou brought to me?

Elisabeth pulled Bruce to her and wrapped her arms around his head, nestling him to her as she had when he was an infant. Suddenly he was wracked with sobs so great that he wailed the mournful cries of a child in the husky, unused voice of a young man. Elisabeth rocked him as his shoulders heaved and every gasp gave power to his howls.

She shielded him from curious eyes, and sensed this was a cleansing keening that, if it did not rid him of the horrors he had experienced, was at least a step toward healing.

When the worst finally subsided, she pulled him to his feet and walked him back to his room. He resisted being led to the bed, however, and sat across from her in a side chair. She held his hands again, and agony showed on his face as he labored to speak.

"I," he began. "I, I, I—" She had the feeling that if he could get out a few words, a torrent would follow. "I k—, k—, ki—"

She nodded and bit her lip. When she looked away he squeezed her hands and leaned close so she was forced to look into his face. When his laryngitic and tremulous words finally came, they haunted her, as if she were hearing a voice from hell.

"I killed Japanese," he whispered desperately. "I shot some full in the face from a foot away! My friends were blown to pieces, their insides splashing on me. Oh, the smell, the heat! And they kept coming and shouting and shooting! I fired and fired, but they were just boys too. So much gunfire. I knew I had to be hit. Men on both sides cried and screamed like children, calling for their mothers. I was covered with blood and flesh. When the Japanese were dead, I turned to my friends. I checked the chest wound of one and my hand slipped inside his ribs and I felt when his heart stopped beating. He looked at me as if I had done it!"

Elisabeth wanted to soothe her son. As he gushed the awful story, he emitted whines and groans such as she had never heard, and she wanted to tell him it was all right and that he need not continue.

But she knew he did. From the corner of her eye she spotted the orderly, Charles, watching from the door. He hurried off, she hoped, to find the doctor. She didn't know whether Bruce might need to be sedated, if dredging these details might do more harm than good.

"Mom, I lay between and beneath my buddies and the only breathing I heard was my own. I expected to die. I expected to see Jesus, I really did. Mom, did you know that most men who die that way don't close their eyes? They stare at you and you wonder how you survived.

"Then I heard the transports, EVAC planes. They buzzed low as if looking for signs of life. Finally one landed in a clearing to my left and someone shouted, 'More Japs! Last call!'

"I fought my way through the gory mess, ran, and dove on board. Three marines jumped in behind me. They said, 'You saved our tails, Bishop!' But they didn't know the price. They thanked me, but I couldn't speak. The transport got off the ground and those guys looked down and swore. I couldn't move.

"'Look, Bishop,' they kept saying. But I couldn't. I was numb; I was afraid I was paralyzed. One of them grabbed me and pointed me toward the opening. There, coming up over the rise, were another two hundred enemy. We were the only four to get out, and we'd have been dead in another minute. When that guy let go of me, I fell over and couldn't pull myself up. I didn't move until I was in San Diego."

Bruce was sweating and hyperventilating. Elisabeth felt his hands go weak. "Let's get you into bed," she said, but he was a dead weight and just sat shaking his head. Charles and the doctor entered and soon had him in bed. The horror on his face had given way to a sadness that broke Elisabeth's heart. She wanted to tell him he'd had no choice, that he was a hero who had done his duty and could be proud. The day would come when the Allied powers would win this awful war and the U.S. would be largely responsible. But Elisabeth knew that paled next to what he had been through. Saying anything to try to make it better would have been as futile as the platitudes she had heard when her father died. Only Pastor Hill and one other had kept silent and grieved with her. Will.

Elisabeth sat by Bruce's bed all night and took the next day off work. He whispered and sang as the sun rose. Whatever had broken free had unfettered his tongue, but Elisabeth would never again raise the subject of his living nightmare, and she doubted he would either.

Joyce treated Bruce like a china doll when she learned he had finally spoken. He started to write her a note, but she swept his hand away.

"No more of that," she said. "If you're talking, you can talk to me."

"I just wanted to tell you that you looked cheery this morning, as usual," he whispered.

"That's the best you can do? I look better than cheery, and you know it. Come up with a better word, and I'll introduce you to the new chaplain next week," she said.

"Pretty," he said.

"Now you're talking."

A week later the doctor began talking about Bruce going home. Elisabeth couldn't wait. She was startled when Joyce showed up that afternoon in her waitress uniform. "Got somebody to cover for me for an hour," Joyce told Elisabeth in Bruce's room. "Had to tell you about the new chaplain. He comes right at you. I ask him questions about the stuff Bruce and I talk about and he asks me if I've ever been led to Christ. I tell him I don't think so. He says he's gonna do that, lead me to Christ. I say, okay, go right ahead. And he did."

Elisabeth blinked. "He did?"

Bruce beamed.

"You knew about this?" Elisabeth asked him. He nodded. "I suppose you've met the new chaplain, too?"

Bruce nodded again and he and Joyce made eye contact.

"What?" Elisabeth said.

"Says he knows you," Joyce said. "Name's Phillips."

Elisabeth sucked in a breath. "Ben Phillips is the new chaplain? Ben Phillips led you to Christ?"

Joyce smiled. "I've got to get to work," she said, and right in front of his mother, she kissed Bruce full on the lips.

Elisabeth had collected herself by the time Joyce was gone. "You've been encouraging a girl who wasn't a believer?" she said.

"It was only a matter of time, Mom," he said.

Elisabeth sat shaking her head. "Have mercy," she said. "Ben Phillips and now this."

Elisabeth knew Ben would check the records and know all about Will. She sent him a note asking that he look her up in Will's room some afternoon. In spite of herself, she couldn't help but be conscious of her clothes and hair, wondering each day if this would the one Ben chose to drop in on her.

She was writing a letter to a missionary when he appeared in the doorway. "Ben," she said, standing. He approached and shook her hand, then looked with sympathy at Will. Ben did something no visitor had done in years. He bent to look into Will's vacant eyes, reached under the sheet, and gripped a gnarled hand. "Will," he said, "it's Ben Phillips, and I'm here to pray for you." Ben pleaded with God for comfort and rest for Will and grace for Elisabeth.

Ben was pushing fifty now. His hair was mostly white and he wore glasses, but he was trim and tastefully dressed. His limp was pronounced, and the scar on his neck still showed.

He said he had served three churches since seminary and jumped at the chance to do something different. "Churches are getting more board-oriented all the time, and I had one too many frustrations." Elisabeth decided not to share her own stories of the same from Christ Church.

"I'm doing more singing now," he said, "like in the old days. And I'm always looking for special music for our chapel services here. I know you have a gift."

"I'm rarely here in the morning," she said.

"If that changes, and you're willing . . ."

"How's your family?" she asked.

"My parents are both gone now," he said. "And I'm alone. What's become of your aunt?"

"Last I heard she was in a rest home, but she never communicates. It's wonderful to see you, Ben."

Over the next several months, Ben greeted her two or three times a week. Once he asked her to play when he sang a solo in the chapel. She made a special trip to do it. "We'll have to try a duet sometime," he said.

Bruce's recovery was not as smooth as Elisabeth had hoped. Once he was home, she had expected him to improve quickly and soon begin work, saving money to attend Moody in the fall of 1944. But he was plagued by dark moods, periods of silence, even nightmares.

He was finally able to work part-time on the line at Fairbanks-Morse, but the highlight of his week was Saturday night when Joyce would visit. Elisabeth arranged the guestroom for her, and Joyce often spent the night and joined them at Christ Church the next day. Trudy Childs, according to her mother, had joined another church. Elisabeth mourned her own estrangement from Frances and prayed they could reconnect one day.

By August, Bruce seemed much better, and he and Joyce were engaged. They married at Christmas and moved into an apartment in the third ward. Elisabeth felt she had nearly reconciled by mail with her daughter Betty, and only bad weather in New Mexico had made it impossible for her and Cliff to come by train for Bruce's wedding.

In May of 1944, Bruce and Joyce announced that a baby was due the following January. Bruce, now working full-time at Fairbanks, still dreamt of attending Moody and began a rigorous series of their correspondence courses.

Elisabeth saw Bruce and Joyce often. They drove her to Jackson when Benjy finally consented to see her. He insisted on seeing only his mother, though in a note dictated to the chaplain he congratulated Bruce and Joyce on their marriage.

Elisabeth trembled with anticipation as she was led to a room where Benjamin was brought to her. She barely recognized him at first, a wasted wisp of a man, looking a decade older than his years. Elisabeth opened her arms to him when he shyly approached, and while he did not hug her back, he let her embrace him. They sat at a steel table.

"How've you been, Benjamin? All right?"

"For a guy doing life."

"You've been getting all my mail?"

He nodded. "I've begun clerking for the chaplain."

"That's wonderful, Benjamin. You need to get back with the Lord."

Benjamin shrugged. "Keep in touch," he said, rising.

Elisabeth was determined not to cry, even though she was afraid it was what she had just said that had made him pull away so quickly. "I will," she said, the tears coming. "May I come again next month?"

He shrugged. "I'll let you know."

Elisabeth left somewhat encouraged about Benjy. Something was better than nothing. She remained optimistic about Betty too, her letters lately sounding more spiritual than her mother recalled.

Elisabeth allowed herself to consider that her own prospects may have changed. She felt fulfilled in her church work, believing that perhaps God had honored her commitment to obedience. Though she worried that was bad theology, she was comforted by a season of relative calm.

The call that made Elisabeth cringe ever after at any ringing phone came just before midnight in the winter of her forty-fifth year.

Only the wealthy had extension phones in Three Rivers, and Elisabeth had not numbered herself among them for decades. Unsure how long the phone had been ringing, she ignored her slippers and tugged her robe on as she hurried stiff-legged toward the stairs. The hardwood creaked as her feet lost feeling on the icy floor. The thermometer outside the kitchen window had read nine below zero just hours before.

There was no one to waken anymore in the big house on Kelsey Street. "Keep ringing, phone," she whispered, "unless you bring bad news."

At the bottom of the stairs Elisabeth breathed a prayer and picked up.

"Mother Bishop, it's Joyce. We've had an accident."

Elisabeth clutched her robe tight at her throat. Her daughter-in-law sounded calm enough, but . . .

"Tell me you didn't lose the baby."

"I'm fine, so I assume the baby is too."

Elisabeth hardly wanted to ask. "And Bruce?"

She heard her own heart as Joyce hesitated. "Bruce seems okay, but he's trapped in the car."

"Oh, no! Did you—"

"The police are on their way."

"Thank God. Where are you?"

"Not far. M–60. We were coming back from visiting—"

"At this hour? Joyce! You're due in what? A month?"

"The road looked clear, but at the big curve over by—"

"I know where it is."

"There was ice. We slid into the ditch. Bruce steered away from the water. He somehow swung back up onto the road, but we flipped over."

"Oh, Joyce!"

"He seems fine, but the wheel and the dashboard have him pinned."

"I'll come."

"Please don't. I'll call you as soon as we get home. He didn't even want me to tell you."

"Just like him. How did you get out?"

"I crawled out the window. We weren't far from a farmhouse. The people are so nice. I hated to wake them."

"Call as soon as you know anything. And have someone check you over, honey."

Elisabeth stood in the darkness of the living room, staring out at the streetlight on the corner. What a marvel, throwing off ten times the light of the gas lamps lit by hand, one by one at twilight, when she was a child. Back then a year could pass before she saw more than three automobiles. Now everyone had one. Some two. Imagine! Well, a flipped horse cart wouldn't have trapped Bruce.

The weight of a lifetime of strife overcame Elisabeth, and she lowered herself to the floor, her face in her palms, the backs of her hands pressed against the gritty carpet. "Oh, God," she began, "you have protected Bruce from so much. You must have great things in mind for him. He is completely yours. Let the police be your agents and may they get there even now to rescue one who wants above all to serve you."

Elisabeth would not sleep. She alternately paced and sat on the couch in the stillness.

Since childhood, prayer had been as natural to Elisabeth as breathing. And during that time, God had required much of her, allowing her to be tested until she was forced to rely solely upon him. Her underpinnings had been ripped away with such regularity that she had often been tempted to settle into a life that didn't shake its fist in the Enemy's face.

Elisabeth didn't want to change her past. But as she shivered in the wee hours of a bitter morning, she struggled with God yet again, as she had so often before, over the safety of her son. She had accepted so much, suffered so much, given so much, that surely God would grant her deepest, most heartfelt wish now, would he not? Hadn't everything in her life and Bruce's pointed to his being a *living* sacrifice?

She had long wondered whether there was any benefit, this side of heaven, for a lifetime commitment to obedience. After years of service, of countless hours in the Word and in prayer, Elisabeth found herself at yet another crossroad. She thought she understood grace, had told herself she understood sovereignty. But unless God spared her son, seemingly unhurt yet trapped in a twisted car on M–60 in the middle of a winter's night, she feared there was something about God she still didn't understand—and didn't like.

Chapter Nineteen

*E*lisabeth could not recall feeling more alone. How she needed Will right now!

Years before, when she first began visiting him every day, she battled resentment that he had disengaged. She knew it wasn't his fault. But when trying to make ends meet, to discipline Benjy, to keep Betty breathing, she could have used help.

Her friends, the women who had grown up in the church with her, backed away too. Mental illness—and there was no other way to describe Will's malady—was simply not talked about. Elisabeth had been naïve to think any of Will's or her friends would go to see him. Everyone found excuses. Frances Childs said she was so distraught over not being able to have her own children that she just couldn't handle the "stress" of seeing Will so ill. For whatever help and comfort it might have been to Will to see familiar faces, no one but Pastor Hill and his wife ever came. The new pastor had never raised the subject.

Maybe it was better that Will had not had to endure the pain and hardship Elisabeth had. But how wonderful it would be on a night like tonight to be held, comforted, prayed with—to have someone with whom to share the load.

"I've asked for years that you would be my portion," she prayed. "And I never really knew what it meant. If it means you're all I've got and all I need, then I need you to be my father, my husband, and my friend right now. How long does it take to pull someone from a car? Forgive me for worrying. Help me rest in you. I know you are sovereign, I believe you love me, and I'm begging for the safety of my son."

Elisabeth could wait no longer. She dialed Bruce and Joyce's number. No answer.

She called the police department.

"Three Rivers police, Officer Fox."

Elisabeth explained what Joyce had told her about the accident. "So I expected to have heard something by now."

"Yes, ma'am. I'm going to have to ask you to call the hospital."

"What happened?"

"I'm not at liberty to—"

"Was Bruce Bishop injured?"

"Ma'am, I'm sorry, but I was directed to—"

"How badly is he hurt?"

"I was about to call you, Mrs. Bishop. Do you need a ride to—"

"I'll drive," Elisabeth said. "But I want to know what to expect."

"I've not been given all the details."

"Is my son dead?"

"I have not gotten that word, ma'am, no."

"But he was injured."

"That's my understanding."

"And my daughter-in-law? She was to call me."

"The request that we call you came from her, Mrs. Bishop."

"Is *she* all right?"

"As far as I know."

"Why didn't *she* call?"

"I don't want to alarm you, but I have been asked to request that you come quickly."

Elisabeth threw her heavy coat on over her bathrobe, stepped into her boots, and gingerly made her way down the back stairs to the garage. People would understand.

The old Ford whined before finally turning over. Elisabeth's bare legs were so cold, she left the sliding garage door open for the first time in her life. Her prayers were incoherent. She quoted verses she'd known since childhood: "Likewise the Spirit also helpeth our infirmities: for we know not what we should pray for as we ought: but the Spirit itself maketh intercession for us with groanings which cannot be uttered. And he that searcheth the hearts knoweth what is the mind of the Spirit, because he maketh intercession for the saints according to the will of God. And we know that all things work together for good to them that love God, to them who are called according to his purpose."

How many times had that last verse been quoted to her in an attempt to persuade her that Will's infirmity, that Benjy's crimes, that Betty's asthma were somehow God's ideas? Elisabeth had no doubt the Scripture was true. But she had become convinced that either she had not been called according to God's purpose, or that things work together for good only once the saints get to heaven.

As for tonight? It made no sense. "God, let him be alive."

Elisabeth pulled up to the emergency room entrance and ran in. Four uniformed police officers looked grave and sneaked glances at her.

"Mrs. Bishop?" a nurse said from behind a desk.

"Is my son alive?"

"He's in surgery right now, ma'am."

"For what?"

"I don't know all the details yet—"

"Of course you do! Why won't anyone tell me anything?"

"The doctor will meet with you as soon as he's out of surgery."

"Where's my daughter-in-law?"

"In the waiting room. She's expecting you."

"What happened anyway? I was told—" Elisabeth whirled to look at the policemen. "Who was there?"

One cop sat with his head in his hands, a cast on his right wrist, and a special shoe on his right foot, protecting bandaged toes. As she started for him, another intercepted her.

"Ma'am, this officer is not ready to talk about what happened. He lost his partner, and he was driving."

"He lost his—you mean, there—"

"Was a fatality, yes, ma'am. And your son is hardly out of the woods, so I would suggest—"

"But what happened?"

"I wasn't there, but I'll not let you demand details of this officer just now."

Elisabeth found Joyce at the end of the hall, grimacing, her hands gently cradling her abdomen. Her feet and legs were wrapped in a huge blanket, her wet shoes and socks near a heat register close by.

"Are you all right, dear?" Elisabeth asked, sitting next to her.

Joyce nodded. "Just uncomfortable."

"What in the world—?"

"The police car hit our car!"

What? This was God's answer to her prayer that the police would get there quickly?

"I guess the cop didn't realize how fast he was going or how icy it was," Joyce said. "Crazy thing is, I know him. Guy Hiestand. He used to drive race cars with my dad."

"Then he ought to know how to drive fast."

"You'd think."

"He hit your car going how fast?"

Joyce shrugged. "It sounded awful. It pushed our car back down into the ditch and it wound up on its side in that water." She began to cry. "Bruce doesn't deserve this! After all he went through, to be trapped in that car with water rising . . ."

"He was under water?"

"He was fighting to keep his nose above the surface. I ran down in there and tried to rock the car, but—"

"Joyce! With a baby due next month!"

"Was I supposed to let him drown? Guy was hurt himself and was working on his partner, who looked unconscious."

"How'd you get Bruce out?"

"The farmer had followed me out, and he helped me lean against the roof of the car and tip it enough for Bruce to breathe. The firemen finally got him out."

"How bad was he?"

Joyce shook her head. "They stabilized him on this board thing, strapped his head down. He was bleeding from the ears. The emergency room doctor said something about internal injuries. They told me the surgeon would talk to me as soon as he could. I asked if someone would call you."

Elisabeth took Joyce's hands in hers. "Father," she began, "I've quit trying to understand your ways. Give the doctors wisdom and use their skill . . ." Elisabeth was flooded with the realization that the last time she prayed that professionals would be used of God, the police made things worse. She feared if she kept praying she'd say things a new Christian shouldn't hear. "Joyce, would you continue?"

Silence. Elisabeth peeked at Joyce.

"Mother, I'm not happy with God right now."

Neither was Elisabeth, but she couldn't admit that. "Careful, honey," she said.

"I mean it! Bruce tells me you're a prayer warrior, that you trust God for everything."

"I try."

"Why? I haven't seen one clue that he's still working."

"But your own salvation . . ."

Joyce struggled heavily to her feet. "When was the last time you had a prayer answered?"

"When Bruce got his voice back, when you became a Christian, when he came home. God is working, Joyce. His ways are not our ways."

"They sure aren't! Hasn't Bruce been through enough? Does he need to learn something more?"

"Maybe *I* do."

"You've learned enough lessons for a lifetime!"

"Please sit," Elisabeth said, reaching for her. "Protect that baby." Joyce sat and Elisabeth helped straighten her blanket and coat. She sighed. "Maybe I put Bruce on too high a pedestal," she said. "Maybe I made him the center of my life instead of the Lord."

"So *Bruce* suffers for that? I wondered if you'd let him go after we were married, but you've been great. I'm telling you, I don't like this. If anything happens to Bruce, I'm not going to forgive God."

"Oh, Joyce, don't say things like that."

Joyce did not respond, and Elisabeth hated that the accusation of the Lord hung in the room. But could she argue? If Bruce died in such a senseless, random, capricious way, what would that say about God? Did faith, prayer, commitment, obedience count for anything?

It was refreshing that her daughter-in-law felt free to speak her mind, but Elisabeth would not express her own doubts in front of so new a Christian. "Joyce, no matter what, we're going to trust God and believe that he loves us."

Joyce hunched her shoulders and pulled her coat collar higher on her neck. She looked at Elisabeth. "No matter what?"

Elisabeth nodded, wishing she felt as sure as she sounded. "Absolutely." *God, handle this one right.*

Joyce shook her head, her hands deep in her pockets. "You're telling me that if Bruce doesn't pull through, you're still going to say God knew what he was doing."

"It won't be easy." Elisabeth felt like a weakling.

Joyce turned away. "God had better give Bruce back to me in one piece," she said. "All Bruce talks about is serving him. He believes he has been exposed to all kinds of tragedy just to make him a better pastor."

"That's why God will spare him."

Joyce faced her again. "What if he doesn't?"

Elisabeth felt as if she were swimming against a strong current. "Don't upset yourself," she said. "Think of the baby."

Joyce threw off her blanket and stood again. She paced ponderously. "I *am!* This baby needs a father!"

"We need to pray."

"I've prayed enough!" Joyce said. "How many things does Bruce have to go through? He's given his whole life to God!"

A nurse appeared. "Excuse me. The doctor has sent word from the operating room that you might want to have someone called. Your pastor, or . . . ?"

"Why?" Joyce demanded. "Is Bruce going to die?"

"They're still working on him, Mrs. Bishop. Is there someone you'd like here with you?"

"Pastor Clarkson is away this week," Elisabeth said.

"I'd rather have Chaplain Phillips anyway," Joyce said.

The nurse went to call him.

Elisabeth said, "We really should keep praying."

"I'm prayed out," Joyce said. "God's going to do what God's going to do. If Bruce pulls through, you'll thank God. If he doesn't, you'll say God's ways aren't our ways. What's the difference?"

"Oh, Joyce . . ."

But Joyce had fallen silent. She put her feet up on a chair and leaned back, supporting herself on her elbows behind her.

Half an hour later, Elisabeth decided that, as usual, no news was good news. "They must be making progress."

Joyce looked at her with disgust. "Are you just incurably cheery? They're probably fighting to keep him alive."

"We have to think positively."

Joyce shook her head. "Maybe our car wasn't totaled. Maybe tonight was *good* for our baby. Look at it this way, it gave you and me some time together."

Elisabeth couldn't hide she was hurt.

"I'm sorry, Mother. I don't mean to be this way."

"I understand, honey, but don't blame God." How Elisabeth wanted to follow her own advice.

As she returned from the washroom a few minutes later, Elisabeth recognized Ben's voice. He was talking with the surgeon near the elevator around the corner.

"Talk with Bruce's mother first. She's strong and can help his wife."

"Yes," the doctor said. "The widow will need her."

Elisabeth's knees cracked hard on the hard floor before she knew she had fallen. She cried out, "No, no, God, please, no!"

Ben and the doctor helped her to the waiting room where Joyce quickly stood. "What? Tell me!"

"Please sit down," the doctor said.

"Just tell me!"

Ben guided Joyce back down. "Mrs. Bishop," the doctor began, "I'm sorry to tell you that your husband has died due to severe brain trauma. We did everything humanly possible."

Elisabeth's knees throbbed and her throat felt constricted.

"I want to see him," Joyce said.

The doctor turned to Elisabeth. "You too, ma'am?"

Elisabeth couldn't find her voice. Nor could she imagine seeing her dead son. She shook her head, afraid she would topple again.

"Come with me, Mother," Joyce said. Ben stayed outside the operating room as the doctor led them in.

"We had to shave his head," the doctor said, pulling the sheet from Bruce's face and quietly leaving. The incision had already been stitched.

His face was smooth and pale, eyes shut, lips slightly parted. "Bruce," Joyce whispered, shuddering. Elisabeth wrapped an arm around her waist. "Bruce," she said again.

Elisabeth fought the urge to embrace him, to kiss him, to will him back to life. This was the nightmare she had feared every minute he was overseas. And now this. She couldn't take her eyes off him, knowing the next time she saw him would be in a funeral parlor, surrounded by friends who would try to make it make sense.

Joyce turned abruptly and strode out, leaving Elisabeth alone with him. She was transported to his birth, which seemed so recent. Bruce had been smooth-skinned and still then too. Elisabeth couldn't stop her hands from shaking, and the muscles in her back and neck coiled. Her emotions scared her. She wanted to scream, to cry, to rail against God. She wanted to grab Bruce's beautiful body in the bloom of its youth and wrestle it off that table and out of that place to keep with her forever. She didn't trust herself to cradle his face and kiss his cheek. If she didn't somehow make her way out of there that instant, she knew they would be picking her up off the floor again.

She felt a strong, gentle hand on her shoulder, and Ben led her out. Joyce scowled at her, then at Ben, as if demanding that they somehow explain. Ben put his arm around Joyce. "Nothing I say," he began, but she cut him off.

"That's right. Why would God do this? Why would he let me fall in love with the most wonderful person I've ever met, then let this happen to him?"

"It's not our place to—"

"I'm not allowed to question God Almighty when he takes my husband before our child is—"

"God didn't take—"

"Who then? What's the point of faith or any of it?"

Elisabeth's shoulders slumped. She knew she should worry about salvaging Joyce, her new faith so fragile. But her anger resonated with Joyce's. She feared what would become of that unborn child, but she was so overcome with revulsion and loss she could barely function.

"Joyce," Ben said. "God would want you to be honest with him."

"I don't want to talk to him."

"But he wants to hear from you. Do you think he doesn't know how you feel?"

"If God had anything to do with this," Joyce said, "he would have protected Bruce."

Elisabeth couldn't have agreed more.

Ben insisted on driving them both to Elisabeth's home in her car, followed by a squad car that would take him back to his own vehicle. Ben urged Joyce to stay with her mother-in-law until her due date, for both their sakes. Though Joyce did not respond, Elisabeth sensed resignation. Joyce allowed Ben to help her up the stairs.

Elisabeth stood in the front hallway, still in her coat, as if unsure what to do next. Ben descended and said, "I don't imagine either of you will be sleeping." She shook her head. "I'm having a hard time with this myself," he added.

Elisabeth clasped her hands and hung her head. The hollowness of her own voice scared her. "I am just hoping to wake up yesterday."

"I'll check in on Will every day for you, and—"

"I'll be there," she said.

"Oh. All right then." He looked at the floor. "I worry about Joyce. Perhaps if we work together on—"

"I'm worried about my own reaction, Ben."

"That's natural."

"Not for me. I'm just at the end."

He cocked his head and sighed. "I learned a long time ago that words are meaningless at this point," he said. "Just let me plead with you to make no decisions until you can get some rest. In the meantime,

if you need the embrace of an old friend, I'm willing. You know me
well enough to know that the last thing I would ever want is to be inappropriate with you."

"I know, Ben."

"May I, then?"

"No. But thank you."

"May I pray for you?"

She shook her head.

"Need help up the stairs?"

She shook her head again.

"I'll be thinking of you," he said, stepping past her into the frigid
night.

Elisabeth left her coat on as she pulled herself up the stairs with a
hand on the banister, aching all the way for Ben Phillips's encouraging embrace.

She sat heavily on the edge of her bed, kicked her shoes off, and
lay on her back, her feet still on the floor. She did not move until
dawn. Neither did she sleep. Nor pray.

Chapter Twenty

*E*lisabeth might have suspected something the next morning, had she not been so debilitated by grief and her tenuous grip on God. It seemed logical when Joyce asked to be driven to Bruce's and her apartment to pick up a few things.

Elisabeth offered to help, but Joyce asked to be alone awhile. "Sure. Shall I pick you up on the way back from Kalamazoo?"

"I'll call you," Joyce said.

Elisabeth wanted to leave her with some encouraging comment, but she was empty. Her own prayers were laced with such bitterness and anger that she felt like Job's advisers and feared cursing God. What did all of it, any of it, mean? Were the promises of Scripture lies? Where was abundant life, the joy of knowing God, things working together for good?

She tried to pray for Joyce, but that just frustrated her more. Joyce was one of the reasons Bruce should still be alive. What would become of her faith?

Elisabeth felt a dark foreboding as she entered the State Hospital. Several regulars appeared surprised to see her and offered condolences. She could not speak. She merely nodded and continued toward Will's room. How could news travel so fast?

The orderlies had learned to leave Will's room the way it had been the night before. They knew Elisabeth liked to open the drapes and blinds herself, to freshen the room for Will. He hadn't moved for years and never acknowledged anyone. Several times during the day some-one would come to turn him, roll him over, helping to prevent bed-sores. Still, Elisabeth's routine was to speak to him and hold his hand and caress him.

Her knees still smarted as she moved slowly down the corridor. The darkness of the room fit her mood and she did not move to open the drapes. She left the lights off and went directly to the still form beneath the blankets. Elisabeth was used to Will's appearance by now, but somehow he looked even smaller this morning. On his side, his bony hips providing the only rise on the bed, he lay in a fetal position. As she had done for years, she dug beneath the cover for his balled-up fist, forced it open, and let it close around her hand.

She leaned close, unable to tell in the darkness whether his eyes were open. His breathing was deep and regular. "Will," she whispered, "we lost our baby. I'm glad you can't take that in. I hardly can. How I would love to drift into unconsciousness myself. But I wish you were here to talk with me. Explain to me Psalm 37 and those verses I have loved so long. I can't pray. I can't sleep. I can't eat. I'm angry with God. I don't understand him. I can't imagine there's another thing I need to learn from tragedy."

Weak from fatigue and grief, Elisabeth released Will's hand, drew the blanket up to his neck, and sat in a reclining chair near the wall. Still bundled against the cold, she kept vigil over the barely alive remains of her husband. Her body ached, her spirit was numb. Sleep would be such sweet relief. Was there any escape from this despair? How could she look forward to her grandchild, due next month? Was it possible to survive this monstrous grief so that somehow she and Joyce could raise that child in Bruce's childhood home?

She was nodding, nearly dozing, when Ben Phillips tiptoed in and pulled a chair next to hers. Elisabeth barely acknowledged him. He took her hand in both of his, and she was transported to the first time she had felt his grip. So warm, so firm, so compassionate.

"Can we chat a minute?" he said quietly.

She shrugged.

"Joyce asked me to handle the funeral at Christ Church. I spoke with Pastor Clarkson, who understands."

Elisabeth nodded. She was surprised to find herself actually grateful that this ugly responsibility was now Joyce's and not hers. She hoped someone would just tell her when to be there.

"Are you all right, Elisabeth?" She turned slowly to look at him, incredulous. "I mean, other than the obvious."

She wasn't suicidal, if that's what he meant. Yet the details of her son's funeral interested her no more than the sweet relief from grief that a moment of sleep would bring. All she could do was shake her head, and still she had not shed a tear. It was as if her grief was dammed up by an unspeakable rage.

"I have some difficult news, Elisabeth."

She was so drained she closed her eyes and could hardly open them again. "Ben, I can't bear another thing. Please."

"It's no tragedy, but it's something you need to know."

He waited for a response, but she could not communicate.

"Joyce is moving out of her apartment."

Elisabeth forced herself to look at him. "That's all right. She can live with me as long as she likes."

Ben let go of her hand and leaned forward, his elbows on his knees. "She asked if I would speak with you. She will not be living with you either."

Elisabeth had to work to keep from slurring. "But surely at least until after the baby comes—"

"She knows your heart is set on that, but she has already moved back to the trailer park."

Elisabeth squinted, trying to make it figure. "Whatever for?"

"Apparently her cousin lives there with a boyfriend—"

"That's no environment—"

"I tried to urge her to stay with you at least a while, but she's angry and dead set—"

"Angry at me?" Elisabeth felt suddenly warm, and when she began to shed her coat, Ben helped her.

"You represent God to her," he said. "And she's furious at him."

So am I, Elisabeth thought. "I need to talk with her," she said.

"Elisabeth, she doesn't want to talk to you."

Elisabeth was disgusted to be brought to the brink of tears over the sting of that insult, when she couldn't weep over the loss of her precious son. "Can't she think of the baby?" she said. "Staying with me for now is ideal."

Ben spread his hands. "I pleaded with her. She's closed to that. I'm sure your place reminds her of her loss, and she——"

"It does me too, Ben, but *I'm* not leaving."

He stood and asked if he could open the drapes and blinds. When she didn't protest, he flooded the room with harsh sunlight, and she covered her eyes. "Joyce is an adult, Elisabeth. Free to make her own decisions."

Elisabeth shook her head, stood, and stretched. That made her dizzy and Ben steadied her. She sat back down. "The thought of being alone in that house now . . ."

"You're going to get through this, you know."

Her eyes adjusted to the light. "I'm not so sure," she said. "My cup is empty, Ben. Where do I turn when I no longer trust where I've turned before?"

"That's grief talking," he said. "And fatigue."

"Truth is, it's a lifetime of disappointment. Can't anything God does ever make sense?"

Ben stepped to the door and kept his back to Elisabeth. "I don't know if you want answers or sympathy. I've never claimed to know the mind of God."

She sighed loudly, near collapse. He returned and sat with her. Elisabeth wanted to fall into his embrace, to weep on his chest, to be held and rocked. Not because this man was the love of her youth, but because he knew her, cared for her, and—she hoped—understood her.

"Delight yourself also in the Lord," she began in a whisper. "And he shall give you the desires of your heart. Commit your way to the Lord, trust also in him, and he shall bring it to pass."

He smiled. "Precious promises."

"They aren't true, Ben! I've delighted myself in the Lord my whole life. Do you think it was the desire of my heart to never know my mother? To lose my father? To be kicked out of my own house? To lose all three of my children? My husband lies here only forty-six years old and could linger many more years. God gives me the son any mother would dream of, dramatically protects him over and over, then lets him die?" She raised her voice and couldn't help it, and with her shouts finally came the tears. "I don't want to understand the mysteries of heaven! I just want God to make sense one time!"

Ben stood. "Walk with me."

"Ben, I'm exhausted. My knees hurt."

"Just to the dayroom," he said.

Elisabeth followed him there and sat on a love seat facing the east windows where the sun streamed in. Ben sat on a table, blocking the light, his frame silhouetted in the window. "I fought God over this same issue. It's clear he does not give us whatever we desire, so either we are not truly delighting ourselves in him—"

"I've searched myself, Ben."

"—or we misinterpret the phrase 'give you the desires of your heart.'"

"What's to misinterpret?" she said.

"Has he given you the desires of your heart?"

"No!"

"Then what's wrong?"

"I'm asking you, Ben. I have nowhere else to turn."

"Consider a possibility: that the phrase 'he will give you the desires of your heart' means he will *tell* you what the desires of your heart should be."

Elisabeth sat staring, blinking.

Ben continued. "In other words, delight yourself in him and he will tell you what to desire. That same passage says, 'He shall bring forth your righteousness as the light, and your justice as the noonday. Rest in the Lord, and wait patiently for him.'"

"How can I, Ben? I'm so angry!"

"The passage gets more personal. 'Cease from anger, and forsake wrath; do not fret; it only causes harm.'"

Elisabeth could barely move. She let her chin fall to her chest and wept.

Ben rested a hand on hers. "In about ten minutes I'm expecting one of the widows from my last church to come and play the piano and sing. Any day other than today Dellarae Shockadance might amuse you."

Elisabeth looked up. "That's her name?"

"Don't get me wrong, she's a wonderful person. But she's a little overweight, a little rosy-cheeked, and little enthusiastic on the keyboard and as a vocalist. Come to chapel, and then let me drive you to Three Rivers."

"But my car—"

"You shouldn't drive without sleep. I'll pick you up again tomorrow and you can drive home after that."

"It's out of your way."

"I don't want to worry about you on the road."

"I appreciate that more than I can say, Ben. I just wish I could sleep."

"You will. I'll look for you at chapel."

Elisabeth sleepwalked to Will's room to gather her things, touched his lean shoulder, and made her way down the hall. She was among the first at chapel and sat in the back. Dellarae was already at the piano and playing too loudly. She wore a red dress slightly too small for her, a hat with a feather, and a huge smile. She played with a flourish, ending every phrase with a high note.

The little chapel soon filled. Dellarae seemed to enjoy herself. She accompanied herself for a solo, and she and Ben sang a duet before he spoke. With her feather keeping time, she transported Elisabeth to childhood when she snorted aloud to keep from laughing at the guest soloist at the protracted meetings.

Ben spoke for twenty minutes. When Mrs. Shockadance began the last song, Elisabeth slipped out and waited for him. Finally he emerged and introduced the women. "I've heard so much about you," Dellarae gushed. "And I'm so sorry about your loss. My husband died almost ten years ago, when I was about your age. Thank God we had twenty-five years together."

Elisabeth tried to smile but could not. Losing a husband after twenty-five years didn't sound so bad. She had allowed her own silver anniversary to pass without notice the previous January.

Elisabeth confronted Joyce at the funeral. "Please," she said, "let's not become strangers. I want to help with the baby."

Eyes hidden behind sunglasses, Joyce nodded and said nothing. A contingent of her old friends and possibly family—none were introduced to Elisabeth—crowded the front row. They smelled of tobacco and body odor and stood in a group smoking while awaiting the ride to the cemetery.

Despite Ben's warm message, Elisabeth's pain was unabated. She feared she would never find her way out of the black hole that entrapped her. Receiving friends was as difficult a chore as she could remember, and she was grateful to finally arrive home.

She changed into her nightgown and robe in the middle of the afternoon and lay atop the covers of her bed. Sleep eluded her, yet exhaustion overwhelmed her. The thought of going back to work and driving to Kalamazoo every afternoon depressed her all the more.

Through Christmas and New Year's she prayed for relief, venting her anger toward God. People at church, at work, and at the hospital were kind but no help. Ben was compassionate and never failed to try to cheer her. She took a break from her Sunday school class and stopped her missionary letters too, feeling hypocritical and not wanting to spread her bitterness.

Late in the evening of January 23, 1946, she was startled to hear the rough voice of an uneducated man on the phone. "This here Mrs. Bishop?"

"Who's calling?"

"Yeah, um, I'm, ah, friend of Joyce Adams, ah, Bishop."

"I'm Elisabeth Bishop."

"Joyce wanted me to tell you that you have a granddaughter."

Something broke loose in Elisabeth as she hurried to the hospital in the middle of the night. For the first time in weeks, she was able to thank God for something. "Restore me!" she pleaded. "Make me what I need to be for this child."

How long had it been since she had heard from God? He seemed to impress upon her afresh something she had known all her life. What he was about, the desire he wanted to plant in her heart, was to bring as many as possible into his family. That still, small voice reminded her,

"I am not willing that any should perish, but that all should come to repentance."

Her granddaughter needed Christ. Her daughter-in-law needed to be brought back to him. Elisabeth herself, as well as Joyce and the baby, could be used to further God's kingdom. She still didn't understand, didn't agree Bruce had to die, still wanted answers. Meanwhile, she was starving from the estrangement. She missed God, needed him, wanted him.

Suddenly, from deep within her memory gushed verses she had memorized as a child. As she drove, blinking away tears, she recited from Psalm 51:9–13: "Hide thy face from my sins, and blot out all mine iniquities. Create in me a clean heart, O God; and renew a right spirit within me. Cast me not away from thy presence; and take not thy holy spirit from me. Restore unto me the joy of thy salvation; and uphold me with thy free spirit. Then will I teach transgressors thy ways; and sinners shall be converted unto thee."

Elisabeth dug in her purse for a hankie and wiped her face. Joy flooded her and she thanked God for not abandoning her. "Be my friend!" she cried. "Be my guide and my companion. All my trust is in you. Though I don't understand you, I love you. You are my rock, my fortress. In you I hide. I have nowhere else to turn."

In the same building where she had lost her son, she was introduced to a squalling baby girl, just under seven pounds. "I'm going to call her Lisa," Joyce said, smiling sadly. "Bruce and I had agreed to name her after you. Elisabeth Grace Bishop."

"I couldn't be more touched."

"I don't believe in grace anymore. You were a great mother, but I wouldn't have given her that middle name, except Bruce wanted me to."

"You need to see that she's raised in the nurture and admonition—"

"That will be up to you," Joyce said. "You're not going to find me in church again."

"Oh, Joyce."

"Don't start. God lost me when he took Bruce."

Elisabeth wanted to argue, to warn Joyce against becoming a miserable old woman as Aunt Agatha had. But Elisabeth herself had nearly lost her faith. Joyce handed her the baby and Elisabeth wept. Holding that precious new life and looking into her dark, curious eyes, she resolved to find Aunt Agatha and give her a look at her great-grandniece.

"I'll be happy to take Lisa anytime."

"Don't worry," Joyce said. "I have to work, so I'll need a lot of help."

"I'd love to show her off at church. Will you come—"

"No, now I told you. You can take Lisa, but don't expect me to go and don't ask me again."

Elisabeth spent the next several months praying that if God could not make clear some purpose in Bruce's death, he would somehow nurture in her heart desires that would please him. She revisited her commitment to obedience and hunkered down to resume her spiritual disciplines and service. She even told Ben she'd try a duet with him in the State Hospital chapel.

Elisabeth cut her work hours in half, determined to sacrifice if necessary so she could watch Lisa frequently, spend more time in Kalamazoo, and enlist Ben's help in locating her aunt. Through his contacts with other healthcare facilities in the state, he finally found Agatha Erastus in the Battle Creek Home for the Aged. She was seventy-five years old, in a wheelchair, and nearly blind from diabetes.

Noting how close Battle Creek was to the penitentiary in Jackson, Elisabeth informed the prison chaplain she was bringing Benjamin Bishop's first niece to meet him. "If you have to surprise him, do it. Don't even give him the option of turning us away."

She and Ben agreed on "When I Survey the Wondrous Cross" for their duet at the State Hospital chapel, and the indefatigable Mrs. Shockadance came early to rehearse. "You're singing my favorite song," she said, and sobbed loudly throughout practice, which was the only thing that kept Elisabeth from doing the same. She had to concentrate on blending with Ben's beautiful baritone. As she sat waiting to sing in front of the audience, she let the lyric echo in her mind. "My richest gain I count but loss, and pour contempt on all my pride."

After the duet, during which Dellarae was able to keep quiet despite torrents of tears, she told Elisabeth, "It's eerie. You two sound as if you were born to sing together. It's almost as if you're related, the blend is so perfect."

Elisabeth stopped to see Will on her way out, feeling guilty over how she enjoyed standing close to Ben. Ben was careful about not touching her, reminding her of how perfectly appropriate Will had been years before when living in the same house with her, secretly loving her, but honoring her engagement to Ben.

As she left, Ben met her in the hallway. "We'll have to do that again sometime," he said. "That sure melted the years away."

"I'd like that," she said.

"I'll play for you two anytime!" Dellarae hollered from the end of the hall, and Ben and Elisabeth smiled at each other.

Elisabeth arrived home to a letter from the chaplain in Jackson. "I suggest you accelerate plans to see your son. He is showing signs of confusion and forgetfulness. Any light you might shed on this would be appreciated, family history, etc."

Elisabeth slumped on the couch, letter in hand. She raised her eyes to the ceiling. "God," she prayed, "don't do this to me."

Transporting a baby by herself reminded Elisabeth she was not as young as she used to be. She encouraged herself by imagining the looks on the faces of Aunt Agatha and Benjy when they saw this beautiful little one.

An orderly wheeled Aunt Agatha to the great room in the Battle Creek Home. Her chair brakes were locked near a couch by the window, and the orderly bent to speak loudly into her ear. "You have visitors, Mrs. Erastus!"

The little old lady, her hair now wisps of white, scowled and looked up at him. "I what?"

"You have visitors!"

"Oh, not too bad. And you?"

"Look, ma'am! Over there! That's your niece, Mrs. Bishop, and your great-grandniece!"

"I don't know any Bishop!" she said.

Elisabeth approached. "Tell her it's Elisabeth LeRoy, her brother's daughter."

Agatha grew rigid. As other patients reached for the baby and cooed at her, Agatha said, "Elisabeth is here? Here to see me?"

"I wanted you to see my granddaughter, Aunt Agatha!" Elisabeth said, holding the baby before her.

"Oh, my!" the woman said, seeming afraid to touch the baby. "James! Bring Elisabeth and come and see the beautiful baby!"

Elisabeth sat across from Agatha with Lisa in her lap. "Do you remember me, Aunt Agatha? I'm Elisabeth!"

Agatha looked at her out of the corner of her eye. "I'm blind," she said. "But I remember you. You hate me."

"I don't! I never did! I've missed you, wanted to see you for a long time! I'm glad I finally found you!"

"And this is your baby?"

"My granddaughter! Can you believe it?"

"You married the soldier then? Such a nice young man."

"I married Will Bishop."

"His dad was crazy. Died in the State Hospital."

After half an hour of bizarre interchange, Elisabeth asked Aunt Agatha if she could read to her from the Bible. The old woman's head bobbed and Elisabeth imagined a smart retort, as she'd heard so many times as a child. "Read me Psalm 23," Agatha said.

Elisabeth was shocked. "Psalm 23?"

"In my room."

The orderly pushed her there and helped her into bed. She appeared sound asleep. Elisabeth balanced Lisa on one knee and found Psalm 23 with her free hand. Convinced her aunt was sleeping, she hesitated.

"Well, are you going to read or not?" Agatha said.

Elisabeth's eye fell on Psalm 22. "Aunt Agatha," she said softly, "before I read Psalm 23, let me read you the chapter before it. This psalm used the same language Jesus would use on the cross."

"Just read it!" Agatha said, eyes still closed.

"'My God, my God, why hast thou forsaken me? Why art thou so far from helping me, and from the words of my roaring? O my God, I cry in the daytime, but thou hearest not; and in the night season, and am not silent. But thou—'"

"What?" Agatha shouted. "Begin again!"

"'My God, my God, why hast thou forsaken me? Why art thou so far from—'"

"He has not forsaken me!" Agatha wailed. "I've forsaken him!" She forced herself up onto her elbows, eyes still shut. "It's too late! Too late!"

"It's never too late, Auntie," Elisabeth said, and the baby began to cry.

"Oh, Elisabeth, will you keep that little one close to God?"

"I'll try."

"It's too late for me."

"No, it isn't."

"I've strayed too far, been stubborn too long."

"It's never too late."

"Go and let me sleep."

"All right, but—"

"Go!"

"I'll pray for you."

"Don't waste your breath."

"Jesus forgave the thief on the cross. He was a believer for only a few minutes, yet Jesus told him, 'Today you will be with me in Paradise.'"

Agatha rolled onto her side and wept. Elisabeth set the Bible down and reached for her, but Agatha wrenched away. "Go!"

Chapter Twenty-One

On the drive from Battle Creek to Jackson, baby Lisa slept and Elisabeth prayed for Agatha. She had hated to leave, but she did not want to agitate her aunt when Agatha seemed as close to repentance as Elisabeth had ever seen her.

That took Elisabeth's mind off Benjy, at least enough to allow her to keep her emotions together. She did not want to break down in front of him, regardless of his state. She only hoped that his dementia, if that's what it was, was in a stage early enough that she could still communicate with him.

The penitentiary was clangy and cold. Lisa was still sound asleep, despite the noise and the fact that a matron had to search even her. "Such a sweetheart," the woman said.

"Yes," Elisabeth said. "And too inexperienced for a breakout attempt."

She was directed to a table in the corner of the large, busy room where families met prisoners. Elisabeth dug two blankets from her bag and built a thick, soft bed in the middle of the table. When she placed Lisa atop them and covered her, the baby moved only to turn her face away from the harsh light. That pointed her tiny features toward where Benjy would sit.

Here he came. Elisabeth was shocked at his appearance. One thing Benjy cared about was dressing a certain way. Last time his hair had been combed just so. His denims were tucked neatly with his cigarette pack rolled crisply in his sleeve. His shoes had been shined. This time his shoes were dingy and untied. He wore one sock. His denims were dirty, he had missed a belt loop, the zipper and button were askew, and his shirt had been buttoned in the wrong holes and had one shirttail out. His hair looked as if he hadn't touched it since he woke up. And he was none too happy.

She rose to embrace him. He did not return her hug. "I didn't know it was you or I would have said no," he said.

"I would have come anyway. You're my son and I love you, and I understand you're having some trouble with your memory."

Benjamin squinted at her and scowled. "I don't remember." He clearly didn't see the humor in his own comment.

"Sit down and meet your niece," Elisabeth said. "Let me talk with you."

Benjy sat and drew in an awestruck breath as he leaned close to Lisa's face. Elisabeth worried his tobacco breath would bother her, but the baby did not stir. "Can I touch her?"

"If your hands are clean, you can touch the back of her hand."

He held his hands up to her, as he had done as a toddler on his way from the bathroom to the dinner table. Elisabeth was pierced. His hands were not clean, but she didn't think running his finger across Lisa's hand would do any harm. She could wash the baby's hands before they left.

"Just feel her velvety skin right there, Benjy," Elisabeth said, realizing immediately she had called him his little boy name, the one he had not liked for years. He touched the baby as if she were fragile as an eggshell, and again he drew a quavery breath.

"Her name is Lisa?" he whispered. Elisabeth nodded. "And she's my sister?"

"She's your niece, honey. She's your brother Bruce's daughter."

He nodded. "Bruce is a marine."

"I wrote you about Bruce," she said. "Remember?"

He nodded, his eyes still on the child. "They wouldn't let me come to the funeral. Bruce was killed in the war."

"It was a car wreck, Benjy."

"His wife was okay. She's going to have a baby."

"This is the baby."

Benjy nodded as if he had finally put it all together. He put his hands in his lap and his eyes darted. "Visitor day," he said. "I'm here forever."

"Benjy, does it scare you that you're having trouble remembering things?"

"Dad lost his memory. He died."

"Your dad is still alive, Benjy."

"Will he come?"

"No."

He nodded. "I don't want to lose my mind."

"Give me your hands," she said, and he let her take them in hers. "More important is that you don't lose your soul."

"I've got Jesus in my heart, Ma."

Elisabeth started. He sounded so much like himself, so sure. "You do?"

He seemed to scold her. "You prayed with me. Don't *you* remember?"

"I do, Benjy, but you can't live like you want and say you've received Jesus. In Matthew 7:16, Jesus says, 'Ye shall know them by their fruits.'"

"I've been bad," he said.

"Yes, you have. But Jesus loves you."

"I know. Jesus loves me, this I know. The chaplain prays with me. I'm a Christian."

"How do you know?"

He seemed calm and looked directly into her eyes. "Romans 8:16," he said. "Romans 8:16."

"What does it say?"

He shook his head. "I used to know. But it's true."

"Let me look it up," she said.

She got out her Bible. Her eyes filled as she read, "'The Spirit himself beareth witness with our spirit, that we are the children of God.'" Elisabeth reached for his hands again. "Do you know what that means?"

He shrugged. "I used to. Chaplain explained it. I want to go to heaven."

"I want you there too, Benjy. I want us all together there someday. My dad is there. Your brother is there. Your father will be there. Someday your sister and I will be there too."

"I'm not good enough," he said, "but I'm going anyway."

"You *do* understand then," she said. "None of us are good enough."

"I'm the worst."

"The apostle Paul said *he* was the chief of sinners, but he was a great evangelist."

"I know him."

"You do?"

Benjy nodded, then looked puzzled. "He comes to our meetings. No wait, he doesn't come. We read about him. We read what he writes."

Elisabeth put her Bible away and sat staring at Benjy, who looked self-conscious. "You realize you probably have the same disease your father has?"

He nodded. "I don't want to lose my mind."

"I know."

"Are you going now? Taking the baby?"

"Soon."

"Good-by, Mom. Good-by, baby."

Lisa stirred on the way out and Elisabeth sat feeding her in the parking lot. How was it possible that Aunt Agatha and Benjy had somehow grown spiritually tender after she had virtually given up on them? God wanted them for his kingdom even more than she did, she realized. Was there something about this baby that changed everyone's perspective of the future?

Elisabeth agonized over Joyce, who was drifting. She coveted Joyce for the church, not just Christ Church but Christ's church. She

believed Joyce's conversion had been real and that God would somehow hound her until she returned.

As Elisabeth drove Lisa back to Three Rivers in the dark, she prayed
up and down her list. Will, Benjy, Betty, Joyce, Lisa, and Ben. Yes, Ben.
He seemed so lonely, and yet he maintained his passion for ministry.
She knew he cared for her, probably even held out hope for rekindling
their romance someday. She loved him. She always had. But her husband was still alive.

Elisabeth was to return Lisa to Joyce the following noon. Back
home, she finally put the baby down for the night and collapsed into
her own bed. Exhausted as she was, she was grateful to God for both
meetings that day. She turned onto her stomach and tucked her knees
up under her so she was kneeling on the bed, her face in her pillow.

"Lord," she said, "I don't know what else to pray except thank you
for the gift of this little one. I'm still wounded, still confused, still angry
over my loss. But the desire you've given me is to see people come into
your kingdom. If there is pain along the way, I'll try to accept it. And
if there is no reward this side of heaven, help me accept that too."

Elisabeth hummed "Trust and Obey," and sang, "When we walk
with the Lord, in the light of his Word, what a glory he sheds on our
way. As we do his good will, he abides with us still, and with all who
will trust and obey. Trust and obey, for there's no other way, to be
happy in Jesus, but to trust and obey."

Happy in Jesus, she thought as she fell asleep. *That alone would be
worth it all.*

The next afternoon, Elisabeth stood in the bare dirt yard, if it could
be called that, of the trailer Joyce shared with a cousin and the cousin's
boyfriend. A playpen sat outside next to a girl who sat smoking in a
plastic lawn chair. "Just put her in here," the girl said. "I'm Joyce's
cousin."

"I'd like to speak with Joyce first, if you don't mind."

"She's sleeping."

"I'll wake her."

"She won't like that."

Elisabeth entered the trailer, where she was met by the barefoot, bare-chested man of the house. He lolled around in jeans and carried a steaming cup of coffee.

"Mornin', ma'am," he said.

"It's not morning anymore," she said. "Where's Joyce?"

"It's my morning!" he said, laughing heartily until disintegrating into a raspy cough. "Joyce!" he said. "Git up! It's yer ma or in-law or somethin'!"

Elisabeth heard movement in a back room, and Joyce swore. She hurried to find Joyce sitting on the bed, wrapped in a blanket, squinting at the sun. "Whoa," she said. "Hi. What time is it?"

"Almost one. I thought you'd be worried."

"I never worry when she's with you," Joyce said.

"I wish I could say the same when she's here."

"Don't worry about her. Everybody loves her here. My cousin's watching her this afternoon. She set up a pl—"

"I'd rather keep her, if you don't mind."

"I mind. I want to see her when I get off work."

"She should be in bed by then."

"I can raise my own kid."

"I wish that were true. Joyce, look at you. Look at this place. This is nowhere to raise a baby."

Joyce stood and threw the blanket on the bed. She yanked on a blouse and slacks, stepped into a pair of sandals, and reached for Lisa. Elisabeth pulled away. "If you ever want to see her again," Joyce said, "you'll give her to me! This happens to be how I was raised, and I was good enough for your son!"

"I'm sorry, Joyce. I didn't mean to insult you. I—"

"You did a good job of it. Now I said you could take her to church Sunday, so you can come get her Saturday night. Meantime, she's my daughter, she stays with me, and I raise her. You don't like it, kiss her good-by right now."

Elisabeth reluctantly handed Lisa over. "Think about letting her live with me awhile. Will you?"

Joyce glared at her. "Give Lisa up to you?"

"I'm just saying there might come a time when you'll see she'd be better off—now don't look at me that way—staying with me in town for a while."

"In the first ward, you mean."

"That has nothing to do with it."

"Just come Saturday night," Joyce said. "And I want her back Sunday night."

Elisabeth put in several hours at the Fairbanks plant, then drove to Kalamazoo. She prayed for Lisa every time she thought about her, seemingly every second.

"Ben! Hi!" she said as she entered Will's room. "To what do I owe the—"

"Dr. Fitzgerald wanted to know when you arrived," Ben said, rising. "I'll get him."

"Fitzgerald from Three Rivers? I haven't seen him in years. What's the matter?"

"Something with Will, of course, but I don't understand it, Elisabeth. Let me get him."

Dr. Fitzgerald had been sent Will's weekly charts for years but had made clear to Elisabeth that the daily care provided at the State Hospital virtually took him off the case, except as the physician of record. "It's good to see you again," he said as he entered. Ben had disappeared.

She smiled guardedly. "Should I be happy to see *you*, Doctor?"

He cocked his head. "That depends. I understand you have been consistent in your visits. Please sit down."

Elisabeth was way past the need for gentility. "So is the end finally in sight?"

"I'm afraid so. He'll soon need to be put on some sort of life support, and—"

"No. If he'd had the choice, he'd have said good-by a long time ago. I don't want him to suffer, that's all." Elisabeth's voice sounded hollow and flat to her. She knew this day was coming, but that took away none of the pain of its finality.

The doctor looked at Will. "Ma'am, he has felt nothing for years. We would continue to feed him and give him oxygen so he can breathe on his own."

"And how will he die?"

"His heart will give out."

"He won't struggle?"

"Nothing he would be conscious of. I would like to move him to Three Rivers Hospital. That should make things easier for you."

Elisabeth nodded, numb. Will's breathing was labored. She heard every sound in his throat. "How long do you guess?"

Dr. Fitzgerald leafed through his chart. "There's heart and liver damage now. A few weeks. A month at most."

Elisabeth sighed. "I've had people tell me for years what a relief this should be. And I suppose it will be. He's been dead to me, but I'll miss him still. I would love to be with him when he goes."

"I'll check with the ambulance company."

"I mean when he goes to heaven," she said.

When Dr. Fitzgerald left, Elisabeth took Will's hand. "When you're ready, love," she said. "When you're ready. I'll be along later with all three of our children. We can be happy about that."

She heard footsteps outside the door and fell silent. "The doctor thought you might need to chat with someone," Ben said from the hall.

"In a moment," she said.

Elisabeth covered Will. She sat, weary but relieved. "Come in, Ben."

He sat across from her, only a night light near the bed illuminating them. "You okay?" Ben said.

She nodded, tears welling up. "I'm going to miss him so."

"You've been a wonderful wife, Elisabeth. A man could not ask for more."

She felt as if his words were from God to encourage her. "Thank you, Ben."

He nodded.

"I'd appreciate if you'd sing at the funeral."

"I'd be honored."

"I love 'I Have Decided to Follow Jesus.' The preacher referenced it the night Will and I dedicated our lives."

"It's the story of your life, Elisabeth."

"How I wish that were true."

Ben leaned forward. "May I pray for you, Elisabeth?" She nodded. "And may I take your hand?" She nodded again, appreciating his asking. He thanked God for Will's life and for the love Will and Elisabeth had shared, "that has been an example to me and many others of true commitment."

As he finished, Elisabeth felt pressure on her knuckle. As he let go and they opened their eyes, she saw the glint of metal. "Ben," she said, "are you wearing a ring?"

He nodded.

Elisabeth wondered if she could draw a breath. She fought for composure. "A wedding ring?"

"I was going to tell you."

"Tell me?" she said, pretending the offense was merely that she didn't know. "Invite me, you mean?"

"We invited no one. One of my old seminary profs officiated, and he and his wife were witnesses."

Elisabeth hated that this news devastated her as much as the word about Will. She wished she were somewhere she could scream, bang her fists on the wall, something. She forced herself to act normal. But what was normal now?

"So, someone I know?"

Ben looked surprised. "Dellarae."

Elisabeth was speechless.

Ben walked with her out into the hall. "Doesn't seem like my type?"

Elisabeth shrugged, not trusting herself to speak.

"I need a little flamboyance, wouldn't you say?"

Elisabeth whispered, "You're fine the way you are."

"She's a woman of God, Elisabeth. Transparent. What you see is what you get. She's fond of you."

Elisabeth wanted to say, "And I of her," but she could not respond. She was fighting rage, even hatred against Dellarae. Hatred?

"She's hoping we'll all be friends," Ben said.

Elisabeth teetered on the edge of actually asking Ben if he would have chosen Mrs. Shockadance had he known Will's prospects. His awful news brought clarity to what she had not admitted even to herself: that her one hope, dream, and consolation was that Ben would one day be waiting at the end of her long and painful journey. She, and she had assumed he, had been obsessive about remaining appropriate until she was free. But hadn't they both been harboring hopes that the day would come when they could freely reveal their feelings toward each other? Had she only assumed he shared her longing?

Maybe he had simply wearied of waiting. Perhaps she had played her part so well that Ben had lost hope she would ever return to him. Fortunately, he had to assume it was the news about Will that rendered her uncommunicative. He walked her to her car and accepted her assurances that she was all right. Elisabeth pulled out, but rather than head south on Oakland Drive, she turned left and drove north to the deserted parking lot at University High School.

There she broke down and let the tears flow, pounding on the steering wheel and raging in the darkness at the injustice of it all. Exhausted and unable to pray, Elisabeth rued the future. Ben would naturally expect his new wife to accompany his solo at Will's funeral. Elisabeth would have to sit there, mourning her husband, mourning her firstborn and his inherited dementia, mourning the miles between her and her daughter, mourning the memory of her youngest child, and mourning the death of any future she had dreamed of with Ben. All the while she would see his choice of a life's mate, in all her glory, playing the piano.

When Elisabeth finally pulled herself together and headed toward Three Rivers, she sensed God checking her spirit as she itemized her sacrifices. Each time she dwelt on Bruce, something niggled at her brain. Something she had never considered. Was it possible that Bruce was spared by dying young?

Would he not have had a tendency toward the same affliction that affected his paternal grandfather, his father, and his older brother? In truth there was little consolation that Bruce may have avoided an ugly end by suffering what appeared a premature one. Yet this was something she had to consider.

That night in bed she tried to pray. "So it is to be just you and me the rest of the way?" she began. "No husband who can see me, talk with me, pray with me, touch me, hold me, kiss me, sleep with me? I don't understand your timing, and I wonder if Ben does. Take Will peacefully, that's all I ask."

If this was a test, Elisabeth wanted to pass it. If God wanted to know he had her attention, her whole heart and soul and mind for the desire he had given her to increase his kingdom, she wanted to assure him he had it. Though it had never been easy and apparently never would be, she wanted to leave her situation, her circumstances, to him. She would serve and obey, not resignedly or only because she knew no other way. Rather, she would fulfill her commitment to a God she believed was trustworthy even when he didn't seem so.

For the next three weeks she visited Will every day at Three Rivers Hospital and kept little Lisa on weekends. Now that Will was dying, rather than vegetating as a mental patient, several friends from Christ Church also visited. Even Pastor Clarkson came, and Elisabeth had to give him credit. He was not afraid to look at Will and touch him and even address him. Most others talked with her as if Will were not there.

Elisabeth corresponded with Betty, pleading with her to somehow make it back for the funeral. Betty wanted to but made no promises.

At about three in the morning, Friday, October 4, 1946, Elisabeth was dreaming of the weekend with Lisa, now nearly ten months old. The phone awakened her. Elisabeth did not hurry. She knew what this message bore.

Making her way down the stairs, she prayed only that Will would hang on at least another hour. By the time she dressed, drove to the hospital, and reached his room, Will's breathing had decreased to nine respirations a minute.

"He doesn't appear to be struggling," Dr. Fitzgerald said. "His respiration should slow until it stops. I'll leave you with him. If you detect any discomfort, we can medicate him."

Elisabeth sensed she was in the presence of God from the instant she was alone with Will. He lay on his side, his face to the wall. She pulled a chair there and forced his hand open, placing hers inside. His eyes were closed and he breathed deeply. She counted. Just barely nine a minute. A couple of minutes later, he was down to eight, then seven.

Slowly, slowly his breathing became shallower. When he was respiring only four times a minute, she wondered if each breath was his last. She spoke softly to him. "You're about to see Jesus," she said. "I envy you. Say hello to our dads, will you? And Bruce? And would you tell God I have a lot to ask him?"

He took a long, deep breath, and let it out, and she heard nothing for more than twenty seconds. "Go quietly, my sweetheart. I love you with all my heart, and I always will. I'll love you with all that is in me until I see you again."

Will inhaled deeply yet again. Elisabeth stood and pried her hand from his, leaning to embrace his bony frame. She pressed her face into his neck, one arm on his back, the other in his thinning hair. "Goodby, Will," she said. "Good-by, my love."

He exhaled and was gone.

The evening before the funeral, Elisabeth spent more than an hour with Pastor Clarkson. He seemed deeply impressed with her account of Will's life and their love story. They planned a simple ceremony for one o'clock: a welcome, an obituary, Ben's solo, Pastor's message, and the burial.

"Would you like a viewing in advance of the service?" Pastor said.

She shook her head. "I put myself in his place. I would not want people to see me that way." She chose to place atop the casket his Fairbanks-Morse executive photograph from just before he was hospitalized.

The next day was unseasonably warm. Elisabeth put on a thin raincoat and waited outside her front door. She was moved by the offer of Frances Childs that she and Art swing by and drive her the few blocks to Christ Church.

"We'll sit with you, if you'd like," Frances said. But Elisabeth declined. Benjy was not cleared to attend and Betty was under the weather in New Mexico, so Elisabeth had decided to sit alone with her thoughts in the first pew. Had she known how nice it would be outside, she'd have declined the ride as well.

Art and Frances were clearly uncomfortable, he clamming up and she jabbering. Elisabeth felt no need to humor her. She hoped one day she and Frances would again become the friends they had once been, ones who told each other everything.

Will's closed coffin stood beneath the pulpit, and the mourners shuffled past, smiling at the picture, some softly touching it, most pausing to greet Elisabeth.

She had felt so alone for so long in her vigil over Will that she was amazed at how many people filed by. The little sanctuary quickly filled with people from Snyder's Pharmacy, Fairbanks-Morse, the State Hospital (including staff and even family of other long-term patients), Three Rivers Hospital, the church, and the neighborhood. Elisabeth was grateful that Ben and Dellarae just silently shook her hand. A sinking feeling reminded her that she had lost both the men in her life yet again.

The seven junior girls from Elisabeth's Sunday school class were the last to be herded past. Their substitute teacher led the way with a stern look and a finger to her lips, obviously having scared the girls into silence. Elisabeth found herself suddenly animated, thrilled to see them. She greeted each by name and thanked them for coming. The last handed her a thick, business-size envelope with "Mrs. Bishop" hand-printed on it.

"It's from all of us," towheaded Irene whispered. Her teacher shushed her, but Elisabeth winked and thanked her.

Elisabeth quietly worked open the envelope. Inside was an oversized sheet of lined writing paper that Elisabeth couldn't unfold all the way without making it visible to everyone. From what she could decipher, each girl had written a brief paragraph and signed her name.

One had written, "Mrs. Bishop, I'm sorry your husband died, even if he was in the State Hospital. From you I learned to pray and forgive people."

Elisabeth couldn't wait to get to the rest of them, but she quickly put the sheet away when Joyce was ushered in next to her, carrying a sleeping Lisa. "Oh!" Elisabeth said, and the tears came. "I thought you weren't—"

"I know," Joyce said. "I just thought she ought to be at her grandfather's funeral."

"I'm so grateful," Elisabeth said. Lisa awoke when Elisabeth took her, but she didn't stir during the ceremony.

Pastor Clarkson began with an obituary reciting Will Bishop's dates of birth and death, his employment and community service record, the names of his late son and survivors, and a litany of his spiritual life.

After Ben's solo, Pastor Clarkson told Will and Elisabeth's unusual story. "This was a man," he concluded, "I would love to have known."

Elisabeth pressed her lips together. *And I would have loved to have known him longer.*

Joyce took Lisa and left immediately after the service, so Elisabeth was alone at the burial. She had to steel herself as she watched the casket being lowered in the churchyard cemetery. But that was not as difficult as enduring yet again the condolences of nearly everyone present. Elisabeth knew they meant well, every one. She simply wanted to go home with her memories and her too-fresh grief.

Propriety kept Elisabeth there until the last mourner left. She thanked Frances for the offer of a ride home but told her she preferred walking. She finally started home when the sun began flirting with the top of the trees. Two blocks away Elisabeth stopped and turned to see Christ Church silhouetted against the twilight. "Thank you, Lord," she said, grateful for a church to come to not only several times a week, but also during every crisis in her life.

As she turned again toward home, Elisabeth's reverie was broken by the figure of a little girl poking a stick into a mud puddle at the next corner. She wore oversized black rubber boots and a red raincoat. As Elisabeth drew near, the blond hair told her it was Irene.

"Does your mother know you're still out, honey?"

"Mm-hm," Irene said, staring at the water. "Daddy too."

"Your Daddy's home?"

Irene nodded.

"I didn't see him at—"

"Didn't want to come. Said your husband really died a long time ago."

"In a way, he did."

"I know, Miz Bishop. You told us. I already changed my prayer list."

"You did?"

Irene threw her stick into the street and turned to look at Elisabeth. "I took him off the top and put you there. That's all right, isn't it? I mean, he's dead now, right?"

"You put me on top?"

"You were second already, so now you're first."

"I'm so happy you still have your prayer list, Irene."

Irene took her glove off and picked a stone out of the mud. "We all do. All your girls."

"That means a lot to me."

"You need a lot of prayer."

Elisabeth had to smile in spite of everything. "I do?"

"'Course! You have a boy in prison, a sick daughter you haven't seen for years, a dead husband, a dead boy, a daughter-in-law who doesn't come to church, and a new granddaughter. See you Sunday. Bye!"

Irene ran off before Elisabeth could respond. The little girl ran around the back of her house, and a door slammed.

Elisabeth finally made her way home and walked across the painted wood porch that led to the door that had survived the fire and had been on that house since the day Will bought it. She entered to the dark comfort of familiarity.

Upstairs Elisabeth sat on her bed and gathered her well-worn Bible into her lap. She let out a low chuckle. There was something to be said for the uncultured frankness of a child. "I do need a lot of prayer, don't I?" she prayed silently. "And I have a lot to do."

Part Four

Chapter Twenty-Two

At eight forty-two A.M., January 1, 1965, the sun bullied its way through heavy draperies in Elisabeth's front room. The old woman's lids fluttered and she squinted from her overstuffed chair. Her feet remained asleep, angrily pinpricking her from their woolen cocoons. A bulky terrycloth robe covered her flannel nightgown, long sleeves enveloping balled fists, palms perspiring.

As usual, Elisabeth had padded gingerly down the steps in the middle of the night, unable to sleep. Even with the three-way bulb at high power, reading had not been the answer. She had outed the light, tucked her feet beneath her, hid her frigid hands from the draft, and drew her knees up, hoping, praying, waiting for the charity of sleep.

It had been years since Elisabeth had slept through the night. When first she had found herself staring at the ceiling in the wee hours, she attributed it to worry, worry she tried to pray away. She prayed for Joyce, for Betty, for Lisa, for Benjy. Betty and Benjy had finally, mercifully, died within months of each other more than six years before. Elisabeth had not seen her daughter for more than fifteen years except in pictures, and to see her in repose, her weeping Cliff standing guard, was almost more than she could bear. Why had it taken Betty's death

to finally push her to scrape together the funds and head west? Yet the
funeral strangely warmed Elisabeth, who learned of Betty's vibrant faith
and many friends. She even saw hints of what her daughter had seen
in her husband, a gigantic, softhearted man. Elisabeth had returned
with a modicum of peace and no more anxiety over her daughter, imagining her reuniting with her father and her brothers in heaven.

Elisabeth had outlived her whole immediate family. The losses, all
but Bruce, muted as the years passed. But Elisabeth had often awakened, eyes popping open and mind as alert as at midday, at the precise hour she had taken the fateful phone call from Joyce about Bruce
so many years before.

Joyce. How she had prayed for that precious girl who now seemed
beyond hope. Her former daughter-in-law had kept her end of the
bargain anyway; Elisabeth had to give her that. She had allowed Lisa
many weekends at Grandma's, Sunday after Sunday at Christ Church.
Elisabeth stretched painfully as she recalled Lisa as a student in her
own primary girls' Sunday school class. How it both thrilled and
wounded her to see so much of Bruce in her granddaughter's deep,
beautiful eyes.

Had Elisabeth had her druthers, Lisa would have lived with her full-
time. What a thing to do to a child! During the week Lisa lived in a
trailer with her bitter mother and her succession of live-in lovers,
short-term husbands, alcohol, violence, foul language, and who knew
what else. Friday night she was dropped off at her grandmother's
echoing three-story house in the old section of the first ward.

Elisabeth had fought for every hour with the child. She made it her
business to counteract every evil influence, insisting Lisa bathe, keep
a schedule, obey, learn manners, study, memorize Scripture, pray, and
go to church. Lisa was remarkably compliant at first.

Lisa reminded Elisabeth of herself as a child, enamored of church
and God and Jesus. She prayed to receive Christ as a youngster and
got in trouble with her mother for becoming judgmental and "too
religious." Joyce threatened to keep Lisa from her own grandmother,
but the two pleaded so strenuously that she had to relent. Plus, it was
clear Joyce wanted her freedom, especially on weekends.

Lisa had blossomed into a nineteen-year-old beauty with dark hair and eyes. Elisabeth felt the differences in their generation every time she saw her now, and, yes, she worried—mostly about the men in Lisa's life. "Don't badger me about my dates, Grandma," Lisa said. "I know what I'm doing."

But knowing what she was doing included thinking she could be a good influence on boys who had no interest in God. "It doesn't work that way," Elisabeth would tell her, and quoted Proverbs about how evil drags down good rather than vice versa. Lisa would roll her eyes, and Elisabeth feared coming off as a taskmaster.

None of Lisa's male friends were from Christ Church, and she hardly ever made it to Sunday school and church anymore. She had never really rebelled, as far as Elisabeth could tell, and Lisa still claimed to be a believer. But neither did they have the spiritual discussions Elisabeth so enjoyed when Lisa had been in junior high. Now that she had graduated high school, their relationship had changed.

Lisa was a student at Western Michigan and worked as a nurse's aide at Borgess Hospital. She seemed so grown up, and yet Elisabeth couldn't shake the image of her as a newborn. "You'll be the perfect nurse," Elisabeth told her often. "So caring, compassionate, gentle."

Lisa would blush. "Where do you think I got that?" she said. "Certainly not from Joyce."

"Honey, don't call your mother by her name. That's not respect."

"That's why I do it."

"We have to love her."

"Do *you*, Grandma? *Can* you, the way she treats you?"

Elisabeth wanted desperately to say that she loved Joyce, but she could not. She was not capable in herself of loving the unlovable. "God loves her."

"You let her walk on you."

"Oh, she doesn't—"

"Of course she does! She knows you'll do anything for her, but does she ever act like she appreciates it?"

"I don't do it for appreciation."

"Still—"

"That's enough now, honey," Elisabeth would say, and they would talk about other things.

Now, in her chair on a bitter New Year's Day, Elisabeth closed her eyes again and prayed for Lisa. And for Joyce. Lisa was good enough to drop in on Elisabeth at least once a week. Joyce she hardly ever saw. Frances Childs remained a friend, and they had socialized more since Art's accidental death in the welding shop at Fairbanks-Morse two years before. But still Elisabeth found herself desperately lonely. She was as close to God as she had ever been, despite that her increasing physical infirmities had made her drop her church service projects one by one. And while the Lord remained her refuge, as she liked to say, she had quit praying for relief from the crushing aloneness.

The phone rang. Though it had been twenty years since the call about Bruce, still she hated that sound. Elisabeth planted her palms on the arms of the chair and remembered when she could lift her weight and swing her feet to the floor. Now it was all she could do to shift enough to force them out from under her. They caught in her robe and she had to painfully wiggle free.

Elisabeth felt every one of her sixty-five years as she mince-stepped toward the phone. It rang and rang. Only one who loved her and knew she was home would be patient enough to wait. It was Lisa.

"How are you, dear heart?" Elisabeth said. "Tell me you're on your way to see me."

"I am!"

"Oh, sweetie, that will be nice!"

"Happy birthday, Grandma."

"So it is," Elisabeth said. "And it will be happier when you get here."

"I'm coming to give you a bath."

"I'm sorry?"

"Grandma! Do you have the phone up to your good ear?"

"Agh! Just a minute . . . There. Now what?"

"Bath! I'm coming to give you a bath."

"Heaven knows I need one, but don't go to any trouble."

"You haven't forgotten your luncheon today, have you?"

"My what? My lunch—oh, that's right! I tried every which way to talk Frances out of that. I don't know why she insists."

"This is a milestone, Grandma! Sixty-five is nothing to sneeze at."

"Then why have I been sneezing all week?"

"Are you ill?"

"I'm still here. Can't see, can't hear, can hardly taste. Short of breath, hot flashes, aches and pains in every joint. But you know what?"

"Yes, I know."

"Do you?"

"Of course I do."

"What am I going to say next?"

"That the joy of the Lord is your strength."

"Amen and amen! I love you, Lisa."

"I love you too, Grandma. I'll be there in an hour or so."

Elisabeth stretched the phone cord so she could lower herself to the piano bench. "Just let me call Frances and beg off. It's supposed to be below zero today, too cold even to snow."

"It's nearly ten below now," Lisa said, "but it's bound to rocket up to zero by noon."

"I don't have anything to wear. No sense polishin' and powderin' me for the old dress I'd put on."

"Get yourself some breakfast and be ready for me, because I'm coming. And I just might have a present that will hush you up."

"Say! I thought grandmas hushed grandchildren!"

"Then act your age and watch for me. Your driveway shoveled?"

"Now don't be volunteering for that—"

"Grandma! I just need to know if I can pull in there."

Elisabeth leaned forward and pulled back the drape. The sun blinded her. "I can't see a thing," she said. "But the neighbor boy never misses."

Feeling gradually returned to her feet as Elisabeth turned on the burner for her tea. But when she sat to drink it she could hardly move. It was sweet of Lisa to come on her birthday, and Elisabeth never ceased to be moved by her granddaughter's sense of propriety when bathing her. Lisa helped her sit on a wood bench across the tub and had never once made her feel exposed or embarrassed. The girl merely helped her in and out and with extremities she couldn't reach.

That morning Lisa hurried in and put a large shopping bag on the table before rushing to the stove. "Grandma, you must remember to turn the flame off under the tea. You don't want to lose another kettle, or worse."

Elisabeth, alarmed at herself, was too embarrassed to respond.

"I gave the boy next door two dollars for the shoveling," Lisa said.

"I've never given him more than one-fifty. You'll spoil him."

"It's a new year. Give him a raise."

Lisa guided Elisabeth by the elbow toward the bathroom. "I expected you to have your robe and slippers off. Tuckered out today?"

Elisabeth nodded. What would she do without Lisa? Her granddaughter washed her back and her calves and feet with such gentleness that Elisabeth nearly wept. "Your patients must love you," she whispered.

"They do," Lisa said with a grin. "Especially the men."

"Stop that!"

"I'm kidding, Grandma. You know I'm holding out for someone you'll approve of."

"That'd be no one you've introduced me to so far."

"Tell me something I don't know." She wrapped Elisabeth in a huge towel and walked her upstairs, holding her close. Elisabeth found herself transported to her childhood. Hardly aware of her surroundings, she remembered her father enveloping her in a towel and gently rubbing her dry.

Lisa set out Elisabeth's undergarments, told her she'd help her with her hose, and said, "I'll be right back." Elisabeth's lower back ached as she sat on the side of the bed and put on what she could. Lisa returned presently with the shopping bag.

"Ooh, let me see," Elisabeth said, but Lisa made her wait.

She helped her with everything else, then said, "I'll show you your new outfit, but don't put it on until just before Frances gets here. Wear your robe till then."

Lisa pulled from the bag a box containing patent leather shoes. They were still sensible, thick, and heavy on support, but they were definitely party shoes. Elisabeth smiled.

Then came the matching purse. "Lisa! I expected a dress, not all this!"

"Patience, Grandma." She produced a red wool, shirtwaist dress with a white Peter Pan collar and buttons down the front. Elisabeth tried to exult, to tell her it was the handsomest outfit she had ever seen, but Lisa was already on to accessorizing. "This will take a large brooch," she said. "How about the white cameo? You're going to look so festive, so wintry. I wish you'd had this for Christmas."

They rummaged through Elisabeth's bureau for the right necklace, earrings, and bracelet. "Too many pieces?" Elisabeth asked. "I've never worn much."

"You've never been sixty-five either."

Elisabeth chuckled and covered her mouth.

"What?"

She shook her head, her shoulders heaving.

"Come on, Grandma. Out with it."

"I'm going to be way overdressed for Frances!" And she convulsed with laughter. Lisa dropped onto the bed, howling.

"You're awful!"

"Aren't I just the worst?" Elisabeth said. "Now if I could find a feather boa I could look like Dellarae Shockadance Phillips, Lord rest her soul."

Lisa sat up and leaned against Elisabeth and they supported each other on the soft mattress. "I haven't heard that name in a while," Lisa said.

"You know the story."

"Of course. How long has she been gone now?"

Elisabeth shrugged. "I used to get their Christmas card, always signed by her." She sighed. "'With Christmas love, Dellarae and Ben.' Never heard from them otherwise. Then two Christmases ago the card just read, 'Merry Christmas, '63. Benjamin.'"

"Not that you memorized it."

Elisabeth felt the urge to stand and look out the window, as she often did when lost in memories. But her left knee was stiff and her right ankle throbbed. She shook her head. "I hurt for him. I really did. I didn't know he'd lost her. A carbon copied note said something about it being his first Christmas without her and how, 'as many of you know,' she had passed that spring. Well, I wasn't one of the many who knew."

Elisabeth felt Lisa's embrace. "An oversight," she said. "He was grieving."

"I let him know when Betty passed."

"That was a long time ago, Grandma."

"He sent a nice note."

"I remember."

"I might have been able to help him."

"I know," Lisa said. "People in pain are your specialty."

"I should have written or called, but what could I say after so many months? He didn't bother to let me know, so—"

"So you didn't even send him a card that year."

"Or last year. Or this. I think he finally got the message."

"No card from him this year?"

Elisabeth shook her head.

"It's never too late to send one."

Elisabeth was desperate to change the subject. "Stay with me."

"Can't. Gotta go."

"I won't be able to button this dress."

"Sure you will. I'll button all but the top two, and Frances can help with those, if necessary."

"Come with us. Frances won't mind—"

"Grandma, stop! I'd love to, but I, uh, have a lunch date already."

"A date?"

"If you must know."

"With whom?"

"None of your business."

"Of course it is! Now who?"

"Well, it's not just one."

"Lisa!"

"And they're not all men."

"Well, then tell me."

"I'll tell you all about it later." Lisa stood.

"You'll come by then, promise?"

"Promise. Now let's get you downstairs and get your outfit ready so all you have to do is slip into it."

The house felt colder with Lisa gone. Most weekdays when she didn't check in, Elisabeth usually stayed in her robe. It was all she could do to get from the kitchen to the bathroom and to her chair. Lisa had bought her a used black and white, but reception was so poor that she hardly ever watched except for fifteen minutes of Walter Cronkite late in the afternoon and the occasional *This Is Your Life* with Ralph Edwards.

Lisa had set the newspaper on the table next to Elisabeth's chair and unfolded it for her. It still felt cold as she tried to smooth it with swollen-knuckled fingers. She passed up the entire front page and the editorial page blather about LBJ's Great Society and what the first family was doing over the holidays. She skipped any article with Vietnam in the headline and pored over the engagement announcements and the obituaries. Then it was straight to the comics. Blondie, Out Our Way, and The Berrys amused her, but then her lack of sleep came calling and she began to nod.

The paper slipped to cover her legs from just above the knees. It felt so toasty she didn't try to retrieve it. She tucked her hands into the large pockets of her robe and let her chin fall to her chest. Her neck would ache when she roused, she knew, but for now it felt so good, so cozy, so . . .

Elisabeth dreamt of a woman, a large, loud, red-dress wearing amalgam of Dellarae and Frances. Frances had expanded in her maturity and her voice had become fluttery but no less voluble. The woman in Elisabeth's dream looked and dressed like Dellarae but moved and sounded like Frances.

Elisabeth and the woman were playing in the schoolyard, kneeling to tend to their jump ropes. Though they were their present ages, Elisabeth moved like a little girl and Frances had a huge head of ringlets. "I could vomit!" she said.

"Regurgitate," Elisabeth corrected, and her large, old playmate pointed at her, threw back her head, and laughed so heartily that Elisabeth had to laugh along.

She woke herself laughing, or was it the blast of frigid air from the front door, the squeaking of the hinge, the stomping, that voice?

"Elisabeth, I expected you'd be ready!" Frances bellowed, shutting the door and moving heavy-footed into the front room. "You're not even dressed!"

"I'm sorry, Frances," she said weakly. "I don't feel much like going."

"Nonsense! Here are your things. Now on your feet, up you go. That's my girl. So many people waiting."

"Where?"

"Well, down at the cafeteria, like I said. Only place open today. Turkey dinner for two-ninety-five. My treat."

"How do you know people are waiting?" Elisabeth said, as Frances helped her out of her robe and into the dress. The cold emanated from her friend's coat.

"Because I called them, that's all."

"You didn't tell them this was a birthday lunch, did you?"

"Well—"

"Please, no."

"They're not going to any fuss—"

"Oh, Frances!"

"I had to make sure we could get in. They assured me we could, and they're holding a table, that's all."

"But I don't want people making a big show—"

"I told them that, all right? Now come on. They're holding a table. The least we can do is not make them hold it too long. Elisabeth, this dress is stunning! And the rest of the ensemble! My! Lisa had to have put this together."

"What's that supposed to mean?"

"Not that you don't have taste and style, Elisabeth. Of course you do. But you so seldom buy for yourself. Lisa did this, didn't she?"

"Of course."

"What a sweet girl."

Elisabeth's boots and winter coat didn't do justice to her look, but she could not venture out without them. She covered her glasses with an oversized sunshade and held Frances's arm as they carefully managed the steps.

"What's that thermometer say?" Elisabeth said.

"I don't want to know and neither do you," Frances said, and Elisabeth could see only the huge vapor cloud her friend emitted. But she heard something from next door.

"What're they doing?" she said. "Going somewhere?"

"Looks like it," Frances said, holding open the car door. "In you go now."

Elisabeth felt the ice in her lungs with each breath. "Where would they be going?"

Frances bent to help lift her feet and swing them into the car. "Honestly, Elisabeth, you are the curiousest woman I've ever known!"

"Curiousest?" Elisabeth said, laughing as Frances shut the door and hurried to the driver's side.

As she slid behind the wheel, Frances said, "You know what I meant. How would I know where your neighbors are going?"

"Well, what are they wearing? Going sledding?"

"A sled would freeze to the hill today. They're bundled up but sort of dressed up. Satisfied?"

"Could you just ask them—"

"I am not about to stick my nose into your neighbors' business. I don't care where they're going and neither should you!"

"All right, all right, Frances. When did you stop that?"

"Stop what?" Frances said as she backed into the street.

"Caring about the neighbors' business."

Frances grinned. "Don't start with me, Elisabeth. You know it's only my own neighbors' business I care about."

The day was bright and clear, the roads packed with squeaky snow. Frances drove very slowly, and as Elisabeth's eyes gradually adjusted to the glare, she peered out to see why. Cars were parked on both sides of the street.

"Can't anyone get into their driveways?" Elisabeth said. "You'd think boys would want all this shoveling money. Wouldn't you? Hm? Well, what do you make of it, Frances?"

"Make of what?"

"All these cars!"

"Honestly, Elisabeth, I don't know! How *could* I know? I don't care! I'm just trying to get you to lunch in one piece."

"Then why'd you turn here?"

"What?"

"You turned the wrong way. The new cafeteria is straight down the hill next to the drugstore."

"I know where it is! I made the arrangements."

"You're going to the church?"

"I need to pick up something."

"I thought we were making the people at the cafeteria wait."

Frances pulled in to the church lot, which was full except for one cleanly shoveled place right by the back door. "Will you shush while I run my errand?"

"You're the second person who's shushed me this morning. What in the world is going on here today?"

"Sit tight a minute and try not to think of any more questions!"

Frances left the car running and waddled to the back door. The sun glared off the windshield, so Elisabeth covered her eyes with her hand and felt as if she could nap again. She racked her brain for what might be going on at Christ Church. She remembered nothing in the bulletin Sunday, but that had been five days before.

She started at a light tap on her window and squinted through the frost at Walt Burke and Ike Slater, two of the elders. They were in shirts and ties, but no coats.

"You'll catch your death," she said, as Walt opened her door. "I'm just waiting for Frances Childs."

"Yeah, she asked if you'd come in a minute."

"Oh, I don't mind waiting."

"It's a lot warmer in there," Ike said, reaching to help her out.

"Well, all right then," she said, wishing she could muster the courage to refuse. If they'd let her be, she'd have been as comfortable as a woman could be on a day like that.

The big men all but lifted her across the sidewalk and inside. Ike Slater's wife beamed at her. "Let me take your coat and boots," she said.

"Oh, I'm not staying, Gladys," she said.

"Just for a minute," Gladys said, kneeling to unfasten her boots. Elisabeth was half a heartbeat from snapping that she would just as soon be left alone, but the men steadied her as her boots came off. "Such lovely shoes!" Gladys exulted. Elisabeth sighed.

Then it was off with her coat and Ike and Walt helping her down the stairs with her feet barely touching the steps. Gladys followed, clucking about her dress. "Where *is* Frances anyway?" Elisabeth said, as she emerged into the fellowship hall.

The men let go of her and Gladys stepped past her with a self-satisfied grin. Elisabeth's eyes worked overtime to take it all in, but from what she could make out, hundreds of smiling people had packed the place and stood staring at her.

"Well, hello," she said, and they broke into applause and a raucous chorus of *Happy Birthday*.

How could she have been so dense? She had been had! Frances, yes, and even Lisa had pulled it off. This was all for her. She wobbled at the weight of it, and Ike and Walt steadied her, then led her to the seat of honor. *Oh, no, anything but this!*

Her padded chair was on an elevated platform decorated with white streamers and balloons under a latticework arch. Spotlights illuminated her as her lips quivered—as much from embarrassment as emotion—and she felt conspicuous and rude sitting there while everyone stood applauding and singing.

She caught Walt Burke's eye and beckoned him. He leaned toward her and she grabbed his tie to pull his ear to her mouth. The crowd laughed as it sang, obviously assuming she was scolding him for this surprise.

"Is my Lisa here?"

"Of course, ma'am."

"Get a chair for her and get her up here next to me."

"But this is your place of hon—"

The song wound down and people cheered.

"How well do you know me, Walter?"

"Known you all my life, ma'am."

"Then you know I mean it. Get her up here with me or I'm walking out on my own party."

Chapter Twenty-Three

"Are you all right, Grandma?" Lisa asked as she mounted the makeshift platform. "Do you need a pill?"

"I need a paddle for you," Elisabeth scolded. "And I'm not going to sit up here eating alone in front of all these people."

"They're not even looking at you," Lisa said. "Look."

"I don't dare."

"Come on, I mean it. Look out there."

Elisabeth didn't trust her aging eyes, but she tried to peer past the spotlights. Lisa was right. People paid her no attention.

"Feel better?"

"A little. What's for lunch?"

Pastor David Clarkson, no youngster himself anymore, prayed for the food and for the "occasion and the woman responsible for our celebrating," then sent the hungry toward tables heaping with hot dishes, salads, and desserts. It was potluck and Lisa went to the front of the line to fetch plates for herself and the guest of honor.

"You know just what I like," Elisabeth said when Lisa returned. "But you forget my appetite has shrunk."

"I'm just here to serve," Lisa said. "I like what you like, so I'll clean both our plates."

"Not unless you want to look like me before your time."

"I'd love to look like you at your age."

"I'd love to feel like you look," Elisabeth said. She only picked at a meatball and a chicken casserole, but two large cups of iced tea didn't slake her thirst. "I wish they'd turn off these spotlights."

"And leave you in the dark? Not likely."

"I suppose there's some program. I've been to these before."

"You've never been to one like this, Grandma. Wait till you see who's here."

"People outside the church, you mean?"

"Almost half from outside, I'd say. Didn't you see all the traffic, the cars parked up and down the streets?"

"Yes, but—"

"All because of your bash."

"Nonsense."

"You'll see. Look in the back."

"I can't see that far."

"I'm not asking you to look at faces. Look at the tables, the chairs, the crowd."

Elisabeth looked. The place was jammed. "Has the fire marshal seen this?"

"Oh, Grandma!"

"I'd better not be expected to say anything."

"What do you think?"

"They can stick a microphone in my face, but I don't have to say anything."

"Unless you want to."

"Unless I want to."

"You'll want to."

"Don't bet the farm."

"You pass up an opportunity to *testify*? I'd bet my life." Elisabeth caught the hint of sarcasm, and it pierced her.

Elisabeth worried she would need a bathroom break before this shindig was over, and she wasn't about to make that obvious.

"This is thoughtful, Lisa," she said, "but you know all I care about is the people. Can't I just say hello to them one at a time?"

"Of course. That comes later. People want to greet you corporately first."

"Oh, please."

"You don't have to like it. It's as much for them as it is for you. Many of them came great distances."

"There aren't going to be gifts, are there? You know an old lady gets to where she couldn't use one more blessed thing. Except a party outfit, of course."

"The invitations said 'no gifts,'" Lisa said.

"You sent individual invitations?"

"All over the world."

"Wherever did you get the names and addresses?"

Lisa smiled at her as someone came to clear their places. "This was a huge effort," she said. "A committee, leads, lists, you name it."

"I'm touched."

Lisa squeezed her grandmother's shoulder. "I should hope you would be. It seemed like everyone we located knew of someone else who wanted to be here."

Still, Elisabeth was puzzled at who would be there and from where.

The program began with music. An ensemble from the choir sang. Two soloists followed, then a primary girls Sunday school class. It had been many years since Elisabeth had taught that age, but Pastor Clarkson explained that the singers mirrored "her most representative classes."

"And now," he added with a flourish, "we have a particular surprise for you, because, Elisabeth Grace LeRoy Bishop, this is your life!"

Just like Ralph Edwards, the pastor read from a big scrapbook. Slides were projected on the wall, depicting converted black and white photos of Elisabeth as an infant, a young girl, an adolescent, and so on. Many elicited gales of laughter as well-known church members were also portrayed younger, thinner, and with more or different-colored hair. The changes in fashion also amused everyone. Elisabeth was stunned to silence to be reminded of so many students and fellow parishioners from years hence.

From out of her field of vision came the mature voice of a young woman. "You may not remember me," she said, "but I was in your Sunday school class twenty years ago. I'm thirty now, and my hair is darker. Back then you called me a towhead, and I was offended until I learned that simply meant that I was blond."

The pastor announced, "Mrs. Bishop, welcome one of your many students from the 1940s, Irene Gammil, now Irene Hamilton!"

"Irene?" Elisabeth gasped, as the woman mounted the platform and hugged her.

"We all made it," Irene said, as Elisabeth tilted her head back to search for some vestige of the little girl she remembered.

"All of you?"

"That's right," Pastor Clarkson said. "All seven of your primary girls are here from your class of 1945."

One by one the women took the microphone and told what Elisabeth had meant to them, how she had taught them to pray, to memorize Bible verses, to tell others about Jesus. All but one were married and had children. Those had Christian husbands, and all seven were active in their local churches. Three were Sunday school teachers.

Elisabeth wanted to spend time with each of them but barely had time to collect herself before an elderly woman was ushered in. The bent lady held the microphone close to her mouth in shaking hands and spoke so quietly that a hush fell over the place. "You don't need to hear my voice from offstage, Elisabeth, because you wouldn't recognize me anyway. I haven't seen you for exactly forty-four years. This white hair was red back then, when I attended your wedding right here in this church. I'm eighty-four years old now, but I wouldn't have missed this for the world."

She looked at Elisabeth expectantly, but all Elisabeth could do was open her hands in puzzlement. "You knew me as Rose," the woman said. "Rose Morton. I worked with your father, and truth be told, I explained to you the facts of life."

Elisabeth covered her face in embarrassment while Miss Morton absorbed the laughter and applause. "Now if I can be serious for a moment," she said, "I want you to know, if you ever doubted it, that you were the apple of your father's eye. He was so proud of you and loved you with all his heart."

Elisabeth felt tears welling and a sob rising, but she merely smiled and applauded, glad she did not have the floor. What a treat it would be to greet her father's nurse again after so many years.

Frances Childs strode out with the microphone, eschewing mystery and announcing that "Elspeth would know my voice from down the block!" She recounted their lifelong friendship, the ups and downs, and how she was once told not to call Elisabeth Elspeth anymore. "I found out that was her beloved Will's name for her, and I gladly relinquished it to his memory until now. It's no secret Elisabeth was and is more spiritual than I. I'm grateful she never condescended to me over it. With her husband in the hospital for all those years, still she taught, sang, played, attended, and everything. I couldn't be happier than to call her my friend. I just hope I outlive her, because I'd like to say this at her funeral."

Elisabeth laughed as she waved off her old friend, then embraced her, knowing she would soon lose the battle with her tears.

The daughter of missionaries Elisabeth had written to for decades spoke next and told how much her faithfulness had meant to them. Pastor Jack Hill's daughter, whom Elisabeth had never met, was now retired from the mission field herself and spoke of her parents' glowing letters about young Elisabeth.

A middle-aged man was next. "I met you only once," he said, "and I would not expect you to remember. I was an aide at the rest home where your Aunt Agatha spent her last days. Anyone who knew her knew how she was perceived, and however bad that was, it was probably accurate. But she loved you, Elisabeth. If you ever wondered what happened to the list of blessings you wrote out as a child, I'm here to tell you. She entrusted it to me." He pulled a sheet from his pocket and unfolded it. "'My blessings: God. Christ. Holy Spirit. Bible. Church. Father. House. Warmth. Brain. Curiosity. Books. Lamp. Food. Bed. Clothes. Training Hour. Friends. Aunt Agatha (sometimes).'"

He turned to face her. "As you know, your aunt made her peace with God before she died."

The now sixty-year-old son of itinerant evangelist Kendall Hasper told of how his father never forgot the night Elisabeth dedicated herself to God as a thirteen-year-old. A girl Elisabeth had not seen since camp as a teenager said Elisabeth had been a model to her "of devotion to Christ, of how even the most menial task could be done for the glory of God."

A woman's voice came through the P.A. system. "Being five years younger than you seemed like a big deal forty-five years ago, Elisabeth. That was when I was working at Snyder's with you, and getting away with murder because I was A.W.'s niece. Is it too late to say I'm sorry?"

A man with a thick southern accent drawled, "Ah 'member you and yore husband-to-be bein' more'n kind to me and my brother and sister and cousins when we was living with y'all at the boarding house. I'm Carl, Will's nephew."

The tears finally burst from Elisabeth when she heard the unmistakable voice of Charles Jackson, the orderly at the State Hospital who had tended to both Will and Bruce. He was white-haired now, but she recognized his voice immediately and would have known him anywhere. "I'm a believer and have been for 's long as I can remember," he said, "but I don't guess I'll ever see a better example of love and faithfulness than I saw in you, ma'am, standing by your husband and then your son. Sitting there singing, reading your Bible, writing them letters, why, you were an example to me, ma'am, and I'll always say I was proud to know you."

Elisabeth saw the tears roll down his cheeks as he bent to hug her, and they both held tight as they wept.

A man in his late thirties recounted growing up on the same street as the Bishops and told the story of Bruce working the donut man for five for a nickel. "We all knew he got that negotiating skill from his mama," he said.

The next man said, "I don't reckon there are too many people in this room that's done time in the Jackson pen, but I was a cellmate of Ben Bishop for nearly two years before he died. He was a troubled guy and gradually lost his memory. But somethin' that never left him was thoughts of his mama. We all knew ya without meetin' ya, ma'am, 'cause of what Ben told us and because of all them letters and packages you sent. I finally found the Lord myself a coupla years back, and you had more to do with that than you'll ever know."

Another voice from offstage, but Elisabeth knew immediately to whom it belonged. "I only met you once, ma'am, and that was at your daughter's funeral. I wasn't much to speak of as a son-in-law prospect, bein' older than you and havin' a past like I did. But you never once made me feel low-class, and your constant letters always encouraged us, and me especially, in my faith."

Cliff lumbered into view and Elisabeth stood to embrace him. She couldn't wait to talk more with him.

She leaned to Lisa, who held her hand in both of hers. "I have to go to the bathroom in the worst way. Is there anybody I've ever known anywhere who's *not* here?"

"It's almost over," Lisa whispered. "But everybody's going to want to hear from you."

"No, I said—"

"Just keep it short."

"Trust me. If I say anything it'll be, 'I'll be right back.'"

Elisabeth didn't recognize Ben's voice at first. How long had it been since she had seen him? She did the math. He was seventy now, and his voice sounded it. "I was your first fiancé," he began. "God and life had different plans for us, Elisabeth, but you need to know that you always shone in my mind as the kind of a Christian we all can and should be. No longer can Henry Varley say, as he said to D. L. Moody, 'The world has yet to see what God can do through one totally dedicated to him.' Moody said that by the grace of God he would be that one. You made that commitment in your heart, and we here all bear witness to what God has done with your total dedication.

"I asked to be last today so that I could sing one of your favorite songs." A pianist began with a quiet introduction to "I Have Decided to Follow Jesus," but as Benjamin Phillips stepped out to sing, Elisabeth interrupted him.

"Excuse me," she said, and Ike Slater quickly passed her a microphone and the pianist stopped playing. "Hold that thought, Ben. I want to hear that song, and I don't guess there's any way out of me having to say a few words, but I'm an old lady and I need a break. My granddaughter is going to accompany me, and I'll be right back."

The crowd responded with laughter and applause, and many others followed her lead. Elisabeth was stunned to get a peek at Ben as she made her way out on Lisa's arm. He was dressed dapper as usual with two-tone spats, beige slacks, and a checked jacket and tie. But he was thin to the point of being almost gaunt, and his hair was pure white and wispy. He still had those sparkling eyes and the olive skin, but the scar on his neck was obvious and his limp severe. Her heart broke for him and all he'd been through. It would be good to get a few minutes with him as well.

In the rest room Lisa submerged a washcloth in cold water and patted her grandmother's face. "My heart is so full," Elisabeth said, "I can't imagine saying anything without blubbering."

"You'll do fine, Grandma."

When they returned to the platform, Ben stood waiting on the floor. Elisabeth caught her breath while others returned to their seats, then she merely nodded to the pianist and to Ben, and the music began again. He turned to look at her as he introduced the song again, and she felt the years melt away. It was as if he could look into her soul. Could this be the same young man who had walked her to her cabin that night at camp so many summers ago?

"Listen to the words," he said, "and imagine our beloved birthday girl praying these to her Lord every day of her life." He turned to sing in his weaker but still precise baritone.

I have decided to follow Jesus;
I have decided to follow Jesus;
I have decided to follow Jesus,
No turning back, no turning back.
The world behind me, the cross before me;
The world behind me, the cross before me;
The world behind me, the cross before me,
No turning back, no turning back.
Though none go with me,
Still I will follow;
Though none go with me,

Still I will follow;
Though none go with me,
Still I will follow.
No turning back, no turning back.

"May it ever be, Lord," Elisabeth prayed, closing her eyes and imagining Ben singing as a college student, and her occasionally singing with him. As Ben stepped out of the spotlight and Ike Slater handed her the other microphone, she continued silently, "Calm me and let me say what you want me to say and may these dear ones hear what you want them to hear."

"Do you want to stand?" Lisa whispered, reaching for her.

"I suppose I should."

Lisa helped her up, and Elisabeth quickly realized what a toll the party had taken. Her throat felt dry, her heart cracked against her ribs, and she felt unsteady. Yet she owed these precious people her thanks, and Lisa was more right than she knew: Elisabeth would never pass up an opportunity to speak for God.

"I cannot begin to express," she began, her voice thick with emotion, "what you have put in my heart today. All I can say is thank you, thank you, thank you. For coming so far. For investing your holiday this way. For reminding me just how old this body is. I can't wait to greet every one of you, to look you in the eye, to hug you, to celebrate our brotherhood and sisterhood in our Savior.

"It will come as no surprise to you that whatever spiritual gifts God gave me, public speaking was not one of them. As humbled as I have been with everything that has been said, I will be more than thrilled when my part of this is over. But if you'll bear with me, I want to tell you a story."

She started with the tale of her birth, as her father had recounted so many times. She quickly moved to her conversation with the late Pastor Jack Hill and his wife, Margaret. And then the fateful night, the first session of the protracted meetings with Dr. Kendall Hasper in the summer of 1913.

"My heart told me that though it was a simple decision, a choice, it was also profound. The knowledge that God was there and that I was talking directly to him flattened me to the ground and made me wish I could dig myself even lower. I felt called, compelled, to make the rest of my life an experiment in obedience. Though I had been warned of the consequences, I could not have imagined what would follow.

"Many of you know what my life has been like, but many of you don't. Few would know or remember that it was that very night I learned my dear father was dying of cancer. He was my rock, my everything from a human standpoint. It was as if God were telling me, 'All right, Elisabeth, if you really want to depend on me, it will have to be on only me.'

"From that day to this, from outward appearances my life has been chaotic. I survived a fire, rescued a child from drowning, and saw my family spin out of control. I outlived my husband and all three of my children. In many ways I wouldn't wish my history on my worst enemy."

Elisabeth shifted her weight and swallowed, willing away the lump in her throat that might make her point less clear. Her voice was still quavery, but she merely slowed and spoke as directly into the mike as she could: "And yet I am here to tell you that God is faithful." She was interrupted by *amens*, something she hadn't heard in her church in a long time. "He is sovereign. He knows best." More agreement. "I don't know or understand or even like every decision he has made on my behalf, but I trust him. The joy of the Lord is my strength. He is my rock and my shield, whom shall I fear?" Elisabeth was nonplussed by actual applause.

"I remember days," she forged on, "when I would not have predicted I would reach this birthday. At times I'd rather have been in heaven with the ones I love. But you have made me glad I made it, grateful to be here, to get this tiny glimpse of heaven in advance.

"If I could be so bold as to leave you with a challenge, it would be to put all your faith in Christ, to make the truth of that song the theme of your heart, and to make your whole life an experiment in obedience. You will be putting your trust in the faithfulness of the Creator of the universe. Though you may look at my life and wonder at the wisdom of that counsel, take it from one who has also sometimes wondered, sometimes regretted, sometimes rebelled: in the end you will not regret it. God is real. He is trustworthy. And he who has begun a good work in you will be faithful to complete it."

Elisabeth was grateful for Lisa's young strength as she dropped back into her chair. She worried she had not done justice to what was in her heart, but everyone in the room rose, and their applause warmed and lifted her. She believed they were honoring God, and she couldn't ask for more than that.

The pastor stepped up next to her and took her microphone, waiting for the ovation to fade. "I know you'll want to greet Elisabeth before you leave," he said finally, but he was interrupted.

"Excuse me, Pastor," Ben said. "I'm grateful for the opportunity to have sung my old friend's theme song, but I would like also to say a word, if I may."

"Certainly," the pastor said, and he stepped back into the shadows.

"I plan," Ben began, "to go to the back of the line and take my turn embracing Elisabeth and wishing her well on her birthday. I will shake her hand and try to tell her what she has meant to me over the years, from when we were young and in love to when we grew old and loved others.

"But I will not be quickly letting go of her hand. I have other plans. I am proud to declare that I will risk rejection from a woman I have loved my whole life. I will somehow find my way down to one of these bony old knees and ask her to consider spending the rest of whatever time God allows us as my wife."

The ovation began again, but Elisabeth wrestled the microphone back from Pastor Clarkson and stood, waving for silence.

"Ben Phillips, I have always known you to be bold to the point of nervy. If you think that declaring yourself in front of all these people will make it harder for me to turn you down, you should see how far my children got when they challenged my authority in public. But you're an old man, and I'm inclined to forgive you. And if by the time you finally get your audience with me I still have the energy to hear your proposal, I just might be inclined to accept it."

Joyce had not spoken and Elisabeth was not aware she was in the room until her turn in line came more than an hour later and she knelt to take Elisabeth's hands in hers. Elisabeth jumped at the hard coldness of Joyce's fingers and felt for the woman who looked so much older than her years.

Joyce whispered, "If anyone could make me want to come back to God, Elisabeth, it's you. No promises, but just know that I've been watching you all these years. That's all I want to say. That and thanks for your influence on Lisa." Elisabeth tried to hang on and assure Joyce that God was still waiting for her, but she hurried away.

Lisa, who had been distracted and heard none of it, put her arm around her grandmother and pulled her close, while the line waited a moment.

"Grandma," she whispered, "I want you to know I heard you today. I'm making the same commitment you made. I want the rest of my life to be an experiment in obedience to God."

Elisabeth held Lisa close and couldn't imagine hearing anything that thrilled her more on this special day—with the possible exception of what she expected from the distinguished old gentleman at the end of the line.

We want to hear from you. Please send your comments about this book to us in care of the address below. Thank you.

ZondervanPublishingHouse
Grand Rapids, Michigan 49530
http://www.zondervan.com